Praise for

"*The Silent Gi[...]* [...] Eric Rickstad ma[...] and single father [...] but never backs [...]rs, a moody rural-noir vibe, and a compulsively readable story make this a stunner of a crime novel!"

— Steve Ulfelder, Edgar® finalist author of *Wolverine Bros. Freight & Storage*

"Eric Rickstad's *The Silent Girls* is a bone-chilling mystery set in one of New England's darkest corners, the kind of place travelers are well-advised to avoid after nightfall. This well-crafted book will have you staying up late, turning pages and afraid to turn off the light."

— Paul Doiron, author of *The Poacher's Son*

"Finely drawn characters, a narrative that beguiles and surprises and stark, poetic writing make for a novel as dark and brooding as its rural Vermont setting. *The Silent Girls* is both an exceptional detective story and a terrifying meditation on good and evil."

— Roger Smith, international bestselling author of *Wake Up Dead, Dust Devils, Mixed Blood,* and *Sacrifices*

"*The Silent Girls* is a thrilling ride to very dark places. I kept turning pages, scared of what I'd find but compelled to look. It'll keep you reading all the way up to its shattering conclusion."

—Jake Hinkson, author of *Hell on Church Street* and *The Big Ugly*

"Eric Rickstad writes with the ferocious passion a father has for his deeply loved child and with the precision of a verbal surgeon versed in terror. From the very first, a feeling of dread crept over me and stayed with me until the end, and remains with me days later. *The Silent Girls* is love and terror, a mix of intense feelings that seeps into your heart and does not go away."

— Stephen Foreman, author of the novels *Watching Gideon* and *Toe Hold*

Also by Eric Rickstad

REAP

LIE IN WAIT

ATTENTION: ORGANIZATIONS AND CORPORATIONS
HarperCollins books may be purchased for educational, business, or sales promotional use. For information, please e-mail the Special Markets Department at SPsales@harpercollins.com.

THE SILENT GIRLS

A Novel

ERIC RICKSTAD

WITNESS

An Imprint of HarperCollins Publishers

HarperCollins
PUBLISHERS
Since 1817

Excerpt from *Lie in Wait* copyright © 2015 by Eric Rickstad.

First Witness premium printing: March 2017
First Witness Impulse paperback printing: January 2015

ISBN 978-0-06-267665-8

17 18 19 20 21   QGM   10 9 8 7 6 5 4 3 2

For my wife, Meridith

Crime. From the Latin *Cernô*: *I* decide.
I give judgment.

THE
SILENT
GIRLS

CHAPTER 1

Under the dim porch light, the child's gruesome mask looked real, as if molten rubber had been poured over the poor thing's skull and melted the flesh, the features hideous and deformed.

The woman caught her breath and shrank back, the bowl of candy nearly slipping from her hand. *What kind of mother lets a young child wear such a grotesquerie,* the woman wondered. *And where are the child's parents?* Sometimes, parents who drove their kids to these better neighborhoods waited in their cars as they sipped beer from cans and prodded kids too young for Halloween to *Go on up and get your goodies. Grab Mommy a big handful.* But the woman didn't see any adults or vehicles at the shadowy curb.

She stooped to better see the child's mask.

"And what are we supposed to be?" she said.

"Dead."

The child's voice was reedy and phlegmy, genderless.

The woman searched the child's mask, unable to tell where the mask ended and the child's face began. There seemed to be no gaps around the unblinking eyes; the irises, as black as the pupils, wet and animal, swam in the oddly large eye whites.

"You're very scary," the woman said.

"You're scary," the child said in its strangled voice.

"Me?" the woman said.

The child nodded. "You're a monster."

"I am, am I?"

"Mmm. Hmmm."

The woman started to laugh, but the laugh died in the back of her throat, gagged on a sharp bone of sudden, inexplicable dread. She looked over the child's shoulder, toward the street, which was quiet and still and dark. *Where were all the children from earlier, so ecstatic with greed?*

"There's no such thing as monsters," the woman said.

"Mmm. Hmm."

"Who says?"

"My mom."

"Oh? And who's your mom?"

"You."

"I see. And who told you I was your mom?"

"My mom."

A greasy sickness bubbled in her stomach. The dread. Irrational. But mounting. Her blood electric. She reached back to grip the doorknob as blood thrummed at her temples.

A child shrieked. The woman flinched and looked up as a pair of kids in black capes floated along the sidewalk and melted back into the darkness.

Wait! Come back! the woman wanted to scream.

She looked down at the child again. It held something in its hand now: something gleaming. A knife. The blade long and slender. Wicked.

The woman held out the bowl of candy.

"Take all you want," she croaked, "and go."

The child's black eyes stared.

The woman's eyes caught the silver glint of the knife blade as the child jabbed it at her belly.

"Jesus!" she cried. "You little shi—" But she could not finish. Pain cleaved her open, turned her inside out. Her hand slipped from the doorknob, and the candy bowl clattered to the porch.

Oh God.

She clutched her belly—too terrified to look—feeling a warm stickiness seep between her fingers.

The child drove the knife blade clean through her hand, and the woman howled with pain. The child plunged the knife again, just above the waistband of the woman's jeans and yanked upward.

Oh God.

She was being . . .

. . . *unzipped.*

She staggered backward, crumpling in the foyer.

The child stepped into the house and shut the door with a soft *click.* Its face hovered above the woman's. The woman reached up, clutched the mask's rubbery skin. Pulled. The mask would not come off. She dug her fingers in. Clawed. The mask stretched. The knife sliced. She tore at the mask, gasping. The child had been right.

Monsters did exist.

CHAPTER 2

October 22, 2011

The blood on Frank Rath's hands steamed in the cold October air as he slung one end of a rope over the barn's crossbeam, tied the other end to the center of the tomato stake skewered through the gutted carcass's legs, and yanked.

Pain erupted in his lower back as if he'd been struck with an axe. He dropped to his knees, the dead deer sagging back in a puddle of its own sad blood on the frozen dirt.

Rath remained still, breathing slowly through his nose, counting backward from ten. *Erector spinae.* He'd learned the Latin from studying the anatomy model while whiling away his autumn in Doc Rankin's office.

Rath's cell phone vibrated in his shirt pocket. Rachel, he hoped. For seven weeks now, she'd been away for her first semester at Johnson State, and in that time, loneliness had nested in Rath's heart. The house felt lifeless, no hum of Rachel's hair dryer in the morning, no insistent burble of incoming texts when she left her cell phone idle for even a second on the kitchen table.

Rath reached for his cell phone, but the skewering pain insisted he lower himself onto his back, where he performed an inept pelvic tilt. Doc Rankin had sent him to a whack-job physical therapist, who'd prescribed a contortionist's regimen of humiliating stretches that made Rath feel as though he were about to shit himself: stretches better suited to rich housewives who performed them in steamy rooms while listening to didgeridoo music than to a man whose idea of stretching was reaching in the top cupboard for his Lagavulin 16 and chocolate Pop Tarts. Rath gained his feet with a groan.

What worried him wasn't the pain but that the pain seemed to have no source. He'd simply awoken one morning as if someone had punched a hole in his back and ripped the *erector spinae* from his spine.

He looked down at the deer. He had to get it hung. First the deer. Then a beer. Or three.

Rath's cell phone buzzed: Harland Grout.

The lone, lead detective on the anemic Canaan police force, Grout was as green as the back of a wet frog. He was also a dart player in Rath's dart league. Most importantly, he had a strong young back good for lifting a dead deer.

Rath answered. "Grout. I'm trying to hang a deer here. Maybe you'd like to earn a six-pack and lend your—"

"There's a car. Out on Route fifteen," Grout said.

"That sort of specificity and twenty bucks Canadian will buy you a lap dance at The Dirty Girl over the border in Richelieu."

"Yeah," Grout said, and Rath noted a barb of severity in his voice that made him regret his initial glibness.

"What?" Rath said, and wandered out of the barn to lean against the fender of the '74 International Scout it seemed he'd been restoring since Lincoln was a Whig.

"The car appears abandoned." Grout paused to wait for the static of the weak signal to pass. Up here, near the border, there wasn't one cell tower within five thousand miles. God bless Vermont. Or not. "The car belongs to my wife's cousin's daughter."

"Shit," Rath said, not even trying to untangle that snarl of family-tree branches.

"She's sixteen."

"Shit." Rath slumped against the Scout. "You think something happened?"

Something happened. What euphemistic bullshit for the images—none pretty—that leapt into Rath's mind the instant he heard of a girl gone missing.

"It's hard telling," Grout said. "I just got the call on the car. When I called her mom, she was worried. Hasn't heard from her in days and asked me to look into it."

"Why call me? She's a minor, you can investigate it straightaway as an MP."

"She's emancipated."

"Shit," Rath said again. His repertoire of blue language needed work.

Unless foul play was clearly evident, seventy-two hours had to pass before an official investigation could begin on a missing adult. And, by Vermont law, an emancipated girl, sixteen or not, was an adult. It made no sense. Sixteen was a *child*, and any adult who looked at a girl that young and saw anything *but* a child was deluded or a pervert.

"I'm on my way there now," Grout said. "For all we know, the car's clean, and she's just off banging a boyfriend or crashed at a girlfriend's. Or something. I got Sonja Test headed there, on her own time, giving up her Saturday training to bumper-to-bumper it best she can *in situ*. That itself is against protocol without probable. But Chief Barrons is out three more days fishing the Bahamas, and—"

"That bastard," Rath said. Barrons had been Rath's senior the three years Rath was a state-police detective in the 1990s. Barrons was an exceptional cop and an even better fisherman. Rath wasn't sure for which trait he resented and envied Barrons more.

"So," Grout said, "I'm taking liberties as it is without leaving my entire nutsack hanging out for Barrons to lop off and brine when he gets back. This girl is, technically, family; if it looks like I'm playing favorites or expending resources without due cause, and the girl just strolls in, my ass is in a sling, right when it's looking like the budget might open up, and there's a shot at a promotion. At the same time—"

"Fuck protocol," Rath said. The hard consonants felt good to bite off and spit out. *But, what promotion?* If Grout wanted to excel in law enforcement, he should have taken Rath's advice several years back and gone to the staties. And he shouldn't have been calling Rath for help. Grout needed to take the helm himself, damn the repercussions: Protocol never outweighed doing what was right. Rath knew that if he wanted to help Grout and his career, he should force Grout to see this through on his own and be either tempered or turned to ash by the heat he'd feel from Barrons.

But there was a missing girl. That came before any career.

"I could use your help," Grout said. "Even if it becomes official, it's still just an MP, a low priority unless it becomes something else."

Something else.

The sun glared on the skin of snow that had fallen overnight, melting fast, water dripping from the barn roof to tick on a sheet of rusted tin that had been leaning against the barn since the Pleistocene ice age.

Rath lit a cigarette and drew in the smoke. All he got from it was trembling fingertips and a numb nose. He needed to go back to dipping.

His cell-phone screen glowed with an incoming call: Stan Laroche. Rath let it go.

"Where's the car?" Rath asked Grout.

Grout told him, and Rath tossed his cigarette into a rag of snow, where it settled with a paling hiss. He ended the call and looked back at the dead deer on the barn floor.

"Not today, pal."

He yanked shut the barn door, to keep out the coyotes that skulked around the place at night; he had a draining feeling that he'd be occupied until long after dark.

In his kitchen, an ember of pain glowing in the old *erector spinae*, Rath scrubbed his hands with Lava soap, the water foaming pink with deer blood. He searched the freezer for an ice pack, remembered he'd left it in bed where it was now thawed, and dug out a pack of frozen peas. He snatched a bottle of Vicodin off the counter, slugged back two pills with a half bottle of Molson Golden left in the sink from the night before, then listened to Laroche's message: "Rath. Laroche. Call me."

Laroche. Mr. Department of Corrections; no doubt calling to weasel out of darts so his wife could strut off to some scrapbooking or karaoke night with the gals. Supposedly. Rath suspected there was a man involved. He deleted the message. Let Laroche swing.

In the Scout, Rath tucked the pack of peas behind his back, sighing at the minor temporary relief it brought. He worked the Scout's choke and fired up the old lady. With 350,670 miles on her, she had leaky gaskets and bad springs, but she kept on stubbornly plugging along. Not unlike Rath.

CHAPTER 3

Rath drove north on his dirt road, past the enormous, looming, granite face of Canaan Monadnock, which gave way to flat farmland with the abruptness of the Fundy Escarpment smacking up to the Atlantic's edge; a geologic anomaly in a state of worn, aged mountains that folded into gentle foothills and gradually leveled out into Lake Champlain to the west and the Connecticut River to the east.

As a boy, Rath had been fascinated by this peculiarity and spent nights tucked under his covers, his sister asleep in her bed beside his, enrapt by books on plate tectonics, volcanoes, and the Earth's molten core. In 1862, whalebones had been unearthed by a farmer's plow blade in the surrounding fields; eleven thousand years before the world's most famed carpenter supposedly rose again, the glaciers had retreated, and the Atlantic had rushed in, creating a paratropical ocean that for three thousand years reached north to the Saint Lawrence and west to Ottawa. Hence: whalebones. Those early years, Rath had been obsessed with the violence of nature and how it shaped the physical world. As he'd grown older, his fixation had shifted from the violence of nature to the nature of violence, and how to stop it.

Rath turned north onto Route 15, toward Canada, lighting a cigarette and wondering about this missing girl.

Up ahead, the mountain foliage was set ablaze with the beauty of autumn's death, a supreme loveliness that people traveled across the globe to view from Peter Pan buses.

Regional tourists, those rocketing up I-89 to flee Boston in their Beemers, cruising in Volvo Cross Countrys up I-91 North from Connecticut, and oozing south from Montreal in Jag XJs were lulled by the pastoral idyll, the dairy farms dotted with black-and-white Holsteins; sugar shacks tucked tidily among the sugarbush; general stores painted "barn red" to approximate the original nineteenth-century pigment created from rust.

As soon as the sightseers crossed into the land where billboards were banned for their affront to nature's aesthetics, they settled into their heated leather seats, bathed in a Rockwellian serenity and liberated from the gray grind of urban life. They'd power down their windows to breathe in the crisp mountain air, buoyed and intoxicated by the setting and by a pang of nostalgia for a past they'd never lived but could taste on their tongues nonetheless. Here, the air was sweeter. Here, they were alive. Safe.

Safe. Rath snorted as he adjusted his back against the pack of thawing peas. Nowhere was safe. No one. Violence lurked here as it did the world over, most often exacted by known parties. Intimate, familial, and unspeakable.

He'd always wondered why people in rural areas, when interviewed after appalling violence, said, "This isn't supposed to happen here." As if violence had forgotten to keep itself within some prescribed geographic boundary.

Rath drove along a piece of road that annually made the *New York Times's Top 10 Fall Foliage Drives,* but was known to locals as Murder Road: the stretch where Gabe Hoyt shot his cousin. The two men had been arguing over a woman in Hoyt's truck when Hoyt crashed his rig. As his cousin staggered away, Hoyt shot him in the head with a .45 he kept in his glove box. Panicking, Hoyt ran over his cousin's skull with his truck, believing it would hide the evidence. Good theory, for a pickled redneck. The blood still stained the road here, a dark smear like that left by a deer mauled by a logging truck.

Rath flicked cigarette ash in the Scout's ashtray.

There was last year's home invasion of two married Vermont Law School professors who had been tied up, tortured with a blowtorch, and bludgeoned with the fire poker they'd last used to stoke a Christmas fire. The fifteen-year-old killers recorded the crime on their cell phones. Neither boy had even a whiff of a violent past. They'd simply skipped school on a whim and along the way gotten it in their heads it would be "freaky" to kill someone. So. Knock knock.

How did one explain such acts? What word did you put to them other than evil?

Rath drew in smoke from his cigarette. The tobacco crackled.

Then, of course, there were the Pritchards, slaughtered on Monday, May 3, 1995, a notorious crime, because of the baby.

At 4:30 P.M., Laura Pritchard had returned home from the farmer's market, put the baby to sleep upstairs, and was preparing a birthday dinner for her younger brother, when the doorbell rang. Her brother was supposed to have met her at the farmer's market. But he'd not shown, as usual. With a woman, as usual. No regard for anyone but himself. So she'd gone to the door, likely expecting it was him.

But it wasn't him. It was the man who had once mown Laura's lawn. A Mr. Fix It who drove a jalopy truck with power tools clanking around in the bed and a sign on the door that boasted FREE ESTIMATES. Ned Preacher. Though that wasn't the name he used then.

Laura must have been surprised to see him. Not just because he wasn't her brother but because, sixteen months earlier, Ned had skipped town, leaving a check due him for $150. Perhaps she'd thought Preacher had finally come to collect.

Rath had been first on the scene, and in the years since then, he'd imagined every possible scenario that might have transpired in that doorway. He'd found the front door open and a lake of blood soaking the carpet, clots and strings of it slopped on the walls like some macabre Pollack painting.

Laura's body had lain at the bottom of the stairs in an undignified pose: her legs pinned abnormally beneath her torso, her lacerated face turned to the side as if in shame. The plush, wall-to-wall carpet, once as white as a fresh snowdrift, now so drenched with her blood it squished underfoot. Her neck had been broken, and she'd been rudely violated with objects other than the male anatomy though that would prove to have been used, too.

Rath shuddered now, his flesh cold and rubbery.

The broken neck had killed Laura, but she'd have bled out in seconds from where the knife had nicked her superior *vena cava*, preventing the flow of deoxygenated blood from her brain to her right atrium.

Daniel Pritchard's body had been draped over his wife's chest as if trying to protect her even in death, a tableau out of some twisted *Romeo and Juliet*, these players done in by another's dark impulses.

Daniel had been stabbed as he'd walked in, Preacher hiding behind the door, the knife plunged between Daniel's third and fourth ribs, slicing the liver's caudate lobe and hepatic artery. He'd suffered four defense wounds in the palms of his right hand, his right thumb dangling by a flap of skin, and two more wounds in the back of the neck, both puncturing his posterior external jugular vein beneath the splenius and trapezius muscles: death by catastrophic blood loss.

Even now, the images cast a shadow over Rath's soul and left a bitter metallic taste on his tongue. Even now, he tried to beg off the misery squeezing his heart in its ugly, unforgiving grip.

Standing there with the two bodies at his feet, it had suddenly struck Rath: the vacuum of ominous horrific soundlessness. Then. Faintly. A nearly inaudible whine, like the sound of a wet finger traced on the rim of a crystal glass, piercing his brain.

The baby.

He'd scrambled over the bodies, slipping in the blood, mindless of physical evidence, as he sprang up the stairs to thunder down the hallway and smashed open the door across from the master bedroom.

He'd rushed to the crib.

There she'd lain, tiny legs and arms pumping spasmodically, as if she'd been set afire, her mouth agape but just that shrill escape of air rising from the back of her throat, air leaking from a balloon's pinched neck.

Rath had clenched the wooden rails of the crib until they'd cracked. Downstairs lay the baby's mother, raped and murdered by a man who'd prove no stranger to rape and murder. Laura Pritchard. Loving wife. Adoring mother. Older sister to a sole sibling whose presence would have prevented the murder if he'd been on time as promised, but, as always, had failed to be, just like their old man. Laura's only sibling, her younger brother.

Frank Rath.

Rath shivered, that day as alive and crawling inside him now as then. Nothing dulled the guilt or the loss. Not even his deep love for the baby girl.

Rachel.

At the moment Rath had picked Rachel up from her crib, he'd felt an abrupt shift within him, a permanent upheaval like one plate of the Earth's lithosphere slipping beneath another; his selfish past life subducting beneath a selfless future life, a deep rift created in him, altering his inner landscape. A niece transformed into a daughter by acts of violent cruelty.

For six months after the murder, Rath had kept Rachel's crib beside his bed and lain sleepless each night as he'd listened to her frayed breathing, her every sigh and whimper. He'd panicked when she'd fallen too quiet, shaken her lightly to make certain she was alive, been flooded with relief when she'd wriggled in her swaddle. He'd picked her up and cradled her to him as she'd broken into the loneliest cry he'd ever heard, her baby heart pattering as he'd promised to keep her safe. Thinking, *If we just get through this phase with its SIDS and spiking fevers and odd diseases, you'll be OK, and I won't ever have to worry like this again.*

But peril pressed in at the edges of a girl's life, and worry planted roots in Rath's heart and bloomed wild and reckless. As Rachel had grown, Rath's worry had grown, and he'd kept vigilant for the lone man who stood with his hands jammed in his trouser pockets behind the playground fence. In public, Rath had gripped Rachel's hand fiercely, his love ferocious and animal.

If anyone *ever* did anything to her.

CHAPTER 4

The missing girl's metallic brown 1989 Monte Carlo was parked at a strange angle. Its trunk was backed up to the side of a dilapidated hay barn, so close to the road that the nose of the Monte Carlo jutted out into the soft shoulder.

Rath stood at the road's edge with Grout to study the scene.

A logging truck howled past with a load of cedar logs, its horn wailing as it kicked up a wind that ruffled Rath's thatch of black hair.

Rath spit road grit from his mouth and pulled the collar of his Johnson wool coat up around his neck.

Grout blew his nose into a red bandana. "The car is registered to Mandy Wilks, the girl," he said.

Rath knew Grout hadn't wanted to ask for help. They were friends, and they threw darts together, and Grout respected Rath. Still, no young man wanted to ask for help. Especially involving career.

"Her mother reported her missing this morning, after

she got a call about the car." Grout peeked at a sheet of paper in his hand. "Sixteen," he said. "Last seen Thursday night at about eleven."

"Where?" Rath said.

"Where she washed dishes. The Lost Mountain Inn."

"Odd."

"What?"

"Washing dishes. Odd for a girl," Rath said. "I was a dishwasher as a kid. The girls always worked out front."

"Things change," Grout said.

"Some don't. Like missing girls."

"She could have taken off of her own free will with a friend," Grout said, but his voice carried no conviction. It was a loathsome fact about the human condition: Wherever there were girls, some would go missing, plucked like errant threads from the fabric of everyday life and cast into a lurid nightmare of someone else's making. Movies created suspense out of a "forty-eight-hour window" cops had to find a girl alive, as if kidnapped girls had a "kill-by" date. The colder reality remained: A girl gone missing against her will, nine times out of ten, was dead within three hours. Usually after being raped.

"Nobody's touched anything?" Rath said.

"Not me," Grout said.

Rath rubbed his jaw, his fingers still stained pink with deer blood. "Why's it parked like that?" he muttered.

The snow had melted. Rath surveyed the ground and stepped toward the car with the mindful, deliberate motion of a soldier navigating a minefield.

"No sign of another car," Grout said. "No tire tracks. Snow is gone, but the cold snap froze the ground pretty solid last few nights."

"The other car stayed on the road," Rath said.

"If there was another car."

"There was." Rath gazed at the long, deserted stretch of road that ran north into Canada in just under a mile, then looked south to a length of road equally long and deserted. "Unless we think Mandy got out and walked because she was struck with an urge to stroll a country road in the middle of the night with a windchill of ten degrees. Not much chance of getting a boot print."

He inched closer to the car, analyzing the ground. The search was like being hungry but not knowing what you wanted to eat. You had to open the fridge and peer inside until something made your mouth water: a piece of chocolate cake, a stick of pepperoni. When you saw it, you knew it was just the thing you'd been looking for, but you had to look to *know*. His mother used to tell him when he stood with the refrigerator door open: *If you can't decide what you want, you must not be hungry. Shut the door.* But she'd only been concerned with the electric bill.

"What are you looking for?" Grout said.

"Chocolate cake. A stick of pepperoni."

Grout shook his head.

Rath craned his neck to peer inside the car as a late nineties white Peugeot, scabbed with rust at the rear fenders, rumbled up roadside, its hazards flashing.

Out stepped Canaan Police Department's forensics team-of-one and lone part-time junior detective, Sonja Test. Dartmouth graduate, *summa cum laude*, crazed marathon runner with the lean, taut physique to match; wife of Claude Test, wildlife oil-paint artist of limited regional renown; mother of Elizabeth and George, ages six and three.

"Gentlemen," Sonja said as she hefted her kit from the Peugeot's front seat and nodded.

She caught her short red hair in her hand, pulled it back taut to wrap a rubber band around it and make a stunted ponytail. She tugged a white shower cap over it, then peeled surgical gloves on over her long, slender fingers.

As she set to work on the Monte Carlo, Rath turned to Grout. "What else is in that folder of yours?"

The two men sat in Rath's Scout, the folder open between them on the bench seat.

"Sixteen," Rath said. A year younger than Rachel. His stomach felt as if he'd swallowed crystal Drano.

"Hard age," Grout said.

"What age isn't? Emancipated. Nice family you got."

"Extended."

"And you personally spoke to the mother?" Rath said.

"Briefly. This morning, after the car was found, and she got worried."

"Who discovered the car?"

"Lee Storrow. He was spreading salt with the town rig before dawn. Called the dispatcher, pissed off that a car was *parked in the fucking road.*"

Rath pushed the lighter into the dash. If for no other reason, he'd kept the Scout because it had a lighter and a solid metal ashtray.

"So," Grout said, "we can discount any connection between the person who discovered the car and the disappearance of the girl driving it."

"If it was her driving it," Rath said.

"Naturally," Grout said, though Rath could see that possibility had not occurred to Grout.

Rath lit his cigarette, drew the smoke deep. It tasted

like dryer lint, but he'd suck it to the filter anyway. That's why they called it addiction. At least his lips weren't suctioned to a bottle of Beam. Lung cancer instead of cirrhosis. Here's to you.

"What's so funny?" Grout said, catching the shine in Rath's eyes.

"Me. I'm an idiot."

"And that's funny to you?"

"I rest my case."

"Can you roll down your window? Your cigarette smoke—"

"My window hasn't rolled down since Letterman wore sneakers," Rath said.

Grout rolled down his window and coughed.

"Now that the drama's out of the way," Rath said. He swept cigarette ash from the report. "I wonder—"

A rap came at Rath's window, startling him. He dropped his cigarette in his lap, snatched it and stuck it back in his mouth.

Sonja stood at his window, a grin pasted to her face. It was a pretty face.

Rath opened the truck door.

"I'm done with cursory," Sonja said.

"You shouldn't sneak up on people," Rath said.

"*I* saw her from ten feet away," Grout said.

Rath made to get out of the Scout, and the nerves in his back exploded. He clutched the door, sweat flooding his brow.

"Bad back?" Sonja said, squinting at him.

"You could say that."

"Heat's good for it."

"My doc says ice."

"He's the doctor, I guess."

Rath flicked his cigarette to the road and stood erect with a wince.

"What's the short version?" Grout asked Sonja.

"Tons of prints. It's like an iPad screen in there. Some hair. Long, red. Probably hers. No blood, to the naked eye. I'll know better once I put the Luminol to it."

"You won't find anything," Rath said. "The car's clean."

"That'll have to wait till Barrons is back anyway," Grout said.

"It shouldn't. We should move on this," Sonja said. "No sign of a struggle either. Which means if she was taken, it was someone she knew and trusted, or—"

"—someone who tricked her," Grout finished.

"Right," Sonja said, not one to be interrupted apparently, even by her pseudosuperior. "Nothing in the trunk but a tire iron, a spare, jumper cables."

She led them to the Monte Carlo, her pert runner's backside pushing snugly against her faded jeans. Rath looked off toward plowed-under cornfields.

Sonja pointed at the ignition. The keys were in it. "There's cash on the floor," she said. "Three fives and twenty-eight ones."

"Forty-three dollars," Grout said.

"Math whiz here," Sonja said.

"Her share of tips," Rath said.

"This isn't going to end the way the mother hopes, is it?" Grout said.

CHAPTER 5

Rath drove toward Mandy's mother's house, trying not to think of Sonja's ass. With Rachel's absence, he felt long-dormant urges of his awakening. He didn't like them. They worried and upset him. Ghosts from a past life he wished would remain dead.

His cell phone vibrated. Laroche. Rath let it go, thinking of Sonja's ass. Women. His failing. The old man's.

The day of Laura's murder, Rath had been at the height of his promising detective career, working under Barrons on the Connecticut River Valley Killer case. From May 1994 to July 1995, the CRVK had raped and strangled five female victims in the region, then dumped their bodies in the woods. The case had thrust Barrons and Rath into the national spotlight, the crimes being the only serial-murder investigation known to Vermont, then or since. It could have made Rath's career.

Rath had also been at the apex of his bachelorhood: broad-shouldered, muscled, arrogant, his lightning blue eyes, the old man's eyes, not yet dimmed by the vulgarities to come. Women had been drawn to him in or out of uniform though the gun and cuffs at his hips hadn't hurt. He'd made no qualms about wanting zero ties with the women. We're adults. No harm done.

Except that while Laura was being raped and stabbed, her neck broken, Rath had been with a waitress who'd been wild in bed in a way Rath pegged then as an animal sexuality but knew now was born of loneliness. The same way he knew now his behavior then had been anything but adult. His callousness and lack of perspective then startled him now when he thought of it, something he tried not to do.

By the time he'd pulled into Laura's drive an hour late, buzzing from his conquest, he'd crafted a lie about having to work on the CRVK case. Who could fault him? Besides, it had been his birthday. He was entitled. Wasn't he?

After he'd found Laura, he'd vowed he'd never lie again.

He'd discover soon enough just how impossible that was.

Rath hated this part.

He got out of the Scout and let the autumn sun bathe his face with warmth that betrayed the brisk mountain air. Lately, when he came in from the cold, lines that had once gone away as his skin warmed now remained.

Mandy's mother's house was a fifties ranch with faded, beige, vinyl siding that hung just off level, likely from being slapped up by a guy who eked a living out of the same van in which he trucked his kids to Little League. A birdbath was wedged out in the lawn, dried up and crusted with moss.

Rath knew this house. It was the same house he'd

grown up in; the same house as a million others from Portland, Maine, to Portland, Oregon. Common. What troubled Rath was that inside the house nothing was any longer common. And nothing ever would be again, whether Mandy came home after crashing on a friend's couch or her desecrated body was found in the dank reek of a rapist's cellar.

Rath told himself to remain hopeful. Maybe Mandy *had* run off with a boy for a romp in a Montreal hotel, where the two could drink legally and play adults and enjoy more of life than what these back roads offered. And once they got their ya-yas out, they'd come back. Safe.

Except Mandy's tips were left on the Monte Carlo's floor, the keys in the ignition. No. Hope was a luxury. And Rath had to knock on the door and ask the missing girl's mother painful, intrusive questions, yank scabs off tender wounds and gouge old sores, let the blood run fresh.

He craved a cigarette.

A shade pulled back from the living-room window, then settled again.

Rath knocked on a metal storm door caved in from being slammed against the porch rail, perhaps by the savage mountain winds up here, perhaps by a savage temper.

Faint footsteps came from inside, and a bony woman with hair heaped in the unkempt tangle of the sleepless opened the main door. She wore a sweat suit the color of mold and stared with eyes whose only glint was that of pain. She pushed the storm door open. "Yeah?" she said.

"Mrs. Wilks?"

"I suppose."

"Sorry?"

"I use the name, but we're divorced. They charge a ransom for a woman to get her own name back. Didn't have it in me to suffer one more humiliation."

"I understand."

"I doubt it."

"My mom was married to a lout," Rath said, giving louts everywhere a bad name.

The corner of the woman's mouth twitched, as close to a smile as he'd get, he supposed.

"I'm Frank Rath. Harland Grout's friend. What do you prefer I call you?"

"Doris. Come in. I don't need to be heating the outdoors."

Rath stepped inside. Doris Wilks shut the door, and the living room fell as dark and silent as a confessional, the room's velour shades drawn and not a single bulb burning. A chemical pine scent made Rath's nose itch. In the quiet shadows sat a sectional sofa of the sort found at a Rent-A-Center: purple velveteen marshmallow cushions that suggested sumptuous comfort but swallowed you whole with all the support of overcooked pasta. On the wall above it, crooked shelves displayed dusty Beanie Babies.

Doris pulled the chain on a floor lamp to shed a funereal glow on the room. A dog, if that's what you'd call the lint ball perched on the ottoman, yapped.

"*Shut* it," Doris croaked. Lint Ball curled on itself like a pill bug.

"Sit." Doris nodded at the couch. Rath knew he'd sink into the atrocity and look even less official than he already was, so he said, "Bad back. I'd better stand."

"In the kitchen," Doris said, swinging her head toward a doorway. "The chairs are sturdier. Couch is a black hole."

Doris flipped a switch on the kitchen wall, and a naked fluorescent ceiling light spit to life. The Z-Brick linoleum was tacky beneath Rath's boots, reminding him of the meat markets on 25¢-Draft Nite during his BU days. He and Doris sat across from each other at a chipped Formica table.

"Mind I smoke?" She brought a Salem Light to her lips, lit it with a paper match.

"Mind if I do?" Rath said, figuring their common vice might gain him an edge.

"Have at it."

Rath lit up, getting nothing for his effort but a faint headache.

"Tell me about your daughter," he said.

Doris drew a deep drag and exhaled.

Mandy was her only child. Doris had been pregnant twice, "a million years ago." After that, she and the ex had given up on a family and pretty much everything else. Then she got pregnant at thirty-five. "It took," she said. "There was something wrong with the others." She waved smoke from her face. "I had to, you know."

Rath didn't need this information, but he let her tell it because she needed to tell it. And it would loosen her up.

"Mandy was a miracle," she said. "The ex didn't see it that way. Wanted to terminate her, too. Not because anything was wrong. Argued he was too old for tantrums. This from a man who still has tantrums."

"Is he why Mandy sought emancipation? Because—"

"—He's an asshole? Pretty much." Doris's face sagged as she tapped cigarette ash in a foil TV-dinner tray puddled with congealed gravy.

"When was the last time you saw Mandy?"

"Five days ago."

"What happened?"

"I had taken her to a job interview at the Lost Mountain Inn. She got the job, and they wanted her to start that night. I wanted to celebrate for once, take her to lunch or something. But she was too nervous to eat. So we went to the Dress Shoppe. They have a good clearance going on."

Doris made a squeaky sound with her lips, and Lint Ball leapt in her lap and bared its rat teeth at Rath. "Idiot," she said, scratching the dog's ear. "Mandy found her as a pup, in a box on the side of the road. A whole litter. The others were dead. Mandy nursed her from a bottle. But her new roomie has mean cats, so. Who does such a thing? Leaves puppies to die?"

Rath wondered if she was trying to distract him. "Why'd you drive her to her interview?" He flicked ashes in the TV-dinner tray, seeing no other place to do so.

"She has the Monte Carlo."

"I'm her mother."

"But she sought emancipation."

"Because of Asshole. I ain't a saint. I make mistakes. But she was right. I shoulda divorced him long ago. Shoulda never taken it."

"He abuse you?"

She shrugged. Rath made a note. Underlined it.

"He abuse her?" Rath said.

"Phh. He couldn't be bothered."

Rath didn't believe her.

"You sure?" he said.

"Of course I'm sure. He's too lazy. Besides, he'd so

much as touched her, she'd have cut his nuts off." She laughed. "She's stronger than me that way. And smart. Not test smart maybe. But commonsense smart."

"Where's your ex-husband live?"

"Some shit hole with his new wife—139 Pine Street."

"When did you divorce?"

"Nine months ago."

"And he's married again already?"

"Like I said. Asshole."

"What's his name?"

"Larry."

Rath made a note. "And you're on good terms now, with Mandy?"

"Pretty good. She's sixteen. I hated my mother when I was sixteen."

"Why's that?"

"I was *sixteen*."

"Did you and Mandy argue recently?"

"She'd never let me drive her if she were pissed. She don't compromise. Not Mandy."

"And you haven't heard from her since?"

"She said she'd call and let me know how her first night went. She never did. I figured she got busy. *Teenagers*. Then I found out about the car." She sighed heavily and collapsed on herself like a punctured tire. "She's a good girl. Smile that'd break your heart. Ask anyone."

"I will." Rath snubbed his cigarette as Doris tamped her pack and knocked one free. Lit a match.

"Did anything strange happen that day?" Rath said.

"Strange?" The match burned down toward her fingers as she stared beyond it, her eyes emptying. The flame reached her fingertips, and Rath was about to snuff it out when Doris finally shook the match, a tendril of smoke spinning in the air between them, leaving the bite of sulfur in Rath's nostrils.

Doris reflected, her eyes clouding.

Rath let Doris untangle her cat's cradle of thoughts.

"We were in the Dress Shoppe." Clarity returned to her eyes. "I asked Mandy about a dress. But she was distracted." Doris paused and closed her eyes. She opened her eyes and resumed. "Then she said, 'Hold on' and went out. I was going to spy. *Nosey mom.* But the salesgirl came up and started going on about how gorgeous Mandy is and hauled me off to show me just the *perfect* full-price dress. Before I knew it, Mandy was back. I figured she'd seen a friend, or wanted to sneak a cigarette. She smokes and thinks I don't know it."

"How long was she gone?"

"Five minutes. Tops."

"How was she after that? If you could use just one word to describe it."

"One word?"

"One."

Memory was a devil that wore many disguises. Wrong in detail and fact. In court, a prosecutor or DA shot more holes in testimony based on eyewitness recollection than a redneck shooting a road sign with a .12 gauge. Witnesses seldom stopped to actually *remember.* To get them to focus, Rath asked them to use one word to describe a detail, a person's height or the color of a car driving from a crime scene.

"Close your eyes," Rath said. "See her face."

Doris closed her eyes, eyeballs spasming beneath their lids.

She opened her eyes. "Done," she said. "Exhausted.

She wanted to get home. She didn't seem excited anymore. About the new job or the clothes."

"Did you ask her about it?"

"She thinks I pry. So, no." She blew out a breath.

"You can't beat yourself up over these things."

"Yes you can," she said.

Yes, Rath thought, you can. Forever. Without it ever changing a thing. "You know anyone who might want to hurt your daughter?" Rath said.

She nodded without hesitation.

He leaned forward, surprised. "Who?"

"No one in particular."

Rath frowned, confused.

"You haven't seen her, have you?" Doris said.

"I have a snapshot Grout had from a family thing." The photo wasn't great, a candid taken at a cookout, a bit at a distance with people around her, but it did show a clearly pretty girl with red hair, a heart-shaped face, and caramel eyes that locked on you.

"You've never *seen her*," Doris said. "In person. When I told you the salesgirl was prattling about Mandy being gorgeous, she wasn't *just* trying to sell a dress. Mandy's a jaw-dropper. She *radiates*. A smile like sunshine's pouring from her. Her eyes, that red hair. But, she don't photograph that way. In photos, she looks pretty. But in *life*. She *stops* people."

Doris smiled, sadly. Then in a hushed, confessional tone, said: "She attracts men, Mr. Rath. All kinds. All ages. They get this *glaze*. Like they want to *own* her, bring her home, and put her in a glass cage, keep her *safe* from the bad men, which, of course, *they're* not. They're the only one who can save her."

Doris shivered. She seemed caught in the whirlwind

of speaking about Mandy, as if doing so might conjure her up here and now, and they could be done with the mystery of her whereabouts and go on with life.

"Mandy makes boys crazy, Mr. Rath, and middle-aged men insane for their lost youth. They say such *desperate* things to her."

"Does anyone in particular get this 'glaze'?"

"*Everyone.* You would."

"I doubt—"

"You would. Even women get it. Some people like to hurt a girl like that. Just because she exists. You need to find her."

"We'll find her," Rath said, meaning it.

"Alive?"

"Yes," Rath said, lying.

CHAPTER 6

Endorphins slammed through Sonja as she ran up Gamble Hill, a sublime ache in her calves and thighs, body sheathed in sweat, the deep, steady rhythm of her breathing accompanying the metronomic pace of her Asics striking the dirt road as she gained the top of the hill at the same speed she'd started with a quarter mile back at the bottom. There was no better rush than being awash in her chemical high. Marijuana in high school had left her lobotomized, and her one-time dalliance with coke at Dartmouth had left her nerve endings feeling raked raw and dipped in kerosene. Not even sex with Claude got her blood surging like running did, not that they'd found the time of late.

She wiped stinging sweat from her eyes with the hem of her running shirt, tipped on her toes to flex her calves, then jogged lightly in place, her mind clearing.

Her house sat far below in the valley, a cottage that had been added onto three times since a Civil War veteran had built the original home in 1867. She could just make it out from here. It squatted in a small field that had once been an apple orchard, of which only a few fruitless trees remained. The golden autumn sunlight glanced off the slate-shingle roof whose weight caused the roofline to sag like the spine of an old mare. She loved the old house. Did not want to restore or remodel it. She loved it for what it was. Old. And a long way from Chicago and her parents. It was home, where she would spend the rest of her life. Where she would die. Knowing this filled her with the peace of mind that came with certainty.

She touched her toes, cracked her back. The road ahead traversed Gamble Ridge for 2.8 miles then took a steep descent into the river valley, where she'd take River Road north four miles back to home.

She popped in her iPod's earbuds and cranked R.E.M.'s "E-Bow The Letter," set it to loop, preferring its melancholic throb to music that assailed, like the System of a Down or AC/DC that inspired Claude. His clients would be aghast to know their pastoral paintings were created to such *tasteless* music.

As Stipe's voice incanted *Look up, what do you see? All of you, and all of me*, Sonja set out leisurely to get her blood flowing again, pacing herself.

Up ahead, a woman with a lovely black mane of hair was at her mailbox. As Sonja approached, she saw that the woman was a man. His bare feet were grimed, his faded jeans torn, and his blousy tunic stained with what looked like strawberries. Or blood. Back in the day, he'd probably followed The Dead until Jerry had croaked, then toured with Phish; a UNH or UVM English major who'd retreated to where land was still cheap, and he could be left alone with his LSD flashbacks.

But Sonja thought he'd been a woman. Her radar was off, and it bothered her.

She settled into a languid stride, working up to a refreshing six-minute pace. A heart-attack pace, Claude would say. They used to jog together, before the kids. After jogging, they'd make love, shower together, then sit out on the back porch in the dark, drink a sixer of Long Trail as they listened to the tree frogs sing.

When Sonja hadn't been able to jog the last few months of carrying George, Claude had given it up. After George had arrived, Sonja had grown depressed by her inactivity, felt like a dirty gym sock filled with custard.

When she'd finally been cleared to jog, and was able to squeeze in time for it, a trigger had been pulled, and she found she'd needed the rush to start her day right and to think straight. She'd morphed from jogging casually in whatever shorts and T she threw on, into a gearhead runner seeking the perfect two-hundred-dollar running shoe, synthetic sweat-wicking garb, and heart-rate wristband, fanatical about improving time. She'd run every weekend 5k race within a hundred miles, May through October.

Then 5k had become 10k. Then half marathons. Now, finally, the Burlington City marathon. Her eating had become regimented. Food, which she'd always indulged in for the sheer pleasure of taste—from sushi or a bloody burger, to a chocolate shake or a Velveeta & Wonder Bread grilled cheese—had been reduced to fuel ingested solely for its grams of protein, fat, and complex carbs.

She was unclear on what compelled her to run with such mania. Exhilaration and competition played a part.

But there was something else. She needed something of her own; though this notion had a Virginia Woolf smack to it that gagged her. Claude had his painting, which had many times taken him deep into the night in the carriage-house studio. It also fed a part of him she never could. She loved and resented him for it. But she understood. Her own career fed her similarly. It was purposeful and gratifying work that required intelligence and precision, cunning and nerve and study. It gave her satisfaction.

She ran, the dirt road testing her ankle strength as she thought about Mandy's car. Against protocol, against Grout's wishes, she'd had the Monte Carlo towed to the department's evidence garage and put the Luminol to it. The car was clean, as Rath had supposed. He was good at his work. Remote, perhaps. But there was much to learn from him, and she kept alert, particularly with the rumors of new positions possible. If Rath hinted at an angle on this missing girl, she'd pursue it in a blink. As of now, they had zilch. Even the tip money could easily have fallen out of Mandy's handbag. And Mandy was, legally, an adult. If alive, she had the freedom to do as she wished.

Running was Sonja's freedom. Sixty minutes a day. She paid for even that. Last night in bed, Claude had rested his latest Jim Harrison novel on his softening stomach, peered over his Rite Aid reading glasses, and said, "You think you could eat what the rest of us eat just one night a week instead of gulping juiced broccoli and fish oil?"

No, she'd said. She'd been clear about the sacrifice the marathon would demand. He shouldn't act so wounded. Besides, once she ran Burlington, that'd be it. He said he'd heard that before. True. She was obsessed. She'd once mocked weekend-warrior athletes who never broke from their crazy diets. At George's last birthday, she'd downed a protein shake instead of hot dogs; nibbled cake as if it were poison—a bakery cake at that. She'd always baked the kids' cakes. But baking would have cut into her running time.

The worst was that her period had stopped and wouldn't return until after the marathon, months from now. She and Claude had planned to have three children. An only child seemed too lonely an existence for the child. Two kids seemed like a census-bureau statistic. Three kids were ideal. She'd had a bad miscarriage between Elizabeth and George. And after the half marathon last year, she hadn't gotten her cycle straight for six months. "What if it screws you up permanently?" Claude had said.

She'd been furious. And scared. She would be thirty-two in May, and while that was young, she was edging closer to being on the bubble with the risk of Down syndrome and other conditions. Conditions that, they agreed, would result in ending the pregnancy.

She was gambling her family's future for a race. As much as she was capable at deciphering the motives of others, she was dreadful at doing the same for herself.

She ran hard now, her heart pounding like a madman's fist at the asylum door, the air redolent with the metallic tang of minerals in the roadside ledge, wetted darkly with leaking groundwater.

The road began its descent toward the river as she fell more on her heels now, a pronounced strain on the body, the jamming of joints, the constant resistance to gravity's wanting its way with her as she thought about the

man at the mailbox. He'd looked so much like a woman.
Fooled her until she was right upon him. It was perfectly reasonable to think such long hair had belonged
to a woman. So why did it bother her so much?

Nearer, nearer, Patti Smith intoned hauntingly, promising over and over to take Sonja there.

Sonja's work cell phone buzzed in its Velcro hip pouch.
She slowed and took the phone out. Lou McCreary,
medical examiner here in Victory County, just south of
Canaan County, and Sonja's neighbor. He could only be
calling for one reason. A body.

Sonja stopped running.

CHAPTER 7

The Dress Shoppe welcomed Rath with the aroma he thought would have a name like Sandalwood or Beach Dunes. The jangle of the bell above the door brought three female clerks capering toward him in unison, as if performing a Broadway number for the easy mark: the husband in the doghouse or the boyfriend looking to get into his girlfriend's pants, thinking the perfect ensemble would do the trick.

A woman in her forties, the oldest of the three, glided over to Rath, her canary yellow dress, splashed with vibrant daffodils, swishing at the hem, her white bangle bracelets clacking. She was tanned and fit. The tan did not have the orange tint of a spray. It was a glow he suspected came from time outdoors hiking or gardening, not splayed out on a beach towel, what was once thought of as a healthy tan. He imagined her calves and arms were sculpted from being active in the natural, physical world. Rath detected the faintest scent of lilac as the woman reached out a hand, her fingernails blunt, a hint of pale pink from an unassuming manicure.

Rath shook her hand to find her skin soft as a flower petal, her grip lingering for a split second.

"I'm Madeline," she said with plucky ebullience. "May I help you?"

"A mother and a daughter were in here five days ago," Rath said. "I'm helping the mother." Rath handed the clerk Mandy's photo, wishing he'd asked Doris for a "good" one.

"I don't understand," the clerk said.

"The girl seems to have disappeared."

The clerk's pupils bloomed with fear. "You're the police?"

"I'm helping. Officially, the police can't be involved for a couple days."

"But by then—"

"That's why I'm helping out." Rath showed her his ID. "I want to find this girl as soon as possible." He nodded at the photo of Mandy in the clerk's hand.

The clerk seemed rightfully guarded and was about to shake her head *no* when recognition lit her face. "They were in here. Bought a few of the marked-down summer dresses we're pushing." She spread her palms over the dress she was wearing. "Thus my drastically out-of-season attire. I didn't recognize her in the photo at first. It doesn't do her justice. It's like a photo of her ugly-duckling cousin."

"So you assisted her, miss?"

"Madeline. Come with me," she said, her fingernails just grazing the inside of Rath's wrist as she slid away. An electric warmth spread up Rath's arm at the kiss of Madeline's touch.

She led Rath to the back, through a curtained doorway and into a break room that consisted of a card table with mismatched folding chairs. On the table, an empty coffeepot sat ticking on a hot plate next to a microwave, electrical cords stretched to an outlet in the wall. The room smelled of burned coffee. OSHA'd love this setup. "How can I help?" Madeline said.

"Was there anything you sensed that was odd about her?"

The coffeepot ticked.

"No," she said. "No strange vibe."

"What *was* their vibe? In one word."

"Alive. Whatever *IT* is, this girl had *IT.* For her mom, I'd say tickled. The girl went outside, and I brought the mom over to a just-the-most-perfect dress. When I glanced out, I saw the girl across the street. Just. Staring."

"At what?"

"I don't know."

"No one was with her?" Rath said.

"Might have been, but not that I saw."

"How did she seem when she came back in?"

"One word? Remote."

"And the mother?"

"Bothered."

Rath gave her his card and told her to call, day or night, if she recalled anything.

As he made to leave, Madeline said, "No dress for your wife?"

Rath brandished a ring finger that was not living up to its name.

Madeline's ring finger was bare, too, a detail he'd have noted straight away in his earlier days. Since Laura's murder, the closest Rath had come to dating were the days strolling Rachel in the park where local moms brought their kids. Flirting had consisted of asking about potty training techniques, when to bribe with stickers. If any of the mothers had hit on him, he'd been unaware in his fugue of sleeplessness and blind infatuation with Rachel. His depression had left him with barely enough energy to focus on work and Rachel, and none for chasing women, a pursuit that only sickened him now as he could not help but equate it with the death of Laura.

"Girlfriend?" Madeline said, raising an eyebrow.

Was she flirting? No. She was looking to sell a dress.

"I'm. In between," Rath said.

"Good in between or bad in between?"

He felt the warmth wash through him as when her fingernails grazed his wrist.

"Good, I guess," he said.

"So. No one in your life at all who could use a dress?"

"My daughter."

"Oh. How old?"

"Seventeen." A year older than Mandy. The thought chilled him. "I don't know the last time I saw her wear a dress, though. I stopped buying her clothes years ago. I just hand over the money. I never got it right anyway."

"Maybe I could help."

"Maybe another time." He slipped out through the curtain.

Satan. Divorce, however, had nothing to do with possession. It was humas selfishness. The gravest sin. She must
said he'd pray for her but she was no longer a welcome

CHAPTER 8

Rath stepped onto the sidewalk outside the Dress
Shoppe. Dark clouds skidded across the sun, and a
north wind raked down the street, snapping flags in
front of shops.

He crossed the street and stood where Mandy had
stood, trying to get a feel for the location. He looked up
to the top of the street.

The Church of Unity served as the village's anchor
at the head of Main Street, with its majestic spire. He
walked up the street toward it, passing the firehouse and
a fire engine parked at the curb, around which several
young volunteer firemen stood bullshitting, nodding at
Rath as he passed.

Rath stood across from the Church of Unity. A sign
in front announced a Ham and Bean Supper Friday at
7 P.M. ALL SOULS WELCOME. Rath didn't know what de-
nomination Church of Unity was but guessed it was one
of those that cast as wide a net as possible to keep the
coffers full.

When Rath was ten, his mother had finally decided to divorce his father and confided in Father Morency, the priest who'd baptized, confirmed, and married her in the church where she'd worshipped each Sunday of her life. Father Morency had told her that marriage was a holy bond and to break it was a sin. She'd asked if serial adultery wasn't a sin. Of course, but her husband had the devil in him, and only her love could help expel Satan. Divorce, however, had nothing to do with possession. It was human selfishness. The graver sin. She must forgive. Pray for her husband. It was her duty. When she'd gone forward with the divorce, Father Morency said he'd pray for her but she was no longer a welcome member of his flock.

Along the street, pedestrians scurried, heads bowed to the wind as they soldiered in and out of shops. Down the street, a similar unremarkable scene. Rath waited and watched. Who or what had Mandy seen? There was the head shop, A Kind Place, masquerading as a purveyor of tobacco pipes and products. Had she gone in there, or into another clothes shop? Had she seen a friend? Who had seen her? A nagging need to call Rachel struck him, as it did about once an hour. Most often he fought it, wanting to grant her the space she needed to live her new college life. He could resist no longer. He pulled out his cell phone. Two whole bars. Miracle of miracles. The phone vibrated in his hand, giving him a start. Laroche. Rath ignored it.

He dialed Rachel's number and waited. Johnson State was tucked in the shadow of Mount Eden, and if two bars here in Canaan was a miracle, then a single bar on campus was The Second Coming: The faithful could hope for it, but not realistically expect any hard evidence. He knew Rachel checked messages and returned them when she was in Johnson Village.

Rath was kicked to voice mail and gladdened by the simple joy of hearing his daughter's voice: "If it's important enough to call, it's important enough to leave a message. Sooo, go for it. Love yah. Mwaaah."

"Hey, sweetie, it's Dad. Calling to see how you are. And—" He paused at a jab of guilt. He had been about to tell her he had a question about an important case. But thought better of it. "I hope classes are OK. Give a call. Sometime. Miss you."

He hit END and felt nostalgia creep into him for a time when 4 P.M. had meant Rachel would pop through the door after school to enliven the house with her enthusiastic spirit.

He didn't have a question for Rachel about the case but knew if he had left a message saying he did, it would compel her to call. He'd done such things before and felt guilty for lying. Manipulative. He had trouble with lying. Like his father. Lying seemed so simple, even necessary, but it always led to unforeseen problems. Still, he wished he'd lied to get Rachel to call back, to hear her voice.

Since she'd been eleven years old, Rachel had assisted him on cases. At first, the simple, nonviolent cases: deadbeat dads, a town clerk embezzling $623. He'd given Rachel transcripts of interviews, phone bills, and e-mails to sift for connections and patterns. It had been something to share, and they'd work on building a case the way other families worked on jigsaw puzzles.

Even then, he'd involved her out of selfishness. When he'd felt he was losing his sunny and open daughter to a private, darker imposter, it had frightened him. So he'd lured her to the kitchen table by playing to her interest in mysteries and all things vaguely sinister. She was the kid who never covered her eyes at the scary part of a movie, but awaited it giddily. When her friends had gone through their *Goosebumps* and *Harry Potter* phases, she'd been into *Gashlycrumb Tinies* and the *Complete Works of Poe.*

At work on a case, she'd hunch over files with a Fluffernutter sandwich in hand, circle details with a red pencil, and dash off notes in the Moleskine she'd bought with birthday money. When Rath had ventured over to see how things were coming, she'd shielded her work like the smart kid warding off the dimwit during finals. "Dad. *Please.* I'll report when I'm done."

Then, late last spring, a disturbing turn had taken place. Rath had been vacuuming under Rachel's bed when he'd knocked over a box of books with titles like *Serial Killers: The Method and Madness of Monsters, Blood Lust, Fiend, Houses of Death, Extreme Evil. Female Serial Killers: How and Why Women Become Monsters.*

His heartbeat had slowed, and he'd sat on the edge of her bed, terrified.

He'd fired up her laptop and found her Netflix queue showed nothing but movies like *Evil Inside Me, Black Soul, Carnage, Deranged.* No comedies, no teen flicks, no TV shows. She'd watched fifty depraved B movies and had another fifty waiting.

When he'd told Rachel he'd discovered the books, she'd laughed, "Sick, right?"

Her reaction had worried him even more.

"They worry me," he'd confessed, afraid he'd spook her away if he pressed too hard, the ice thin beneath him.

"They're for a school *report*, Dad," she'd said.

When he'd told her it was a lot of books for a report,

she'd moaned, and insisted, "It's my biggest paper. I need to investigate!"

They'd not spoken of it again.

But he wondered: As a baby, had she heard her parents' murders? Her mother's rape? What ungodly sounds had escaped Laura? What bloody, evil thumbprint might have been pressed into Rachel's soul? What demonic sound track recorded in the coils of her brain? How else to explain her craving for such base filth?

He'd never told Rachel the truth about her parents. He'd told her they'd died in a car crash. What good would it have done for her to become *The Girl Whose Parents Were Slaughtered*? Here was the bottom line: If you were associated with a violent murder like Laura's, you were stained by it. It was the most powerful lens, the only lens, through which people viewed you and through which you viewed the world. This was inalterable and absolute. This was violence's reach, and he'd wanted to spare Rachel its alienating pain.

Her parents had been killed seventy miles south, nearly seventeen years ago, and none of her friends or friends' parents knew. When he'd adopted her, he'd changed her surname to his, so there was no connection with her mother's married name. The only people who knew were in the criminal-justice profession, and they knew better than to mention it to Rath. The past year, she'd asked about her mother more, and he'd lived in fear that her curiosity would lead her to the truth. At any moment, she could discover something online. What would it do to her, to them, to find out the truth, learn he'd lied? Was that why she wasn't calling him back? She'd found out?

This was the trouble with lying: it bred paranoia.

CHAPTER 9

As Rath drove up into Aver's Gore, the Scout shuddering so hard on the dirt road that his molars ached, his back pain was ludicrous.

His cell phone vibrated on the dash. PRIVATE. Rachel? Calling from a friend's?

He answered.

"A girl's body was found, near St. J.," Sonja Test said.

"Where?"

"Victory."

Victory was situated twenty-five miles south of Canaan and ten minutes outside St. J. It had once been a booming logging town, but only a few folks still carved a living for Northern Dynasty Mills. A quiet town of fewer than a thousand souls, it had a Main Street of local establishments like Northwoods Outfitters and The Wilderness Restaurant alongside McDonald's and Dunkin' Donuts.

Sonja lived in Victory.

Rath pulled over onto an old logging road. "Is it Mandy?"

"I'm waiting to hear more from Lou. I gave him our girl's description."

Rath leaned back and stared out the windshield. The sky was a blinding blue. It was one of those days that looked balmy from inside, but bitch-slapped you with its cold hand when you stepped into it.

"I hope it's not her," he said. "I'm about to visit her roommate. Then her father. I can't inform them of a death officially. That needs to come from a cop."

"Nothing's official. I have squat except it's a dead girl."

Why is she calling me and not Grout? Rath wondered.

"Listen," she said. "Not a word to Grout. Not until we have something. OK." It wasn't a request. It was a demand. And it answered Rath's question. She was playing a dangerous game, keeping information from her superior.

"OK," Rath said, and ended the call.

He dialed Rachel. Got her voice mail. "Hey it's Dad. Call me."

It wasn't a request.

Rath drove by mailboxes crammed into rusted milk cans and boasting French names, the progeny of drunken fur traders whose feral stock lived on in a legion of loggers and roofers, masons and dairy farmers: LaSalle, Lepage, Leduc, LaValle, Lavec. The names made Rath thirst for a Laphroaig as he came upon a dented mailbox with the name Duffy scribbled on it with black marker. Which one of these names doesn't belong?

A crummy split-level house sat atop a steep, gravel drive, the gravel washed to the side in fans by runoff. Rath pulled the Scout up the drive and parked on a patch of dead grass next to a nineties Corolla with a faded FREE TIBET bumper sticker. He walked past the Corolla, black beads dangling from the car's rearview, the rear floor littered with candy wrappers and spent Diet Coke cans. A child's car seat polluted with pet hair. The house's cheap T-111 panel siding was diseased with lichen, skirt chewed ragged by porcupines seeking salt in the glue.

Rath glanced at the Monadnock River Valley. The river cleaved through the open farmland, its surface mirroring the afternoon sun, so it shone like a skein of molten silver. The hardwoods' autumn colors luminescent in the golden afternoon light, a beauty discordant with the shambled house before him. The door opened, and a woman in her early twenties stood behind the torn screen, and said, "Can I help you?"

Gale Duffy had the gaping eyes of a frog. Her cheeks were peppered with moles, her lips plump and bunched like a guppy's. She wore a pink Gronkowski Patriots jersey draped over a belly that suggested her idea of home cooking was frozen pizza and Eggos. The jersey fell to her knees. Barefoot, she seemed to be wearing nothing but the jersey, her toenails painted Patriots' red and blue. She leaned against the doorjamb, hugging herself, her cleavage deepening. She seemed oblivious to it.

"Gronk's off to a good start, if he can remain healthy," Rath said. "Too bad the secondary is a sieve."

"You lost, or just a lonely Pats fan?"

"I'm a—"

"A cop? You don't look it."

"What do cops look like?"

"Not you." She peered out at the Scout, raised her eyebrows like *Really?*

"I work privately," Rath said.

"You guys actually exist?"

"I do." He showed her his ID.

"I wouldn't know that from a Gold's Gym card," she said.

"A Gold's Gym card says Gold's Gym on it."

"What do you want?" she said.

So much for levity, Rath thought.

"To ask you questions about Mandy," he said.

"What's she done?"

"What makes you think she's done something?"

"Umm. You?"

"May I come in?"

She groaned and pushed open the screen door.

The house reeked of kitty litter and of the cat piss that kitty litter was supposed to cover but never did. One of many reasons Rath disliked house cats, the first reason being his allergies. Rath sneezed, his eyes weepy.

As shoddy as the outside of the house was, the inside was staggeringly tidy. The shag carpet had deep, vacuum-wheel marks running in it like ski tracks in fresh powder.

The couch and chairs had modern lines of bent birchwood arms and white linen fabric that lent an illusion of upscale Euro design. Rachel had similar furniture he'd helped her haul back from Ikea in Montreal. It looked good, but was cheaply made. He hadn't expressed that to Rachel though, not wishing to dampen her enthusiasm.

On the wall hung photos of Gale with several middle-aged women, arms draped about one another, each a tad disheveled and sweating. Easy smiles like the women were on a tropical vacation. The women's matching T-shirts read: RACE FOR LIFE. A race for curing cancer. Under the photo was a plaque with Gale as the recipient: Hero for Life 2010.

Bookcases were so crammed that books lay horizontally atop those arranged upright. Rath read a few spines. *Edie: American Girl; Vamps and Tramps* by Camille Paglia. *Wonderland Avenue: Tales of Glamour and Excess;* Sarah Vowell's *Take the Cannoli.*

"Those are Mandy's," Gale said. "She's into all that. Woman empowerment, sexual *revolution.*"

"Why are her books out here? It's your place, right?"

"Her room's a shoebox. And she sort of gamed me. I think she likes showing them off in case a smart guy ever comes over."

"Have any smart guys come over?"

"No guys at all. Hard to believe as it is."

"What's that mean?"

"Have you *seen* her? She can wear a burlap bag, and still guys slobber and girls get pissy with envy."

"Do you envy her?"

"Envy may be a sin. But. I'm only human. Imagine if you were roomies with a real slab."

"Slab?"

She rolled her eyes. "What you old guys call a hunk. Like, say, Gronk. You know. If he were running around your apartment with his shirt off, showing off his build, and you're like, you know, *you.* Anyway, her looks make you feel like mud. Until you get to know her."

"How so?"

"She's quiet. Private. She's not in your face about her looks. Which can rankle some girls more. Because you know, if a good-looking girl is a witch, you can at least nail her on that. You know, she's got it all in the looks category, *but what a witch.* That Mandy's nice and seemingly oblivious to her looks makes girls go ballistic. Because how can a girl not *know* she's *that* gorgeous? If *I* were, *I'd* be a witch. See what I mean?"

He did, and he didn't.

She laughed. "Girls are strange."

"You think?"

"Especially when it involves other, prettier girls. What's this about?"

"She's missing."

"She'll turn up," Gale said.

"You seem pretty sure." Rath studied her face, surprised by her quick response.

"When I was her age"—a lost look came over her face—"I *disappeared* a lot."

"So. What's she like?"

"Like I said. Freakin' *private*. She comes in, says *hey*, flashes her smile, grabs a book, and sneaks into her bedroom. Then *stays* in there and doesn't come out. Not even for, like, snacks. I doubt she even reads half those books."

"You said she gamed you?"

"I didn't want the books out here. I *suggested* she put them in the cellar, but she said the cellar was damp, and her books meant a lot. I was like, they're just books. It's not like they're the Bible. Then she said if I want to use her furniture . . . and I need a place to plop and watch the tube. All I had before was milk crates and beanbag chairs. So—"

"So you and Mandy don't get along?"

"My ad said *Roommate* wanted, not *Friend* wanted."

"Can I see her room?"

"Not much to see." She scratched at a rash on her neck and flung her eyes toward the narrow corridor. "Last room on the left."

The bedroom was as promised: a shoebox. A twin bed without a headboard or a footboard was centered on the opposite wall from the door, maybe three feet of space around it. Above the bed, a faded poster of Warhol's *Monroe* was tacked crookedly. The rest of the bare white walls were peppered with nail and tack holes.

The bedsheets were tossed back in a twisted heap. On a pink bedspread, an image of Betty Boop performed a jig. Rath pinched a corner of the top sheet between his fingers and thumb and lifted it. An open book sat beneath it. *Black and Blue*. Rath had never heard of it. He read the jacket cover. The book was about a mother who fled an abusive husband and changed her identity. *Is that what you've done*, Rath wondered, *fled, changed your identity?* He scribbled the book's title in his notebook.

The drawer of an Ikea nightstand was ajar. Rath stuck the pencil in the drawer's gap and pulled the drawer open to find a hairbrush, nail polish in hot colors named Rupture, Purge, Hipnotic. Pens and pencils, a raffle-ticket stub, Midol, a pad of paper. He paused and looked at the header of the notepad. Starmont Hotels and Resorts.

The notepad was pristine, no indentations from writing. He tucked it in his jacket pocket, then looked under the bed. A cat raked his face with its claws, then squirted past him. Wincing, Rath stood and wiped at blood on his cheek, the scratch itching and swelling. "Cat Scratch Fever." That right-wing nutjob Nugent had gotten it right in the one crummy song on which he'd based his entire offensive life.

Rath opened the closet's folding doors to find clothes spilling from milk crates. Acid-washed jeans in black and blue. Corduroys and sundresses. Tank tops and

T-shirts with Wonder Woman, Betty Boop, and Marilyn. Black Ts that read, JOHN DEERE and GOT CHOICE?

Panties, plain white cotton, tossed in a pile. No bras.

He searched pockets and found one business card. It had been through the wash, and he could not read it. He closed the closet door.

On the way down the hall, he slipped into the bathroom and shut the door. The bathroom was spotless, the chrome-sink fixtures mirroring his distorted image back at him in miniature. The room smelled strongly of bleach though not strongly enough to cover the stench of the litter box next to the toilet. He wondered what Luminol would pick up: The place seemed somehow too immaculate. Had it been cleaned and scoured after an altercation?

Under the sink were boxes of panty liners, tampons, creams and ointments and powders, a toilet-bowl scrubber.

He opened the medicine cabinet, a metal job with a scratched mirror on the face. The interior was rusty where the shelves were riveted to the sides. The usual. Cough syrup. Allergy pills. Contact-lens solution. Pink disposable razors. Tweezers. Cosmetics. Red and blue Halloween hair dye. Birth-control pills.

He shut the medicine cabinet and stepped toward the door. Something was stuck to his shoe. A Post-it note. He unstuck it and looked at it. A childish scrawl. One word. Hard to make out. Impossible. *argtbrongcin*? He folded it and tucked it in his shirt pocket.

His heart leapt as his cell phone buzzed.

Laroche. Again. Rath wasn't going to let the son of a bitch bail on dart night without finding his own substitute. That's what he deserved for not having a spine to tell his wife he was owed one night out for every ten of her supposed girls nights.

In the living room, Rath found Gale slouched on the couch, watching *Judge Judy*. Evil Cat sat in her lap, giving him the evil eye.

"You scared my cat," she said.

"Did Mandy have a laptop or a PC?" he asked.

"No way. She just got a job. She scraped together rent, but she couldn't afford toys. Besides, we get nothing but dial-up here. It's like watching TV with rabbit ears."

Rath nodded. Parts of Vermont were still locked in a perpetual time warp.

"You keep a tidy house," he said.

"Cleanliness is next to godliness," she quipped.

"You have reason to think she's been hurt or in trouble?" Rath asked.

"Not unless she's gotten over her head in something."

"Like?"

"How would I know?"

"Are you on the pill?"

She laughed. The harsh bray of a mule, a spray of spittle misting from her nose.

"I'm a *virgin*," she said, laughing and giving a burst of spittle again.

Rath laughed with her, sharing in the joke.

Anger seared Gale's face. "Not every woman—"

"Of course not," Rath said, mortified that she'd been serious. "I just—"

"Judged. Poor-white-trash girl who lives in a dump and talks about hunks must be doing half the loggers this side of Canada, right? Mandy can read all those snobby books about feminism, but I'm the true feminist. Because when you control your body, you control your life." Her ire was up, her eyes jumpy and mad. The girl had a temper, was a hot head.

"I apologize," Rath said.

"Don't. You'd be right ninety-nine times out of a hundred. But you're wrong now."

"I only thought. The baby seat, in the car?"

"*Oh*," she said brightly, the outrage in her face melting like snow on a sunny spring day. "Now I apologize. I can be a bit testy at times."

"Yeah?"

"I work for a day care. I have the seat in case of an emergency. It's the law."

Rath nodded.

"The cats are my babies," she said.

"If you think of anything, call me." Rath handed her his card. "One more thing." He took out the Post-it note and showed it to her. "This yours?"

She considered it. "No."

"Well. If you think of anything."

Out in the Scout, Rath stuck the Post-it note to the dash above the ashtray.

In the valley, he tried Rachel's number and was kicked to voice mail. "Hey," he said. "It's Dad. Just. Being Dad."

CHAPTER 10

Rath watched the front of Larry Wilks's apartment from the Scout parked across the street and down the block several houses. The narrow street's asphalt was cracked and broken from frost heaves, a forgotten street crowded by and darkened beneath red pines that had been set in eerily precise rows by FDR's Tree Army.

The unkempt yards were littered with rusted pine needles and broken branches. In the few minutes the Scout had been parked, sap had already dappled the windshield like viscous birdshit. From some backyard, a rooster crowed, as if the shadows of the pines left the confused bird announcing an eternal dawn.

These were homes built in the eighties' real-estate boom that had died as quickly as it had been born, leaving housing developments unfinished, cellars filling with rainwater that turned to a soup of green algae and drowned frogs. This street had been finished, but archaeological artifacts of its heyday being circa 1987 remained everywhere. Windows sported long-faded

Tot-Finder stickers. To the side of most of the crushed-stone driveways stood basketball hoops. The metal backboards pocked with rust, the scraps of gray nets flitting in the breeze like the frayed strings of an old mop. The backboard posts leaned dejectedly, the cement in which they were affixed twenty-five years ago breaking down and loosening its grip. No new backboards in sight, the ones made of fiberglass with black plastic bases easily moved on wheels, adjustable arms to set the hoop's height relative to that of the child.

Rath could all but hear the shrieks of the ghost kids who had once overrun the forlorn street on Big Wheels, could see the cardboard lemonade stands, the lawn sprinklers spraying water in silver arcs, fathers washing wood-paneled station wagons and mothers gabbing over fences that had long since fallen over and were now being reclaimed by the Earth.

His childhood years. Long gone.

He double-checked the address in his notepad: Apartment #2, 139 Pine Street. He checked the glove box, considered his .22 revolver. He closed the glove box and got out and shut the Scout's door quietly. The rooster crowed.

At 139 Pine, a purple Dodge Neon and a white Ford F150, both with their hoods up, sat in a driveway spoiled with oil and other engine fluids.

Apartment #2 was in the upstairs half of the cape at the top of an iron stairway that looked like a fire escape lag bolted straight into the cape's vinyl siding.

Rath took the steep, creaking stairs, the whole rig swaying with his weight. The door at the top was black with mildew. A shade on the inside of the small window prevented him from seeing inside. He rapped on the door.

A girl answered immediately, as if she'd been expecting him, and Rath's heart jumped. The girl possessed the round and runny eyes of a foundling. Her plump rump was squished into Daisy Dukes two sizes too small. She sported pigtails and a tight pink tank top with the word PINK scrawled across it, Rath guessed in case you were color-blind you'd know what color shirt she was wearing. The shirt was stained with chocolate and threadbare enough to be nearly transparent. She wasn't wearing a bra, and her dark nipples were visible. The look on her face said she had indeed been expecting someone, just not *this* someone.

"Who are you?" she said.

"Is Larry around?"

She made to slam the door, but Rath stuck his foot inside.

"What the hell?" the girl said. Her breath was sour with gin. It was 1 P.M. The girl shouted over her shoulder: "*Dad,*" she said in a mocking tone, "one of your coke-head buddies is here!"

A model of discretion, this girl.

She plopped down on a sunken couch befouled with dog hair and started playing an ancient video game, jerking a joystick obscenely between her thighs. Larry, *Dad,* lumbered in from the kitchen, his pale, whale-blubber gut stretching his wife beater and threadbare boxers to their limits. He wore one white, sagging sock. The other foot was bare, the toes deformed and hairy. Two toenails black with decay. He was unshaven and had either been eating powdered donuts or burying his face and fingers in a bowl of before-mentioned coke.

"What the *fuck*?" he grunted. "You tell Porkchop you're here for coke? Where you get off making her think I deal coke? I don't know your ass. Who the fuck you think you are?" He moved close to Rath, and Rath caught a stench akin to a clogged sewer pipe.

"I need to talk to you about your daughter," Rath said, meeting Dad's eyes.

"I don't have a daughter."

"Mandy, your—"

"She ain't my daughter."

Rath stared, confused. "I just came from your wife's house, and—"

"*Ex*-wife."

"Your daughter, *Mandy,* is missing," Rath said, his voice sharp, insistent.

Wilks curled his upper lip and wagged his head like a bulldog. "A bitch just like her mother. Probably run off as usual. The Ex tell you why I divorced her?"

"She said she divorced you."

"She says whatever she needs to say to make herself look good."

As opposed to you, Rath thought, who can speak his mind openly because he's of such high social standing he's beyond reproach.

Dad plodded into the kitchen. Rath walked past the couch where Porkchop lay on her side, jerking the joystick with one hand, her other hand crammed down her Daisy Duke's, scratching furiously.

Rath entered the kitchen, and a pride of tomcats preened at his feet, then leapt one by one up onto the counter, where they prowled anxiously. From a rusted chain, the leg of a slaughtered deer hung in the corner, dripping blood into a baking pan. The cats licked their whiskers and tongued their eyeballs. They blinked in their drowsy, feline manner. Rath sneezed wetly.

Dad sat at a Formica table littered with comic books, video-game cartridges, and donut boxes. Two revolvers lay on the table, within easy reach of Dad. One was an old, cheap .22, the bluing worn and rusted. The second was a .45. A model 625 JM, its stainless steel polished to a mirror finish. A round from it would go clean through Rath, through the wall behind him, and sail out into FDR's forest.

On the table sat tiny vials, glassine envelopes, and a minuscule electronic hand scale. Dad leered up at Rath. His eyes were milky.

"Sit," Dad said.

"I'm good," Rath said.

"*Sit.*" Dad rested his paw on the 625 JM.

Rath sat. The chair was sticky. What made it so sticky Rath did not want to know. He thought about the .22 back in his glove box, where it wasn't doing him much good. But a .22 bullet, even at point-blank range, would likely just get lodged in the first ten inches of Dad's fat. Rath would have to shoot Dad in the head, and he didn't come here to shoot anyone in the head. The kitchen stank of warm blood, filthy cats, and whatever bodily stench was pouring off Dad, who fidgeted with the scale.

"What do you mean she's not your daughter?" Rath asked. His shirt was pasted to his spine with sweat. Blood dripped from the calf leg into the baking pan. *Ping ping.*

"Found out three years ago. Was in for some tests to see if I didn't have cancer in my balls. Found out my boys are too fucked up to take proper hold to an egg. That's why the first two brats never took. You follow?"

A pair of cats leapt from the counter and raked their claws down the muscled hank of deer leg in a sensual manner, leaving tattered furrows in the meat. They slurped blood from the baking pan.

"Well. Even so. She's missing."

"Good," Porkchop muttered from the sofa.

Dad grunted like a hog. "Jealous like the rest." His hand squeezed around the 625 JM. It dwarfed the revolver, made it seem like a squirt gun. "So. What you want?"

"I need to know where you were night before last—"

His eyes sparked. "*Here.*"

"Was anyone here with you?"

"Yeah," he said, and wagged his three chins toward Porkchop. "She was."

Porkchop looked up and stared at him.

"Weren't you," he said.

"Yeah, sure," Porkchop muttered, and went back to jerking her joystick.

"Just who the fuck are *you*, anyway," Dad said to Rath, "coming into my home like some needle Dick? You ain't a cop, sure's shit, and—"

"A friend of the family. I just want to see if there's anything you can tell me—"

Porkchop got up and wandered past down the hall, her breasts all but falling out of her top now. A nipple exposed. The bottom crescent of her ass cheek jiggled out from her Daisy Dukes as she disappeared into another room. Rath tore his eyes away.

"You wanna taste of Porkchop?" Dad said, and smiled, teeth gray as dirty dishwater.

Rath recoiled, felt his stomach churn.

"Way you're eyeing her," Dad said, "thought maybe you'd like a piece o' Porkchop."

"I'm good," Rath said.

"*She's* good. Fifty bucks." His finger slipped inside the 625 JM's trigger guard.

Rath felt his balls tighten. He had to get out of there. He inched his chair back.

A tomcat the size of a Labrador retriever lapped blood from the baking pan, hissed at the other feral felines who eyed the blood.

"Cheapskate, huh?" Dad moved his hand from the .45 and picked up the .22. It nearly disappeared in his palm. He folded his arms across his chest, tipping back a bit in a chair two sizes too small for him. "Or are you queer?"

"Yeah, that's it."

Rath glanced at the deer leg.

Drip. Drip.

"Well," Rath said, "it seems you'd rather speak to a real cop."

Dad considered this as if he were trying to figure out the quantum physics of Time's Arrow. He looked hard at Rath. His eyes had lost their milkiness and were bright and clear now, crazed.

A cat stood on its hind legs, stretched to rip its claws along the meat, shredding it.

Dad kicked the cat, and it bared its fangs. Dad aimed the pistol square at Rath's chest. Smiled. Then he swung the .22 at the deer leg and fired a round. The cats didn't flinch. They seemed used to it. It was only a .22, but would still kill Rath at that range. It might take awhile, hours, but it'd do the trick eventually.

Dad leaned back, a madman's smirk seeping across his face. Rath sprang then, shoved the table hard so it struck Dad's fat gut, and Dad sucked in air with a *whump*, his chair teetering, arms pinwheeling, and eyes blowing up. "What—"

Rath shoved the table harder. Dad toppled back

and hit the floor so hard, empty beer bottles fell and smashed. The back of Dad's head struck the counter edge as he went down, and he lay there making blubbering, snoring sounds, blood leaking from an ear.

Porkchop ran into the room, pupils huge, teeth clenched. She eyed the .22 on the floor. Rath kicked it under the stove and glared at her. "Get out," he said. She glared back. "*Now*," he ordered. And suddenly all her teen bravado evaporated, and she was a scared child. She ran out through the living room and threw open the door and crashed down the fire escape.

Dad was hoisting himself up, eyes locked on Rath, homicidal. Rath grabbed the .45 as Dad came at him, his head down and his arms wide. Rath raised the .45, but Dad hit him square in the solar plexus before he got it all the way up. The wind left Rath, and his vision splintered in silver explosions as he landed on his back. He howled when Dad fell on him, and his spine felt as if it were being crushed.

Rath tried to get the .45 out from between him and Dad as Dad rose, hauling Rath up by the neck, and tossed him across the kitchen as if he were a dirty sock. Rath smashed hard against the cold slickness of the deer leg, then struck the refrigerator's door handle with his spine as a blinding pain ignited in him, and he collapsed on the floor. He thought he would pass out, his vision spongy, the world warbly. A hive of bees droned in his ears, and he smelled the ocean.

The .45 lay on the floor beside him, light-years away. He stretched his fingers for it, his eyes leaking hot tears of pain. He got a hand on the revolver's grip as Dad tossed the table aside and bore down on him.

Dad was reaching for the .45, and Rath shook his head, *no no*. Dad backhanded Rath across the face, the stone of his ring taking a chunk of Rath's cheek.

Rath kicked Dad hard, square in the ankle. Dad hopped in pain, and Rath drove the heel of his boot into Dad's kneecap. Dad crashed on the table, the table imploding under his mass.

Rath stood, grinding his teeth against the savage wreck of his back, and grabbed the .45. He caught Dad trying to gain his feet again and jammed the .45 to his forehead. "I'll paint the floor with whatever's inside that fucking skull of yours instead of brains." He pressed the muzzle tighter between Dad's eyes, cocked the hammer with his thumb, his finger on the trigger, itchy. "Lie down."

Dad lay down.

"Good dog," Rath said, grimacing and fighting nausea.

Rath turned and hobbled out of the place. He scrambled down the stairs, the fire escape swaying, making him puke. In the driveway, between the Neon and the F150, his ankles got wrapped in jumper cables strung between the vehicles, and he did a header, planting his face into the Neon's bumper. He struggled back to his feet and staggered out to the Scout, each step more painful than the last.

CHAPTER 11

Battered and exhausted, Rath looked at his sad paunch in the bathroom mirror, a body whose muscles were once taut without any work no matter the beers or the pizza. No more.

He poured hydrogen peroxide on his gashed cheek, gritting his teeth. Pain spiderwebbed from his spine. He filled the sink with cold water and sank his face into it. He put back two Vicodin with a belt of Lagavulin.

He dipped a toe in the bath. Icy. Perfect. He set the bottle of Lagavulin beside the tub then eased in, the pain in his back relenting some as he shut his eyes. His eye was swollen, his jaw stiff. The tub felt damn good. There were, he had to admit, upsides to having the place to himself again. He was allowed to spread out, let the laundry stack up, the dishes pile in the sink, leave a beer bottle where he finished it without Rachel's swooping in and scolding. Still.

He picked up his home phone from the floor beside him and dialed.

"Hello?" Grout answered.

"Grout, Rath."

"Why did you come up *Private*?"

"It's my home number. I don't want clients calling it, or trouble finding me."

"OK, Jason Bourne. How'd it go today?"

"Fabulous. My back feels like a shattered windshield. Mandy's father is a real gem. HE fucked up my back even worse."

"You want to press charges?"

"Nothing'd stick. I pushed my way into his home, unwanted. He can say whatever he likes. His stepdaughter would likely cover. Out of fear." Rath couldn't help but feel empathy for Porkchop. What happened to cause a girl of her tender age to behave the way she did? "If I were you I'd bring Dad in as soon as you can though. Grill him."

"You think he's got something to do with Mandy?"

"I wouldn't put anything past him. I don't trust the girl's alibi for him. You can get him for dealing coke at least. Possibly pimping, though I think he was just yanking my chain on that one. Address is 139 Pine Street."

"Shitty area."

"You think?" Rath took a pull of Lagavulin. "There any Starmont resorts in Vermont?"

"You have any questions Google can't answer?"

"I'm on dial-up here."

"Move down from the hills. Leave the ice age behind."

"I like the ice age. You wish you lived here and not Deer Meadow Townhouses."

"Pheasant Run Condos."

Rath heard Grout's fingers typing.

"There's a Starmont hotel in Stowe," Grout said. "The Double Black Diamond. Real *la-di-da. Starts* at 350 bucks a night. What's this about?"

"A notepad in Mandy's room was from a Starmont. Would be worth checking if she stayed there. You'd need to do it. Hotels are tight with info to anyone not a cop."

"Even to cops. Mandy couldn't afford this joint."

"It'd have been on someone else's dime. Mandy, by all accounts, is a stunner. Maybe she had some rich guy wanting to get hooks into her. If any staff saw her, they might remember her. If I've learned anything, it's that she's memorable. Men want her. Women envy her."

Rath readjusted himself in the tub, water sloshing.

"Are you in the *tub*?" Grout said.

"For medical reasons. My back. It was bad before, now—"

"Snoop around the Double Black Diamond with me, and you can throw a massage on your expense account. Maybe they give Happy Endings."

"The only place in Stowe that gives a Happy Ending is Friendly's restaurant," Rath said.

"They don't allow Friendly's in Stowe. What else you got?"

"I stopped by the Lost Mountain Inn. Nothing. No one there saw anything odd about her behavior. She punched out as usual, and said 'See you tomorrow.' Listen. Let's catch up in person after Stowe. I'm wiped." Rath rested the bottle of Lagavulin on his chest. "Get *yourself* a massage at the Double Black Diamond while you're there."

"The wife'd just love that."

"She'll be too pissed you're volunteering a Sunday to care."

"Don't bet on it."

Rath hung up, took a slug of scotch, and lay back in the bath, looking at his notes. So. So. So.

Sew your own buttons, his mother would say.

Her old-fashioned sense of humor had gotten her through tough times. Rath wondered if it would have gotten her through the aftermath of Laura's murder? Not for the first time, he was glad she'd not lived to suffer that. She'd suffered enough.

The winter Rath was nine his mother had broken an ankle on an icy sidewalk. When his father had come home to see her in a cast, he'd said, "They shoot horses for less," and strode into the kitchen to clank glasses and crack ice trays, giving sound to his inner fury as he poured a highball of straight club soda.

He'd been on the wagon for weeks, and Rath had wished he'd fall back off it. When drinking, Rath's father tossed the ball around, took the family out for ice cream, bought his wife candy—gestures unheard of when sober. Rath preferred him this way. But when his father drank, he also never got to work at his barbershop, and the place would go shuttered for days. Rath's mother would pick up nightly waitressing gigs to supplement her full-time job as a drugstore clerk, working doubles all weekend until sick with exhaustion.

When the old man sobered, he'd find his clientele had dwindled, and his mood would darken. Each day sober, each second, was more ominously tense than the last. He became a stick of lit dynamite, his smoldering fuse sucking up the oxygen in the house as the inevitable explosion approached.

He'd never struck any of them. In moments of self-pity, he'd return to the refrain: "At least I never hit none of you." It made Rath wonder what abuses the old man had suffered as a boy to make this a shining accomplishment. He'd never hit them. But he'd broken chairs. Broken his hand driving it through a wall, a hairsbreadth from his wife's face. Broken his wife's heart.

When sober, his eyes wandered, too. He'd had the broad build, blue eyes, and black hair he'd passed to his son, and women were readily sucked into his orbit. Before Laura's murder, Rath had shunned relationships because he'd felt the old man's weakness for women festering inside him and had never wanted to hurt a woman as his father had hurt his mother.

Rath glanced at his notes now.

Mandy: a knockout. People react strongly to her looks. Glaze over.

Mandy's mother was biased about her daughter's looks. But Gale wasn't. Nor was Madeline. Gale admitted she envied Mandy. He looked at his next note: *Mandy on pill.*

She was likely having sex though that was not a certainty. She never brought boys home. Not one person he'd spoken with knew of a boy in her life.

Double Black Diamond Resort.

She could have picked the Starmont notepad up anywhere. Rath's junk drawer was choked with refrigerator magnets and notepads from places he'd never been, without his having a clue how they'd ended up in his drawer.

His mind came back to the birth-control pills. If she was on the pill, would she have left the apartment without the prescription if she intended to be gone for more than a day? He should have checked the date on the package. For all he knew, they were months old. Did she have a boyfriend? If so, where was he?

CHAPTER 12

Grout barged past the Double Black Diamond's bellhop. One look at the kid's flat, wide-faced bone structure, the pugged Frenchman's nose, and the pinched eyes set too closely, the teeth that begged for braces they would never get, and you could see he was a local yokel from Morrisville or some other piss-poor town that bordered Stowe. And as soon as he shed his Double Black Diamond disguise, he'd be out tooling around on his ATV to sate that inflated insatiable macho urge found in rednecks everywhere to burn up gasoline. Grout despised ATVs and snow machines and the lazy asses who rode them for shits and grins. Same for the yahoos who churned the quiet of Lake Canaan into froth with their Jet Skis. Wherever they towed their Big Boy Toys, they left behind shattered beer bottles, spent condoms, and McDonald's trash. A real nice sight for his two kids and wife when they were trying to enjoy a day outside.

The bellhop probably despised the folks who passed through these doors and gave him his livelihood, resentful of their money. Grout had no use for them either, but not because of their money. He'd have liked to have himself a piece of *this* pie. He'd even played with the idea of applying for a head security position at the resort. He'd heard they made good money. They worked more normal hours, too, and were less likely to get their ass shot while investigating a domestic. Jen had all but begged him to apply for an opening she'd seen in the paper. He'd driven up to get an application but had decided against it at the last minute and sat in the car for an hour listening to ESPN radio. After all, what kind of life was it for a man, a detective, being a rent-a-cop for the rich? Still, he had to admit, it was good money.

It was the privileged class's ignorance, not their money that rankled Grout. They skied here and shot their wad when they saw a black bear scrounging from the Dumpster at their slope-side condo, oblivious to the fact that the ski area's development was destroying bear habitat, putting the population on the edge of collapse, and forcing the bears to seek food at the Dumpster to begin with. They whined about how the old swimming hole they'd loved when they'd "summered" here as kids was now muck, blind to the ski area sucking water from the river for snowmaking. Not that Grout gave a shit about the environment. He was no tree hugger. He was one of a few locals who had approved of the Ravens Way estates on Canaan Ridge. It was stupidity Grout hated.

He elbowed past the moneyed guests on his way to the customer-service desk.

A young woman with a pixie haircut and the requisite black slacks and blouse of the Double Black Diamond looked up from a laptop. FAWN, her nametag announced.

Was that her real name? If so, where could her next stop be except a Montreal strip joint?

"Can I help you?" Fawn said, arcing an eyebrow plucked in an already unnatural perpetual arc.

"I'm here to speak with Cynthia Mann," Grout said, and flashed his badge. Fawn gaped at the badge.

"Cool," she said, beaming. "I'll grab her." She turned toward a shut door behind her, then turned back to Grout, and whispered, "What did she do?"

"I can't say," Grout whispered.

"You never know."

"You never do." Fawn opened the door and slipped inside the back room.

Grout looked at his wristwatch. He could devote a half hour to Cynthia before he headed back north. It was his "official" day off, and he needed to get back for Liam's basketball game and family-dinner night at the Pizza Palace, a place that fell pathetically short of its name. Still, Sunday was the only day he didn't arrive late from work or have to head out for work; and aware as Jen was about his career demands, she was as impatient with its cutting into his supposed day off. Family Day. He saw her point. But what else could he do? Sniffing out scum was his innate talent. His job. What he wanted was to be Senior Detective, then interim chief when Barrons shoved off to live his Caribbean dream. Grout expected he'd advance when the new budget passed. Jen expected it, too. As she saw it, he should have been Senior Detective long ago, and she was beginning to hint that his lack of advancement had had less to do with a shit budget than it did with him. It pissed him off. Maybe if she wasn't always after him to be home.

Fawn came out of the back room, trailing a woman

with long silver hair strung in a ponytail so taut it seemed to pull back the skin of her face, as if she'd had work done by a plastic surgeon who received his certification online. Grout had an urge to rip out the barrette holding her ponytail in place to relax her face.

With a sideways glance, she sent Fawn off on some mission then said, "My office would serve us better. The lobby is chaos."

Grout followed her into the office. She did not wear the resort's black ensemble but a wool dress the rusty orange of an autumn leaf past its peak. "Have a seat." When she sat behind her ornate white desk, he saw she was pregnant.

Grout eased into a chair as ornate as the desk.

"So?" Cynthia Mann clasped her hands atop her desk.

"A young girl up our way has disappeared. We found a notepad in her bedroom." He pointed at a notepad on the desk. "Like that one. We need to follow up every possibility. She might have come by the notepad in any manner of ways, of course."

"What was her full name?"

Grout told her.

Cynthia clicked keys on her laptop, sipped tea from a DBD mug. Waited.

"No one's registered in that name the past three months."

He asked if she could go back farther than that.

"These notepads didn't exist before August," she said. "We rebranded the entire resort when the new ownership took over and sank 20 million into remodeling."

Grout whistled. One more dead end. He should have known not to waste time on such an improbable thread. But what other threads were there? If he could just find one and pull it, a thread of motive, opportunity, means, physical evidence that brought a pattern into clarity, even if, especially if, it proved Mandy was alive. But he needed the single thread to start. Right now, he had squat. At least he'd make Liam's game.

"She likely stayed here with someone else," he said. "She could hardly afford a room."

"She and every other Vermonter. I can't, even at my 40 percent off."

"Do you recognize her?" he asked, and slid a photograph across the desk. It was a better photo than the one Rath had; Grout had stopped by to speak with Doris, and she'd given him the best one she could find.

Cynthia shook her head. "I'd remember her. She's from where?"

"Canaan."

"She's darling. A real Boondocks Beauty. She could make it in New York or—" She snapped her fingers. "You *know*. We get modeling agencies here. Casting calls, too. Out of Boston mostly, they rent a conference room to skim the cream of local talent. We did more of them before the remodeling and the new water park."

Another waste of water, Grout thought. Maybe he *was* a closet tree hugger.

"We had a casting call for extras in a Ben Affleck movie a year ago. I can look into the list of agencies who booked and get back?"

Grout told her to keep the photo, make copies and pass it around. He had more.

As he left, he thought perhaps something was gained. If Mandy had come to one of these modeling or talent-agency auditions, she might have met someone, some

Hollywood dipshit, or someone more sinister. It was a long shot. But it was a shot.

In the parking lot, Grout backed out his Subaru and was nearly clipped by a Land Rover that swept into the space next to his.

Grout got out as the Rover's driver, a tall man dressed in a waxed Barbour coat, wide-wale cords, and suede chukkas strode past.

"Hey," Grout said.

The man didn't break stride.

"Hey," Grout said louder.

The man stopped, his wispy blond hair blowing in the breeze. He looked about to scold Grout, and Grout was about to launch into him when he recognized the man. Boyd Hale Pratt, *III*. The Pratts were as close to the Kennedys as Vermont had. Hailing from a lineage of railroad and steel barons, the clan lived on a sixty-thousand-acre estate perched on Lake Champlain and commanding dramatic views of the Adirondacks.

Grout had spoken with Pratt a year ago, at a fund-raising ceremony.

Pratt squinted and thumbed his round, tortoiseshell glasses higher on his nose.

"Detective Harland Grout," Grout said.

"Right, of course," Pratt said, feigning familiarity and clearly growing impatient with Grout, cop or no cop.

Grout considered telling Pratt how they knew each other but refrained. "Just slow it down," Grout said.

"Right, sure," Pratt said, and hurried away, to his spa treatment or tennis game, or whatever a man who'd never worked a day in his life did when slumming it at a five-star resort.

Monday morning, Rath sat erect in a waiting-room chair of the Canaan County Medical Center, a single-story building that had once been the Canaan elementary school, before the school was absorbed into Connecticut Valley District. In 1990, the asbestos had been torn out, the building gutted, and the site remodeled to house general practitioners under one convenient roof. Rath flipped through a *Sports Illustrated* from April that contended the Red Sox were World Series favorites, no hint of their historic September collapse, spurred by fried chicken and beer.

Rath's cell buzzed. Sonja Test. Rath answered. "Detective Test," he said.

"Please. Sonja." Her voice was low, as if someone might be eavesdropping. "I have something you're going to want to hear. Meet me at The Wilderness Restaurant in Victory, say two o'clock."

"Is this about your dead girl?"

"Can you make it?"

He could.

"See you then." She ended the call.

Rath stared at his cell phone. A nurse poked her head in from the door to the back. "Mr. Rath?"

Rath got up gingerly and followed the nurse, in her mid-twenties, short, and wiry, with the requisite tattoo of her generation, an intricate blue vine snaking out from under the sleeve of her short-sleeved shirt. Rath knew of no image he'd want injected into his skin, and had no idea how tattoos were considered art by anybody; especially when every tattoo he'd ever seen looked like it was done with all the artistry of the high-school stoner drop out.

The nurse had Rath stand on the scale. Measured him. He glimpsed her underarm tuft, caught a whiff of patchouli oil as she raised the bar behind his head.

"Six feet," she said.

"And a half."

"No half."

"There's always been a half."

"Not anymore."

He followed the nurse into a cramped room, where he sat on the edge of an examining table covered with crackling waxed paper.

The nurse took his blood pressure. He felt his blood throb beneath the cuff. "One forty over ninety," the nurse said.

"Is that bad?"

"You'll live, tough guy like you. Dr. Snell will be right in."

"Snell? Where's Rankin?"

"In his bow stand, waiting for a big buck, so he says. He's probably asleep on his couch, worn-out from watching game shows."

She pointed at a Johnny. "Toss that on."

Rath waited in his Johnny, his skin prickling in the cool room. Why were doctors' offices always cold? Snell. He knew of him. Young. Early thirties. When Rath had been in his twenties, he'd not trusted anyone over forty and had disliked *old man* Rankin, who was resistant to technology, a dinosaur stuck in a tar pit. Now that Rath was north of forty, he didn't trust a doctor younger than forty-five, kids who couldn't relate to the tolling bell of mortality accompanying daily life.

Snell strolled in, whistling, his dark eyes working crisply over the screen of the iPad he had in hand. If he didn't know what ailed Rath, perhaps Google would.

Snell's skull was as smooth and bare as a marble pestle, with a squeezed bulge of flesh at the back of his neck. He wore a flannel shirt, Carhartt pants, and Merrell hiking boots. On his chin squatted a soulless soul patch. He sat on a stool and looked at Rath, clicking his teeth as if calling a squirrel from a park bench. "The X-rays were negative. I'm thinking we get you an MRI."

"MRI?" Rath's stomach fluttered.

"We tried six weeks of PT. We gave it a chance. It's nothing skeletal, given the X-ray. If it were muscular, the PT should have worked."

Rath knew his liver and pancreas were packed snug to the *erector spinae*. What if it was something internal? Five years earlier, a friend had experienced back pain throughout the fall. On Thanksgiving, when he'd been unable to get up from the couch for dinner, his wife had taken him to the emergency room. He'd died of lung cancer on Christmas.

Rath shifted. "Rankin said I had nothing to worry about." His voice felt weak.

"We just need to make sure."

Sure of what?

"Look," Snell said, clapping a hand on Rath's knee. Rath flinched. "We'll get the MRI, so we can scratch any other concerns off the list. You've been doing the stretches?"

"Religiously," Rath said, not a lie for a man who thought comedian Bill Maher was a zealot.

"And you've been practicing good body mechanics, not overdoing the bending, twisting, or pulling. Pulling's the worst."

Rath thought about the deer he'd dragged two miles through Dufrane's Swamp and over Corser Brook ridge. He'd dragged bigger deer much farther, over worse terrain.

"Not overdoing it," he said.

"I'll set you up for an MRI. Lie down, I'll take a look." Snell pressed cold fingers into Rath's flesh. "What level of pain, zero to ten?"

Rath's pain felt like a big fat eight, an infinite loop of pain, at least with Snell jabbing away. "Not bad, a six."

"A six is *not* 'not bad', four's bad."

"I'm out of Vicodin."

"You *shouldn't* be. I hope you're not taking more than prescribed or selling them on the playground."

"I knocked the open bottle into a sink of dishwater," Rath lied.

"I'll write another. This once. But don't ever take more than prescribed. It can cloud judgment, impair motor skills." Snell pressed the stethoscope to Rath's chest. Cold. Always cold. He listened to Rath's heart. "So, what's cooking?"

Rath might have a tumor the size of an eggplant in his liver, and Snell wanted to know *what's cooking*?

"I'm trying to find a missing girl," Rath said.

Snell pressed the stethoscope to Rath's back. "Breathe. Sounds ominous."

Rath reached for his shirt and plucked Mandy's photo from its pocket. "Seen her?"

Snell considered the photo, calling all squirrels with his clicking tongue. "Pretty."

"Ever seen her?"

Snell shook his head as he clasped the end of his stethoscope. "I don't think so."

"You might have?" Rath sat up.

Snell squeezed the roll of fat at the base of his neck. "She sort of seems familiar. But. In that way that reminds you of someone from TV or a dream." He handed the photo to Rath.

"Give me a call if anything comes to you," Rath said.

"Get dressed. Don't do anything stupid with that back. And don't worry about the MRI. It's probably nothing."

Probably nothing.

One more euphemism by which to live.

Or die.

CHAPTER 14

"You can't let anyone know I leaked this to you," Sonja said. She sat across from Rath in a dark booth at the rear of The Wilderness, the booth replete with forest green plastic cushions that squeaked like a gerbil wheel every time she or Rath blinked. The two perused plastic menus the size of billboards and tattooed with countless greasy fingerprints: a forensic nightmare.

Being 2:30 on a Monday, The Wilderness was dead except for two waitresses rolling up utensils in green napkins and consolidating ketchup in ketchup bottles. The *clack* of billiard balls rose from the establishment's lone pool table in the back bar. Country music played. Johnny Cash sang his rendition of "Hurt," which Rath preferred to the original.

"I don't have sway in Victory," Sonja said, "but we pool depressing resources. And Lou's my neighbor. But if he knew I was passing incomplete reports to an unofficial—"

"I get it," Rath said. "Why not loop in Grout? It's his

investigation. He's your superior. If this girl is Mandy, the state police will contact him anyway. As of midnight last night, Mandy was officially missing."

"Because this has nothing to do with Mandy. Unless we, *you*, find something. My hands are tied, the girl being found outside my jurisdiction, and, well—"

Rath sipped his chocolate shake. Here he was, The Great PI, fifteen-hundred-calorie milk shake in hand, puzzled by The Mystery of His Middle-Age Flab.

Sonja slid a manila folder to Rath. He lifted the cover with his pinkie and glimpsed a ghastly photo, then let the folder fall shut.

"She's not our girl," Sonja said. "The body is partly decomposed."

"I see that."

"It was found in Sugar Brook, a tributary to the Connecticut. Wedged under a blow down." She leaned on her elbows. "Here's the thing—"

Rath pushed his shake aside as a stout waitress in her fifties clonked over, blowing a wisp of gray hair out of her weary eyes. "Decided?" she said, as if peeved customers would have the gall to come in during her dead time. Rath wondered if his mother had ever showed such irritation with customers. No, he decided. Never. "Well?" the waitress said.

"Chicken tenders," Sonja said.

"You?" The waitress bobbed her head at Rath as if accusing him of a crime, perhaps something lecherous.

"A Barnburner Burger, rare, with chipotle sauce, onion rings. And a Molson." Mystery of the Middle-Aged Flab solved.

They sent her on her way.

"Chipotle on a burger?" Sonja said.

"Salsa of the not-so-new millennium."

Rath pushed a fist into his lower back, wishing he'd stopped to get his prescription filled on the way. "Go on," he said.

"She wasn't killed there. She wasn't even *left* there. The way she was crammed up under the logjam looks like she was dumped upstream, maybe in a shallow grave near the brook. Then, along came the flooding we had to unearth her and carry her downstream. There are broken bones, her left zygomatic is crushed, right ulna and radius both shattered, and deep lacerations to the body suffered postmortem. Likely from the body's being washed down the creek, getting stuck, then tearing free again."

"Cause of death?"

"It will be awhile. The abdomen was ripped open, too. By very sharp rocks looks like. Animals had been at her organs and viscera." Sonja twisted her wedding band absentmindedly. "Could be natural causes. Maybe she was hiking, got caught in a storm, and—"

"You don't believe that."

The waitress dropped their plates and walked away in a huff.

Rath stared at his still-sizzling onion rings, deciding to let them cool before he launched into them and burned his mouth as he always did. The burger was the size of a trash-can lid. "How old do we think this girl is?" he said.

"Sixteen to twenty." Sonja peeled the fried breading from a chicken finger to lay bare a hunk of pale meat.

Is she really going to eat that? Rath wondered.

"Any idea on ID?" he asked.

"None." Sonja took a bite of chicken, set it down, and

pushed her plate to the side. She leaned in again, and Rath caught a scent of shampoo: faint and fresh, strawberry? He took a gulp of his shake.

"If this doesn't have anything to do with Mandy, why am I here?" Rath asked.

"I did some digging. Looking for MP reports for girls roughly her and Mandy's age, the last six months or so. Just. To see."

"And?" Rath bit an onion ring. "*Fuck*," he hissed, and spit out his onion ring. "*Hot*." He ran his tongue along the roof of his napalmed mouth, tickling the tender spot of ruined flesh, knowing in the next few days that strands of dead skin would dangle down and distract him to the edge of insanity. He popped the lid off his shake and chugged what was left, waved his hand, "Sorry, go on."

"You gonna make it?" She smiled, and there was nothing Rath could do to stop the blush that shot through his face.

"Go on," he said.

"I came up with zip, within fifty square miles. But." Sonja straightened. Rath knew the proud posture. A bomb was about to be dropped. "When I looked back over sixteen months and expanded the range to a thousand square miles. It sounds like a lot, but isn't when you consider it being just twenty by fifty miles." Sonja took a breath.

A country song played from the bar, the tremulous voice of a girl, all bubble-gum flirtation, singing *If you wanna pick me up, you better drive a pickup truck*. The girl didn't sound a day over nine years old; probably wasn't.

Sonja looked Rath in the eye, her pupils large in the dim amber lighting. Beautiful. She paused, savoring her private information for a moment. "*Three* girls in the greater region have gone missing in the past sixteen months and not been found."

"Is that high?"

"It *is* for this region. In the ten years prior, only seven girls went missing and have never been located. In ten years. Before that, we had—"

"The Connecticut River Valley Killer."

The song on the jukebox ended, and a silence fell on the place. Sonja shifted, and the booth's vinyl seat squeaked.

Rath knew what Sonja was thinking. The CRVK had never been found even though the killings had stopped. To this day, Rath knew, Barrons returned to the case file again and again. At times, Barrons called Rath in the middle of the night to posit a theory.

That there'd been no prime suspect, let alone charges filed, had been Barrons's greatest regret and career failure; the man had aged ten years and gotten divorced in the twenty months of the official investigation. And as much as Rath had wanted to stay on the case, on the force itself, in the aftermath of Laura's death, his need to care for Rachel had left him depleted, scattered. He'd resigned.

That the killings had stopped had meant one of four scenarios: The killer was serving time on other charges; the killer had died; the killer had moved to a new territory, or, for some reason, the killer had been lying in wait to strike again.

"We're talking *girls* here," Sonja said. "Gone. I dove into the reports. The copies are in your folder. A cursory glance, and I could determine only one thing they had in common besides age. No one interviewed thought any of the girls had any reason whatsoever to run away."

"Which means squat."

"Sure, yeah. Nobody knows what's going on in a teenager's life. But none have ever used her cell phone or Facebook or other Internet pages again."

"So why no investigation?"

"There was, for each. Separately. In the end, there was nothing to find. Zero."

Rath's mind wandered to Rachel, her silence.

"Dig into those reports," Sonja said. "Each girl might be an outlier. A runaway. Who knows. But compare them to our dead girl and to Mandy. For any connection."

"We know our dead girl isn't one of these three?"

"Based on dental records and times of death. Yes."

"So that makes four girls."

Sonja nodded.

"You think they're connected," Rath said.

"I don't think one way or the other."

Sonja was treating Rath like he was a parent of a missing child, playing it tight. *I don't have a theory one way or another, Mr. Rath. We must keep an open mind.* She was eager, ambitious, and she wanted a case to get her to the next level. Rath didn't understand what she was doing in northern Vermont instead of Boston or Chicago. But the new industrial park and big box-store wasteland planned for the southern part of the county meant a stronger tax base. The force would get a piece of the pie, and Sonja was fierce. Her digging up old missing-person reports was not a whim. Most young detectives would never think to do it. And while she wouldn't directly fuck over Grout, she'd give herself an edge over him; Rath saw that plainly.

"The flurry of missing girls might just be a random spike," she said, covering her bases, playing a preemptive devil's advocate before Rath could do it. "Like spikes in teen suicide. And sometimes runaways want to run away from everything and everyone, not just parents. Start clean. Explaining the lack of cell-phone and social-media use. Besides, Mandy might show any second. But. I don't like it."

"Why wouldn't four missing girls get on the radar of Vermont State Police as possibly connected?" Rath was playing devil's advocate now, poking at her theory to make her clarify her logic. The fact was, he didn't like it either.

"They weren't all from Vermont. Two were in New Hampshire. Poor communication. New Hampshire and Vermont State Police did make one effort to connect the dots. They even had the FBI look into it, since two states would make it federal. But, the Bureau said *nada*."

Rath knew that scenario intimately. The Bureau had believed the CRVK was bullshit, too. Told Vermont and New Hampshire there was no solid evidence the crimes were committed by the same killer. Barrons had gone ape-shit: *So, you want me to believe there are several perps out there who each decided to rape and strangle a girl on a whim, as a one-off, using the same MO, and it's coincidence the girls have similar physical profiles?* The Bureau had taken exception to his claim that the MO was exactly the same, and to his tone.

"I'll dig into the reports tonight, before my dart game," Rath said.

"Ah. The big night out." Her eyes glimmered, teasing.

OUTSIDE, THE DAY had turned gray and mean, a north wind shrieking out of Canada. Rath pulled up the collar of his jacket and tugged his knit cap over his ears. He took out his cell and dialed Rachel. It stopped ringing on the second ring.

"Rachel—" He was cut off by a cold, automated voice: *The voice mail for the number you have dialed is full. Please try back at another time.* What the hell? He fumbled typing a short text message.

Are you OK? Let me know. Please. xxoo

CHAPTER 15

Rath wedged a sawed-off hockey stick sideways into the deer's frozen rib cage and propped open the cavity so he could work the knife at the inner tenderloins.

He sliced between the muscle and the spine, the knife razor-sharp, wedging his fingers behind it as he peeled an inner loin from the backbone. He freed it, then the one on the other side of the spine, his fingers stiff with cold. Tomorrow, he'd cut through the hide and get the outer tenderloins. It was the least he could do.

In the kitchen, he drank a Lagavulin as he sliced the tenderloin into medallions, set them in a cast-iron frying pan sizzling with butter, searing them. He forked the medallions onto a ceramic plate.

Grout was supposed to have come over for a face-to-face update of his visit to the Double Black Diamond the day before, but Rath had wanted to dig into Sonja's files and had begged off seeing Grout in person. He told him his back was killing him, which it was, and he needed to bathe in ice water before they played darts. They'd catch up at the tavern.

Rath gazed out the window at the darkening woods beyond Ice Pond, the setting sun's mirror image drowning in the pond's silvery dead surface. During the winters of the late 1800s, farmers had harvested ripe ice from the pond, cut massive blocks, using saws as tall as a man, with rows of nasty teeth. The ice blocks were hauled in oxen-drawn sleighs to sheds, where they were packed in sawdust to refrigerate perishables all summer long.

Rath picked up a hot piece of tenderloin, took a bite, and scorched the raw flesh of his mouth's roof. Idiot. He took a belt of scotch, sluicing it around in his mouth. It worsened the pain. He drank cold water from the spigot, cursed his stupidity.

He called Rachel, was kicked to the same mailbox-full message. Where was she? If she did not respond soon, he'd drive to campus even if it meant humiliating himself.

As he sipped his scotch, he looked out at the deer carcass. He had to get it hung. He'd been known to hang a deer for two weeks, until the muscle tissue crusted black and hard as enzymes broke down the muscles' strings to naturally tenderize the meat. Dry aging. Foodies paid north of $50 a rib eye for it at real steak joints.

The sun had set, and the kitchen was sinking into blue shadow. He killed his scotch and took the files into the living room, where he flipped on his desk light, sending shadows scurrying to the corners. He spread out at his desk. Stared at the first name.

Rebecca Thompson. She'd just turned seventeen, lived at home with her parents, a plumber and a grade-school teacher, and two younger brothers. The interviews indicated she was well liked and respected by teachers, family, coaches, friends, and fellow employees at Bob's Sporting Goods. A solid, hardworking student, she was a regional star athlete who'd lettered in soccer and lacrosse. "She's always been gifted in sports," her mother said. "She's been offered scholarships to good colleges."

Several photos of Rebecca were paper-clipped to the file, many of her in action, blue polyester shorts and jerseys riffling in the breeze as she dribbled a ball, long brown pigtails wrapped at the ends by navy blue rubber bands.

Her milk-carton photo was a yearbook headshot. The blunt nose and thin lips framed by cheeks that still carried girlhood chubbiness. She smiled with her mouth closed, restrained, as though she were trying not to laugh at a joke or didn't like her teeth. Or, for some reason, didn't feel like smiling.

Rebecca had last been seen at soccer practice, October 31, 2010. Halloween. Friends said they'd expected her to show up at a party at Lake Francis. She never had.

The police report was filed by Detective Major Harold Jenks of the New Hampshire State Police. He'd determined there was no evidence to cast anyone close to her under suspicion. He and a team of floaters had interviewed Rebecca's family and friends extensively. Rebecca's boyfriend, Caleb Francis, was described as "in shock and desperate to locate his girlfriend, pleading alongside Rebecca's parents for her return." He'd been interviewed and cleared. Caleb seemed more distraught than even Rebecca's parents. He was in love. He and Rebecca planned to go to the same college. He'd given her a pre-engagement ring she'd worn around her neck.

Caleb said in his interview: "She wouldn't just run off. Especially with the girls' state soccer championship coming up."

But. Here. A teammate of Rebecca's dissented on the rosy picture of Rebecca.

It's nothing I could put my finger on, exactly. As friends and co-captains, we share a lot. Everything. I thought anyways. But there was something off with her the last few weeks. She had the University of Virginia and Syracuse and Maryland offering scholarships, but she seemed, um. Blue. Or nostalgic? I don't know. I saw her once after a game, like, just sitting on the bench in front of her locker. She was holding the ring Caleb gave her, squeezing it. She was usually ecstatic after a win. And we crushed the Otters. But she seemed bummed. I think Caleb was scared. He wasn't getting any scholarship offers. He's the best quarterback our high school's ever seen. But that doesn't mean anything to colleges, a great QB from New Hampshire? Like, where's New Hampshire? I think Rebecca wanted to go her own way. Start fresh in college. And she didn't know how to tell Caleb. Because all Caleb talked about was how they were going to be together. Forever.

Forever.

Forever. That was someone of a very immature mind; which, at seventeen, Caleb possessed. Rath would have thought more about Caleb if the kid hadn't been cleared.

Rath snatched a pillow from his couch and set it behind his back and opened the file on Sally Lawrence. No matter how he sat, he could not get comfortable. His back was stiff and sore, a lacerating pain slicing through him.

Sally could not have been more different than Rebecca. She grew up fifty miles north of Rebecca, in the paper-mill town of Granton, New Hampshire on the Pentoscott River, a single child raised by a single mother who had been in a wheelchair since a car accident with a drunk driver in 2001.

Rath had driven through Granton many times on his way to deer hunt in Maine. It was a town he could recognize with his eyes closed by the gagging, sulfuric odor of the paper mills.

Sally and her mother lived in an apartment in the "upscale" part of the town, meaning upwind of the paper plant, in one of hundreds of houses built in the 1870s, when the mills first sprang up. Houses that had dwindled into disrepair since the 1950s, their once-white clapboard now the sullen color of soot from decades of exhaust belched by logging trucks. The slate roofs covered by sheets of blue tarpaulin where shingles had shed. The yards polluted with junk cars up on blocks, ATVs and bass boats perpetually up for sale but never sold, and blow-up Santa and snow-globe lawn decorations left out year-round, their deflated skins looking like monstrous spent condoms January to November. None of the houses were owned by the people who lived in them but by slumlords. They were the same style of house as showcased in magazines and found in affluent towns like Woodstock, Vermont, where money beat back the scourge of time with fresh paint, landscaped flowerbeds, and fertilized lawns.

Sally's photo showed a grotesquely obese girl. To be so overweight had to be torture. If so, she dumped her anguish into getting stellar grades, topping her school's honor roll. And she gave back. She was, as one teacher commented, "an exemplary citizen." She had a small circle of close friends, and a boyfriend. A shy kid named Shawn Plant, so devastated by her disappearance he'd attempted suicide with prescription pills. This had alerted cops to his potential as a suspect. But he'd been with his family in Florida at the time of Sally's disappearance.

Sally was a "serious but cheerful girl, smart as a whip, caring, and kind. We want her found," said a woman who helped run the Boys and Girls Club where Sally had volunteered, right up to the day she'd disappeared. May 2, 2010.

Rath opened the third file.

Fiona Lemieux. Seventeen. From St. Johnsbury, Vermont. Fifteen miles southwest of Rebecca, sixty-five miles south of Sally. Twenty-five miles southeast of Mandy. Last seen Friday, April 22, 2011, coming out of River Road Market, where she'd purchased cigarettes. The owner had said: "She was rare. A lot of kids distrust adults, but she was bubbly. 'Hello, Mr. L!' she'd shout, and give a big smile, especially after she got her braces off." The store owner recalled looking out the window to see Fiona walking down the sidewalk. "Just before she reached Elm, a car pulled up. She chatted with someone inside, then got in." He couldn't say what model or make the car was. It was too far away. And a customer had come in, and his attention was divided by then.

Fiona was a petite girl, 4' 11", ninety-five pounds soaked. She wore kohl on her eyes and preferred black clothes and army boots. She was an exceptional musician, trained classically on the piano and violin since age six. She'd rebelled as a teen by starting a band called F U, in which she sang and played upright acoustic bass.

Her mother had called the police at 9 A.M. the next morning, the day before Easter. "Straight off," her mother, a stay-at-home mom, said, "I knew something was wrong. She wasn't in bed, and the bed was still made from the housekeeper. Fiona never made her bed, ever. So I knew."

Police interviewed the family, her classmates and boyfriend, and came up with nothing. As the investigation progressed, it was deemed that Fiona had left on her own. Run away. Her parents were outraged though a few friends thought it was possible.

Fiona was unlike Sally and Rebecca. Her family was wealthy, her father a successful intellectual-property attorney who had done smashingly well during the dot-com boom and cashed out just before the bubble burst.

A girlfriend stated that Fiona had called her father a tyrant, with his rules and curfew, and Fiona had wanted to run away. But the friend had not thought she was serious. "Who doesn't bitch about their parents? Dream about getting out of this town? Nothing happens here. I hope she left. I hope she went to try out for *American Idol,* like we kept telling her to do, though the thought of doing that made her puke."

Her boyfriend, Hank Sewal, who played guitar in F U, seemed more angry than upset. "We were going to lay down new tracks on her iMac. Then she skips out? So not cool."

Fiona's bank account had seen no recent withdrawals, all of her clothes, except the black sweatshirt, Diesel jeans, and army boots she'd worn that day, still hung in her closet. All the toiletries a girl might take with her remained on her bathroom sink. Unless she'd *wanted* it to look like an abduction, or had left on an utter whim, it did not exactly seem like a girl who planned to leave.

They were all young girls similar in age, all girls everybody knows. But their family, school lives, and interests were not at all alike. Most markedly, they looked nothing like one another, and there was no evidence that they were anything more than missing. Perhaps they had all run off. For Fiona, it wasn't a huge stretch. But for none of them to ever contact a friend again? Not a single cellphone call made since they'd disappeared. No ATM withdrawals. And they'd all had a lot to look forward to. They had nothing to run from. Nothing in the files, anyway.

If someone had *done something* to them, odds were it was the same perpetrator. The probability that five girls had each been taken by five different people was as likely as snow in July. But it confused Rath. Usually, there was a physical resemblance among victims. With rape, that wasn't the case. But with murder and torture itself as the intent, which is what the dead girl's corpse found in Victory suggested, more often than not there was a common look among victims, surrogates who represented a woman who had betrayed the murderer in his past. Here, the girls had nothing in common: obese, prepubescently petite, athletic. And *if* Mandy had been taken by the same person, her looks further made the physical link improbable. She was leagues beyond the others. A genetic specimen, if ever there was one.

Still, there had to be something between them, a single trait that made them stand out to whoever had taken them. They had been taken. Rath felt it. But he needed motive. Find the *why*, and you'll find the who, he thought. But he could not see a why.

It was six o'clock. Time to shut down and throw darts.

CHAPTER 16

Rath undid the brass latch and opened the cover on the lacquered walnut box he'd built himself, complete with a purple velvet lining that looked refined but was cut from a Crown Royal sack. He hated Crown Royal. But the velvet looked good.

A set of three darts lay on the velvet. He picked up a dart, rolled it in his fingers, a solid, balanced heft. He'd made the darts, too. Tungsten tips, barrels of solid lead, the long, trim fletching made from the primary wing feathers of a mallard drake he'd shot on Ice Pond. The guys had given him shit about his "special" darts; but the guys knew he could throw a crushing game of Super Cricket or 21 with plastic Kmart darts better than any of their sorry asses could with these beauties. He'd made the darts out of boredom. A man could only do so much ice fishing during a Vermont February.

He took out the other two darts and set them down on his table in the alcove at the back of the Olde Mill Tavern. He'd come early. It was just 6:30 and the place, not being an after-work watering hole, was quiet, the jukebox sleeping, the TV above the bar, where a bartender cut up limes, was set to mute and CLOSED CAPTION. The house lights shone on hardwood tabletops that middle-aged waitresses wiped down with cider vinegar. He thought of his mother again. In her day, restaurants and bars had been choked with cigarette smoke she'd breathed in for twenty years until it had killed her.

A few old sods sat at the bar nursing beers and watching the news as Rath sipped a Johnny Walker Black, the best option the place offered. No single-malt here. He'd stopped by the drugstore and learned it would be several days before his Vicodin prescription could be filled. He tossed a few darts, turning over the missing girls' files in his mind. Drank his Walker.

He was pulling the trio of darts out of the corkboard when he saw Laroche striding toward him.

Rath tossed back his Walker. "Couldn't find a sub after all?"

"Why haven't you returned my calls?" Laroche said, his face fraught with frustration. "I must have left ten messages."

"I thought I'd let you swing in the breeze." Rath winked.

Laroche loosened his tie, took off his ill-fitting sport coat fraying at the cuffs, and draped it over a chair. His wrinkled white oxford was stained mustard at the pits. He ran his long fingers through his thinning hair, then signaled the sole young waitress who hopped over jauntily, her eyes alert and inviting.

"What can I get yah," she trilled.

"Bud bottle," Laroche said.

"Another Walker black," Rath said. "With ice."

"Easy-peasy," she chirped.

Rath shot another trio of darts, letting Laroche stew.

The girl danced back over with a Bud longneck and Walker, set them on the table. Laroche handed her a twenty and told her to keep the change. "Thanks, mister," she said, and sashayed off, high on life or one of its substances.

Rath stared at Laroche. Why was he paying for Rath's drink when Rath had tugged his chain? Laroche sat in the chair where he'd tossed his coat. He looked stricken.

Had Laroche learned his wife's night involved a man? Rath suddenly felt like a bit of a heel. Laroche was a good guy.

Rath glanced at the TV to see Senator Renstrom of Missouri, a long-shot candidate in the GOP presidential primary. He was planning an early fundraising stop in Vermont.

"I have news," Laroche said, his face long and old now. Rath felt badly. He'd strung the joke out too long, not returning calls. The guy was clearly pained by learning about his wife.

Then, suddenly, Rath knew. He killed his Walker, his face going numb.

"It's Ned Preacher," Laroche said.

"What about Preacher?" he said, his voice a whisper.

"He's up for parole."

Rath felt a stab of pain in his eyes. "No," he said. "He got twenty-five to life." His voice rose with desperation. "It's only been sixteen years."

"You know how these things happen," Laroche said, his voice coming from down a long, dark tunnel. Rath knew all right. *These things* happened because the system *let* them happen. *Why they were let to happen*, that was the question. The answer stoked a rage in Rath: money.

In January 1989, Preacher had sodomized a twelve-year-old girl in Glens Falls, New York. Afterward, feeling "a kindness," he'd let her go, naked and bleeding, into the Adirondack wilderness. "If God wanted her to live, she would," he'd said. He'd stripped a child of her dignity and her trust in humanity, soiled her for his own cruel satisfaction, but since he'd "cooperated" and pled down from the aggravated first-degree rape and kidnapping he'd actually committed to a fabricated third-degree sexual assault of a minor that saved the state the *money*, the judge had set a $5,000 bail, stating: "I trust Mr. Preacher will honor the court's decision to appear."

Mr. Preacher had jumped bail straight from the courthouse steps. Three months later, he'd been fingered in mug shots by a sixteen-year-old girl who'd been sexually assaulted in Rhode Island. By then, Preacher had moved on to Maine.

In 1990, he'd kidnapped a fifteen-year-old girl, clubbed her with an axe handle in a Portland Gas 'n' Go parking lot, and driven her to a forest, where he'd raped her while he described in detail how he was going to kill her. After five hours of being victimized, the girl had managed to flee while Preacher had slept like a baby from exhaustion. He was caught. Again, he'd pleaded down, and again was given a lesser sentence on fabricated charges that did not speak toward the awful truth of what he'd done. He got five-to-fifteen. Served five. *Five.* In a minimum-security *corrections center* nicer than Rachel's dormitory; moved from a maximum-security prison to the correction center after mental-health tests revealed: "Mr. Preacher is a *victim* of a low IQ. His actions feed his base needs and are not done with 'criminal intent.' He, and society, will profit from behavior modification. He accepts blame for his role."

A victim? His role? As if the girls he'd raped had played a role? As if Laura had played a role by opening her door. Who were these people who made such atrocious decisions? They had to be childless.

Preacher had been paroled after just five years of behavioral modification. He'd moved to Vermont and assumed a new identity, worked his odd jobs for folks like Laura and Daniel, then lit out for Maine, where he was suspected of trying to kidnap a woman and her daughter though they could not testify that it was him for sure.

His next stop had been a return to Vermont. To Laura.

Why he'd come back to Laura's house was unclear. Perhaps because he knew her pattern and knew she'd likely be home alone during the day, even if he hadn't known about the baby. Rath remembered Preacher's laugh when he was hauled away by the bailiff, as if he knew he'd be out much earlier—a cold, dead laugh.

"So. He's been a *good boy,*" Rath said, stung by humiliation, by his own impotency in the face of a system that gave lenience to perpetrators and forgot their victims. Time and again when Rath turned on the TV to see a rapist or a child molester brought into court, he learned that the perp had priors for similar crimes and had been released early. Every crime committed after the perp's early release had been preventable.

During Rath's first two years as a detective, he'd learned his idea of justice was a delusion. Cops reacted to violent crime. They could not stop it. Violence was an entwined thread in human DNA. Cops came in to clean up and hopefully arrest who'd done it. They were janitors. And once the system got the criminals, it was out of the cops' hands. The DA charged perps as the DA saw fit, not the cops. And the system let freaks out for being *good*.

Rath had thought there would be satisfaction in sending rapists or murderers to prison. There was a professional satisfaction. But not a personal one. Because this subspecies did not care about being in prison. They embraced being put among their own kind, where they could brag and learn from each other, wallow in a shared self-pity for all the wrongs exacted against them by parents and teachers and cops and wives, plot for another stab at things when they got on the outside. The only part of prison they resented was not being able to act on the animal urges that had put them inside to start. The criminal life was a state of mind, a belief as powerful and influential as any religion. Unapologetic and self-righteous. And you couldn't put a belief in prison.

A look of embarrassment sullied Laroche's face. "Good behavior gets a con up to six weeks served per year now. Multiply that over sixteen years." He drank.

Rath stood, every cell humming like a high-voltage power line.

"Easy," Laroche said.

"He killed my sister."

"I know."

"No. You don't."

A heat spread in Rath's palms, and he looked to see blood leaking from between his fingers, his fingernails cutting his flesh. "He can't be let out," he said.

"Odds are he won't be."

"Odds? We gamble on the Preachers of the world with the lives of little girls."

"You have a right to attend the hearing," Laroche said. "That's why I've been calling you. You have a right to be heard."

Rath fought to find words. "He gets out, he'll do it again."

"It's possible."

"It's fact."

"He'll likely never see the outside his first go. It's a flawed system. Agreed. But we have to accept it. If you don't respect the law, how are you any different than the Preachers of the world?"

Rath smashed his hand on the table. "I don't rape and slaughter mothers while their babies sleep, that's how I'm different. Don't dare compare me to that fucking animal."

Laroche recoiled, face reddening. "Look," he said, trying to gain composure. "We're on the same side. Guys like us, we don't have any power."

"I have power."

"Don't talk that way."

"What way should I talk?"

"In a way your sister would respect."

Rath pressed in close to the seated Laroche, towering over him. He felt as if he would shake apart. "You might want to look into who your wife is fucking," Rath hissed and stalked out.

CHAPTER 17

Rath pushed through the porch door into his kitchen, regretting his savagery toward Laroche, the innocent messenger. His back roared with pain, and his head smoldered with vengeful thoughts of Preacher. He took a long drink of Lagavulin straight from the bottle. He needed to talk to Rachel. To see her. Be with the only family he had. He dialed her number. *Mailbox full.* Damn it. Where was she? He took another pull of scotch, texted Rachel. The screen was bleary.

I'm coming to take you out for a bite so you can have something besides Ramen noodles. I Love You, Dad

Rachel always laughed at his proper grammar and correct spelling. "That's *not* texting. I don't have time to read a novel."

Rath headed out.

The Scout's tires barked as he gunned it out onto

County Road 15. He stopped at the Gas 'n' Go to fill up the Scout, let the pump run, and stalked inside and bought beef jerky and a tin of Copenhagen. When he came out, the Scout was still gobbling down gas.

Down the street, the sign outside the Beehive Diner was lit, as were the signs for the Buck Rub Pub and Bistro Henry, a new restaurant trying to make a go with the localvore shtick.

He recalled Madeline from the Dress Shoppe asking when the last time was that he'd bought Rachel something on a whim. He'd bought her an iPhone in August, for his own selfish reasons—the latest, greatest way for her to keep in touch. That had certainly panned out. A gift would be nice. Rath ambled down Main Street to the Dress Shoppe.

A crowd of folks paced on the darkened sidewalk outside the Universal Church, toting picket signs he couldn't quite read. A sandwich board outside Casablanca Video read: GOING OUT OF BUSINESS (thanks Netflix!) DVD SALE OF "TITANIC" PROPORTIONS (PUN INTENDED).

Rath popped a Tic Tac in his mouth, breathed in his cupped hands to check for boozy breath as he ventured inside with what he hoped was an easygoing air.

The toe of his boot caught on the edge of the carpet and he tripped, grabbing a mannequin in a corduroy jumper to keep himself upright.

He felt eyes on him, burning, a hand at his elbow.

"You really like that jumper," a voice said.

He stood staring at Madeline with no comeback. He had none of the rapport he'd had as a young man. No chiseled physique to bolster his confidence. He wasn't the young man he'd once been, and he did not grieve the loss.

He was more buzzed than he thought now that he was inside a warm, well-lit place. He stared at Madeline in her corduroy jumper the pale purple of lupine, her long, rich hair swept back from her forehead and kept in place by a velvet band of a dark purple. She took his wrist in her warm hand. She smelled vaguely of violets. The woman knew how to pull together a motif. "Do you bring good news?" she said.

Rath was confused.

"About the girl?" Madeline clarified.

Rath wondered if she thought investigators updated every witness.

Madeline let go of his wrist.

"No news," Rath said, swallowing.

"No news is good news, right?"

In this case it usually means a corpse, Rath thought. "I'm looking for something for my daughter," he said. Had he slurred his words?

Madeline gave the bracelets on her wrist a smart jangle. "Wonderful."

"I'd like to get something for a seventeen-year-old. Not the twenty-eight-year-old she thinks she is."

"Daughters." Madeline sighed.

"You have one?" He was feeling more at ease now.

"Two. From my first husband. *Only* husband. I make it sound like I bothered with a second." Her eyes flicked over a rack of dresses nearby, then alighted on his face. "And, of course, *I* was one. A young daughter. I know the trouble we can be."

"She's no trouble."

"Well, the heartache we cause whether we mean to or not."

Yes, Rath thought, *exactly.*

"Your daughter, Rachel, doesn't like dresses, correct?"

Rath was impressed Madeline had remembered Rachel's name and her taste.

"I don't know the last time I saw her in one," he said. "She balked at going to her prom because of the mandatory dresses. She and her girlfriends had their own party instead of attending a dance of *forced institutionalized romance*." Was he talking too much?

Madeline laughed, the sound of a bubbling brook. "I remember *those* days." She escorted him through the store, inquiring about Rachel's height and weight, eye and hair color. He told her: 5' 3", 115 pounds. Long black hair. Blue eyes.

Madeline asked how Rachel got across her *look*.

"Jeans and T-shirts," Rath said. "She goes barefoot all she can. As a toddler, she was always yanking off her diapers, shrieking, *naaay-kid*. Lately, she seems fond of overalls." He was talking too much.

"We have great jumpers," Madeline said.

"I noticed," Rath said, meaning the jumper on the mannequin, but as he was looking at Madeline and her jumper, she said *thank you,* and touched her fingers to the jumper's strap, color rising from beneath her tanned cheeks.

"How's this?" Madeline pulled a jumper off a rack with a flourish, spreading it on her open palm and smoothing it out with the other hand. "The straps with brass snaps and chest pocket hearken to overalls. And the wide wale is more youthful, a bit rogue."

"I see," he said. Though he didn't see. His head pounded.

"If she doesn't like it, she can return it. Or you can."

"OK."

"You're easy," Madeline said. "Wait at the counter."
She glanced at her watch.

He ambled to the counter as she dimmed the lighting
to that of a romantic restaurant, then locked the door
and flipped the sign in the window: CLOSED.

At the register, she folded the jumper precisely,
wrapped it in tissue paper, and seated it in a box. "Would
you like it gift-wrapped?" she asked.

"It's no special occasion. Just. Because."

"That's a good dad," she said. "I'll wrap it. Just because."

Rath handed her his credit card and driver's license.

She considered them, looking up at his face from beneath eyelids like tulip petals, dusted with a faint purple eye shadow.

"The card's good," he said, nervous in the silent store.
He'd not been alone in such close proximity to a striking woman in years. When he swallowed, the sound of
it seemed as loud as a waterfall.

CHAPTER 18

The night was so black, Rath seemed to be driving through deep space on the desolate tract of Route 105 that wound through cedar bogs known as Moose Alley. By night, moose haunted the roadsides, licking salt left by plows. By day, one of the creatures might be spied farther off in the swamp, dipping its great head into the bog, then lifting it ponderously, water pouring in strings from a head of an outsized, prehistoric horse, sullen eyes of a cow, and drooping lower lip of a giraffe. In the summer, the slow beasts sought refuge in shoulder-deep waters to escape the clouds of gnats that crawled into and gnawed every orifice, causing the moose to toss its head madly: the largest animal of the land unable to defend itself from the most minuscule of pests.

Rath kept an eye out for moose now. The creature's dark coat concealed it in the night, and it stood so high on its gangly legs that headlight beams shot under its belly, and suddenly you were upon it and you stomped the brakes too late, your car shattering the beast's legs as

1,000 pounds of moose exploded the windshield, crushing you. In the time it took to flick on your high beams, you were dead.

Death lurked everywhere. Death was alive and well.

Rath shivered and cranked the heat, dead leaves rattling behind the dashboard. He eased back on the accelerator as fog swam in from the swamp, headlights illuminating it like a wall of snow.

He turned on the radio to the crackle of 980 AM for the Patriots and Jets game, catching the tail end of the regional news. A string of break-ins of vacation camps on Unknown Pond continued. Local teenagers, no doubt. The foliage season was proving to be the best in years and had drawn an historic number of tourists.

The national news broke; Senator Renstrom was refusing to backtrack on previous remarks. The candidate's nasal voice was laced with a vitriol that brought to mind a sweat-soaked preacher under a leaky canvas tent, promising cures and salvation to the infirm—for a fee. "Government-funded murder stops with me!" Renstrom whined to cheers.

The president then spoke with the calm certitude his opponents condemned as a tone of arrogant elitism. Rath thought he simply sounded presidential. "Federal funding is audited. The funds go strictly to non-profit health services to women and girls who otherwise have no access."

Rath yawned as he drove over the bridge into Johnson, the lights of the village as bombastic as Times Square after driving in the blackness of the swamps. The NFL broadcasters jabbered about how Belichick was in the head of Rex Ryan. Rath had heard it all before.

At the center of sleepy Johnson Village, he turned up

the steep road that led to campus. The road was dark as a tar pit. The Scout heaved past a knot of kids, shadows hugging the dark shoulder as they hiked down to the pubs. The headlights illuminated three girls hitchhiking with a disturbing nonchalance. A car stopped, and the girls piled into the backseat, their nervous laughs cut off from the world as the car door slammed shut. Rath filed to memory the car's make and license-plate number.

What were those girls thinking? They were young. Dangerously foolish. Immortal. Like everyone before them. Like Rachel.

Rath imagined that after the pubs closed, bands of drunken girls swayed up the hill, numb to the hazard of being struck by a car, never mind this road being a rapist's fantasy.

The Scout's headlights gashed the dark around a tight bend. Rath gasped as a girl skipped across the road in front of him like a fawn. She wagged a hand at him, smiling.

That's all it took. One girl. One car. The car slows. The passenger door swings open. The dome light is out. The driver's face ill lit, but smiling. He seems nice. Cute. "Wanna lift?" he asks, smiling. The girl leans in. The driver pats the seat. "It's cold. C'mon. Hop in." The girl hesitates. Her head cocks, like an animal attuned to the snap of a branch, some primal instinct working deep inside her, warning her that getting into this car with this stranger goes against all she was ever taught as a child about protecting herself.

But she's not a child anymore, is she? She's capable. Her own person. She'd know if this guy meant her harm. There'd be something about him. A look. A smell. An aura to raise the alarm to a screeching pitch. But she senses no prickling sensation of dread. The boy's right. It is cold out. The other girls catch rides all the time. Nothing *ever* happened to them. Bad things happen. She's not *stupid*. Bad things happen to good girls. But not to her. Never to her. The laughter of students comes from behind her. No one is crazy enough to do something with *witnesses* just feet away.

She looks at him once more. "Why not?" she says, and gets in the car.

In fewer than thirty seconds, he'll answer her question in unmistakable terms.

Rath pulled into the guest parking lot watching students come and go from the library and the Mountain View Café. He rested a hand on the Dress Shoppe box, wrapped with a flourish of red ribbon. He undid the ribbon. It was too much. He felt confused. Why was he here? Was he really worried just because Rachel hadn't called in a couple days? It was absurd.

He got out of the Scout and grabbed the box.

The night was brutally cold, the temperature in free fall, and the air smelled of snow. The frozen-dirt lot was poorly lit by fluorescent lights too few and far between, and by a weak glow from the Mountain View Café windows. Students hustled out of the café. Rath's eyes followed a girl with long, braided hair like Rachel's trailing from beneath a wool cap, the braids slapping a puffy winter coat like Rachel's. The girl's gait was purposeful as she made for the glass doors of River Dorms. But the girl was not Rachel. Her jacket was zipped. Rachel had always run hot. As a baby, she'd tossed blankets off herself in the crib, and to this day, she left her jacket flapping open in the coldest temperatures, so she could *breathe*.

Rath entered the dorm, welcomed by an invisible wall of warmth and music crashing from the two hallways that met at the lobby. The canary yellow cinderblock walls pained his eyes, and the linoleum floor was scuffed with black hieroglyphic boot and tire marks. The lounge to his right was sparingly furnished with the functional, beleaguered chairs and sofas.

Several students were parked in the chairs and splayed lazily on the couch, oblivious to all but the screens of their smartphones. Rath doubted that the students would glance up if he set fire to himself. A flatscreen TV played unwatched reruns.

As he passed, the students proved him wrong, gawked at the middle-aged man with a wonder reserved for a Big Foot sighting.

The hallway smelled of pizza and pot smoke, and the doors to the rooms were pasted with collages of fashion-magazine covers, quotes from dead rock gods, and the standard old white eraser board with a magic marker hanging from a string. Apparently no one had yet figured out a digital alternative for leaving important notes like *Gone 2 do laundry* or *U suck* on your friend's door.

Rath stood in front of Rachel's door, confronted by his daughter's magazine clips and quotes meant to give passersby a quick glimpse into her life. A photo of the girl from *Hunger Games* was altered with a mustache and the phrase *Hunger Lame.* There was also a mug shot of Charles Manson and a gruesome magazine cover for *Fangoria.* A poster of a band called Dethknot. Under these were two quotes in Rachel's calligraphic hand:

Women who seek to be equal with men lack ambition.
—Timothy Leary
People call me a feminist whenever I express sentiments that differentiate me from a doormat or a prostitute.
—Rebecca West, 1913

Rath was swept up in a rush of melancholy by the naked honesty. He felt as though he were about to take a sledgehammer to the fragile sovereignty Rachel was just starting to piece together. Still, he possessed an urgent *need* to see his daughter's face. To *know* she was safe. It was the only way to quiet the anxiety pressing from the inside of his chest so it felt his ribs would crack. He felt stricken with the same helpless terror he'd known when Rachel had been four years old, and she'd let go of his hand in the Littleton, NH, mall. Her hand could not have been out of his own for more than two seconds. When he'd turned around, Rachel had vanished, and he'd felt such an instant, consuming anguish and paralyzing horror that he'd been unable to move or breathe or think. A saleswoman had looked at him as if he were having a stroke. He'd whipped his head around, scanning frantically for his daughter, who, he knew, just knew, had been taken. "My daughter," he said in a squeezed whisper.

"Daddy," Rachel's voice had said, and he'd looked down to see her peeking out from under a circular rack of men's shirts. The relief had nearly felled him.

He put his ear to her dorm door. No sound. No light from under the door. He raised his hand to knock when he was struck with the idea that she was in there. And wasn't alone. And he was about to interrupt her. Them. He envisioned her tossing open the door wearing some boy's tee, disheveled and flush and ready to tear into whatever lame friend was knocking, only to find her father. He could not do that to her.

He was turning away when he saw the note scrawled on her eraser board:

Ray Ray, Where R U?!!! You've friggin disappeared! Have you gone off the friggin grid or what? <u>Call me</u> - B.

His blood turned to ice.

"Excuse me," a far-off voice said.

Rath turned slowly to see a girl with Play Doh blue hair shaved tight to her skull except for the long, straight bangs cascading in her eyes. Her eyelashes were done up as lush as a carnival teddy bear's. She stood no more than five feet tall and was glaring up at him from behind her bangs and snapping her gum at him. Tiny as she was, her arms had a pudge to them, and a bit of bare belly peeped from under the hem of a purple hippie frock. Her faded jeans flared to bellbottoms that brushed the floor, her bare, ringed toes peeking out.

"What are you doing?" she said, her voice barbed.

"Looking for my daughter."

She stared unblinking.

"I'm Frank," he said, "I'm——"

"Ray Ray's Pops?"

Ray Ray, again.

"Do you know her?" he asked.

"Everyone knows Ray Ray."

"Do you know where she might be?"

"You tried knocking?"

Rath shrugged.

"Maybe try that." The girl flung her eyes at the ceiling, rapped a knuckle on the door.

The door remained unopened.

She rapped again. Shrugged. "Got me."

"Do you normally see her every day?" Rath said.

She blew a bubble with her gum. "Pretty much. Especially Mondays, Wednesdays, and Fridays in Romantic Lit. Not *romance* romance, like chick-lit shit, but Romanticism with a capital R. Shelley, Byron, Coleridge, Whitman. You know?"

"I know," Rath said. "And you haven't seen her since when?"

"She wasn't in class Friday. Or today. And I didn't see her over the weekend. But I was holed up banging out a term paper. Like everyone. She's probably hunkered down. I wouldn't *worry*. You're paler than Jack White. Ray Ray hangs on the third floor, in back, the periodical stacks. Try there." She rolled on her bare heels to leave.

"You know who 'B' is?" He pointed at the "B" below the note on the eraser board.

She blew her bangs from her eyes. "Nope."

"Who would I see about getting inside her room?"

Her eyes squinched with suspicion. "That's *extreme*."

"I'm her father, and I've been calling for days. And—"

She was staring at him, her mouth slack, gum wad hanging out. "OK. Slow down. The dorm monitor. First room back down the hall. Don't look so glum." She wandered down the hallway, scratching the back of her shorn skull.

The dorm monitor, bespectacled and sober in a Johnson State sweat suit, listened to Rath intently from her wicker chair, a pile of biochemistry books on her lap.

"I don't *know*," she said. "You have ID?"

Rath handed her his driver's license. She studied it, then him. Unsure. He handed her his wallet and she rifled through his credit cards, insurance card, and legion of other cards that verified his existence.

She tapped the wallet on her knee, relishing this unexpected sense of control thrust upon her in the midst of her bleary gray world of study. "This is a subjective call," she said. "Mine alone to make." She tapped the wallet.

"This is about my *daughter.*" Rath felt like smacking some humility into that smug face.

"It involves privacy matters," she said, voice tight with newfound authority.

"All I want is to make sure my daughter is OK. I don't have time for—"

"Don't bull-rush me, sir. Your daughter has a roommate, and *her* privacy is paramount, too. I'll let you in," she said as if allowing him in to see the Mona Lisa after hours. "But I have to be there." She slapped his wallet back in his hand and stood, a sour odor of sweat rising around her.

The smell of flowers and a whiff of Rachel's powdery deodorant greeted Rath, and he felt a tug of loss. He took in the room without moving, hardly breathing; this felt far too much like investigating a crime scene. The bunk beds took up the wall to the left. Each a cyclone of sheets. He recognized Boo Bear, Rachel's first teddy bear, lying on its side on the pillow of the top bunk.

Rachel's IKEA desk and dresser were squeezed in the far corner by a window that enjoyed a view of the parking lot. The flowers Rath smelled were tucked into the neck of a wine bottle perched on the windowsill. Black-eyed Susans. Rachel's favorite. They were wilted, the inside of the bottle ringed with a watermark from evaporation. Two dead petals lay at the base of the wine bottle.

Clothes lay scattered on the floor and draped over chairs. The cinder-block walls, the same appalling yellow as the lobby, were plastered with posters for bands like The Dolls, Skeletons on Holiday, Xup, Deathcapades.

An odor reached Rath's nose, stale and oniony. The dorm monitor's breath. She was standing just behind him, breathing through her mouth.

He took a step and looked around, at the photo of a girl hugging a dog, some sort of mutt. The girl wore ink black hair long and straight, and big, bookish glasses. She was smiling, wearing translucent braces. She must have been Rachel's roommate.

"Don't touch anything unless it's your daughter's," the voice behind him said.

Rachel's laptop was nowhere to be seen. He peeked up at her bed. Pulled back a tousled sheet to see several books: *House of Horrors: True Life Accounts of Sadist Killers, Urges: The Compulsion to Kill, Pure Evil.* Rath stared at them, dumbly. He flipped open *Pure Evil.* The pages were littered with notes in a frantic hand. What was this? She certainly didn't have a report due on such subject matter. Through his shock, he felt fear and confusion. He stepped over to Rachel's desk and pulled open the drawer, afraid of what he might find.

"That desk hers?" the voice said.

"I bought it for her."

"Students aren't allowed their own furniture. I'd like to know where the college's desk and dresser are."

Rath's back ached, a hot spark of pain bellowed into flames by the monitor's tone.

There was nothing in the desk drawer but pocket change and paper clips.

Perhaps it was a good sign that Rachel and her roommate's laptops were not here. Perhaps they were actually squirreled away in the library. Rachel was an industrious and serious student who worked hard, even if it did not always result in straight As. She put herself into her studies. How was her not answering his messages any different than when she'd deemed her bedroom *off-limits* while boning up for high-school exams?

Nurse Ratchet cleared her throat. Rath glimpsed her reflection in the window, seeing the stab wound of her impatient mouth.

The room offered nothing. He turned slowly, in a circle, taking it in, Nurse Ratchet sighing with dramatic relief.

"Sorry to exasperate you," he said.

"No need to be nasty."

"If you see her, give me a call."

She nodded primly.

Rath gave his number and stepped into the hall.

For the next hour, he searched the library exhaustively, for his daughter. Nothing. But the library was a labyrinth and swimming with students. She had to be there somewhere, studying like the rest of her peers. Finally, he set out for the long drive back toward his empty house.

MOOSE ALLEY WAS a hazard of black ice covered with falling snow, making travel treacherous. All Rath wanted was to get home and into bed. Sleep, if he could. He drove in a near-catatonic state, drained from searching for Rachel and feeling squeezed dry of all emotion save a raw rage from the news of Preacher's parole hearing. If that monster ever saw the light of day. The Scout felt claustrophobic and hot. He reached across the cab,

cranked down the passenger's window to get a good
bracing dose of night air.

Monday Night Football resumed from halftime as Rath
turned north off Moose Alley. The Pats received the
opening kickoff, as usual. Why Welker was returning
kickoffs was beyond Rath. Welker was driven to the
ground at the thirty-yard line and was slow to get up.
Great.

As Rath came back into cell range, his phone buzzed.
A text from Sonja:

meet me & grout @ the station 10AM
developments with dead
girl had 2 clue him in

Rath rolled the window back up, and the Scout hit a
patch of ice and slid sideways. The Scout spun into the
oncoming lane. As it did, his headlights illuminated a
bull moose standing in the road. He counter-steered,
the moose looming, unfazed as the Scout skidded toward it then whipsawed back into Rath's own lane, just
missing the moose. Rath let the Scout come to a rest
alongside the road, his heart crashing in his chest.

CHAPTER 19

Grout showed Sonja and Rath into his office, which offered all the square footage of an ice-fishing shanty, his crowded desk a shipwreck of exploding folders. The shelves on the left wall showed off his son's sports trophies among a stack of books on home brewing. *When did eight-year-olds start getting trophies?* Rath wondered. The wall to the right was peppered with tiny holes as if a woodpecker had been at it, a dartboard at the center of it. The threadbare carpet stank of sour beer, likely spilled by Rath himself. Many nights, he and Grout had shared a pop here before heading out for darts.

Sonja and Rath kept their coats on, the office situated at the farthest end of the hall from the sole thermostat, which clicked on about once every space-shuttle launch, which was now never.

Rath sat, and the chair, an ergonomic torture device from Staples, tilted wildly. The room swam. His throat felt as if he'd swallowed bits of shaved steel. Even his eyelashes hurt. After arriving home, he'd spent the night out on his steps with the rest of the Lagavulin, his body numb by the time the dawn sun lit the frosted tree branches into a world of delicate spun sugar. The pain in his back radiated down his legs. He was famished too. His MRI was scheduled for the afternoon and he could not recall if he was allowed to eat beforehand or not, so he'd skipped having as much as toast this morning to quiet his stomach.

Sonja unpeeled the wrapper from a Power Bar, and Rath felt his stomach turn.

Grout shut the door and sat in a swivel chair behind his desk. He shot Sonja an icy gaze. "Apparently we have a dead girl found in Victory, who's not Mandy?"

Sonja nodded.

"So, tell me again," Grout said, "why we're talking about her? Don't get me wrong. It's sad. But she was found in another county. She's not our problem. It's a state police matter."

"I think maybe she's connected to Mandy," Sonja said.

"We don't even know if Mandy was abducted. You said yourself, Mandy's forty bucks could have fallen out of her purse by accident."

"Forty-three bucks," Sonja corrected. "Three fives and twenty-eight ones."

"I don't think three bucks will keep me awake at night," Grout said.

They should keep you up at night, Rath thought. "Let's hear her out," he said.

"Fine," Grout said. "Proceed Detective Test."

Sonja drew a deep breath and opened the folder to photos of the girl's corpse. If Rath had not known he was looking at a bloated corpse, it would have taken him several minutes to figure it out. Grout glanced at the photos and looked away.

"The body was found two days ago in Victory," Sonja said. "Her name is Julia Pearl. She was seventeen, reported missing last March, the eleventh. The ME report states the body was exposed to the elements for six weeks, tops. As decomposed as it is, it would be far more so if it had been any longer than six weeks because at the end of August and start of September, we had ten straight days in the nineties."

"There's no such thing as global warming," Grout said.

Sonja gave him a schoolmarm's frown.

"Sorry. Photos like this make me nervous," Grout said.

Rath didn't think Grout had ever seen photos like this. The girl's stomach was torn open and her internal organs and viscera, what little were left, were slopping out of her gaping cavity. Her swollen body was twisted in an unnatural pose of torment. He could not help but think of Laura. And Preacher. He began to sweat in the cold room.

"This girl disappeared six months ago?" Rath said.

Sonja turned to Rath, her eyes bright. "Seven."

"And her body is dumped six weeks ago?"

"At most," Sonja said.

Rath leaned forward in an attempt to relieve his back pain. No such luck. He was trembling with exhaustion and pain and hunger. "So. Where did he keep the body for the six months, a meat locker? And what did he *do* to it while he had it?"

Grout pulled a pack of Big League gum from his desk drawer and grabbed a tangled wad, popped it in his mouth, and chewed like a cow with cud.

"Lou says she died just before the body was dumped,"

Sonja said. "Close as he can gather, the death and dumping were on the same day. Forensics says the body wasn't kept frozen. And it would be far more decomposed if this girl had been killed soon after her original disappearance. So she was kept alive for six months, give or take. Likely tortured. Then killed and dumped."

Grout tossed his wad of gum toward the overflowing wastebasket in the corner. It stuck to the rim, then peeled away onto the floor. "We're overlooking entirely the possibility that the girl wasn't abducted when she first went missing. She could easily have run away. Then trouble found her, months later. Runaways have that vulnerable look about them. They're a trouble magnet. There was no indication she did anything but run away at the outset, was there?"

"No. But—" Sonja cleared her throat and drank from a bottled water she pulled from her backpack.

"There's nothing here to connect her to Mandy. Nothing." Grout turned to Rath, dismissing detective Test. "Sunday, I checked on that lead at the Double Black Diamond. You'd have known about it if you hadn't blown off darts. The resort held model searches and casting calls for production companies out of Boston. Nothing for Mandy comes up, yet. Patrol Officer Larkin is digging around for me."

Larkin was a young officer that looked nineteen years old but was serious-minded and earnest, if dull. He spent most days at road-repair sites or speed traps.

Sonja took another sip of water. "There's more," she said. "Julie was cut open navel to sternum. With a *very* sharp blade, *not* by sharp rocks as first thought. More forensics is needed to determine what kind of blade. But it was as if she were, well, unzipped. But, because the internal organs are so decayed and many consumed by animals, Lou can't determine if this killed her."

"*Unzipped*? Seems pretty clear to me," Grout said.

"It may not have been deep enough," Sonja said. "May not have hit a vital organ or artery. And. There's this." She plucked a photo up, another blowup of sallow and purpled suet flesh.

Rath and Grout leaned in.

Part of the purple was not bruised flesh but a—

"If you look closely, you can see—" Sonja said.

"What is *that*?" Grout said, sucking in a breath.

Sonja spun the photo around. "There," she said.

Grout whistled a long, slow, graveyard whistle.

Silence bloomed, the walls pressed in. A fly ticked in the ceiling light fixture.

"Is that—" Rath began.

"A goat's head," Sonja said.

"I don't see it," Grout said, wiping his mouth. "But whatever the fuck it is—"

A strand of hair fell across Sonja's eyes. Rath sat up straight, focusing on the photo.

"And," Sonja said, "the girl's heart is gone."

Rath felt his throat clench. "Her heart?" He and Grout said it at the same time.

"That's what killed her then," Grout said, grasping, clearly wanting this to go away.

"We're not sure if it was taken. Purposely," Sonja said. "What with the animals. But. Add the carving. The thing is, most of her lungs are gone, too. Intestines. Stomach. Uterus. Not entirely. There's some of each organ left, though clearly eaten by wildlife. The heart, though. No trace. We can reason that perhaps whoever carved her might have taken her heart for, well. Purposes unknown."

"Are you seriously positing rituals or sacrifices?" Grout mumbled. "What is this, 1987?"

"Far-fetched. I *know*. The heart could've gone the way of the raccoon, she'd been picked over pretty good."

"So we have a girl who disappeared seven months ago," Rath said. "Maybe abducted, maybe she ran off, then was abducted. Murdered. Maybe from being cut open. Maybe not. What else could she have died from?"

Sonja shrugged. "Lou will let us know. But there's no blunt-force trauma to the cranium that could have caused her death. All the damage done to the crushed zygomatic bone would have been nonlethal. Besides, that was done by her being washed down the stream postmortem. That's conclusive."

"So, what do we think she has to do with the others?" Rath said.

Sonja winced, and Rath realized his slipup too late.

"Others?" Grout said, his eyes sharp.

"Three other girls about the same age have gone missing within seventy miles of here in the past year or so," Sonja said.

"Christ." Grout flicked his hand at papers on his desk. "I should have been informed. Why the hell was I not informed?"

"I've found no links between them," Rath said. "But my gut—"

"*You?* Maybe I would have found something. And fuck your *gut*. I hired you because—"

Sonja held up a hand to stop him. "Look. I set Rath on it because *he's* not getting paid, and *you* can't afford to be casting such a wide net, budget-wise or politically, especially while Barrons was gone. You can't look like you're playing gunslinger."

She was smart, playing the exact cards she needed to play.

"That's *no* reason not to keep me apprised," Grout snapped. "I'm your superior."

"You're right," Sonja said, saving face. Rath was impressed. Most people would not have said it, preferring to save their pride. "I should have brought you in. I was wrong."

"Damn right," Grout said, and glanced at Rath, letting out a sigh. "Barrons will want to hear about it, but officially we can't try to make a link if there is no proof. You're casting far too wide of a net here, Detective Test. We can't afford that. We've got Mandy missing."

"I hate to think what that poor thing—" Sonja began.

Grout locked eyes with Sonja. "Shove that out of your mind."

Rath saw he was clearly sore. But he was right. During a cop's training, it was hammered home to avoid emotional ties to victims. The victim was an object to provide evidence of the crime against it and could not exist as a human being in the cop's mental or emotional world. To sympathize was to jeopardize objectivity. If you couldn't manage it, it would be your ruin.

Rath was glad he did not have to play by these flawed rules. The photos of Julia, combined with the idea of Preacher's release, were working him into a heady lather of anger. And he worked best angry; it brought a pure clarity.

"Right," Sonja said to Grout, "best to stay detached. To your point: If Mandy, or these other girls are linked—"

"No," Grout said. "Rath said himself he couldn't find a link."

"I just started," Rath said. "I think there's something there. If they *prove* to be linked, and Julia was kept alive for months, there is a chance that Mandy, if she was taken by the same perp, is still alive."

Grout brightened at this. But said: "I won't make that leap. We don't have jack. If Barrons asks, we play it tight. He should be in by now. I'll go see if he's rolled in. This will make him bullshit, our first briefing on his return. Lovely." He got up and pushed past Rath to exit the office.

"Pissy," Sonja said to Rath.

"You should have brought him in on it." Rath stood.

"I just did." Sonja rose and adjusted the file under her arm. "And I think I subjugated myself plenty in here. You think the part about my worrying about Mandy's possible suffering was laying it on too thick to pump his superiority complex?"

Rath blinked. Stunned. She had purposely played up her empathy for a victim to let Grout scold her. She was more politically oiled than Rath thought.

As Rath and Test entered the hall, Grout strode toward them. "He's in. I can't tell if he's happy to have had ten days in fishing nirvana or pissed it's over."

They strode down the hall in silence.

CHAPTER 20

Chief Barrons proved to be in high spirits, launching into the misfortune of his hot, sunny week on North Andros, fly-fishing for bonefish by day and putting down Kaliks and conch fritters by night. According to deprived Barrons, October wasn't the best time for bonefishing in the Bahamas: hurricane season, and all that, a chance of clouds and wind that made for piss-poor fishing. But this year the bonefishing gods had graced him with sunny, windless days. "A bonefisher-man's wet dream."

Before he let his underlings get down to business, he showed them photos on his iPad of the first permit he'd ever caught on a fly, a bonus that had made his trip.

Now, Barrons sat at his desk, his meaty fingers clasped behind his big, square, bald head, his eyes closed, sup-posedly listening to Sonja make a case that Mandy's disappearance was linked to the other girls' and needed official backing though Barrons looked to Rath like he was daydreaming about bonefish.

Sonja leaned toward Barron's desk from her chair. "We think the missing girls *may* be linked. Including Mandy."

Grout shot Sonja a look that could fell a redwood for taking the lead on the conversation. "I don't think that," he snipped.

"*May* be linked?" Barrons ran a palm over his skull, not opening his eyes. "How?"

"What are the odds that these girls—" Rath started, but Sonja snapped him a cold look, and he sat back feeling like a puppy smacked on the nose with a newspaper. Police-force protocol was to let whoever was making their case make it. Never interrupt. Then again, Rath wasn't force.

"As Mr. Rath was saying," Sonja said. "What are the odds that these girls go missing without a trace, then we find this dead girl? And Mandy? And *none* are linked?"

"We don't even know if Mandy is—" Grout started and suffered the same hard smack on the snout from Sonja. He was livid now at Sonja's jockeying.

"What's the farthest distance from the missing girls?" Barrons asked Sonja.

"Seventy-eight miles," Sonja said.

"Christ. That's more than half the length of the state," Barrons said dismissively. "And some of these girls are in New Hampshire?"

Grout folded his fingers behind his head, relishing Sonja's slap down.

"But. State borders aren't going to stop a sicko," Sonja said.

"*But but but.*" Barrons blinked his eyes open. He smoothed his mustache with an index finger and thumb. "No *buts*. I'm not saying there isn't a connection. God help us if there is. But you need proof. That's your job."

"Exactly," Grout jumped in, shooting his own bitter look at Sonja. "What I'm requesting is the ability to focus on Mandy's case. She's our priority."

"Mandy a relative?" Barron's cool gray eyes settled on Grout.

Grout rolled his tongue along the inside of his cheek. "Yes, sir."

"Family can cloud your judgment." Barrons glanced at Rath. Before Rath had resigned from the state police, he'd insisted he be part of Laura's murder investigation. Barrons had flatly refused. For good reason. Though at the time, Rath had wanted to strangle him.

"I don't even know the girl," Grout said, defensively. "She's my wife's cousin's daughter. I met her mom once, at a funeral."

"Just watch playing favorites," Barrons said. "We can't be spending valuable—"

"I'm *aware*," Grout snapped. He cleared his throat. "That's why I brought Rath in, sir. To get a start while it was fresh but unofficial. He's been doing it pro bono, for fuck's sake."

"Don't get riled," Barrons said.

"I'm not riled. The fact is, she's sixteen and missing."

"She's emancipated," Barrons said.

"Yes, but."

"No *buts*. We're police officers. Emancipated means she's a legal adult. She fought for that status. She's entitled to go wherever she likes without telling anyone or cops hounding her."

Barrons's stickler approach rankled Rath more with each word. Perhaps Barrons sensed it because he clapped his hands together, and said, "Look. I don't like it either. And, she's officially missing as an adult now anyway. So I'll grant resources. We treat it officially as a suspicious disappearance until proven otherwise. We'll get her photo in the media to the general public, and I'll give a presser. At least I got a nice tan for the cameras. What I *won't* do, publicly or privately, is tie Mandy or this new body to each other, and certainly *not* to the other disappearances. Not without proof. Murder investigations are headed by the state police, we work only in a support role. For now, we deal with this dead girl under the radar, using Rath. He has more leeway. And he's cheaper."

"Thanks," Rath said.

"And see to it that you do get paid," Barrons said to Rath. "You can't work for free. Make it official. A 1099 form, all that. Find evidence to connect any of them, you'll get more support." He glanced at his iPad, the slide show of his trip.

Ass, Rath thought, though maybe Rath was jealous. Nothing was stopping Rath from going to the Bahamas for a week. Hell, a month. And even though he'd been a spin fisherman chucking bait his whole life, he'd always been tempted to try fly-fishing.

Rath's cell buzzed in his jacket pocket. He eyed the screen. A text. From Rachel. At last.

I'm sorry to be so lame. I've just
been swamped. I'll call you soon.
I promise. Love you, Rachel

Relief rushed through Rath.

"What do you think?" a voice was saying.

Rath blinked to see the three cops staring at him.

"Hmm," he said, feeling as though he were in grade

school, caught daydreaming at his desk. "I was following a thread in my own head," he said.

The cops stared. Never bullshit a roomful of detectives.

"What do you think?" Barrons said.

"I don't think we're talking just a sexual predator. Sonja's gut that they're connected feels right. This new girl. It doesn't feel sexual."

"I disagree," Grout said.

Barrons nodded for Rath to continue. "It suggests a psychotic mind, driven by a concrete, logical, if insane motive," Rath said. "The motive is the link. The *why*. There's something about these girls, dissimilar as they seem, that ties, makes them similarly attractive to the same predator."

"Find it," Barrons said. "Any theories from any of you on the *why*?"

"Some sort of cult," Sonja said, "judging by the goat's head."

"Bull." Barrons picked up a photo from Sonja's folder on his desk. "This doesn't even look like a goat's head. How do we get a goat's head out of this mess?"

"Lou McCreary—" Sonja said.

"Loony Lou? He's suddenly an expert on occult flesh carvings?" Grout barked a laugh.

"Well. No," Sonja said, "I think it looks like—"

"You *think*. *Looks like*?" Barrons said. "You need to do better. Satanists. Christ."

"Not Satanists," Sonja said, prickling. "Not exactly."

"What, exactly?" Barrons said.

"I don't know," Sonja said.

"You do know, it just has to come to you," Rath said. "I feel it, too."

"Jesus," Grout muttered. "You two and your feelings. Join a commune."

Barrons fired a look at Grout. "You got a theory rattling in that gourd?"

"Mandy's not connected. If the others are connected, it is sexual. A twisted perv. Who's to say that"—he caught Rath's eye—"mutilation, carvings, cutting out the heart, aren't a sexual turn-on?"

"If they're connected," Sonja said, "we haven't seen anything like it since"—her eyes caught Barrons's—"the Connecticut River Valley Killer." There. Somebody had said it out loud.

"Well," Barrons said, cracking his knuckles and stretching as he stood. He grimaced at Grout. "You've checked back a few years to crimes involving occult symbols or any of that shit, just in case, to at least eliminate it, I gather?"

"I just got the information," Grout said. "Detective Test just decided this morning to communicate it to me. But, I was thinking that I'd do that."

"Don't think. Do." Barrons's gaze swung on Sonja. "And you. Share everything with your superior. Got it. And put together something I can use at Mandy's presser. I'll avoid any connection to Victory's dead girl. If it gets big, we'll have those turds from NECN up here, national stringers after that. I go away for one week and I come back to a shit storm . . ."

Sonja and Grout made to leave the room. Rath followed, reading Rachel's text again. He smiled. Then, a feeling struck him, that—

"Rath," Barrons said. "Stay."

Rath stared at Barrons.

"I want to talk about your rates," Barrons said.

"Good luck bleeding that stone," Grout said, as he and Sonja made down the hall.

"Shut the door," Barrons said.

Rath shut the door.

"Sit," Barrons said.

Stay. Sit. Good dog.

Rath sat. Barrons sat. He turned the iPad to Rath to show a series of photos he hadn't earlier, grip-and-grins of his prized permit, fly rod clenched in his teeth. "That's a fish," Barrons said.

"That it is," Rath said, "you son of a bitch."

"They fight like a fucker," Barrons said, spreading his arms expansively. A late middle-aged divorced man, full-blown and magnanimous with ease and self-satisfaction, his two kids having flown the coop and his ex having remarried to absolve him of all guilt and responsibilities toward anything but his own pleasure and work. But something worked at the corner of his eyes when he smiled: a splinter of what? Regret?

"And are they ever *hard* to get to take a fly," Barrons continued. "You'd love it. You're out there on the flats, and those flats *are* wild. Let me tell you. An hour by boat, twenty miles from the nearest shack. Nothing but mangroves and flats as far as the eye can see. Monstrous sea turtles gliding beneath you, terns drifting above, and the lemon sharks. Holy Jesus. Sharks all over the place. I had one-in-every-three bonefish get mauled by lemon sharks right at the boat, or right at my leg when I was wading. Bitten clean in half. A bloodbath." He grinned, his teeth stained the color of antique piano keys. "And the permit, you *hunt* them. See maybe three a day and get maybe one good shot and likely no take. But when you do get a take, it's like hooking into a bee-stung bull.

Wild. The natives, too, the females, wild. Real welcoming, the native ladies."

"You don't have to work at all at being an asshole, do you?" Rath said, and smiled.

"Practice, practice."

"You keep me back just to rub my face in your adventurous life?"

"Mostly." Barrons looked at Rath, his eyes hard and the lines in his face deepening. "What do you think you're doing?" he said.

"Doing? Trying to help on a case."

"Not that. With your life?"

"What the hell is this?"

"You're forty-five."

"Forty-*two*."

"Unemployed."

"I work plenty."

"But you keep coming back to help us."

"You need help."

"Don't I know it. So. Come back."

Rath laughed, the sound of escaping air after being sucker punched. "Why would I ever do that?"

"You got nothing better to do. You're all alone now. You don't have something to sink your teeth into, you'll end up pathetic. And because it's in you. It's not like you left because you hated it."

"The way I work now, it's my way."

"*Chairman of the Board* here."

"No politics, no protocol."

"What if you didn't have to put up with protocol? One of the new positions is going to be Senior Detective." Barrons lifted a fly reel from his desk and worked its handle. It made a soft, purring *clickclickclick*.

"You'd want me to just jump ahead of those two?" Rath said.

"Why not?"

"You're not that stupid."

"Sure I am."

"I'd be despised by two good detectives."

"What vet isn't? They're good. But. He *still* needs time. A mentor. They both do."

"You served me OK."

"I got another eighteen months, and I'm Bahamas bound for good."

Rath was taken aback. Could Barrons be fifty already? He did the math. Shit, he was, and he was taking the earliest retirement possible with a pension at fifty-two? "So, I'd be left with some new asshole chief," Rath said.

"By then, I could anoint you chief. Interim anyway."

"This gets worse and worse."

"You saw how I had to lead Grout by the nose on digging up past petty crimes with links to 'Satanic' symbols. The thought hadn't even occurred to him."

"He'd have got to it—"

"Eventually." *Clickclickclick.* "Not good enough. You really think these girls are connected? Mandy, too?"

"But I don't know how, yet," Rath said. "When you give your presser and announce a girl has gone missing and it's learned another girl's body was found, what's the first question by the media?"

"'Are they connected?'"

"Why?" Rath said.

"Because they probably are. But I won't say it aloud. It's *you* who dares say it aloud without a lick of proof."

"Detective Test did, too."

"Junior Detective Test. And she hedges. '*But but but.*

I think. May-be.' They both pussyfoot, weigh their options. Their jobs aren't to *appease* me. Their jobs are to push the fuck back. Jesus. They don't even know *that* much yet."

"She wasn't appeasing when she brought up the CRVK—that was a good jab."

"There are good jabs, then there's swinging wildly, like a girl."

Rath shrugged.

"You don't think this has anything to do with the CRVK—" Barrons started.

"No," Rath lied. "I don't."

"You never tried to appease anyone. You say it like you mean it, even when you don't."

"If I were on the payroll, I wouldn't speak up as much; I wouldn't have that freedom."

"I'd see you did."

"You can't just appoint me Senior Detective. There's a process, and—"

"It's a fucking board of farmers and insurance salesmen. I think I know the process, and saved up a lifetime of favors to negotiate road bumps."

"No."

"Look. The ground's shifting. The world is finding its way into the Kingdom. South from Montreal. North from Boston."

"You sound like an old man."

"I'm telling you. The Montreal strip joints, the pole dancers aren't just McGill University nursing coeds anymore, looking to make a buck by rubbing their wares against a stainless-steel pole to the tune of 'Pour Some Sugar On Me,' then marrying an MBA. Those places are linked to hard-core-porn rings now, Eastern

European sex trafficking. That's *fifty* minutes away, and they're reaching their tentacles into *our homes* to groom new *talent.*"

"You think that's where Mandy is?"

"I don't *think* anything. My head is still marinated with Bacardi. But we're seeing that bath-salts shit. Heroin. I thought *that* shit went out when Cobain gave a BJ to his shotgun."

"I like how things are."

"You've never liked how things are. That's why I put it out there. Think about it."

"I'll think about thinking about it."

"You're pretty good at the asshole shtick yourself."

"That's why you like me so much."

"Probably." Barrons comported his bulk. "I heard about Preacher. *Whatever* happens with him, don't let it get to you."

Whatever happens.

"You hear me?" Barrons said.

Rath shrugged.

"Then do me a favor," Barrons said. "I don't want to see you fucked up by this. Going after that scum. Nothing good can come of it."

CHAPTER 21

Rath sat in Rankin's waiting room, his empty stomach groaning as he ate half a Snickers in a bite. The receptionist had told him he hadn't needed to fast. He popped the other half of the Snickers in his mouth. A nurse entered. "Mr. Rath?"

Rath followed the nurse, a soft, amorphous, middle-aged woman with frizzy hair so unnaturally blond she ought to just let it go gray. She had runs in her nylons, just above the heel of her white sneakers. She pushed her hip into a bar in the middle of a door, and the door opened to the outside of the building, what looked like a loading zone.

Rath raised an eyebrow. "You kicking me out?"

"We have a temporary setup out here."

A temporary MRI machine? Rath followed her to a trailer a few feet away.

"Go on in," she said.

Rath climbed the metal folding stairs up into the trailer, the nurse close behind, shutting them inside with the swing of the metal door.

The trailer was as tight as a coffin, immediately in

front of him was a panel of gadgetry. To his left was, apparently, the MRI machine. It took up the width of the trailer. A cylindrical apparatus made of cream-colored plastic, a cushioned bed he'd lie on before he was shoved into the machine like a loaf of bread into an oven on a baker's paddle. It looked like something out of *Star Trek*.

"It looks more ominous than it is," the nurse said. "I swear it doesn't hurt."

"Can't hurt more than my back does."

"Won't hurt at all. I'll slide you in, and all you have to do is lie still and relax. I'll speak to you through an intercom. You'll hear a few noises, and that's it."

Rath took a breath, wondered what they might find inside his body. His liver. His pancreas. There was nothing that could be done for the pancreas. If Steve Jobs couldn't buy his way out of it, no one could.

"Don't worry," the nurse said. "If you'd take off your belt and anything else that is metal. Coins, keys—in this basket." She handed him a plastic basket that looked like something fried clams would be served in up in a Maine seafood shack.

He did as asked, and she guided him to the MRI machine and helped him rest back on it, her cold palm flat on his chest. "Some of the noises will be a bit loud, so you can wear these."

She handed him a pair of foam earplugs like those he used when sighting in his .30-06. He wedged them in his ears.

As the foam expanded in his ear canal, the world grew muted and remote, while the sounds of his own body grew pronounced: his heartbeat, swallowing and breathing and blinking.

The nurse slid him in and shut the door to leave him in the silent, claustrophobic tube. A distant whir rose, then a sound like a lug-nut gun in a mechanic's garage. *Clackclack clack*. Silence again.

"OK," a faraway, gauzy voice said, "I'm going to move you farther back."

He slid back with the padding beneath him.

He closed his eyes and breathed. A clicking sound arose around him. The sound of a camera shooting pictures rapid fire.

"Turn on your left side please," the voice said.

He struggled to turn, pain shooting from his back down his leg.

Clickclick clack.

"Your right side please."

His palms were sticky. His heart skipping.

The machine whirred, a soft, low, pleasant hum. He drifted on the sound.

"OK," the voice said.

Rath jolted.

Had he fallen asleep?

The door to the MRI machine opened, and he was slid out.

"Fall asleep?" the nurse said.

"Hmm, no," he lied. Embarrassed somehow.

"A lot of people do," she said kindly.

He gathered his belongings from the fried-clam basket. Saw images of the internal workings of a body on a computer screen, each muscle as distinct as a poster of a steer in a butcher shop. "Is that me?" he said.

"That's you."

"Can you tell if there's anything wrong?"

"I just take the pictures. I'm sure your doctor will be in touch. It'll be all right."

Rath left unconvinced.

He was pulling out of the parking lot as his cell phone buzzed on the seat. He picked it up. The Dress Shoppe. A current of electricity sang in him. The phone buzzed again. He stared at it, picked it up, and answered.

"Is Frank there?" a woman's voice said.

"Speaking," Rath said. *Speaking?* Who spoke so formally? The woman was saying something.

"What? I lost you for a moment," he said, lying.

"It's Madeline." Her voice was bright and musical, and his tension from thinking about the MRI subsided to hear it. "I was calling to see how your daughter liked the jumper and to remind you that you can always return it for an exchange. We don't do full returns for worn clothes, but . . ." She paused. "Anyway, did she like it?" Was this business?

"She loved it," Rath lied again, wanting Madeline to feel as good about her choice of jumpers as he surprisingly felt at hearing her voice.

"Well," she said. "Great." He knew he'd messed up. She'd tossed him a big fat easy softball that hung up belt high over the plate, and he'd look it into the glove. She didn't care about the jumper; she was calling for him. Or was she? Damn it. He couldn't tell. What did it matter anyway?

"Hello," Madeline said. "You there?"

"Sorry, I'm in a bad place, a bad section of road."

"I'll let you go. I'm glad your daughter liked it."

"Maybe I'll stop in sometime, get her another one." He sucked a breath through teeth. He sounded desperate.

"Great." Her voice had lost its warmth, grown distracted. "I have a customer—"

"Of course. Sorry."

"No need to apologize." Her voice cool now. "Good-bye."

He ended the call and looked at himself in the rearview mirror. "Idiot."

CHAPTER 22

That night, Rath watched Barrons's presser on WKDM, unsurprised by the reporters asking how the police could possibly have waited more than seventy-two hours to have made public a missing *sixteen-year-old girl*. Barrons had tried to impress upon them that it was a matter of the law. Miss Wilks had won her right to emancipation, adulthood. But since the logic of the law flew in the face of common sense, the reporters hammered away: "She's *sixteen*."

The deer carcass had frozen solid to the barn's dirt floor, and Rath had called Grout to help with it. But Grout was too busy with running down files on old crimes involving Satanists and sadists and other assorted twisted fucks, and attending his son's basketball game to be bothered with such a nuisance. Or so he'd said. Rath knew Grout had taken exception when Rath hadn't backed him in front of Barrons. Grout probably wondered why Barrons had kept Rath back in his office, too. Rath wanted nothing to do with politics or a legitimate role in the force, especially now with Preacher having a chance to enter society a free man. If Preacher were released, Rath did not want to be bound by the law.

A raw northeast blow and sleet storm swept the last of autumn's leaves from the trees and kept Rath inside with his Lagavulin and his case notes.

Halloween would soon be here. No trick-or-treaters came to his house—they never ventured down his dead-end road—but the thought of Halloween made him think of Rachel. He'd called her several times only to get her full-voice-mail message. He'd texted, to no avail. At least he had her text to refer to, and knew she was OK. He knew how it was: midterms, first year of college. His first semester, he'd had every intention of calling his mother; he had just never gotten around to it. It was part and parcel of college life.

So, he decided to surrender to his own new independence, relax into the silence of the house, and try to take a break from details of the case and from stewing about Preacher.

He spread out deer hunting gear in the living room to prepare for the upcoming rifle season. He hung his Johnson hunting jacket out on the back porch to air it out and get traces of human scent off of it. He broke out a box of grunt calls and compasses, sharpened his knife, and laid out his topo maps. He'd considered buying a GPS, a technology he'd sworn he'd never cave in to, and in the end hadn't. If a man could not get by in the woods with a compass and topo map, what kind of outdoorsman was he?

The next day, he took a day trip across New Hampshire to Kittery, Maine Trading Post, where he bought a Zeiss scope that cost nearly a grand, without a hint of buyer's remorse. Afterward, in Portsmouth, he indulged in fresh, deep-fried, whole-belly clams dipped in melted butter and washed them down with a couple Narragansett pints.

Back home, he broke out his old Lee reloader press and knocked out fifty rounds of hand-pressed superhot 190 grain, round-nose .30-06 rifle cartridges. He took his Springfield pump out back along Ice Pond and sighted in the Zeiss with his hand-loaded rounds, dialed the rifle in until it drove tacks at two hundred yards.

He plinked cans with the .22 revolver he kept in the Scout's glove box.

Still. Thoughts of Preacher and the missing girls crawled into the back of his mind like a burglar slipping in through a cellar window. Snatches of each missing girl's circumstances plagued him, and he returned to the files again and again. Much as he tried not to, he obsessed about Preacher's parole hearing. He didn't know if he could bring himself to go. During a late-afternoon nap, he dreamt of Laura at the bottom of the stairs, her face turned away in shame. And when he leaned at her side, he saw that her face was Rachel's face. In his dream, Rath would jump back as the sound of Preacher's cruel laughter broke around him. When he looked up the staircase, he'd see Preacher standing at the top, laughing, his lecherous eyes gleaming. In his arms, he held baby Rachel. What disturbed Rath most was that Rachel wasn't squirming to escape Preacher's grasp, but was calm and quiet; at peace in this monster's arms. He awoke with a jolt to the sadistic laughter echoing in his head, icy sweat soaking him.

What good would it do for him to show at the hearing?

To be subjected to a person with such a filthy soul and watch as that person was treated with respect and due process. What respect had he shown Laura and Daniel, or the young girls before them? But. If Rath didn't go. What would his absence say? That he didn't care? If he didn't care, why should anyone else? He didn't know what he could say that would convey his sense of loss. He worried his anger would get the best of him.

He was pondering what to do the next morning while out at the barn, standing over the dead deer with a Saws All to cut it up into chunks when his cell buzzed.

"Yeah," he said, distracted.

"We found something. Lou did. The girl's feet were bruised and cut." It was Sonja.

"So our psycho's a foot fetishist, too."

"Cut up from running. Barefoot. She wasn't dumped. She escaped. Her feet suffered so many cuts no one in their right mind could have kept running like she did. The St. J. force and staties have scoured the area. They found a cabin near where she was found. Nothing obvious that anyone was kept there. We'll see. They figure she either came from there or escaped from a car on the road below. She died of exposure. She wasn't murdered. Then, when the flood came—" She paused. "And—"

"And what?"

"She was pregnant."

"How did Lou miss that in the initial?"

"The condition of the body, for one. And, there was no fetus."

"What? How? Animals?" Rath felt ill.

"So to speak. Lou thinks someone took it."

Took it. Rath swallowed hard. "How far along was she?"

"Impossible to say. No one close to her so far has claimed they knew about it."

Rath slumped and sat, a hand resting on the frozen deer. Jesus, what was *this*?

"We need to meet. First chance. Grout's got something, too."

CHAPTER 23

Rath lobbed a dart over Detective Test's head to hit the triple 12 on the dartboard behind her.

"Watch it," she said.

"Before we get to our pregnant dead girl," Grout said, brusquely, "I have two things. First, I admit I may have been wrong. Maybe the girls are connected. And maybe it is something other than a straight-out rape killing. Second. A Mandy update. Larkin vacuumed all of her e-mails, interactions on Facebook, social-media crap. Zip. She only has six friends on Facebook, all girls, and has not posted anything since August. All her friends were girls. Plenty of guys sent friend requests. Larkin's looking into them. But Mandy wasn't active online. She had no computer. Good for her. That online shit's pathetic. The older you are, the more so."

"I'm on Facebook," Sonja said.

"Right," Grout said. "Anyway. She's a loner. No close friends. Maybe because of the upheaval in her family life."

"Anything there?" Rath said, "The coke-dealing dad?"

"A real winner, as you know," Grout said. "Landscaper in the summer. Ski-lift operator in the winters. Not a sign of coke dealing when I stopped by to interview him. Your visit must have put him on high alert. He claims he was razzing you about pimping the girl because *you*, as he put it, were *fucking her with your eyes.*"

"I—" Rath said.

"Forget it. He's a fucktard," Grout said. "I grilled him like a sirloin about Mandy. He tried to come off as genuinely baffled why we're even looking for her. Said she took off. That's why she got emancipated after all. Called her a *little bitch*. She's always done just what she wanted, according to him. Apparently, he doesn't like people doing what they want unless it's him. I think the girl, Porkchop, Abby Land, was covering for him though, as far as an alibi. There was definitely something there. She was scared."

"I wonder why," Rath said.

"I don't," Grout said. "Guy's a fucking animal. His new wife, she's been in Arizona the past two weeks because her mother's dying. I don't think Abby's covering because she thinks he did something to Mandy. I asked her in private if she thought he did it. She looked me dead in the eyes and said no. She was telling the truth. But, I think she's covering for him for something else. Maybe an affair. Or the coke dealing. It's a fucked-up situation in that house. Much as I'd like to fuck this guy up, regarding Mandy, I think he's a nonstarter, especially if the girls are all connected."

Grout took a breath. Smiled. He handed a folder each to Sonja and Rath. He was taking control. Rath and Sonja had pissed him off in Barrons's office, and it was fueling him to find focus and command. About time. Grout smiled again. "I ran down recent activity involving Satanic graffiti, sadism, the like," he said. "I dug up these two model citizens."

Rath opened the folder and looked at the mug shots from nineteen months prior of George Waters and Jeff Barber, both eighteen years old. Waters had the pale skin of a drowning victim pocked with acne craters and a nose that looked like a malformed tuber. His long hair was black and oily as hot tar and was plastered to his caved cheeks. His narrow eyes were black, the irises as dark as the pupils, reptilian. Peach fuzz traced his upper lip like a child's scribble, and his left earlobe sported an earring: a silver pentagram.

The other mug shot showed a kid who looked somewhat normal in comparison, which wasn't saying much. His hair was buzz cut; the first impression Rath had was *skinhead*. Odd how the same cut on another person might have made Rath think *military* or *monk*.

The kid's bulging eyes gave him a startled, anxious look if you didn't recognize symptoms of drug use. The kid's eyes were jaundiced and set in a squeezed face that, paired with his sharp teeth, gave him a Nosferatu look. A sinister smile slashed his face, as if he thought getting a mug shot was a joke. Which he probably did.

"Real studs," Sonja said.

"They were arrested for vandalism of a construction site. May of 2009. Along with—" Grout flipped a page of the report. "Desecration of a cemetery and animal cruelty."

"Shit," Sonja said. "These are the two lowlifes that killed that dog and left it on a headstone."

Grout nodded. "*Gutted* the dog. And knocked over headstones with their pickup."

"I should have thought of them. I missed the connection because I mostly remember the dog. Poisoned with hamburger laced with crystal Drano."

Rath vaguely remembered something about the case now.

"But it didn't die from that," Grout said. "They sliced it open along its belly and pulled out all its insides while it was still alive."

"They killed the puppies with a hammer," Sonja said.

"Puppies?" Rath said.

"All five puppies," Grout said. "Smashed to pulp with a hammer on headstones."

"Practice for babies?" Sonja said, pale-faced.

"The graffiti they sprayed was of swastikas and pentagrams and *goats' heads*," Grout admitted, not without some regret. "It's not as much *that* they painted the headstones as it is *what* they *painted the headstones with*."

Rath read down the page. "They drained the dog's blood into spray bottles?"

"Rust-Oleum red wasn't good enough for these clowns," Grout said.

This sort of viciousness wasn't found in your average rebellious teen. It wasn't even rebellion. It was an ecstatic pleasure taken from the debasement of other living creatures. Pure sadism. "So where are our two celebrated-citizen youths these days?" Rath said.

"Not in jail, where they should be," Grout said. "They did Juvie. Community service. Same old shit. Blame it on their losing the parent lottery. Being minors. Give them a break."

"No crimes committed since then?" Sonja asked.

"No arrests," Grout said.

"Which isn't the same thing," Sonja said.

"Sick kids like these, how long do you think they still get their kicks from animal cruelty before they graduate to something *better*?" Grout said.

"They still in the area?" Rath asked.

"You'll love this. Barber is in Afghanistan. Joined the fucking army. They'll take anyone these days, apparently," Grout said. "Waters is a house painter and is working on a construction site down in Bloomfield. I got a line on his address. But I might try to catch him off guard at work, first thing in the morning. I spoke to the general contractor, and he said the painters are in first this week, the electricians and plumbers done. I told him to have the other painters arrive about twenty minutes later than usual, so I can nab Waters alone. Brush up on how to remain neutral in the face of life's shit."

CHAPTER 24

Grout waited in his Outback at the construction site, listening to CHOM FM out of Montreal and eating a fresh Clear Brook Farm cider donut. If there was one thing about fall he looked forward to, it was these donuts. That, and good sleeping weather. Every August he put AC units in the bedroom windows. The AC put Jen into a catatonic state, but the meat-locker clamminess kept Grout awake. The AC was a wash when it came to the kids; with the AC off, they swam in their own sweat. With the AC on, they were comfortable but kept awake by the AC's racket. And sleepless children were demonic children. Autumn always came just as it seemed the family would implode into mutual homicide against one another. Now, with the cold nights, and the windows cracked a hair the family slept like victims of a carbon-monoxide leak.

Grout had awoken this morning invigorated instead of feeling like a slab of leftover meat loaf. He and Jen had fallen asleep in bed while watching a *Columbo* DVD. Jen

liked *Columbo* for the seventies' fashion. Grout watched
it for the classic cars and the banter. The investigations
themselves were ridiculous. The episode the previous
night had starred Robert Culp as a blackmailing and
murdering private eye. It seemed Robert Culp was in
half the episodes. Grout liked him. Jen had fallen asleep
a half-hour into the show. So tonight, as usual, they'd
rewind to where she'd drifted off. It usually took three
nights to watch an episode.

Grout pulled a second cider donut from the paper
bag, the donut warm and smelling pleasantly of yeasty
dough and warm sugar. The donuts were the only junk
food in which he indulged; otherwise, sweets had no
grip on him as they did the kids, who could stand to
lose a few pounds by playing outside. Liam's basketball and Jill's gymnastics did not make up for running your brains out in the yard, something he and his
brother had done growing up but which was apparently
stripped from today's kids' genes. Grout and his brother
had fought like cats dragged to water to stay outside.
Summers, they'd roamed the woods behind the house
until the mosquitoes drove them inside; winters, they'd
sledded until they couldn't feel their fingers. The whole
world was weakening. He wondered if in two hundred
years, humans would be reduced to gelatinous blobs
hooked up to feeding tubes.

Grout ate his second donut. They were made from
scratch at dawn, September through November only.
This morning, he'd arrived at six A.M., the farm shrouded
in fog, to watch the girl roll and cut the dough, then
drop it in hot, foaming oil. She'd scooped each donut
out, rolled them in sugar then tonged five into his bag,
handing him the sixth. When he took that first bite,

sugar clung to his lips and melted, and the donut's crisp golden skin gave way to a hot, doughy inside. He was lucky Clear Brook only made donuts in the fall. He'd weigh three hundred pounds and have arteries as clogged as old sewer pipes if they had them year-round. Shit. He'd be dead by now.

He tore a third donut in two; the sugar melted to a sweet film, and popped half in his mouth. He licked his fingers as he watched through the windshield.

A clunker Chevy Suburban out of a *Starsky & Hutch* episode rattled into the site, the radio blasting death metal. George Waters.

Waters stepped from the truck wearing painter's overalls and carrying a canvas tool bag. From fifty feet away, the eruptions of pustules on his cheeks were plainly visible. Greasy black hair like rotted kelp pasted to his ugly mug.

Grout opened his car door slowly and got out.

Waters dropped his bag and bolted across the lot toward the fields behind the site.

Grout stood frozen for a moment. Then he took pursuit.

The kid sprang across the lot, weaved between parked dozers and bucket loaders, then leapt a barbed-wire fence and broke across a cow pasture. He had two hundred feet on Grout when Grout had to stop at the fence, unable to hurdle it. As he swung a leg over the fence, his pant cuff tore as he fell over the fence onto his face. He jumped up and started across the field, pushing hard. He was in reasonable shape, but the pale and sickly-looking kid had two things going for him: youth and fear.

Grout kept pace across a knobby field that tortured

his ankles. His lungs burned as the kid leapt another fence, putting more distance between them.

Grout trudged on, climbed the next fence. When he looked up, the field was empty. The kid was gone. Then, Grout saw him. The kid popped up from the grass. He'd fallen and now hobbled lamely. Grout took off. Slowly, he closed, shouting, "Stop! Police!" like an imbecile. As if a fleeing criminal had ever stopped because a cop had yelled after him. Grout sucked breath between his teeth, a stitch in his side slowing him. But he was gaining. The kid was hurt.

Grout was nearly within reach. He lunged at the kid's legs and found only air, then frozen mud. The kid kicked Grout's hand, and Grout felt the knuckles of two fingers pop and break. He gritted his teeth. *Motherfucker.* He scrambled after the limping kid and dove again, wrapping the kid's ankles in his arms as the kid hit the ground hard.

"Fucker," the kid shouted, kicking. But Grout was too strong for the scrawny youth. He cranked the kid's foot, and Waters wailed in pain. Grout cranked some more.

Then reefed the kid's hands behind his back, cuffed him, and slammed his face into the frozen ground, growling as adrenaline raged in him, "You piece of shit!"

CHAPTER 25

"Sit," Grout ordered Waters in the interrogation room, with Officer Larkin watching from behind the two-way. The kid glowered, his face muddied and bruised.

"I'm going to tell them you abused me," the kid sneered.

"Tell who? My boss? He could use a laugh."

Grout sat opposite, taking an aloof posture, his legs out and crossed leisurely at the ankles, as if he were on a park bench enjoying the sun. He took a donut from his bag. They were cold but still good. He took a bite. His throbbing knuckles were swollen three times their normal size, broken for sure. He held them up to the kid. "Assault of a police officer," Grout said absently. He looked up at the video camera in the corner. "Lead Detective Harland Grout interviewing one George Henry Waters, October 27, 2011."

The kid made a snoring sound.

"Assault's small potatoes." Grout held up his hand. "Compared to murder."

The kid cracked his back. "What the fuck are you jabbering about?"

"You tell me, you little sadist." Grout fished another donut from the bag.

"You're a walking, fucking cliché," the kid snapped. "*Donuts?*"

Grout held up the donut. "Not just any donut, you twat. A Clear Brook Farm donut. And look at you, speaking of clichés. Mister Satanist. With your dyed black hair and your black-painted fingernails filed sharp, your repulsive cadaver skin and pentagram tattoos. You look like a *Twilight* extra. I bet you got Aleister Crowley books at home."

"Kafka and Camus actually."

Grout had never heard of them. "Maybe a pet python?"

"You don't know shit."

"I know you like gutting dogs."

The kid cackled.

"Desecrating gravesites of the dead who've rested in peace for two centuries," Grout pressed.

The kid yawned, picked at a loose thumb cuticle. "Who says they rest in peace?"

Grout took out a photo of Mandy, the good one, slid toward the kid.

The kid looked at it. "Hot bitch. Who is she?"

"Don't you know?"

"I think I'd remember a piece of ass like that."

"I think you do remember."

"You don't know shit." The kid stared, eyes blazing with hatred.

"I guess a high-school dropout knows more than anyone, right?"

"Ooh, you've been in my file. School don't mean squat when it comes to smarts. Bill Gates dropped out."

"Yeah, you're a real Bill Gates."

The kid stared at Grout. "I guess I should aspire to be a civil servant who risks his life for shit pay and can't even afford to take the family to Six Flags. A real genius, like you."

Grout felt his blood lather. If the knuckles of his right hand weren't busted, he'd hammer the punk in the face. "Where were you on March 11 this past spring?"

The kid laughed. "*March?* You shitting me? Where were *you?*"

"In bed watching *Columbo*."

The kid stared, baffled.

"Maybe you were abducting *her?*" Grout slid a photo of Julia alive to the kid. "Dogs weren't fun anymore. So you decide you'd like carving goats' heads into girls instead to hear them scream, or was she unconscious when you did it?"

"Never seen her," the kid said.

"How about her?" Grout slid a photo of Julia's corpse. The kid flinched. Then, a smile, disturbingly gleeful, broke on his face. "That shit for real?"

Grout sat stone-faced.

The kid fell back in his seat. "Wow. Sick. What's it got to do with me?"

"I thought you'd like to know what she looked like after you were done with her."

"Me?" The kid snapped his posture so straight, his chair skidded backward. "No fucking way. That's sick shit."

"Whereas gutting a dog while it's alive isn't? Using its blood to paint pentagrams on headstones." Grout perked up, fixed his eyes on the kid. "Smashing fucking puppies with a ball-peen hammer. That's just a run-of-the-fucking-mill good time. You got bored with dogs. Maybe they didn't struggle enough. Plead enough."

The kid sprang up from his chair, eyeing the door.

"Sit the fuck down!" Grout roared, and shot up to standing, his muscles twitching to hurt the kid.

The kid sat. "I'm not into that shit anymore," he said.

"Turned over a new leaf, did you?"

"I'm clean. And sober. For a year. I got a job. Or had one till you ran after me."

"*You* ran *from* me."

"I run from cops, so?"

"How'd you know I was a cop?"

The kid grunted and sniffed. "I could smell your pussy."

This kid was begging for it. A fucking masochist and a sadist. Worst of the nuts to crack: the ones who didn't care what happened to themselves. "Why'd you run? Who'd you think I was?" Grout let the question hang, the silence bloom. Silence was a key tactic to get someone to talk. Most people couldn't stand it. It was like a big invisible finger of accusation.

"I thought you were sent by this other guy I know," the kid finally said.

"Who?"

"I can't say."

"You better. Otherwise, I'm liable to think you were running because you knew we'd tied you to kidnapping, torture, murder. That's life behind bars. With fellow rapists."

"He's just a guy after me to do some work. Break-ins. But I'm not doing it."

"Then why run? Why not tell him?"

"You don't *tell* guys like him anything. They *tell* you. What day did that hottie disappear?"

"Late night October the twenty-second or early in the morning the twenty-third."

The kid muttered, wedged his bony hands between his knees, rocked in place.

"I was home. Sick. I was supposed to be at AA earlier in the evening on the twenty-second. But, I felt like shit."

"Anybody home with you?"

"I live alone."

"Right." Grout tapped the photo of dead Julia. "You see that? Look at it."

The kid moved his eyes over the photo.

"See that carving there." Grout tapped the photo. "That's a goat's head."

"Looks like bullshit to me."

It was true. Grout still didn't see the supposed goat's head Test claimed to see so plainly.

"Your signature work. If you were me, and you were looking for someone sick enough to do something like that, you'd have to think it was pretty select company."

The kid wrinkled his lip.

"Now, if you had these two kids who'd done similar things to a dog," Grout said. "And only one kid was in the States, and he had no alibi, what would you think?" The kid's eyes locked on Julia's corpse, his left eye twitching.

"You got off mutilating some kid's pet," Grout said. "You're way into the Satanism."

The kid mumbled something unintelligible.

"What?" Grout said. "What the fuck did you say? Get the cock out of your mouth."

"I don't *believe* in that shit," the kid said, chuckling. "I never did." He looked up from under his brow and gave Grout a cold, mischievous stare as if he'd studied that sicko movie. What was it? *A Clockwork Orange*?

"We did it for fun," Waters said. "And it *was* fun. At the time. To get at old fucks like you. How easily you sheep fall for stupid fucking symbols. We carved goats' heads and pentagrams because it was fun to watch people go all crazy."

Grout ground his teeth. This kid had no place walking around in society.

"Pentagrams, swastikas, nooses, crosses. All that shit. It means fuck-all to *me*," Waters sneered. "*You* old superstitious fucks give symbols power. Not me." He smiled, his eyes black, depthless. "Do you believe in the devil? Because I sure as fuck *don't*."

Grout didn't know if he believed. Neither he nor Jen had stepped inside a church since they'd been kids. Then, their own kids had started asking about God, and Grout had felt *why not* expose them to church, let them decide for themselves?

Besides, if this kid wasn't spawned from the devil, who was?

The kid was rambling, " . . . we carved goats' heads and pentagrams because it was fun to watch people go all crazy."

Grout leaned in, close enough to Waters's face to taste the kid's foul breath.

"What *do* you believe in?" Grout said.

"Nothing," the kid said. He nodded at the photos of Julia. "It wasn't me. And what's some girl who disappeared in March got to do with the hot chick?"

The kid was right. There was no real proof of a connection between Mandy and the others. He'd been going on gut. And it could come back to bite him in the ass.

"We done?" the kid said. "Cuz, unless you're going to arrest me, I—"

"I am arresting you."

"What the fuck for?"

"Assault of a police officer." Grout held up his injured hand and gave the kid the finger.

CHAPTER 26

"I think Waters did Julia," Grout said, as he and Rath sat in the Bee Hive, working on their third beers. "I don't know about Mandy."

"What happened to your fingers?" Rath said, nodding at the finger splints.

"Waters kicks like a girl," Grout said.

Rath drank his Molson. Pain spiderwebbed from either side of his spine, so he felt he was cracking open out of his own skin. He needed to stop in and get his Vicodin. The prescription had been delayed another day because the pharmacist had been unable to read Snell's handwriting, and he'd had to contact Snell to confirm it.

Grout fished a couple pretzels from a wicker basket, crunched them down.

"What makes you think Waters is the doer?" Rath said.

"What *doesn't?* Carving up dogs, the Satanist bullshit. I hate to admit it, but your angle looks better than mine about now. Still, I don't see how Mandy fits. Yet."

"Is the carving the same on the dog as on the girl?"

"We're talking flesh carvings here, not paint by numbers. And I still don't see any damn goat head or whatever. But—" Grout looked at Rath. "What? You don't think he's our boy now? As soon as I come around to your line of thinking."

"I didn't say he wasn't—"

"But?"

"It doesn't feel like something someone does alone. Carve up a girl, torture her, and the fetus thing." Rath rolled his beer bottle between his palms. "It lends itself to the alchemy of two sickos prodding each other. Two halves of one evil. Like those two who did the professors. Waters did the dog with his buddy, probably because they fed off each other. Now. His buddy is in Afghanistan so is he going to have the guts to act alone?"

"OK. So it was two perps. So maybe Waters got a new recruit," Grout said, latching onto Rath's theory. "The kid *is* evil. The type to prey on weaker, troubled kids, lure them in—I'd buy that, put it on Lay-Away at least. And Waters has no alibi."

"Whoever did it, won't need an alibi. Can't even be expected to have an alibi for eight months ago. There is no fixed time of death."

"She disappeared March 11, that's a concrete date."

"But not a concrete time. And you said yourself she could have run away on that date. Been abducted later. There's no way we can tie Waters or anyone else without hard physical evidence."

"Why are you shooting holes in this?"

"Don't get defensive."

"I'm *not*, I'm looking at the facts."

"That's the problem."

"Looking *at facts,* that's the problem?" Grout shook his head angrily. "Or is it because *I* found Waters?"

"I'll walk now if you want. I'm fine with that," Rath said, though he wasn't fine. He wouldn't extract himself from the case even if he were kicked off it. He'd pursue it on his own. "Look," he said. "I know you want Barrons's desk. And should get it—"

"What the hell did he tell you in his office?" Grout said.

"Nothing you have to worry about."

"I'll decide what I need to worry about."

Rath jabbed a finger onto a cork coaster and spun the coaster around. "The only thing you need to worry about is this case. Not politics. Not positioning. Not who came up with what lead first. Not your kids' basketball games or gymnastics. If you want to get ahead, focus. And take more chances. It's not just the facts, it's how you *interpret* them."

"*You* can say that. You can follow any old hunch. You don't have a career or wife to lose."

"You think I waste time on any old hunch? I get a hundred hunches a day and ignore a hundred and one of them. You don't think maybe I'd like to find who's cutting up girls? You think maybe I haven't seen enough of that?"

They sat in shrieking silence.

"Of course not," Grout said. "No."

"Say it is Waters, and some other degenerate. Do you think lowlifes like that could keep quiet under pressure?"

"I haven't turned the screws that tight yet."

"What did the search of his apartment show?"

"Nothing."

"His truck?"

"Nothing, but—"

"Computer?"

"Larkin's only halfway there with it. But nothing so far. But he fits. He *does*. More than anything you have. I don't give a shit if he's going to AA. For all I know, maybe he's trolling the bottom of the barrel for fucked-up chicks to get a girl involved. Maybe this is some sexual thing with a sick chick. It happens."

It did. Too often. And AA was full of lost types ripe for the picking.

The waitress brought over Grout's Bud, and he stared at it without picking it up.

"I admit you're right about one thing. I can spend as much time on more unlikely scenarios of a case because I have no life. Darts and deer hunting." Rath raised his beer. "Here's to my thrilling life."

"Try being married with kids."

"Married. I haven't had a date in sixteen years."

Grout stared in disbelief.

Rath slid his Molson from one hand to the other. "I was never interested. I'd see other single parents bringing home dates, having someone move in with them and their kids. I never wanted to do that to Rachel." He finished his beer. "If married parents like you and Jen can't find more than their anniversary to get out on a real date, how could I justify dating as a single parent?"

"Who says we get out on our anniversary," Grout said, breaking the remaining tension with a laugh.

"There may be a woman now," Rath said. "Maybe. She works at a dress shop and called to see if Rachel liked the jumper she helped me pick—"

"She called to ask if you liked what you bought? Jen has single and divorced girlfriends cackling all the time about this shit. Women don't waste a second with any man unless they're interested. That's not gut. That's fact. Call her."

IN THE PARKING lot, Rath dialed the Dress Shoppe.

"Dress Shoppe," a woman's voice said.

Rath realized he was holding his breath. He exhaled. "Is Madeline there?" he said, his voice cracking like a twelve-year-old Peter Brady.

"Speaking."

"It's Frank."

The silence of a nunnery at 3 A.M. He considered hanging up. "Who?"

"Frank Rath. The father who bought his daughter the jumper."

"Oh. Yes. What can I do for you?"

Christ, what a blunder.

"Hmmm?" he managed.

"What can I *do* for you?" she said.

"I was wondering. What are you doing Friday?"

"Friday day?"

"Day. Night. Either."

Silence. Then voices in the background, muffled by a hand over the phone.

"Sorry, customer," she said. "Friday. Well."

"Look, I think maybe I got my wires crossed. I—"

"You didn't."

His pulse quickened. "No?" he said.

"No."

"So, are you free?"

"No. But I could change that if you're asking me out. Are you asking me out?"

"I guess."

"You guess?"

"I am. I am asking you out."

"So. You're just shy?"

"Shit no."

She laughed.

He relaxed. Some.

"So . . . day or night?" she said.

"Evening. Seven?"

"Where?"

"I hadn't thought that far."

She laughed harder, a spirited laugh that caused all the stress to flow out of him, leaving him loose. Humming.

"What do you like to eat?" His voice was thick, from the back of his throat.

"Depends on my mood."

Every word seemed an unintentional double entendre now. It was a sticky web of flirtation, and he felt tangled in it.

"Comfort food," she said. "So, where do you want to take me?"

"Some place quiet."

"How about the new place, Bistro Henry?"

Bistro Henry was fine. Bistro Henry was perfect.

CHAPTER 27

Rath stood before his living-room wall. He'd taken down his two Proseck prints and two deer mounts to tack up all the information he had about the missing girls. He'd tried to lay it out on his PC, but the computer's screen was too small, the windows overlapped, and his mind ended up a tangled confusion of barbed wire. He needed to see the information laid out before him, big and bold and sprawling.

He'd taken a copy of the good photo of Mandy from Grout and tacked it to the wall, around which he'd pinned the photos and info of the other missing girls. He studied the photos of the girls up close, then backed away and took them all in at once. *Look.*

He'd been looking for five hours now. It was one in the afternoon. He had been at it since four in the morning. *Look.*

The girls looked back. Silent.

Nothing in common besides sex and age.

No one close to the girls proved suspicious under

interrogation. If even one girl had a relative or friend as a genuine suspect, it would put a hole in the theory that they were linked. But not one of the disappearances could be even remotely tied to someone they knew. Each of them had to have known someone, the same person. Or one person had known them. Fiona Lemieux had been seen by the owner of the corner store, getting into a nondescript car. Why? Had she and the other girls had their instincts to help others used against them? Maybe. Maybe.

But. How did one person, or even two people, choose these girls? And why?

He looked at the photos of Julia's corpse. They were hard to stomach. He focused on the close-up shots of the carving. What sort of evil were they dealing with? Someone who wanted to leave such a mark on a girl, to show just how depraved, how evil, they were, while the girl was still alive. He poured over the biographies as he glanced at the photos.

Sally Lawrence: Lived with a single mom. Poor, obese but confident, honor roll.

Rebecca Thompson: Working-class, loving parents, well liked, ordinary looks, extraordinary athlete.

Fiona Lemieux: Wealthy, influential family, petite, pretty, gifted musician, golden voice.

Julia Pearl: White-collar parents, teacher mother, CPA father, only child. Pregnant.

Mandy: Average grades. Emancipated. Asshole father. Private. Gorgeous.

The girls shared nothing *except* dissimilarity.

He let his mind wander. Fishing. At times, you hunted with focus. Other times, you fished, let your thoughts cast about and see what your unconscious mind hooked.

He considered the good photo of Mandy. It was much better than his first photo.

Her warm, caramel eyes were flaked with gold, inviting and intimate; they suggested secrecy, a promise, a sense that she had a confession to whisper in your ear, to you and you alone. It was a look that could confuse the wrong person into believing he was exceptional. Chosen. And anger in him when he found he wasn't either.

Rath stared at the photos and his notes, feeling a thought begin to rise to the surface, like a trout about to sip down a mayfly. He closed his eyes and waited. The connection was just about there, a fine, clear theory, when his phone buzzed on his desk. He let it go to voice mail, but the thought had been submerged. He kept his eyes closed, trying to find a tranquil state and let ephemeral thought materialize into a concrete image he could use.

The phone buzzed.

He ignored it, breathed.

The phone buzzed again. A bee in his ear.

The thought was gone.

He grabbed the phone: PRIVATE.

He answered.

"Yeah?" he said, distracted, his voice the snap of a branch.

"Mr. Rath?"

"Yes."

"Dr. Snell. I remembered where I saw the girl."

Rath caught his breath and felt his legs go weak.

"I don't know if it will be of any help or not," Snell was saying.

"Where are you?" Rath reached for his jacket.

"My office."

"I'd like to speak in person as soon as possible."

"I'm straight out all day. My last appointment is at five. I have some paperwork, but should be done by seven. Just let yourself in."

CHAPTER 28

Dr. Snell's office was as quiet as the deep woods on a winter night. The recessed lights dimmed to leave the office in a perpetual dusk. Rath had let himself in, as instructed. He peered around the empty waiting room, looked for a bell or something to get the doctor's attention. There was nothing. He cleared his throat, the sound loud as the crack of a whip in the dead silence.

"Out back!" a voice shouted from down a hall.

Rath pushed the gate at the reception area open and worked his way down the hall to find Dr. Snell in a spacious, high-ceilinged office adorned with an Executive Mission desk of quarter-sawn red oak and hammered-copper hardware and accents. The bookcases were crafted of the same handsome oak. Pricy, heirloom pieces. Alongside the diplomas on the wall, hung oil paintings of desolate, windswept landscapes with decrepit barns and lonely farmhouses, bringing to mind Wyeth. Rath's favorite. The paintings weren't prints. They were originals, each lit from above with a pair of sconced lights set at exact angles. The gilded frames alone must have run a couple grand each.

The place was a long ways from the impression Snell gave of himself to patients, with his Carhartt jeans and flannel shirts and Merrells.

Snell finished buttoning up a smart slate blue tailored shirt, then tucked it into designer jeans held up by a polished, hand-tooled leather belt. He nodded at a chair that looked like a Stickley, all dark oak and sumptuous leather.

Rath sat. Damn, what comfort. He thought he might never want to get up again. The pain in his back vanished. He'd sell the farm for a chair like this. It'd probably cost him that, too.

"Drink?" Snell said.

"Why not?" Rath said.

"Ice? Water?"

Rath always took ice, but he sensed, somehow, such practice was taboo in this office, so shook his head.

"Good man," Snell said, and pulled down the top of what looked like a small rolltop mail desk to reveal a full bar of top-shelf liquor. Clever. Snell took a bottle of Caol Ila 18 and poured two fingers into a snifter he handed to Rath, then poured the same for himself.

His snifter was solid and supremely balanced in the hand. A regal specimen of lead crystal. Rath took a sip. Fine scotch from a fine glass. The familiar glow spread through him and slowed the world to a more manageable pace.

Snell sat behind his desk, set his drink on the chair's generous arm.

Rath rested his drink on his knee. He wanted a second sip but decided to hold off until Snell took his.

"So," Rath said.

"The girl," Snell said. "Yes."

"Where'd you see her?" A feeling of insecurity crept down Rath's spine. Such sensations were foreign to him. Could it be because he sat amid an abundance of wealth and success that, although displayed tastefully, was nevertheless meant to put a visitor in his place? No. He'd interviewed plenty of people who could buy the doctor fifty times over without this reaction. Some were friends. So, what was it?

"I met the girl in a hallway," Snell said.

"Can you be more specific?"

"The Northern Medical Center."

Snell put his nose in the snifter, breathed, swirled his glass but did not drink.

Rath kept his glass fixed on his knee. "Tell me," he said. "Leave nothing out."

"I don't plan to," Snell said. "Leave anything out." He rolled his glass between his palms. "It's simply that. While I saw her in a hallway, it's where she went into that might be both helpful to you, but also . . . Let's say if circumstances weren't what they were, I would never—"

"Circumstances are what they are, Dr. Snell. In my business, one thing you learn is to accept circumstances as they are and to recognize that cruel acts are done by the hands of some against the will of others, often only to get supreme satisfaction from the cruelty."

Snell took a long drink of scotch. "I saw her going into the office of a Dr. Langevine."

Rath sipped his drink, let the mellow smokiness dissolve into his tongue and further soften the edges of the world. "Dr. Langevine?"

"A general practitioner with a focus in gynecology."

Rath resisted the urge to stand and pace. "Not so unusual then," he said flatly.

Snell raised an eyebrow. "True. But. I saw her again, later that day. That's why she stuck with me. That and she's quite—" He seemed unsure how to say it, struggled with the implications. "Exquisite. It took me a while to realize she was your girl. That photo you tote around isn't—"

"I've got a better one now."

"Anyway. I saw her later the same day. Coming out of Family Matters."

Rath sipped, mulling over what he was hearing, trying to make sense of it. "Are you saying . . ."

"I'm not *saying* anything. I don't *know* anything. Except that I saw her at these two places in a matter of a few hours."

"What was the date?"

"A few Tuesdays ago. October fourth."

"How can you be sure?"

"I was down there for a meeting."

What was Mandy Wilks doing at these places? Was she pregnant? Was this what she shared with Julia? His mind was a hive of theories, each a buzzing bee on a cold morning, twitching its wings and wanting, but unable, to take flight. Yet.

"What time?" Rath said.

"At Langevine's, anywhere from nine to eleven in the morning. I was in the hallway several times. That afternoon, the best I could say was between two and three."

It struck Rath that as disparate as all the girls were, they did have one thing in common. It had stared him in the face the whole time, and he'd thought of it just before Snell had called. It had been the thought that had escaped him as the phone buzzed. Regardless of the girls' upbringings, talents, tastes, or looks, they all had had boyfriends. They *could* all have been pregnant. George Waters couldn't know that the girls were pregnant when the girls hadn't known each other and would have been pregnant at several different times. How would any one person know that? Perhaps a doctor, like this Langevine? Except the girls lived too far apart to share the same doctor, and doctors would have no access to each others' patients' files. It made no sense. If true, of course, it would eventually make sense. Logic pulled back the veil of mystery that clouded every crime. Always.

"I hope I was of some help," Snell said.

Rath finished his drink and stood.

Snell remained seated, as if he might stay there and ponder for some time the cruelty and exquisiteness of the world while he put a good dent in his bottle of Caol Ila.

CHAPTER 29

It was 8:30 P.M. when Rath stepped out into the dark night. The shock of winter air felt cold enough to crack glass, and the grass crunched beneath his boots.

In the Scout, he realized his jaw was numb and vision gauzy with scotch. He worked the Scout's choke and got the beast running and let it idle as the embattled heater sluggishly warmed the rig to a balmy 40°. He needed to get his prescription filled before the drugstore closed.

The Scout's engine raced, and Rath pumped the gas pedal to bring the idle back down. He stared at Mandy's Post-it stuck to the dash. Her handwriting as indecipherable as a doctor's. Even Gale hadn't been able to decipher it.

Jesus. Gale. Of course. He dialed her number.

"Hello," Gale said. "Is this the private eye?"

"We don't use that term," he said. "You mentioned Mandy left you notes."

She paused. "Sure. Grocery lists. Roommate stuff."

"Do you have any of those notes?"

"Why?"

"I'd like to compare it to the Post-it I found."

"Umm." There was a rustling of papers. "There's a note on the fridge from like a month ago."

"Can you read it?"

"Of course I *can* read." Gale sighed. "But. Her handwriting is a first grader's. I'll give it my best."

"Please."

"'I picked up . . . laundry detergent? But didn't have time to' Umm . . . 'do a load. Could you do a load of lights? Thanks.'"

Rath could hear the ice clacking in a glass.

"That's my best guess," she said.

"Can I come by and take a look at the note?" Rath said.

Another pause and sigh. "I'm just watching a TiVo of *So You Think You Can Dance.*"

Gale answered the door in a pink Wes Welker jersey. She let Rath in and plunked down on the sofa, her bare, pudgy feet stuffed with cotton between each toe, propped on the coffee table as she painted the nails precisely with red and blue stripes. "It's on the fridge," she said, blowing on a toe. "Have at it."

The kitchen's linoleum floor was peeling at the edges, and beneath the stench of kitty litter the odor of garlic and sour milk rose. Rath plucked the hieroglyphic note from under a Patriots' refrigerator magnet and went out to the living room.

"I—" Rath began.

Gale waved a hand at him, as if fending off a swarm of killer bees. "Shhh!" She chewed her fingernails, gaping at the TV, where a pair of dancers were being harangued by a coiffed man clearly in his seventies, despite the plastic surgery meant to conceal that fact.

"Oh bull!" Gale screamed. She snatched the remote and turned off the TV. "Show should be called *So You Think You Can Judge*."

"Could I use your bathroom, to scrub my hands, I got gasoline on them at the Gas 'n' Go earlier."

"Go for it."

In the bathroom, he ran the water in the sink. Then he opened the lower door on the vanity and found the birth-control pills. The date of the last pill taken was August 20. He slipped the package in his jacket pocket, turned off the water, and went back out.

"Could you read this note again for me?" He held out the note. "Word for word."

Gale had some difficulty but read it slowly as Rath leaned over her, the Post-it in his hand.

"One more time, please," he said. She read the note again, this time more easily. "But you can't read this?" he said, and handed her the Post-it.

She squinted at the note, sighed. "No."

"Why not?"

She looked up into his face. "Can you? It's gobblede-gook."

He couldn't disagree. He'd been unable to read it before. But now, he could. After following closely as Gale read the other note. But he still didn't know what it meant.

He thanked her and went out into a night that was growing colder by the second.

He got into the Scout, thinking. When Gale had read the note, Rath had seen how Mandy wrote certain let-ters that made them easily mistaken for other letters. Her *y* and her *g* looked like. Her *e* looked like an *a*. Her *h* looked like a *b*. Her *m* like an *n*. Rath looked at Mandy's

Post-it and compared it to the refrigerator note. The handwriting was the same. He did not know what the word meant, but suspected it was a prescription drug. He'd ask Rankin when he saw him in the morning, right before Preacher's parole hearing.

CHAPTER 30

The door opened, and Rath looked up nervously from studying the anatomy model in Doc Rankin's office.

Rankin shuffled in, rummaging his fingers in his Santa's beard as if searching for loose change, worked his eyes over his clipboard. "Well," he said, and sat on a stool, legs spread, bear-paw hands rubbing the knees of his green Dickies. If you didn't know he was a doctor, you'd have thought he was a dairy farmer. Rath liked that.

He examined Rath's eyes and throat, listened to his heart, glanced at the clipboard.

"Well," he said.

Out with it, Rath thought.

"I know you were concerned," Doc said, "about the pain being a symptom of something else."

Something else.

"The MRI shows nothing of the sort," Rankin said.

Rath nodded, expecting to feel relief. Instead, he felt disquiet, as if someone were eavesdropping on the other side of the door and waiting to bring the real news.

"What it *does* show is your pelvic bone has torn away a bit." Doc leaned toward the anatomy model to grab hold of its pelvic area. "See here, the largest of the pelvic bone, the palmate part. The ilium. Where it connects the tissue is a bit torn. We're talking less than a millimeter, a tenth of a millimeter actually."

"That little? How can it possibly—"

"To your body, it's seismic. It causes pain, so you compensate with your standing, lifting, and walking, which stresses other areas, other muscles, like the *erecta spinae*."

"I know that one."

"The new stress means more pain. So you compensate for that. Get the picture?"

"My hip's fucked up, and it's fucking up everything else?"

"So to speak."

"What can be done?"

"Nothing. Not with PT. You hadn't been doing your stretches anyway, had you?"

Rath shrugged.

"Uh-huh. Well. The way to correct it," Doc said, "and it's not really correcting it, but the way to give you the most permanent relief is to mask the pain, so you no longer compensate and recompensate. Exacerbate the issue. I suggest an appointment at the Spine Center for a series of cortisone shots. That will block the pain."

"When can I go about doing what I've always done?"

"You act as if you'd stopped."

"Without it killing me."

"After the shot. Within days, pain-free. The 'injury' is an anomaly. But it gets those nerves rankled. So we'll shoot you up and tell the nerves a lie, that all is OK, and they will quiet down."

"That's it?"

"That's it. You can't reinjure it or make it worse."

"I don't know if it can get worse."

"Pain can always get worse." Rankin clapped a hand on Rath's knee in a gesture of finality and rose. Rath stood, the pain in his back coursing along his spine, as if in protest to their conspiracy to kill it. He took the Post-it note from his pocket. "Doc. What does this mean to you?" he said, and held out the note.

Rankin read the note, scratched his beard. "What is this?"

"It's the word *erythromycin*."

"Sure doesn't look it. What's it all about?"

"What's it used for, erythromycin?"

"It's a macrolide antibiotic used to prevent bacterial infection, usually postop, often for individuals who have an allergic reaction to penicillin. Though not always."

"What would the use of this drug among several teenage girls tell you. If you could give me one word."

Rankin told him.

IN THE HALL, Rath dialed Grout and told him his theory.

"Christ. That's ghoulish," Grout said.

"We're not after the Hardy Boys here," Rath said. "We need to interview Langevine and whoever's in charge of the Family Matters in St. J. Later. I have somewhere to be right now."

An uncomfortable silence bled between them.

"Preacher," Grout said. "That today? No wonder you've been an asshole."

"We'll need a subpoena. Short notice, I know."

"I'll run it up the flagpole for Barrons. Judge Charbonneau owes him for a New Year's DUI that never was."

In the Scout, Rath stared out the windshield at Mount Monadnock. The woods bare of leaves, the trees gray as ash. Winter now had the woods clenched in its tight, unforgiving fist.

Rath rested his head on the steering wheel for a moment, trying to collect himself. He'd go home and shower and work on what he was going to say to the parole board even though he knew he'd end up sweating like a wrestler and have every rational thought fly from his mind like bats from a cave at dusk once he saw Preacher in the flesh.

CHAPTER 31

Ned Preacher had aged well, and this fact sent a wave of hatred through Rath that made his muscles go rigid. He'd expected a fat, grizzled, ruined man.

At the time of the murders Preacher had been rough and seedy, but fit, too, the hard, sinewy body of a laborer, a smile that could be both menacing and charming. He had disarming, persuasive, roguish good looks. Rath supposed this was what kept people off guard—and kept them from believing he was capable of what he'd done. He'd come off as the knowing bad boy. But he'd also had a haggard look around his eyes, and in a certain light, back then, he'd looked fifteen years older than his actual age.

Now, Preacher was 53 but looked 40. Younger and more virile than Rath, he was fit and trim, the bags under his eyes miraculously gone. His skin was weathered but tan. A man who'd spent time soaking up the rays in the prison yard. A man who'd made use of the prison gym. On the public dime. He stood up straight. His easy, *don't-give-a-fuck* swagger had vanished, and as he was led by the guards into the old judge's quarters used for the hearing, shackled and cuffed, he walked with a slow, easy confidence, shoulders squared, chin up, eyes forward. His demeanor was one of humility and pride.

Rath felt his utter repulsion for Preacher expand inside himself, suffocate all other emotion, leaving it hard to breathe.

As Preacher was aided into his seat by the guards, he locked eyes with Rath, and a smirk oozed across his face, as if he might break into a fit of his soulless laughter, his eyes brilliant with evil. Then it was gone. His face full again with false reverence. An act. This room his theater. The five people on the board, the only audience he had to impress. In his hands, he held a book. The Bible.

Rath fought a mounting urge to spring from his folding chair and drive his fist through Preacher's teeth, through the back of his throat, grab hold of his spine, and rip it out. He closed his eyes, trying to master his rage.

Laura had never been a vengeful person. She'd been forgiving, a study in patience and understanding. But that had been toward transgressions of the everyday variety. How patient would she be after what she'd suffered? After what her husband had suffered? Would she be so forgiving? She'd forgiven Rath's selfish youthful ways partly because she herself had struggled with promiscuity in high school and college, until she'd met Daniel.

If I'd been on time. The thought knifed through Rath's heart. If not for Preacher, Laura and Daniel would be the ones worrying about Rachel these days. And where would Rath be? Still a bachelor? Unmoored and indifferent, sating his base desires? Unable to commit because he could feel the old man's blood like a toxin in his veins. A man alone because he was unable or unwilling to suppress his own ugly appetite? He could imagine it, and it chilled him. Laura's death had been his rebirth into a better life. Her death had saved him. And this thought sickened him most of all. The simple truth: Rath loathed himself even more than he loathed Preacher.

Preacher looked at Rath, a malicious glint in his eye, the look of one accomplice to the other: *Without you, I could not have done it.* As the parole board readied at its table with the shuffling of papers, Preacher clutched his Bible to his chest, eyes on Rath, and winked. Rath, trembling, willed himself to keep calm.

That Preacher was even here today, given a pulpit from which to spin his web in a civil procedure, was a mockery of the system, or perhaps it revealed the system for what it was: inept and inadequate. Justice was blind all right—blind to its own failings.

This was a waking nightmare.

A female parole-board member, a former public defender, for God's sake, was nattering about procedure. How the victims and family of victims would have a say. Rath was the only family. He and Rachel. And Rachel had no idea Ned Preacher had murdered her parents. He'd not spared her pain she didn't deserve but robbed her of a truth she did deserve. However hard it would have been to tell it. He'd been weak.

The parole-board members cleared their throats, adjusted microphones, and poured springwater from plastic bottles into glasses etched with the scale of justice.

Rath's hatred radiated from his every pore.

"Mr. Rath. Would you care to speak?" a parole-board member, Jonas Kron, said, staring at Rath as if he knew what Rath had been thinking. Kron was a liberal who used *human-rights* issues to benefit and free criminals rather than think of the victim's rights to keep the criminal locked up.

Rath stood, and the Earth's rotation had slowed, gravity had lessened, and he felt he'd float away. He held fast to the back of the chair in front of him to keep from doing just that.

"This," he nodded toward Preacher. He wanted to say pervert, sociopath, *monster.* But hot emotion did not play as well as cold fact in this theater. Unless you were the criminal sobbing false tears of regret, not for what you'd done but for being caught. Then, emotion worked.

Rath continued. "This man killed my sister. He stabbed her and he cut her throat and he broke her neck. He raped her. While her baby slept. And when her husband came home, he killed him, too. The mother and father of a sleeping baby. My niece. My daughter." Rath tried to swallow, but couldn't, his throat tight, as if a pair of hands were squeezing it. "What he did was not the result of a momentary fit of passion. It was planned. Calculated. Sport. His entire life, this *man* has committed violent crimes, ruined lives, then plea-bargained, knowing the law would go easier on him for saving the state money. He has it figured out, what the state's priority is. *Money.*"

Rath's heartbeat was accelerating too fast. "He works the system. In prison, he takes every *'self-improvement'* class available. He's a Good Boy. Not because he's changed. But to help *himself* get out. I don't think his appetite has lessened. It's grown, the same way your own appetite grows for something you crave when you are deprived of it, and whatever he tells you, how he's a better man, repentant, changed, *found* Jesus, don't believe it. He can't wait to do it again." The words were gushing forth now, his adrenaline screaming, his blood lit gasoline. "Ask yourselves why men like him *find* Jesus only after being locked up? Why can't *Jesus* find the *man* before the man commits such acts? When 'God' becomes proactive and spares women and children, maybe I'll start to believe in him."

Rath's thoughts were fleeing, his emotions boiling over. To continue was a mistake. But he could not stop himself. "He can't be allowed to do these things again. Ruin more lives. He doesn't have the right. The only way to *guarantee* that he won't is to keep him locked up. If you let him out, when he does it again, and he *will*, those crimes are on your hands."

Rath sat.

The parole board responded with cold stares and the scratching of pencils in notebooks.

CHAPTER 32

Rath waited outside Langevine's office building. The temperature had risen to hover just above freezing, and he was chilled to the bone standing in the raw, damp cold. The sweat that had soaked his shirt during the hearing was icy against his skin now. He shuddered, trying to wipe the hearing from his mind. He'd left before Preacher had spoken, unequipped to deal with such a performance. He was exhausted.

Grout strode down the sidewalk toward him, and they walked toward Langevine's office. "How'd it go?" Grout said.

Rath didn't answer.

"Sorry," Grout said, and clapped a hand on Rath's shoulder.

Inside, an elderly woman showed them to Dr. Langevine's office.

Dr. Langevine sat behind a modest pine desk, a slight man, delicate and diminutive, with narrow, bony shoulders beneath a slightly baggy pink-striped oxford. He was on the phone and extended a hand, his fingers long and fine as he covered the phone's receiver with his other hand. His handshake was certain and warm. He eyed two chairs over large, round eyeglasses of the sort Rath hadn't seen since John Denver on the Muppets.

Rath and Grout sat, Rath noting Langevine's thick but impeccably trimmed red beard and absurd flop of red hair, and, in another throwback, a single wave of bangs hanging to his eyebrows.

Langevine's minimalist office was the opposite of Snell's, the walls absent of painting or prints, displaying a sole diploma and a medical license. Books on a shelf were aligned so precisely it was as if the books were never removed for reading. Langevine hung up the phone and sat with a smile of disarming warmth and kindness. He shook mints from a dispenser and popped them in his mouth, making a tiny, sucking noise, as if slurping the dregs of a milk shake through a straw. Then he folded his thin fingers on his knees and rocked slightly in his chair. "How may I assist you?"

Grout took a tape recorder from his coat. "Mind if I tape this? I hate taking notes."

Langevine smiled again, a waft of mint mouthwash coming from him. "Be my guest."

Grout set the tape recorder on the edge of the desk, where it whirred. "We believe you had a patient by the name of Mandy Wilks," he said.

"Oh, gentlemen, sincerest apologies." The doctor's voice was soft as talcum powder. "I can't comment on patients. I'm afraid—"

Grout plucked the subpoena from the same pocket from which he'd taken the tape recorder, set it on the desk.

Dr. Langevine glanced at it and nodded cordially. "Well, then, at your service."

"Understand," Rath said, "this is also about helping find your patient, who may be the victim of a crime. We can take her records with us, but we'd prefer to have you answer pressing questions now, as well."

"I have to say it does make me a trifle uncomfortable yet. I've never spoken openly about a patient to anyone other than the patient herself or staff."

"Understood," Grout said.

"Proceed." Dr. Langevine dipped his chin at Grout.

"To give context," Grout said, "Mandy disappeared late the night of October twenty-one or early on the twenty-second."

"This world," Dr. Langevine said.

"What was she seeing you for?" Grout said.

"Reproductive health."

"Did she have a venereal disease?"

Dr. Langevine was clearly uncomfortable. But then, he had reason to be. This was a rare circumstance, and the information he might give was of the most personal.

"No," he said, "she did not."

"Was she pregnant?"

"No. At least not at her last scheduled appointment."

Rath felt his shoulders sag with disappointment then straightened himself. "And when was that?" he asked.

"I'd have to check."

"We'll wait."

As Langevine set about typing on his keyboard, Grout asked, "What was she like the last time you saw her? Her behavior. Was she agitated, nervous, distracted? Upset?"

"The last time I saw her?" Langevine stared at Rath

from behind his glasses with big, magnified eyes that made him look a bit of the kook.

"If you could give us one word," Rath said.

"Maybe a bit nervous," Langevine said. "But that's entirely normal for a young girl for such a visit."

"She wasn't depressed or upset or—"

"No. A tad nervous. More shy really. That's it."

"And what did she see you for, her last appointment?"

"Her annual check up. Here it is." Langevine spun his monitor for Rath and Grout to see. "Friday, September 2."

Grout glanced at Rath.

"You're sure?" Grout said.

"Absolutely. Eve, my front-desk administrator, is scrupulous. I insist on it."

Rath stared at Langevine, who met his gaze evenly.

"We have a conflict," Rath said.

"Excuse me?" said Langevine. His voice remained level, unexcited but tinged with that natural curiosity of someone truly at a loss.

Grout tapped a hand on the chair arm, and said, "We have it from a sound witness that your patient was seen here in your office on Tuesday, October 4."

"Impossible."

"This witness is certain," Grout said.

"He's mistaken." Langevine's gaze and voice were resolute.

"Look," Grout said, leaning in, "this witness is reliable. He's the only reason we even knew she was a patient of yours. So you tell us how he sees a girl who is a stranger to him walk into this office on Tuesday, October 4, and you say it's impossible, yet this girl is *your* patient. Do you know the odds of that coincidence?"

"Infinitesimal, I imagine," Langevine said. "Nevertheless, the witness is mistaken."

"Now look," Grout said, rising halfway out of his chair.

Rath cleared his throat, and Grout sat back down.

"Perhaps your calendar is wrong," Rath said, leaning to get a better look at the calendar on the monitor.

"As you see." Langevine pointed to Tuesday, October 25 on his calendar, then the eighteenth, and the eleventh. "My office is closed Tuesdays, gentlemen."

Grout and Rath stared at the calendar.

"If you like," Langevine said, "I can call in Eve to attest to this, or any number of patients sitting out there now, many of whom are peeved I am closed on Tuesdays."

Rath shook his head. "That won't be necessary."

Grout sat back, his jaw set.

"The office is closed," Langevine said, "but the main door only leads to the waiting room, and from there no one can access the back offices and rooms. So, the door to the hallway may have been unlocked to allow cleaners access. It's possible Ms. Wilks stopped in for some reason and, finding that the office door was unlocked, entered."

"Wouldn't she have known you were closed on Tuesdays?" Grout said.

"Apparently, no."

"What could she have wanted to see you about?" Rath asked.

"I wish I could say."

"She also visited Family Matters that day," Grout said.

Rath flinched, wishing Grout had not played that card. It was sloppy.

"Well," Langevine said, "she obviously came here for a purpose, perhaps something pressing, and when she found the office closed, went to them. They might be able to shed more light than I, in that case."

"Let's hope so," Rath said.

"Will there be anything else?" Langevine directed his eyes to Rath.

"Yes," Grout said. "You have CCTV."

"Excuse me?"

"Closed Circuit TV. We will need to look at all the tapes from that Tuesday, along with getting copies of all Ms. Wilks's records."

"The records of course I can give you. The tapes, or digital chips, or whatever they are, unfortunately, I believe, but you can double check with security, are overwritten every couple weeks."

"We will. We'll expect copies of the records sent to this e-mail." Grout handed Langevine his card.

Dr. Langevine escorted them out of his office to the hallway, limping faintly, his leg having apparently fallen asleep with it tossed on top of the other leg's knee. Rath disliked when it happened, the odd prickling sensation that followed a dead numbness.

"Come back anytime with questions, gentlemen," Langevine said. "Except Tuesdays, of course."

CHAPTER 33

Outside, Rath wedged a pinch of dip in his lip. "Think he's telling the truth?"

"At first, when he denied the girl was at his office, no. After. I got no read that he was lying."

"Me either. Let's see what's doing at Family Matters."

At the corner, they stood waiting for the light to change, so they could cross.

"I hate these abortion factories," Grout grumbled with a bitterness that took Rath aback.

"I didn't know you were political," Rath said.

"Screw politics."

"Religious?"

"God, no."

Rath pressed the button on the light post beside him that was meant to speed the changing of the signal but never did. The light finally changed.

They crossed and walked in silence toward the next intersection, across from which was Family Matters. At the corner, a small gang of picketers paced up ahead, directly across from the Family Matters building. There were eight picketers in all. Five were middle-aged, overweight women with tragic faces, each wearing a crucifix necklace. They paced in a drudging circle, picket signs hefted overhead as they babbled some incoherent prayer. Two more picketers were men in their forties. The last picketer was a girl of perhaps eight years old. She hefted a sign that read: THANK GOD MY MOTHER DIDN'T MURDER ME.

As Rath and Grout approached, the picketers parted peaceably.

Inside the Family Matter's reception area, several girls sat awaiting appointments. They each looked up at Rath and Grout with uneasy eyes.

A woman with the cropped pewter hair, wire eyeglasses, and smock of a high-school art teacher bustled anxiously over to them.

Two men in such a setting, Rath thought. Was it cause for alarm? Maybe.

The woman was about to speak when Grout showed his badge. "We phoned."

"Yes," the woman said, glancing about the room of women apologetically. "This way, please." She hurried them down a narrow hallway with the waddle of a penguin.

The room was a hothouse nursery. The spider plants dangling over the sides of suspended pots, rows of African violets on the windowsill behind a metal desk, and two stupendous rubber trees in the back corners overwhelmed the small, overly warm office. The room smelled of dank potting soil and lush plant life. Bookshelves constructed of cinder blocks and two-by-ten planks took up one wall. Even the shelves were given primarily to more plants. On the desk sat framed photos of the woman and what were apparently her children and grandchildren.

"I'm June," the woman said, and sat, the leaf of a spider plant dangling unnoticed in her face. She offered a smile Rath sensed she'd given a million times. A reassuring smile: *I know this is hard, but it will be all right. With time.* She did not ask Rath or Grout to sit, but they sat anyway.

Grout took the subpoena out from his jacket pocket and set it on the desk.

"What's that?" June said, a lilt of surprise in her voice.

"A subpoena," Grout said.

"I wouldn't really know if it was real or not. But, one has to trust in others."

Rath thought June sounded more spiritual than the religious picketers outside.

"This is about Mandy Wilks," Grout said. "She visited you Tuesday, October fourth."

"I have her file." June placed a finger with an unpolished nail rimed with a faint edge of dirt, potting soil likely, on a manila folder. "And on the computer, of course."

"Why did she visit here?" Grout asked.

June took a drink from a Nalgene bottle. "I'm sorry. I should have offered you something to drink."

Grout waved her off. "Why did she come here?"

"For Ortho Tri-Cyclen."

Rath and Grout exchanged looks of confusion.

"The pill," June clarified.

"How long was she on it?" Rath said.

"Is that relevant?" June said.

"We only ask relevant questions," Grout said.

"Since August eleventh. Not long."

"But she could still get pregnant?" Grout said.

"Only abstinence, a vasectomy, or tubal ligation works one hundred percent."

"Was she pregnant?" Rath asked. June's blink rate increased. Just for an instant.

"I—"

Rath sat up straight. If Mandy were pregnant, it would be a link to Julia, a commonality at least.

"Was she?" Grout said.

"It's hard to say exactly. I think—"

Why was she hesitating? Rath wondered.

"Not to be callous," Grout said, impatiently. "But either she was or she wasn't."

"The fact is," June said, "I don't know. I know she wanted to see me badly that day, and I had a strong suspicion it was because she was pregnant or thought she was and wanted to find out for certain."

"There are home tests for that," Grout said brusquely. "My wife used them. Why would Mandy need you?"

"Those tests sometimes give false positives. And some girls, especially if they have no strong figures in their lives and are afraid of the baby's father for some reason, they don't like to find out at home, alone. They want someone they can trust to be there."

"Right," Grout said. "So, you suspect she came here that day because she was pregnant?"

"Yes."

"And if she was, she'd want to get rid of the baby?" Grout cracked.

"Help," June corrected. "She'd want help. Options."

"Mmm," Grout said, chewing the inside of his cheek. Rath noted that June's temple pulsed rapidly. The faint down on her upper lip glistened with perspiration. "Contrary to what some people think, we're not some on-demand, drive-thru abortion mill. The notion that girls just stroll in and get abortions like they're getting their hair done, then stroll out to go party is a manifest lie and a gross under-estimation of the toll it takes and the other services we provide."

"Right," Grout said.

Rath wanted to backhand Grout. Instead, he stretched a leg out to calm the spasm in his back. He was starving, spent. Had not slept well, if at all, in days. His head swam with murderous thoughts of Preacher.

"Can you tell us about her general demeanor, the time before last, when she came in for the pill?" Grout asked.

"She seemed very nervous."

"Is that common?"

"Nervousness is. But this was something more. She seemed more nervous than most. Almost panicked. Or as if she was being pressured to go on the pill."

"Who would pressure her?" Grout said.

"I don't even know if that is what it was—"

"Who? Just going on that assumption. A boyfriend?" June nodded.

"Speak for the tape recorder," Grout said.

"A boyfriend is the most obvious. Perhaps an older boyfriend."

"A man?" Grout said.

"Could be a man. Often older men pressure a girl to get protection, and—"

"And you take exception to that?" Grout said.

June's throat flushed pink. "It's not my place either way, as a professional."

"What about as a person?" Grout said. "You'd prefer a girl not be pressured to use the pill, to be responsible. Then when she ends up in a fix, the same guy that might have pressured her to get contraception has no say if—"

"I prefer protection," June snapped.

"So," Rath said. "If you could explain for me. The last time she came. If she came in because she was pregnant or to find out if she was pregnant, how come you don't know if she was or not?"

"I never ended up seeing her."

Grout folded his arms across his chest, his entire posture closed off to the interview now. It was an alarming transformation that unsettled and embarrassed Rath.

"And why is that?" Rath said, taking over the interview.

June glanced out the window that overlooked a bench on the sidewalk. "The last time I saw her, she was sitting on that bench. She preferred to wait outside. I don't know if she just liked the fresh air or if being around the other girls inside made her uncomfortable. I can't imagine how they could make her any more uncomfortable than those wretched protestors."

"Did you ever see any of the protestors invade her personal space?" Rath said.

"No more than they do anyone else."

"Did you ever see her with anyone, a man or boyfriend, anyone at all who she looked uncomfortable around, or fearful of?"

"No one."

"So, she was just sitting out there alone on that bench?" Rath said.

"Yes. Well. No. There was an older woman sitting on the bench, too."

"How old?"

"Hard to say. But rather frail. I'd see her out there once in a while. Feeding the birds."

"Did she speak to Mandy?"

"Not that I saw. She was at one end of the bench, and Mandy was at the other. But Mandy, she had this look on her face. She was just staring into space, and she looked so stricken. Aggrieved. I wanted to go out there and tell her I would just be a little while longer. But I got tied up in a meeting. I actually set aside protocol and left the meeting and went out there to speak to her." June cleared her throat. "I got stopped on my way out, a nurse with a pressing question. By the time I got out there, Mandy was gone."

OUTSIDE, RATH GRABBED Grout by the shoulder and spun him around. "What was that?" he demanded.

Grout looked fiercely at Rath's hand on his shoulder, shrugged it off. "Nothing."

"You lost professionalism in there."

"Who are you to tell me about professionalism?" Grout started away.

Rath grasped his elbow.

Grout wheeled around, backing Rath against a storefront. His eyes wide, daring. He was ten years younger than Rath and forty pounds heavier. His pupils were pinpricks. "You're not a cop. So don't lecture me about professionalism."

He turned and started away again, and Rath let him.

The protestors were gone now, the sidewalk barren. Rath wondered what had set Grout off. Something had happened. That much was clear. Something ugly.

CHAPTER 34

Rath lay awake in bed, the wind shrieking under the eaves like a succubus in throes, icy air leaking into the bedroom through the ancient window casings. An idea sifted through his sleepy mind. He needed to write it down. But sleep overtook him as the first blue light of dawn bled into the room.

Rath was startled awake by a loud sharp *crack*, like a rifle shot, as a maple tree crashed through his bedroom window. Glass shards scattered on his bed. He leapt up and stood on the cold floor as the icy wind swam around his feet and flapped the hem of his pajamas.

He remembered his last thought before sleep had claimed him. He called Grout, who was short with him. Distant.

"I want to check all the girls' phone records," Rath said.

"Larkin did that."

"I want to check again."

"There are no common numbers between them."

"It may not be a single matching number."

"Fine. I'll e-mail the records to you. You *can* open files on your dial-up, right?"

Rath hung up and stared out his broken window toward the clouds darkening the morning sky. "We're in for it," he said to no one in particular.

It was 10:30 P.M., and the rake of the wind at the windows more insistent as Rath leaned back in his chair. He could hear the flapping sound from his bedroom, where he'd stapled plastic over the broken window. A man had come earlier and cut the tree up with a chain saw while Rath worked on his theory.

Rath stretched, his back catching with pain. He could not wait to get injected and end this torment. All day and into the evening he'd scoured the records of each girl's home and cell phones from the months before the girls had gone missing. In search of a single common number, he'd camped at his desk, gnawing on jerky and drinking from a liter jug of ginger ale that went warm and flat, stopping only to piss off the back porch. He'd not found a phone number that connected the girls. But, he had found something when checking each number against switchboard.com. To make certain what he'd found was accurate, he dialed a number on his cell phone.

A computerized voice answered, "Dr. Stephens's office is not open at the moment—"

Rath hung up and dialed again.

"Northeast Vermont Pediatrics is currently closed—"

He hung up and dialed again. "Dr. Linda Bullock's office is closed for the day—"

Rath wiped his palm over his dry mouth and dialed a fourth number.

"You've reached Monadnock Health Services, we're currently—"

Rath dialed one last number.

"Dr. Langevine's office is closed. Our office hours are Monday and Wednesday through Friday, nine to five. Please leave a clear message at the tone, and we will get back to you during office hours. If this is an emergency, please dial 911."

"Dr. Langevine. This is Frank Rath. Please call me as soon as possible, anytime day or night." He left his home and cell numbers.

"WELL?" GROUT SAID the next morning at 8 A.M. He seemed in a better mood, eating a cider donut as he leaned against the vending machine in the cramped, so-called squad room. It was a reach to call a staff of five, including the chief, a squad. The room was home to a beat-up farm table and a countertop the length of an ironing board, on which were crammed a relic coffeemaker, a microwave, and a minifridge.

"Where's Sonja? She ought to hear this," Rath said.

"She's got downed trees blocking her drive," Grout said.

"Each girl called a doctor of some kind, at least three times in the month before her disappearance," Rath said. "And each girl called a Family Matters. *Different* ones because of where they lived, so the numbers didn't match."

The fluorescent light flickered as the wind outside grew wild and shook the building by its lapels.

"That's not coincidence," Grout said, begrudgingly, finishing his donut and licking his fingers.

"We need to interview each doctor. Maybe the girls were referred by a single person, which links them. Or their respective doctors referred them to a single person or entity that links them. Something."

"Or is on staff at a Family Matters."

"It's there somewhere."

"So, someone, somehow, knew these girls were pregnant and sought them out to, what?" Grout licked sugar from his fingertips, one by one.

"You tell me."

"How would a guy like George Waters get such info?" Grout said.

"It lessens the odds it's him. But maybe he had a girl from the AA meetings, like you said," Rath said.

"Or a girl who went searching for victims at these Family Matters meetings."

"What meetings?" Rath said.

"Family Matters has support groups for girls." Grout reached in the bag for another donut. "They have to keep lists of attendees. Being a non-profit 501(c)(3). I'll get Sonja on all the lists from Family Matters in the greater region. You and I need to talk to some doctors."

CHAPTER 35

Outside Dr. Stephens's office, his second visit on his list, Rath checked his messages as he processed what he'd learned. His phone showed no messages from Langevine. He called again. The receptionist had a young girl's voice, jittery and apologetic. "I don't know why he hasn't called. I gave him the messages. I'm sure he will."

Rath ended his call, and his cell phone buzzed immediately. He picked up.

"Both my girls were pregnant," Grout said.

"Five to seven weeks along?"

"So, yours too," Grout said. "That makes two in Vermont: Saint Johnsbury and Montpelier; and two across the river: in Littleton and Concord."

"We don't know if Mandy was."

"All these girls though. And all called a Family Matters? I'll see if Sonja's gotten anywhere with lists," Grout said.

Rath hung up, staring out the windshield into the dark night, feeling hopeful. He brought Rachel's text up on his phone to buoy him.

I'm sorry to be so lame. I've just
been swamped. I'll call you soon.
I promise. Love you, Rachel

A nagging feeling overcame him again. There was—
His cell buzzed: Dr. Langevine.

Rath answered. "Yes."

"Mr. Rath. My sincerest apologies in not getting back in a timely manner. It's been quite the day. I understand you wish to speak to me about something rather pressing."

"Right away. It's Ms. Wilks. In person would be best. Right away. Where do you live?"

"I'm the last place at the end of Ravens Way, but I'm in my office. A hike for you."

"I'm on my way," Rath said.

Ravens Way, Rath thought as he drove. It was a private community atop Canaan Ridge, the only one of its kind in the Kingdom, and hopefully the last. Against militant local protest, six 20-acre plots had been clearcut to make room for custom homes ten times the size of the average local home. Granite countertops, heated indoor pools, tennis courts, wine cellars, and lanais had replaced wintering deeryards and a wetland that had included trophy brook trout beaver ponds. Swaths of forest had been leveled to afford the homes an emperor's view of the valley. The folks below who had looked up at the ridge for generations to witness the year's first snow or turning of the leaves now were treated to a view of gargantuan trophy homes dropped into treeless voids, two-story windows reflecting glints of sunlight in an obnoxious wink. Dr. Langevine's place, at the end of the road, likely commanded the grandest view. Rath was glad he did not have to stomach a visit to the place.

CHAPTER 36

The past week, Sonja had been too busy to run, and her muscles had come to feel like mud, her mood as edgy as a serrated knife.

She needed to *run*, felt the pang to work her body hard. She'd planned on, finally, a run this afternoon. But the case demanded she sit in place and pore over lists of hundreds of names from Family Matters, going back twenty-two months. Searching for a single name to stand out. A link. She'd built spreadsheets until her eyes bled.

She leaned back from her desk and gazed out the window of her home office at the fields, shadowed in dusk, tornadoes of snow dancing along the edge of the woods. Claude had recognized she needed space, so he'd taken the kids, home for an in-service day, to the Village Picture Shows for a movie.

She'd gone down through the lists, searching for the names of the missing girls. With her heart sinking into her stomach, she'd found them: Sally, Rebecca, and

Fiona, and circled each with a tug of regret. Now, she circled yet another name: Julia Pearl.

The name of each of the missing girls was on the lists. Except Mandy's. So far. But she'd find it, she would. Whoever had done this to Julia and possibly others would get theirs. It was a matter of time now. Of momentum.

No *M. Wilks*. No *Mandy W.* No *M.W.* Nothing.

The lists were short, five names on average, though the number of attendants did spike to as many as seventeen names for a few dates. She felt a dull ache in the hollow of her belly, the type that followed the annual indignity of her gynecological exam. She shivered.

She drank water and ate a handful of pumpkin seeds as she searched, her fingertips humming with excitement to see the girls' circled names. But no Mandy. Why?

Sonja laid the lists out on the floor. More than a hundred of them. She walked among them, looking for a Mandy or an M. Wilks or W. The girls were supposed to use their real last names, but that did not mean they did. Certainly, rights to privacy superseded some sort of protocol for tax regulations and grant allocations.

She stepped among the lists, bowed over with her fingers locked behind her back. Her eye caught on a name. Not the name exactly, but the penmanship. She stopped cold. She'd seen it on another list—she swore it. She crouched, her eyes leaping from one list to the next. There. She picked up the list and compared the writing. Yes, it was the same. The graphologist Canaan Police used would confirm it. Her synapses snapped and sizzled, a string of lit firecrackers. The endorphins flowed. There it was again: that same odd handwriting.

In ten minutes, she'd found a dozen lists with the same penmanship. There was no doubt it was from the same person. What was peculiar was that the names appeared on lists not just from all four different locales, but appeared over the course of twenty-two months, about every four months or so. What jolted Sonja most was that on each list where the odd handwriting appeared, the name of one of the missing girls also appeared. Except for Mandy. Mandy, nor anyone with her combination of initials, appeared anywhere.

Sonja's endorphins screamed through her now, her pulse a frantic staccato throb.

Perhaps there was a better rush than running.

CHAPTER 37

Rath was breathing hard from jogging down the long corridors of the office building as he entered Langevine's office.

Langevine was seated in a chair in the waiting room, his hands folded on the knee of one leg, which was tossed over the other leg. A bottle of springwater and two Dixie cups sat on the table in front of him. He stood to welcome Rath, shook his hand primly, and asked if he cared for a water.

Rath shook his head, catching his breath. "We've had a breakthrough," he said. "With Miss Wilks."

"Good, good. I hope, anyway," Dr. Langevine said. "Sit, at least, please. You look wiped."

"Just out of shape," Rath said. He did not take a seat. Langevine remained standing. He was a slight man, and the sweater he wore was loose on him.

Rath wiped sweat at his temple. "We've found that the missing girls—"

"*Girls?* Plural?" Langevine stiffened with surprise. "However do you mean?"

"We were investigating several other girls who've gone missing in the region the past two years. We believe the disappearances are connected."

"That's ghastly," Langevine said. He shook his head with dismay.

"Each girl was pregnant at the time of her disappearance," Rath said.

"I don't understand. How can I help?"

"I want you to think very hard about Mandy's behavior or what she might have said. You mentioned she was nervous."

"No more so than usual. And more shy."

"Did she mention a boyfriend or any man, or did she, was her nervousness perhaps brought on by, did she seem pressured maybe. It's *very* important."

"She seemed normal. But. No mention of a boyfriend or man. Nothing. I wish I could help. But." He shrugged, his bulky sweater rippling like the flab of a seal's neck over his birdlike shoulders.

Rath reached in his jacket and took out the photos of the girls. "Have you ever seen any of these girls?"

Langevine considered each photo with meticulous intent. After several minutes of serious contemplation, he said, with disappointment, "No." He handed the folder back. "Many girls find themselves in trouble. I suppose they always have. But if these girls went missing so far apart in time, do you think perhaps each left on her own? To have the baby, or run away, or what have you?"

"No," Rath said, thinking of the body of Julia Pearl.

"You sound certain."

Rath nodded grimly.

"These situations"—the doctor sighed, shaking his head—"are the saddest I can think of. A monstrous business."

He offered a gracious smile.

Outside, Rath scooped a handful of fresh snow from the Scout's hood and pressed it to his face and throat.

As he drove the Scout, his cell vibrated. He'd missed two texts and three voice-mail messages. All from Sonja. All with the same urgent tone.

Call me immediately.
Come straight to the Bee Hive.

He did both.

CHAPTER 38

"What do you see?" Sonja said.

Rath and Grout huddled over the table at the back booth at the Bee Hive, looking at the lists as Sonja sat back with an air of unrestrained satisfaction, nibbling a carrot stick from a smuggled Ziploc.

Rath smoothed his palm over a crack in the metallic, red, vinyl seat that sparkled like Dorothy's slippers and tucked a puff of foam back inside the cushion.

"The same handwriting," Grout said.

"Bingo," Sonja said. "You get to pick the small stuffed animal of your choice."

"We need verification," Grout said.

"I scanned and e-mailed it to our graphologist earlier." Sonja snapped a carrot stick in her teeth. "It's verified."

Grout shifted uncomfortably.

A waitress placed a piece of apple pie with vanilla ice cream in front of Rath and Grout with a balletic flourish that made her gingham check skirt puff up, then settle against her gymnast thighs. "Pie's hot. Ice cream's cold. Dig in." She caught sight of Sonja's carrot stick. "Don't let the owner see you with that," she said, and swooshed away.

"The handwriting is from the same person, even though the names are different," Sonja said, animated, fidgeting with excitement. "*And*. Look at the dates."

Rath, feeling the wave building, knowing soon they'd have enough energy and power to ride to a conclusion, said, "Someone *is* scouting for victims."

"This confirms it," Grout added.

"As you thought," Rath said, tossing Grout a bone. He clanked his spoon on his plate. And froze. Stunned. "Wait," he said. "Wait wait wait." He took a list and spun it around. "I *know* this handwriting. This makes *no* sense. This handwriting." Rath fished around in his wallet and set the Post-it note on the table. "It's *Mandy's*."

Sonja and Grout stared at him, spellbound as he compared the note to the list. "Same weird 'g' and 'e' and 'm.' Same everything."

"How do you know the Post-it is hers?" Sonja said.

"I found it in her bathroom. I couldn't figure out what it said for the longest time, until I got the idea to compare it to other handwriting samples of hers. Duh. I got a note from her roommate. The word on the Post-it is *erythromycin*."

"Erythro what?" Grout said.

"*Mycin*," Rath said.

"It's used, among many other things, to prevent infection in women after abortions," Sonja said.

A fly crawled across the table as they sat trapped in a bubble of silence. Rath considered smashing the fly with his palm. Instead, he swiped a hand at it, scaring it into dizzy flight.

"*Mandy* is our girl?" Grout said, breaking the silence. "*Mandy's* the link?"

"She's the *suspect*," Sonja said.

"No. I don't believe that," Grout said. "That's fucked. She's missing just like the rest of them."

"We don't know that," Sonja said. "She could have fled. Or wanted it to look like she was abducted."

"No," Grout said. "That's bullshit."

"Listen," Sonja said, "I know she's family, but—"

"No," Grout spat. "You choose Mandy over any evil dog torturer with no alibi. A flesh carver. And you want to pin it on a pretty young—"

"So we're basing guilt on looks now?" Sonja shot.

"She didn't kill Julia, torture her, and whatever else. You can't possibly believe that. What possible reason could she have?"

"That's our job to find out," Sonja said.

"I won't waste my time going down this road. And tell me this. How'd she get to all those meetings two years ago when she was fourteen?" Grout said.

"I don't know," Sonja said.

"Exactly."

"Maybe an accomplice. Like Rath was saying, it may take two. Or like you were saying, maybe it's some kinky thing she and another guy—"

Grout shook his head, steaming. "I don't want you wasting resources on this."

"We'll see about that," Sonja said.

"What the fuck is that supposed—"

"It *is* her handwriting," Rath interjected.

Grout shook his head and pushed his pie plate away so hard, the ice cream slid off the table onto the floor.

"Maybe we should get into these Family Matters meetings somehow," Sonja said.

"You're too old to fit in with the teenage girls there," Grout said, taking a deep breath.

"Well, I'm going to get with the women who run them, somehow," Sonja said. "Oh. And that cabin near where Julia was found. Clean. No physical evidence whatsoever that Julia was held there, or anyone had been in the cabin in years for any reason."

CHAPTER 39

Rath stood outside the Bee Hive, letting the cold rein-vigorate him as much as it could in his state. The cars on Main Street were dusted with snow. His breath formed clouds as he tried to wrap his mind around this revelation about Mandy.

He stared at Mandy's Post-it and the refrigerator note. The second note ended with *thx*. On the phone, Gale had read *thx* as *thanks*. Shorthand of a generation. Rachel's generation. Rachel, who couldn't write two words in a text without an abbreviation or an acronym. Fear rose in him like a poisonous bubble. Primordial, parental.

He grabbed his cell phone from his pocket, brought up Rachel's text.

> I'm sorry to be so lame. I've just
> been swamped. I'll call you soon.
> I promise. Love you, Rachel

Not a single abbreviation or acronym. No shorthand.
Rath's blood congealed in his heart.

Rachel had not written this text.

He worked his fingers to dial Rachel, screwed up.
Tried again. Panicked. He tried to breathe slowly and
stabbed Rachel's number one digit at a time. Rachel's
phone rang.

The voice mail of the number you have reached is full and—
Damn it.

He needed to get to Johnson State, and this time he
wasn't leaving until he found his daughter.

CHAPTER 40

By the time he parked in the campus lot, the snow was piling up. He leapt from the Scout, grabbing the box with the jumper in it.

Inside the dorm, he stormed down the hallway. He was about to knock on her door when it opened, startling him. The girl from before, with the shaved Play Doh blue hair gave a yelp, covering her chest with a palm.

Rath peered in the room behind her. There was no one else in the room.

"Where's Rachel?" Rath demanded.

The girl shrugged, biting her upper lip and trying to push past him.

Rath blocked her and glanced at the photo on the dresser behind her. It had escaped him on his first visit, the facial bone structure. The girl with the long black hair and the glasses and braces in the photo was the girl standing before him, transformed. "*You're* her room-mate?" Rath said, his surging anger only outdone by his confusion.

The girl tried again to shove past him.

He put his palm on her chest.

"*Hey*," she snapped. "What do you think you're *doing*?"

"Looking for my daughter. Where is she?"

"I *don't* know. The library, probably."

"That's what you said last time. I didn't find her."

"Yeah, well, it's a big library."

"Why didn't you tell me you were her roommate?"

Two boys raced down the hall, tossing a Nerf football and trailing behind them the yeasty odor of beer.

"Why should I tell you anything?" the girl said.

"You intentionally misled me."

"I don't have to tell a strange man *anything* about me," she said, outraged.

She was right. She'd done what he would want Rachel to do if—

The girl jammed an elbow in his gut, making him suck in his breath as she tore off down the hall. He stood stunned for a moment, then set out after her, students in the lobby gawking as he hustled after the coed with a Dress Shoppe box tucked under his arm.

Outside, a blast of wind blew the box out from under his arm, the lid blowing off it, the jumper spilling out on the snowy walk. He grabbed it up, his eye on the girl as she vanished over the rise toward the library. He jogged after her, the snow blowing sideways.

HE REACHED THE rise and looked for the girl. Where had she gone?

"Dad?"

Rath wheeled around, blinking snow out of his eyes.

A tall, young woman with fogged, cat's-eye glasses,

hair as white as cake frosting cut aggressively in a sharp line along her jaw, stood gawking at him from beneath the arm of a lanky Ichabod kid dressed in a Johnson State hoodie and sweatpants two sizes too big for him.

"Dad?" the young woman said again.

Rath blinked, confused.

"What are you *doing* here?" the young woman asked.

Rachel? Was this his daughter? This girl with this *hair* and *glasses* and, he saw now, black boots with blocky heels that elevated her a good four inches. How easily a young woman could transform her identity by coloring and cutting her hair, taking off or putting on glasses. But it was more than that, too. The last of the baby chub of her face had melted away to reveal beneath it a womanly bone structure, a striking face alarmingly similar to her mother's. There she stood in the snow and wind, her jacket unzipped and flapping away, as always. Rachel.

"Me?" Rath said, his voice weak.

"Yeah, *you.*" She held her hands out like *Who else would I be talking to?* "What are you *doing* here?"

Ichabod collected Rachel closer to him, vulture-shouldered, protective, head lolling like a sunflower, as if his skeleton were too frail to hold him fully upright, and he might accordion up on himself. He peered at Rath from under a cap with the flat broad brim that confounded Rath.

"What is that?" Rachel said, pointing at the soggy Dress Shoppe box collapsing sadly.

This was a disaster. His heart pounded to see Rachel alive and well. But now that he knew she was safe, he felt like a peeping Tom caught at the window. "Nothing," he said, tucking the box closer to him.

"Why are you here? Is something wrong?"

"Your text message. It had no abbreviations. It didn't seem like you."

"What are you talking about?"

"I hadn't heard back from you for days, then your text, it put me at ease for a while. But. I just realized. It, it didn't seem written by you, no abbreviations or—"

"*Penny* wrote it. She's an English major. She believes in grammar and language."

"Penny?"

"My roomie. She told me she ran into you when she found me in the library cramming; I was so stressed out and busy I had her text you from my cell so you wouldn't worry." His daughter stared at him, caught in a limbo between being furious and mystified. "So, you *came* here because you thought the worst as always, that I'd been butchered or—"

"No, no," he blurted, the wheels turning. He needed to salvage this scene. "I—"

"Yeah?" she said, bobbing her head, urging him on.

"I came about a case." He swallowed hard, wishing he were swallowing back down the words before he'd spoken them. But it was too late.

"You're a lawyer?" Ichabod said, his voice unexpectedly resonant, the voice of a midnight AM radio host. Had Rachel not told Ichabod anything about her father?

"God, no," Rachel said. "He'd never stoop to that." She smiled. The same old toothy smile that could melt the devil's heart. His heart, anyway. "He solves cases the cops can't solve," she said with pride.

Ichabod awoke, every atom at attention. "Really? Like what?" His radio voice still ambushing Rath.

"I *help* the police. They can solve crimes themselves," Rath said.

"Then why don't they?" Rachel said.

"What case are you on?" Ichabod pressed.

"A missing girl," Rath said.

"Cool," Ichabod said. "No wonder you like all that dark crap," he said to Rachel. "Killers and sadists and madmen and—"

"That's not *why*," Rachel barked, and peeled away from under his arm.

"Oh," Ichabod said, the timbre of his voice rising, alarmed by Rachel's detaching herself. Rachel seemed to sense Ichabod's panic and sagged against him. The snow blew in cyclones about them, and a gang of boys tumbled down the library steps, chucking snowballs at each other as they were sucked into a whorl of darkness.

"*What* case?" Rachel said, her eyes sparkling. Rath had distracted her from his initial pathetic motivation. But he didn't like this place any better.

"If you checked your messages, you'd know," Rath said.

"I'm *busy*," Rachel snapped, using a tone he'd never heard before, not the plaintive tone of teenage angst but the tone of an assured young woman: *I have my own life, and I don't have to defend or justify any of it to you.* It stung. But it pleased him, too. What greater gift could a parent give a child than independence?

"Go easy, bumble bee," Ichabod said.

Rath nodded, feeling an alliance with Ichabod now.

"Don't gang up on me," Rachel said, but the sharpness in her voice was dulled now. "You drove all the way up in crap weather because you need help on a case? Must be some case."

"It is," Rath said.

"You suck so bad at lying," she said.

"Give the guy a break," Ichabod said, and bumped his hip against hers as he squeezed her closer to him. "Who cares *why* he's here."

"Motive is everything," Rachel said, her eyes glimmering.

"My folks don't even want me home for Christmas break," Ichabod said. "Never mind visiting *me*. I had to hitchhike here for orientation." His voice regressed into a boy's voice for an instant. "So. Are you close to finding the missing girl?"

"Maybe. Maybe not," Rath said.

"That's how all cases go," Rachel said, gazing up at Ichabod and hunching her shoulders up against a gust of bitter wind. "Two steps forward, one step back. But he always solves them. Especially with my help."

Ichabod looked down into her face, fawning. "Why didn't you tell me you got this cool old man. And you *help*? How?"

"I go through reports, transcripts of interviews, and try to find LIMPS." She smiled at Rath, and he felt his back muscles uncoil, the pain ease.

"Limps?" Ichabod said.

"Lies, Links, Inconsistencies, Manipulations, and Patterns," Rachel said with a pinch of self-importance.

"I can't believe you *hid* this from me," Ichabod said.

"*You* didn't tell me about *your* cross-country hitchhike."

"Hopped-up truckers. Gay businessmen who wanted favors. Kids in backseats screaming like they're being shish-kebabbed."

"*Love* it. Except the screaming kids. Not ready for that." A far-off look came across her face, sadness or momentary contemplation. Rath wondered what spawned it, but hoped her not wanting kids meant she wasn't having sex with Ichabod. For an instant, Rath thought of the young women he'd picked up back in the day, used, never calling them again, never even getting their names. Never caring. Some of them had been Rachel's age. Or close to it. Eighteen. And in a bad place, coming from shit families that had left them vulnerable and all too eager. Victims. Prey. He winced, mortified at this revelation.

He looked at Rachel. She was smiling. But he felt sucker punched.

"All I know," Ichabod said, "is *if* I did something as sweet as solve murders, I'd have bragged on our first date." He kissed Rachel's forehead.

"Not *murders*," she said. "I'd *kill* to work murders."

Rath waited for Rachel's face to go dark with the realization that he'd lied about her parents. His head swelled with pressure, as if he had fluid on the brain. He knew if she looked in his eyes then, she'd see it, feel it, the lie between them. His act of treason.

Instead, Rachel's smile widened, his head left aching dully, as if in the halo of a migraine.

"So, what's the *case*?" she said.

"Forget it," Rath said, nearly gasping. He'd lied to spare himself humiliation. But he couldn't actually involve her. It was wrong. "You're busy. It was a bad idea."

"You can't *do* that!" Rachel said, and stomped. Her trademark stomp from age two. "You *have* to at *least* tell me what it is. I'll tell you if it's a time suck."

"This isn't rummaging through files," Rath said, trying to push the idea from his mind, but compelled to draw her closer to him, selfishly. "It was a bad idea."

Ichabod licked his lips, as all his energy seemed to swim into his eyes, bright silver beams of intense focus.

"*Tell* me," Rachel insisted.

Rath looked at her. She was beaming, magnificent.

"You can't tell anyone," he said. "It will—"

"—*jeopardize the case*," Ichabod said, conspiratorially.

"*Dad*," Rachel said.

Rath knew the more he spoke of secrecy, the more it would juice up Rachel. She was already ajitter with nerves. He should have told her the truth then. That he'd been worried about her and run up here to see if she was safe. Instead, he blurted, "I had an idea about your sitting in on some meetings." He regretted the words as soon as he spoke them, but he saw Rachel leaning in, coming closer, and his heart lightened. He took his copy of Sonja's list of names and handed it to Rachel, who studied it quizzically.

"I want to match up a person attending the meeting with the handwriting circled in red there on the lists," Rath said.

"Different names, same handwriting," Rachel said. "What kind of meetings?"

"Teen pregnancy meetings."

Rachel's face contorted as if she'd bitten the inside of her cheek. Her free hand drifted toward her belly.

"What am I supposed to *do* there?" Rachel said.

"Pretend you're pregnant."

Her face puckered.

Rath realized now how distasteful his request of desperation was. He hoped the look on her face reflected her response. His way out. "Told you," he said. "Bad idea."

"Tell me the details," Rachel said.

"No. It's a really stupid, irresponsible idea as a matter of fact." Rath drew a deep breath, the cold air crystallizing his nostril hairs.

"*Dad?*" She wasn't going to let it go.

"We think several missing girls and one who turned up dead are linked," Rath said. "That they were all pregnant. We think someone scouted meetings to find specific girls for their . . . needs." He took out the photo of Mandy. "We think she's behind it."

Rachel looked at the photo. "She's gorgeous."

"Wow," Ichabod said. "Wait. This girl is missing, too. I saw it on TV. So—"

"We don't know how or why she's involved," Rath said. "There may be something more behind this. Prostitution maybe. A cult."

Ichabod ran a hand back over his forehead, his knit cap falling off. He didn't seem to notice. "Like, devil worship, or—"

"We don't *know,*" Rath said. He told them the theory about babies.

"Holy cow," Ichabod said, and turned around in a circle. "And all Rach has to do is sit there and look for this hot chick? I could linger outside, take notes on car makes and models, creeps, crazy-looking chicks. Take pics."

Rachel zipped her jacket up, tight. "You're right, Dad. I'm too busy."

Rath sighed with relief. But her cool reaction was unlike her, even if she was busy. Something was off. Her face was shadowed with doubt, and something Rath could not place and had never seen before on his daughter's face.

Ichabod looked crestfallen.

"Too *busy?*" Ichabod said, despondent, his boy voice returning. "For this?"

"Right," Rachel said.

"Good," Rath said, relief settling in him.

"Lame," Ichabod said, and picked up his cap and batted snow from it.

"*Grow up*," Rachel hissed.

"This is a sweet opportunity to *do* something," Ichabod said.

"*No*," Rachel said.

"Listen," Rath said, rocking from one frozen foot to the other and stuffing his hands in his jacket pockets to emphasize the cold. "How about dinner?"

"I'll take a rain check," Rachel said, distracted now. Lost to him. "I got a lot of cramming to do."

"Sure," Rath said. He moved in for a hug and felt his daughter flinch the slightest before she pulled away.

Rath nodded and set off toward the Scout with the soaked gift box falling apart beneath his arm. He looked back once, to wave bye. But Rachel had already vanished.

CHAPTER 41

Rachel sat on the toilet in Felix's apartment as Felix pleaded through the door. "Why don't you want to do this?"

"Why do you *think*?" Rachel said, peeing.

"Because of—"

"Yes, *because of—what the hell else? Because of—*"

"But that's *why* we should do it."

Rachel heard him slump against the door. "I'll *help* you," he pressed. "I know it's still raw—"

"You don't have to tell *me*."

"I *know*. But all of that is the very reason you should do it."

"I know," Rachel shouted, her patience frayed. "I know! OK!" She dabbed herself with toilet paper and tugged up her panties and jeans. She took the crumpled list from her pocket. The girl's photo. Considered them. Felix had a point. As if what they'd been through the last two weeks hadn't been traumatic enough, the protestors outside Family Matters had made it worse. Monsters.

Her father had never been able to slip a lie past her. He'd visited because he'd been worried about her, and she'd caught him off guard; so he'd offered a way to bond, but had no intention of ever letting her actually do it. She knew that. She'd seen the relief on his face when she'd said no. But. Felix was right, what better reason to investigate than what had happened?

"Well?" Felix said, breaking the silence.

Rachel opened the bathroom door. "OK."

CHAPTER 42

Rath arrived half an hour early and parked across the street from Bistro Henry. He could not recall the last time he'd been so anxious with anticipation. He checked his teeth in the rearview, unable to tell if the whitening strips had lightened them. He thought maybe a little, then thought that was the psychological response the marketers counted on. Sucker.

He buttoned the top button of his only dress shirt, unbuttoned it. Took out his wallet and thumbed through his cash. A hundred bucks, fresh bills from the ATM as stiff as his starched collar. He hoped it was enough. What if she ordered a bottle of wine? Did she expect him to pay? He wanted to. Should he insist on it? *Christ*.

A tap at his window startled him, and he turned to see Madeline winking at him. As he got out of the Scout, he caught a whiff of her clean, fresh fragrance. Her hair was a spill of curlicues bouncing at her shoulders. She corkscrewed a finger at him. "Ready?"

No, he thought, *I'm not.*

The restaurant was all dark woodwork and brass and low lighting in a way that he would have found romantic if it had not reminded him of Dr. Langevine's library. A patter of voices and soothing string-instrument music floated around them.

The host, a doughy, middle-aged man who reminded Rath of an old biology teacher, saw them to their table near the fireplace, but not too near. The fire was propane flames and ceramic logs, the temperature even and relaxing. The host pulled out Madeline's chair and asked if either of them cared for a drink. Rath nodded in deference to Madeline, who said, "Your house red is fine."

"Molson. Golden," Rath said.

Madeline sipped her ice water as Rath looked around the restaurant. "I've never been here," he said.

"Really?" Madeline said, and set her water glass down and propped her chin on her palm.

"I don't get much chance to hit the new spots."

"It's been here almost a year."

He supposed it had. "Well. I never had the occasion."

"That *is* rusty."

"As an old farm gate."

"I'll go easy on you then," she said, and gave a slow grin. She liked to tease. It was subtle, but it was there. "Listen to me," she said. "Sounding like I'm out on the town all the time."

"You're not?"

"A divorced mom with two teenage girls and a full-time job? All I want to do by eight o'clock is crawl in bed and zone out to the tube with a glass of wine. Unless the spirit moves me."

The waiter set their drinks down and, seeing they'd not opened their menus, said, "Take your time."

Madeline glimpsed at the menu fleetingly and snapped it shut. She comes here often, Rath thought.

"Cheers," Madeline said, and raised her wineglass.

Rath lifted his beer bottle, not bothering to pour it in the glass provided, and tapped it against her glass.

He took a long drink to cover for the stunned feeling he suddenly had of not knowing at all what to say.

He set his beer down and swallowed.

"So," he said.

"So." Madeline stared at him as she sipped her wine. "I knew your sister."

Rath stared at her, shocked by this revelation. His muscles tightening.

"Laura Rath, right?" Madeline said.

Rath had not heard anyone speak his sister's maiden name in decades, and though Madeline spoke it with a warm regard, the old, deep sorrow cracked open along an emotional fault line within him to hear it.

"She's my sister," he said. Nothing Preacher had done would ever change that.

"I wondered," Madeline said. "When I saw the name on your credit card. I read about you back then. Like everyone else. About that whole thing. I'm sorry."

She cupped her wineglass and looked around the restaurant, embarrassed.

"So," Rath said. "You knew Laura?" Though he'd thought about his sister every day, he hadn't spoken her name in years, and it sounded alien to him, as if he were trying to speak an extinct language.

"In high school," Madeline said. "We were on the field hockey team together. We weren't too close outside that. I invited her to our house once or twice, but I never came over to your house."

No one came to our house, Rath thought. Not with my old man. We never risked it.

"But I considered her a friend," Madeline said. She glanced over his shoulder briefly. "We lost track when she went to Tufts. When I learned she'd moved to southern Vermont, I thought about getting in touch, but by then I was married with one daughter. And. Well. That's life. I wish I had." She traced a slender, smartly manicured finger along the rim of her wineglass. "Your daughter, is she—"

"Yes," Rath said quickly. "I adopted her. My parents were dead by then. And only her father's mom was alive, in a nursing home. Rachel's father had no siblings. So." He shrugged. "She was seven months old when—"

Madeline placed her hand on his, and he could feel her blood beating beneath her smooth, warm skin. Or was it his own blood beating? "That's admirable," she said.

"I was all she had."

"Still. You were young, probably single."

"She was all *I* had," Rath said. "This is the only life I can imagine. Being a father. Her father. The life I had before was meaningless. She's gone now. College." The lonesomeness he'd felt all fall burrowed more deeply than ever into his heart, his marrow, perhaps partly from seeing her just recently. Seeing how much she'd already changed while away so briefly.

"She's lucky to have you." Madeline squeezed his hand. "I never knew you then. The little brother. Funny how just two years makes such a difference at that age."

"Yes."

"It doesn't make much difference now." Her eyes flitted to a point behind him again.

"No," he said.

The waiter returned, and Madeline ordered the lobster roll and Rath ordered a steak au poivre, and they agreed to share an appetizer of calamari.

Rath polished off a third beer, feeling vulnerable and exposed at having spoken of Laura. He'd almost told Madeline about Preacher's parole hearing. But had refrained. The restaurant had grown crowded. The dining area bubbled with conversation punctuated with eruptions of laughter and the clank of utensils on plates. A party at the front of the restaurant was involved in a celebration. The diners were clearly family, with their similar blocky heads, sandy, tousled hair, and ruddy complexions.

Rath waved at the waiter. He should stop at three beers, he knew. But he had an urge to blot out the image of Laura lying at the foot of the stairs. "More wine?" the waiter said to Madeline as he arrived at their table.

"I'm fine," Madeline said.

"Beer here," Rath said to the waiter, feeling Madeline eyeball him. "A pint."

The waiter wandered away.

"I shouldn't have brought it up," Madeline said. "It's not exactly a first-date topic." A smile glimmered on her face, then quickly faded.

The waiter returned, and Rath took his pint from him, his hand trembling and foam sliding down the outside of the Shaker glass onto his fingers.

"You probably hate talking about it," Madeline said. She was regretful now, he saw. The mood soured from cheery and expectant to morose.

"I've never talked about it," he said, and sipped his beer, resisting the urge to gulp at a go.

Madeline's face was trapped between a look of disbelief and suspicion. "You *must* have talked about her at some time," she said.

Rath drank. "Never."

"But. It's been seventeen years."

"I *know* how long it's been," Rath said, more harshly than he'd intended.

"Of course. Sorry."

"For what?" He felt himself winding tight. He took a drink, spying the clear bottom of his pint glass already. When it came to booze, if he had too much, too quickly, his reaction to it was the opposite of what the old man's had been. He retreated, became closed off. Defensive. Mean.

He set the glass down with a *thock*.

Madeline blinked rapidly.

In the early days, when people had tried to speak of Laura to him, it was either with the dumb pity reserved for an orphaned puppy or with guardedness, as if his proximity to evil had infected him. And it had. Laura's slaying had altered his belief in goodness. He lived in the shadow of violent death. And Preacher—

"You OK?"

His vision fogged, Rath blinked Madeline into focus, smiled as a shiver of remorse ran through him.

"Why have you never talked about it?" Madeline said, her eyes bright now, voice clear. She was making an effort, he saw. Doing her best. What had she expected, bringing up a raped and murdered sister? Just what the fuck had she expected?

"Because I never wanted to talk about it," Rath said.

"I shouldn't have—"

"I never wanted to talk about it, before now." He finished his beer. "So, how are your daughters?" he said, wanting to keep himself from falling off into a darker place, to salvage the evening.

Madeline glanced behind him again.

"What's back there?" Rath said.

"Hmm, where?"

"Behind me, you keep glancing over my shoulder, am I missing something?"

"It's just those lunatic protestors going by with their signs for their nightly vigil."

Rath turned around to see two women march past, signs thrust in the air, as if they were carrying the flags on the front lines to battle.

A waitress brought over their basket of calamari and swept away. Rath ignored it, staring out toward the sidewalk, his heart galloping.

"They're always up there," Madeline said. "At the top of the street at the Church of Unity. Raging on about the evils of man, of *women*, to be more accurate."

Rath thought back to when he'd stood out on the street trying to imagine what Mandy had seen that day to change her mood so quickly. The protestors had not been out that day, but they'd been out the time he'd stopped later to see Madeline. He'd been unable to read their signs. Is that what Mandy had seen, women walking up to the church with their horrendous signs? Had she seen someone she knew with a sign?

Rath turned back to Madeline.

"These are not hobbyists." A storm of emotion darkened Madeline's face. "They're organized thugs. The Better Society, my ass. They think a woman's body is God's Body and her child is God's Child. And, since their ilk is God's Chosen, they have a right to terrorize girls. And bring in that psycho presidential candidate to talk."

Rath's blood crackled. He reached his hand in his jacket pocket for his cell phone.

"*Renstrom,*" Madeline continued, foaming, nearly oblivious of Rath now. "Do you *know* he headed some extreme religion, cult I'd call it, a long time ago; and he told a single struggling mom who was a member, who was pregnant again and thinking of abortion, that she would not be welcome in his congregation even if she had the child and kept it. He told her she had to give the baby up, and give up her two other kids, to two parents, a *real* family, or she'd be excommunicated. He denies it, but she's adamant. It's sick. Those people are sick."

Rath felt stricken, trying to focus his frenzy of thought and form a clear sentence from them. "These protests, would there have been one the day Mandy came into the store?"

Madeline thought a moment. "Yes, they'd have been there."

Rath pushed up from the table, the room spinning away from him.

"You OK?" Madeline said.

"If the check comes," Rath said. He plucked the hundred bucks from his wallet, the bills sticking together, and dropped them to the table.

"What—" Madeline said.

Rath strode outside, dialing on his cell, nearly knocking down the patriarch from the table of redheads as the man stood up to make a toast.

Rath pushed through the door, dialing Sonja.

Sonja answered. "You're home early from your date."

"How do you know I'm on a date?"

"I'm a cop."

"I think I know who Mandy saw, or *what* she saw, out in front of the Dress Shoppe. And I think, somehow, it had something to do with her disappearance."

"What?" Sonja's voice sang. "So, are we thinking suspect here, or victim again?"

"I—" Rath's brain churned in its beery murk. "I don't *know*. Maybe both?" He stalked up the street past the firehouse, a sandwich board out front announcing bingo night and last chance for raffle tix. A sign out front of the church was lit boldly by flood lamps: SENATOR RENSTROM SPEAKS! SOLD OUT! PRAISE GOD! MANY THANKS TO THE BETTER SOCIETY!

"Meet me at the station. Call Grout. And Larkin. And have Larkin check into an organization called The Better Society. I'll see you in an hour."

"What's happened?"

"One hour." He ended the call.

He raced back down the street and burst into the restaurant, jostled against the patriarch redhead, who was still giving his toast and who only laughed garrulously at Rath, as if he were part of an interactive comedy troupe.

At the table, Madeline tried to conceal her irritation and disappointment, but failed, her face all sharp edges.

The bill sat unpaid.

"No dessert?" she said.

"Rain check?"

"Is everything all right?"

"I hope." Rath glanced at his watch.

"Of course," Madeline said, and stood. She made a movement with her hand. She might have been leaning in to touch his arm or to take his hand, or she might have only been reaching for the check. Rath was unsure, because he had turned away just as she'd done it, and was already halfway across the dining room to the door. This time, he gave the redhead a wide berth.

CHAPTER 43

As Rachel raced down the sidewalk like a mom late for her child's first recital, her jacket flapping open despite the cold, a woman's shriek needled the frozen air: "God loves you!" Rachel halted to see a woman, her eyes bulging at Rachel from within a parka's hood. "But!" the woman cried, "He hates murderers!"

A clot of homely women stood behind a rope to seal them off from passersby, mumbling, "Amen," their puffy old faces florid as a child's spanked ass. Revulsion quivered through Rachel, and something else: fear and exhilaration.

Rachel thrust her middle fingers at them and strode on.

A voice raged, "You're going to hell!"

Rachel yelled over her shoulder, "Like you'd *know*, you *cunt*!" as she flung open the door to the Family Matters meeting.

She stomped her boots on a rubber mat and lifted her eyes to see the faces of six girls who sat in a tight circle of folding chairs, all of them Rachel's age or younger, but with eyes as tired as those of a middle-aged woman facing trial for murder. Shame flooded Rachel: The Late Girl. The place was quiet; the only sound was that of water dripping from the melting snow on Rachel's boot-laces. She could feel eyes sizing her up.

"Sorry," she mumbled, and slumped into a seat. "Sorry."

A woman in her forties waddled into the room, the frayed hem of her long black wool skirt sweeping the floor as her thunderous hips pendulumed in a manner that made Rachel wince to imagine how chafed the woman's inner thighs must be. Her trim and flat-chested torso did not jibe with her ponderous ass and legs. It was like the two halves of different women had been screwed together at the waist.

The woman caught Rachel staring and smiled a gummy grin as she heaved into a chair with a groan. She scratched at the back of one rashy hand. "So. Who's scared?" she said, her voice booming in the quiet room. Several girls flinched. None spoke.

Rachel studied the girls' faces, trying to commit them to memory. A woman who'd looked at first to be eighteen or nineteen, under scrutiny, seemed closer to twenty-two or twenty-three. She was heavyset, with streaks of purple in her hair. None of the girls was the girl in the photo: Mandy Wilks.

"Well," the woman leading the group said, "I'm Cathy. And I'm scared. Because whatever decision *you* make, it will change your life. I know; I've been there. I'm forty, and I have a twenty-three-year-old daughter."

Mouths twisted as the girls calculated how old Cathy was when she'd given birth: seventeen.

A girl with pigtails crossed a leg over her opposite knee and waggled her Chuck Taylors, soaked through from melted slush. All eyes were on Cathy now.

"I was pregnant two years *before* that," Cathy said. "I won't lie. This is a place of truth. Part of me wanted to keep that baby. But." Her forced smile was heartbreaking. "My uncle." She forced a new smile. Meant to be brave: all the more tragic. "We're here to give facts and support you with whatever decision you make, because, whatever choice you make, you likely aren't getting much support. Are you?"

Crickets.

"Are you?" Cathy said again.

A girl with braces blurted, "I'm getting jack shit."

"Right, jack shit," Cathy said, and smoothed her skirt with fat fingers cluttered with chunky cheapo rings. "If you are getting support, be grateful. If you aren't, or *weren't,* you are *now.*"

Purple Hair opened a notebook and started writing in it with a pencil.

"So," Cathy said, "who's made up her mind?"

Three girls lifted their hands, cautiously. A fourth and fifth wriggled their fingertips tentatively. Slowly, Rachel raised her hand.

Purple Hair took notes.

"You're undecided?" Cathy asked Purple Hair.

"I've made up my mind. *Not to.*" She cupped a hand on her belly. Nodded at the group, *and so should you.*

A girl with a boot cast on her left foot grimaced.

"OK," Cathy said. "Good."

"Then why are you here?" Boot Cast said.

"I still need support," Purple Hair said. "It's not easy when I think about money and how I am going to manage." She pulled at a strand of hair.

The girl with braces stood up. "I gotta piss."

Cathy nodded toward the rear. "Through there. Second door on the left."

Braces lumbered off, tugging at her red leggings where they'd bunched at the backs of her knees.

"Maybe it's time for a break," Cathy said but made no effort to get up. Her body seemed to puddle in the chair.

Rachel got up with the other girls, stretching.

"Make sure you sign in," Cathy said.

Rachel ambled to a corner of the room and took out her iPhone. She'd received texts from Felix, who was outside in Rachel's old Civic, keeping an eye out.

Bored! Zip going down in steak out

Rachel let out a muted laugh and texted Felix:

'Steak' (sp?) out??? How'd u get in2 skool?

"Nice phone," a voice said. Purple Hair. She leaned herself against the wall. "You rich, or did you steal it?"

A chill ran through Rachel. "Neither."

Purple Hair gave a loose, easy grin. "I'm teasing. I grew up in a house of smart-asses. Family rubs off, you know? You can't escape it."

"Sure," Rachel said. She'd never be here if it weren't for her father.

Her iPhone burbled the arrival of a text from Felix. She read it and knocked out a return.

"Boyfriend?" Purple Hair said.

Rachel nodded. Purple Hair stared. "I'm Rachel," Rachel said, absently. She'd considered using a fake name, but had worried she'd not respond instinctively to it.

She'd use a false last name on the list. Sort of. Pritchard. Her mom's married name.

"Glad to meet you," Purple Hair said, without offering her name. "You're really thinking of . . . *doing* it?"

Rachel touched her fingertips to her belly *absently*, or so she hoped, and cast her eyes downward, trying for a *deeply reflective* look, not having to try too hard after what had happened the past weeks. "Yes." She felt a shimmer of dread at lying, a sense that she was jinxing herself, messing with her future Baby Karma. "I worked hard to get to college. I can't mess up *now*."

"Where do you go?"

"Middlebury." Lying came easier the more she did it.

"And you ain't rich?" Purple Hair huffed.

"Scholarships."

"A brainiac then."

"I study my tail off," Rachel said.

"What do you have to get for grades to get in a hoity-toity college like that?"

Rachel didn't know. Better grades than her 3.2 average, for sure, hard as she worked for that average, and as proud as she was of it.

"You can tell a fellow pregger," Purple Hair said.

Pregger. Rachel cringed. "Three point eight."

"Wheeew. I got like a 2.4. That's why I ended up in a crap community college."

Rachel knew girls like Purple Hair, girls who thought even Rachel's 3.2 was lofty. None of them believed she worked hard at it, thinking it was just some natural gift. Anyone with a 3.0 or higher was a brainiac.

"Some community colleges are very good," Rachel said.

"This one was crap. Waste of time. But *Middle-*

bury. What are you doing way out here in the freakin' boonies? Middlebury's like a three-hour drive, and not a hundred feet of straight road on the way."

"I—" Rachel paused to get her lies straight, deciding on a half-truth. "I grew up in the general area. And I'm on break. I didn't want to risk one of my classmates or professors seeing me down there."

"God forbid. *Me.* I'm keeping *my* baby. You should think about it."

"I *have*."

"I'd think with how test-smart you are, you'd realize how wrong what you want to do to your baby is."

Rachel felt as if she'd been slapped hard across her cheek, and she could sense her mouth was hanging open. "I don't think—"

Cathy made a sound like a dog puking up grass. "If you'll take your seats."

Rachel stood over the list. She wanted to take a picture of it with her iPhone, compare the handwriting to later lists. Even if Mandy wasn't here. But she was afraid to get caught. What would happen if she was? Would she be kicked out? Arrested for trespassing?

"Forget your name?" Purple Hair had sidled up and nudged Rachel with her hip. "Hmmm?"

Rachel said. "No."

Purple Hair rocked on the heels of her boots. Why was she just standing there?

"Sign already," Purple Hair urged, pressing closer. Did she know? Was she onto Rachel? How could she be? Rachel pulled away and signed: Rachel Pritchard.

Purple Hair pushed out her bottom lip like a toddler. "Let's talk after, outside," she said, and squeezed Rachel's wrist.

Rachel rubbed her wrist, feeling the ghost of Purple Hair's fingers on her flesh. Then she angled her iPhone at her hip and snapped a photo of the list.

After an hour of hearing the other girls' traumatic stories, and telling a slightly altered version of her own story, still fresh in her memory, Rachel hurried outside, trying to ignore the sensation that her emotions had been sucked down a tub drain and left behind a filmy scum on her heart. Her uterus ached. Her womb. She felt ill as she gulped the icy air.

A hand touched Rachel's back, and Rachel whirled around to face Purple Hair. "Quit *touching* me," she snapped.

"Sorry. I'm pushy. I just. I did what you're thinking of doing, once, and I would never wish it on my worst enemy. You can't undo it. You know?"

Rachel *knew*. She looked across the road toward her Civic. It was parked under dark pine trees, so she couldn't see Felix inside it.

Purple Hair looked up into the black night sky, the stars cloaked by clouds. "I murdered my child," she said, and jerked her head toward the protestors across the street. "I'm not crazy. Like *them*." She looked haunted. "And you. You're so lovely. So smart." Her voice fell to a hush. "You have——" She paused.

"What?" Rachel said, her voice a whimper. Her energy sapped in the face of such a potent plea. "I have what?" she said in a faltering voice.

"Good genes. I thought this baby"——Purple Hair rubbed her belly——"would make it right. But it doesn't." Her nose leaked snot. "They tossed it in a medical waste can. Incinerated it." She wiped her nose with the back of her hand. "*You'll* have to live with that."

Rachel stared, astonished, feeling scraped out. She wanted to tell this girl the truth. This was an act, she was sorry for exploiting the girl's pain by playing amateur sleuth.

"Are you OK?" Rachel asked.

Purple Hair shrugged Rachel's hand off, and Rachel felt deflated. Weakened. But she needed to stick to her script. She needed to continue the lie.

"No. Are you?" Purple Hair said.

Rachel shook her head.

"So you'll . . . reconsider?" Purple Hair's eyes begged.

"I can't just drop out of school."

"You can go to school. Lots of girls do."

"I can't juggle both."

"You *have* to," Purple Hair said, and clutched Rachel's arm, fingers like talons.

"Let go!" Rachel shrieked, and yanked free. She fled across the street, a car horn blaring, its headlights throwing her in a ghastly spotlight.

She dashed to the other side of the road, sobs catching in her throat as she tugged open the door to her car and collapsed into the passenger seat.

"How'd it go?" Felix said, patting her shoulder.

"Don't *touch* me," she screamed.

CHAPTER 44

As Rath hurried into the squad room, Grout looked him up and down and gave a wolf whistle from where he stood looking at the bulletin-board display of missing girls' photos. "You sure got gussied up," Grout said.

"Nice threads," Sonja said as she fixed herself a cup of tea in the microwave.

"I had Larkin look into The Better Society," Grout said. "Ah, speak of the devil."

Larkin shuffled in and gave a courteous nod and clasped his hands behind his back. Unclasped them and clasped them in front, as if he were in a pew at church.

"We were talking about The Better Society," Grout said. "But first, Rath, tell us what's given you such a hard-on."

Rath paced, his blood fizzing in his veins.

"OK. Look." He felt light-headed with excitement, but also from not having eaten. "Mandy saw something outside the Dress Shoppe. Witnesses have told us this. She was upset by what she saw. Well. Just up the street on that day were radical antiabortion protestors."

Larkin nodded enthusiastically.

"I think Mandy saw some protestors. Perhaps some-one she knew but had no idea was such a radical. And she went out to confront her."

"Her?" Sonja said.

"Or him," Rath said.

"Or both," Grout said, nodding to Rath. "Going on your Evil Twins premise that maybe two people were involved."

"Whoever she saw, it upset her. What else could she have possibly seen?"

No one spoke. They nodded. Were glued to him.

"We have a baby cut from a womb."

"Fetus," Sonja said.

"Hear me out," Rath said. "We think that the fetus, baby, was about eight months old?"

"There's no way to know," Sonja said. "If it was taken just before Julia died, then yeah, but it may have been removed at anytime earlier—"

"Say it was taken late. Eight months. That's a baby." Rachel was three weeks premature and weighed 6 lbs. 2 oz. A tiny human; most definitely not been a *fetus*. "So. Who wants a baby that way? What possible reason could compel someone to do that to another human being?"

Larkin was nodding earnestly now, his hands un-clasped and his fingers working nervously, excitedly in his hair.

"If I may," he said.

"That's why you're here," Grout said.

"Right. Yes," Larkin said. He took a laptop from his bag, set it on the table below the bulletin board, and fired up the Web site for The Better Society. They all huddled around it, eyes roving the screen.

Something began to nag Rath. Something some-one had said. Or something he'd seen. But Larkin was launching into his tour of the Web site.

"These people are extremist," he said, speaking fast, keyed up. "See that?" He jabbed a finger at the Mission Statement on the home page. It read: *To confront abortionists and abortion promoters wherever they go: clinics, abortionists' offices, and even homes.*

"Look at some of these bios," Larkin said, flicking his finger over the track pad. "And they're *proud* of them. Look at this one for instance."

He pulled up a page with a photo of a middle-aged woman with big hair like she'd gotten caught in a cotton-candy machine, her face contorted in midscream as she brandished a sign. Under the photo was her bio.

SHARON WALLS: Sharon has proudly pro-tested in front of the White House since the nine-ties, on the Capitol steps, and all around New England. She has acted as an organizer of rallies for 30 years and has been jailed five times for tres-passing and twice for disturbing the peace.

A collective hush overtook the room as they read. Still, something nagged at Rath.

"And here," Larkin said, licking his lips.

Another woman, this one early thirties perhaps, quite striking, her blond hair styled fashionably, her dress that of a professional executive. LINDA MARSH.

Her bio mentioned numerous arrests for protests, and then, a quote about the doctor in Amherst, Massachu-setts, the one murdered by Knopps in his home for performing abortions? Marsh's big bold quote, regarding the murderer Knopps, read:

> *He was God's right hand, meting justice. A savior who saved with one bullet untold human lives.*

"She," Larkin said, straightening up and raking his long fingers in his hair, "was monitored by the FBI for five years after she said that. Nothing came of it. They found little besides an evangelical, fundamentalist woman who did nothing other than speak her faith. A practitioner of her First Amendment rights."

He clicked to another page, packed untidily with biblical quotes.

> *Thou shalt not lie with mankind, as with womankind: It is abomination.*
>
> *But the cowardly, the unbelieving, the vile, the murderers, the sexually immoral—their place will be in the fiery lake of burning sulfur.*
>
> *The body is not meant for sexual immorality, but for the Lord, and the Lord for the body!*
>
> *Now, we must rescue those who are unjustly sentenced to death; don't stand back and let them die.*

"That's our motive," Rath said. "The last quote."

Grout read it again. "How?"

"Someone is cutting babies from mothers who plan to abort?" Larkin piped in, pacing, going to the sink, and grabbing a mug. They stared at him. He went to place the mug under the spigot but knocked it against the faucet, shattering it. He held the broken handle and stared at the other detectives staring back at him.

"That's crazy," Grout said.

"Yes," Rath said. "It is." And it flashed in his mind that his feelings for Preacher were not dissimilar. He would kill Preacher to save others from knowing the pain Preacher caused. He would protect the innocent from evil.

"Then what do they do with the baby?" Grout said. "We're going on the premise of some sort of sacrifice. Ritual. Jesus freaks sacrifice a baby? No."

"If they're Old Testament enough," Sonja said.

"What about your goat's head?" Grout said.

"Maybe it's not a goat's head," Sonja said. "Maybe Barrons was right. *You* had doubts."

"There's more," Larkin said. He dropped the mug handle into the sink with a clatter among the other pieces of the mug and came back over to his laptop. "Lots more."

Rath could feel the energy shimmering off Larkin, a humming electric field.

They were circling now, like vultures over carrion. Still, there was—

"And, the icing," Larkin said. "I hate to call such an ugly thing that, but. The Better Society has what they call infiltrators."

"Infiltrators?" Grout said.

"Girls they send to group pregnancy counseling for places like Planned Parenthood and Family Matters. To try to convert the girls to be Pro Life."

"*That* explains the lists," Sonja said. "But the fact remains it's Mandy's handwriting on the lists. She is the link. She is the suspect now. She saw someone outside the Dress Shoppe all right. Someone that scared her or made her take off. But she was at all those meetings long before. How else do you explain her handwriting on all those lists?"

Rath stared at her, feeling the blood drain from his face. "I can't. But—"

"We'll get to that. What else you have?" Grout said to Larkin, squinting at the laptop screen.

Rath straightened, his back killing him, and gazed at the photos of the missing girls on the bulletin board in front of him. He let his eyes travel over each of their faces, marking the difference in the two photos of Mandy, the *good* one and the *bad* one. If they kept the girls alive long enough to have the baby, and if Mandy were taken by them, and not a suspect, if she'd been at those meeting for some other reason, she would still be alive. *We'll find you,* he thought. *Alive.*

Rath looked at the laptop screen.

"Betty Malroy founded The Better Society," Larkin said.

"What do we know about her?" Grout said.

"Her husband died in Vietnam, in '72. She was a nurse at Boston General, living in Framingham, Mass. Pregnant with a son. She was left a pittance and a mortgage on a ranch house. Never remarried. She gave birth to her son at home and raised the boy on her own, home-schooled him. Then, in early '86, she shipped him off to Europe to some swank private schools."

"How'd she afford that?" Grout said.

"She started Better Society in '73 in response to Roe vs. Wade. Women of similar minds met in her house to try to battle it. She became quite the star fund-raiser. Didn't hurt that she was very attractive. At first she lobbied and rubbed elbows with state legislators. Then she got on AM right-wing talk radio as a recurring guest. Grew a platform."

"Then?" Grout said.

"She cozied up to neocon politicians. Senator Renstrom was her last. Back when he was just a freshman in the House. Late nineties. She hasn't been seen in public since. She'd be seventy-two now. She was living in Wayland, Massachusetts, in '98, but vanished after she sold the place. No trace. No death certificate came up. So, I assume she's alive. But I'll deep dive. Unless she's living under another name. I'll find her."

"What else?" Grout asked.

"With or without Betty, The Better Society continues, stronger than ever. They're sponsoring Renstrom's stop in Vermont. It costs a lot to pull a candidate of his caliber from states that matter to have him show up in northern Vermont, where most people hate him. His Web site says his fund-raiser speech lasts a half an hour and will start at fifteen hundred bucks a plate, more if you want to shake his hand for a photo op. It's being held at the Pratt estate."

"The Pratt estate?" Grout said. He smacked a palm against his forehead, as if his brain had shorted out, and it needed a good thwack, like an old VHF TV. "I ran into a Pratt awhile ago. Boyd. III. I saw him. At the Double Black Diamond." Grout looked at Larkin. "And his estate is holding the Renstrom thing in a few weeks?"

"Yes, sir."

"What are the odds?" Grout said. "He lives more than an hour from the Double Black Diamond. What would bring him there? The place is a dive compared to the estate."

"What if he's got girls he meets there and things got

out of hand with one of them? With Mandy anyway," Sonja said.

"I'll get with him. In person." Grout pointed a finger like a pistol at Larkin.

"Anything else?"

"Yes, sir." Larkin's hands were trembling he was so jacked up. He rubbed them together, as if about to perform a magic trick, then clicked on the Web site.

A video came up.

"This is her," he said. "Betty Malroy, late '97, introducing then House member Renstrom." Larkin clicked the arrow on the video: *PLAY.*

"God knows! He does! This is God's will! Not mine! Not representative Renstrom's! God's! We are but disciples. His army of disciples! This is war, and we are its angel soldiers!" Betty Malroy roared in exultation, a crucifix dangling from her necklace against a bosom heaving for air, her arms raised above her head in a V, her hands thrust up and out of her white satin robe, palms outward and quaking, radiant, rapturous. Her black hair shimmered like a raven's plumage. She was tiny, but she emitted a power and energy unmistakably drawn from a deep reservoir of conviction. And money. Her voice was euphoric. Lunatic. Toxic. It escalated to hysteria now: "We will win this war! We will win this war!"

The crowd chanted back: "We will win this war!"

The picture on the video trembled; the place was rocking like an NFL stadium.

She wagged a finger, and the crowed shushed again, as if she'd cut their throats.

Her face was scarlet with fury. Insanity. A daub of spittle frothed at the corner of her mouth like a spiderweb.

She looked like she might faint from rapturous overload.

Larkin stopped the video.

The detectives stood speechless. Mesmerized. Rath could hear his heart beating.

"Dig more into this nut-job Malroy," Grout said, clapping Larkin on the back. "You and Detective Test. Together. I want to know everything about this woman, especially where she lives. If she's even alive. I want to know other entities The Better Society may partner with, other societies or the like they fund. Run her down like a beagle on a bunny." He turned to Rath, "So. What do we do about Mandy? Detective Test has a point. Mandy was at those Family Matters meetings, but," he turned to Sonja, "with this news, I don't think it was as a so-called infiltrator. But something else—"

"No," Sonja said. "She's still the common denominator. The link."

"She was on the pill," Grout said. "These radicals, they aren't on the pill. They abstain."

"People who convert to a new radical identity often were just the opposite before the conversion," Sonja said. "Same addictive personality, different drug. Instead of sex, it's God."

"True," Rath said.

"And it's Mandy's handwriting," Sonja said. "I think she's more of a suspect than ever."

"I see it the opposite, Detective Test," Grout said with a professional decorum previously lacking. "Honestly, my gut tells me"—he glanced at Rath—"Mandy's dead. Maybe someone was shadowing her and got to these girls *through* her or—frankly, I don't know."

"Where's this leave your pet suspect, that cretin Waters?" Sonja said.

Grout grimaced. "I admit. He looks less likely. Waters was charged with assault on a police officer. But I have nothing on him for Mandy, Julia, or any of the others. *Nada.*"

"So you're satisfied it's not him?" Rath said.

"Not at all. Not with his background. But. No evidence." His eyes flashed. "Here's what we do. Detective Test, you dig more into Malroy and The Better Society on your own."

Larkin's shoulders sagged, nearly imperceptibly.

"Officer Larkin," Grout continued, "you dig deeper into every crime that has *anything* to do with satanic symbols, flesh mutilation, going back years, decades, from Montreal to Hartford. If you find anything that's a match or similar to Julia that's more than a few years old, before our dog-torturing miscreant incident, we may be able to eliminate him. Eliminating a suspect helps gain clarity, although it might open up another Pandora's box for other possible perps. Which we don't need. We have plenty to worry about as it is."

CHAPTER 45

After the others were gone, Grout sat in his office, the door closed, his head bowed, remembering. Karly Martin. Fall of junior year. He'd been sixteen, and he'd loved her. He must have. Because when he'd gotten her pregnant, he hadn't been scared or angry or ashamed. He'd been proud. Happy. If there was a person he'd wanted to know more than he'd wanted to know Karly, it had been that baby. His baby.

When he'd told Karly, her laughter had scalded him. Was he *crazy?* They were *sixteen.*

He'd argued that if she'd just wait until she felt it kick inside her, she'd love it. "No," she'd said. "I'd hate it. I have things I want to do. Important things. Besides, my old man will kill me. Kill *you.*" It had been a dramatic thing to say, but her father probably would have hit her and definitely would have poleaxed Grout. Grout hadn't cared. He'd told her all she had to do was have the baby, and he'd take care of it. He wanted it. She couldn't do this. The baby was his as much as hers.

She'd howled. "There's no friggin' way I'm packing on fifty pounds and getting cottage-cheese thighs to have a brat for you."

Grout leaned back in his chair and stared at a water stain on the ceiling.

In the end, all he'd been able to do was convince her to let him be there during it. He'd thought he was being noble, as if he were at a vet's office witnessing an old dog being put down quietly. It had been nothing like that.

He'd never seen Karly again—she'd left town.

He would have been a good father. "I *am* a good father," he whispered. He'd been young. But he'd known how to love. "That's one thing I know," he whispered.

"What?" a voice said.

Grout looked up to see Larkin at the door. "You need something?" Larkin said.

Grout stared at the young cop for a long time.

"Resolution," he said.

CHAPTER 46

Rachel scoured her flesh in Felix's shower. She felt dirty and cheap. "I'm disgusting," she said.

A shadow fell across the shower curtain.

She tore back the curtain to find Felix seated on the toilet's lid. She yanked the curtain closed, cranked up the hot water, and pressed her forehead against the tile until she was poached.

In the kitchen, Felix had prepared oolong tea in chipped china cups they'd picked up at a tag sale. They liked rummaging about tag sales. They liked being un-cool.

Felix handed her a cup of tea, and she nibbled at the cup's edge and pressed in against his chest. He enfolded her in wiry arms so long it seemed he could wrap them around her twice. She sighed. Waited for him to ask about the night. Angle for details. But she didn't want to talk. And he didn't ask. She treasured that. Other guys would have poked her with questions to get her to open up, let them carry part of the burden. Solve it.

Play Good Listener when what they really wanted was to soften her, get the dramatics behind them, so they could get to the sex.

Not Felix. He remained quiet. The cold of the linoleum floor seeped through Rachel's thin socks, so she stood on the tops of Felix's giant's feet. Felix drew her tighter to his chest, and now she wished he *would* say something. She was fond of quiet people. Quiet men. Like her father. A man whose voice wasn't music to his own ears. Her dad fell into deep silences sometimes, looking at her as if he was about to confess some horrible deed. Some wicked truth he'd kept from her. But then he'd always say something innocuous, like, "Should we go for pizza tonight?"

"Well," Felix said, clearly sensing her discomfort, "how'd undercover go?"

She looked up into his face and felt a spark of confidence in her bones. "I did good. I think. But. *God.* Nerve-wracking. I didn't see Mandy. I met some other quack. I have to go to other meetings in other locations, see if Mandy shows." She took her iPhone from her pocket. "I snapped the list, just in case, to check for comparisons."

"You're a regular Laura Croft."

"That anorexic skank." She shivered. As hot as her flesh was from the shower and the terry-cloth robe, her core was a block of ice. The tea helped. She sipped it. Felt it easing down her throat and melting her from the inside out.

She slipped from Felix and paced, recounting the meeting, the ugliness of the reality and the buzz of playing her role. Told him all about Purple Hair.

"It's weird," she said. "She was insinuating herself into the group, like she was a spy trying to convert me. And I'm in there, a spy myself."

"You need to watch it. There are crazies out there. We should call your dad."

"Not until I can help; he'll be pissed I did this on my own no matter what."

She sat on Felix's lap, slinging an arm around his neck and cupping his rough, unshaven cheek with her palm. "The upcoming meeting. Hopefully, I'll spot Mandy unless this is all just a dead end."

"Why would your old man follow a dead end?"

"It's not like there's a road sign that tells you: DEAD END. Besides you always learn something." She pinched his cheek.

He blushed. "I'm bush-league."

"You'll learn, Watson." She kissed his forehead. "Pizza?"

CHAPTER 47

Grout pulled his cruiser up to the Pratt estate's admission gate and waited as the attendant spoke to the driver of a silver Volvo on the other side. The Pratt estate was legally deemed a non-profit agricultural center that admitted guests and school field trips to observe cheese making and cow milking. *What a ruse*, Grout thought. The driver of the Volvo, who sported aviator shades and a *Magnum P.I.* mustache, was yapping at the guard, giving him grief. Finally, the driver shook his head with a scowl, and the Volvo shot off in a spit of gravel.

The attendant wheeled over on his chair to address Grout. He was surprisingly young. A kid. Maybe seventeen years old. The skin of his narrow face was pink and raw from Retin-A.

"One ticket?" the guard said, glancing in Grout's car's backseat. The whites of the kid's eyes spiderwebbed pink with burst capillaries.

Grout showed him his badge. "I'm here to see Mr. Pratt."

"Which?"

"Boyd," Grout said.

"Which?"

"*The third.*"

The kid looked at a clipboard. Then nodded to Grout, and said, "I guess you don't need a ticket." He pressed a button, and the gate's arm rose.

The road wound tranquilly through undulating hills of impressive oak stands, dipped between vast, sprawling fields. Grout had read on the Web site that the family had hired so-called geniuses to create carriage trails of crushed pink marble, doze earth to mold the rolling hills, and strategically plant thousands of red oaks to replicate some sort of Victorian *pastoral aesthetic*. These hills had been designed and sculpted by a supposedly famous *landscape engineer* named Frederick Law Olmsted Senior. The original land had been flat as a beaver tail, scraped smooth by glaciers. The hills and oaks had all been purchased, were a manufactured deception.

Cars of foreign make with out-of-state plates passed Grout going the other way, kicking up powdered marble that settled as fine as ocean silt on the hood of the cruiser Grout drove to impress upon Pratt the official capacity of his visit.

Grout drove up the swell of a hill and into the shadows of mature oak trees. Squirrels scampered in the road, performing their neurotic jig of indecision. Grout tapped his brakes warily, so he wouldn't crush one with a tire. He hated that sickening *thwump*.

He came out of the trees and to a vista of the estate. The imposing enormity of the inn and mansion and dairy barn left Grout feeling exposed and dwarfed, as perhaps the buildings were meant to do to folks who did not belong among the privileged class. To those who did belong, the buildings likely inflated their dreamy sense of entitlement.

Grout pulled into the lot opposite the carriage house, which, relative to the other buildings, seemed modest, though it was three times that of Grout's cape. He got out, and a gust of wind off Lake Champlain knocked him so full on he had to put his arms out for balance. The day was bright and cold. Out on the choppy lake, a skein of Canadian geese flew low over the water, making slow progress.

Grout crossed the road to stand in front of the old carriage house. He peered up at the widow's watch. The curtains were drawn over the windows. The carriage house still had the classic double doors that had once allowed access for actual carriages but now likely garaged Pratt's Land Rovers and Bentleys. The doors were windowless and not intended for a guest's foot passage.

Grout went to the side of the place and found a door. It had a window, the pane of glass thin and warped. Old. *Antique* would be the word preferred by the Pratts. The glazing was crumbling. A shade was down inside. Grout was about to rap on the door when a shadow fell across him. As he turned, his hand instinctively went inside his jacket to the butt of his 9mm in his side holster.

The man who'd come up behind him stood a head taller than Grout, his fine blond hair whipped across his forehead by a blast of wind. "I doubt you'll need that," Boyd Pratt said, nodding at Grout's hand inside his jacket. Pratt smiled, or attempted a smile, one corner of his mouth pulled tightly upward anyway, like that of a hooked fish.

He was dressed in a checked olive-and-tan shirt that sported a finely corduroyed shoulder shooting patch, over which was a vest of dense, heavily brushed moleskin in the same drab olive color as his moleskin trousers. It was the kind of blueblood ensemble an Orvis catalog would twaddle on about being *distinctive and refined, made of the finest materials for the sporting gentleman afield or about the town.* In a word: ghastly.

Pratt didn't wear the $600 Le Chameau boots you'd expect with such garb, however. Instead, he wore ratty sneakers.

"You're either the cop who called, or I should call the cops," Boyd said without a hint of humor.

Grout retrieved his hand from his jacket and held it out, and said, "I'm the cop."

Boyd didn't acknowledge Grout's hand. "Follow me," he said, and walked off, shouting over his shoulder in the screaming wind, "I'm on my morning stroll before I brunch with my wife at the inn."

Boyd brought Grout to a teakwood bench perched atop a shale cliff that dropped twenty feet to the lake below. He sat with his knees wide apart, plucked dead grass at his sneakers, tossed the grass in the air, and watched it flutter away, like a golfer testing the wind before a long approach shot, except in this case it seemed to have no purpose whatsoever.

Grout sat beside him, which felt odd, not being able to look him square in the eye. But it would have felt stranger to stand in front of him, looking down on him, Boyd's face about zipper high on Grout.

"Hurry up with whatever you want to say, I'm quite pressed." Boyd stared out at a lake the color of lead, spotted by frothy whitecaps. The string of Canadian geese had made no ground, and though the lake was some twenty feet down the bank from them, the crashing waves and the fierce blow misted water against

Grout's face as if he were oceanside. He licked his lips and was half surprised not to taste salt.

"Well, what is it?" Pratt said, squeezing his own kneecaps.

Prig, Grout thought. *Genuine prig.*

"I'll come right out with it," Grout said.

"Do."

"Why were you at the Double Black Diamond when I saw you on the twenty-third?"

Pratt rotated his head on his neck much like an owl and peered at Grout. "I thought you looked familiar." He turned back to the lake.

"Why were you there?" Grout asked. He stood and looked down on Pratt, blocking Pratt's view. *Fuck it.*

"I don't believe that's your business," Pratt said, staring ahead as if Grout weren't there.

"I'll decide that," Grout said.

"No," Pratt said flatly. "I don't believe you will."

"I'll subpoena you. How'd that be?"

"I didn't say I wouldn't tell you. I said it was none of your business. Meaning it won't help you with anything, whatever it is you are up to."

"I am *up to* the investigation of a missing girl and a murdered girl."

Pratt lifted his eyes slowly to meet Grout's. They were the palest of green, nearly transparent, nearly as white as the whites of his eye.

"So?" Grout said.

"I was there to meet someone."

"Who?"

"A woman."

Who'd have thought this pasty weed of a man could attract a lover? Grout guessed money compensated for a lot, with certain women anyway.

"Who?" Grout said.

"That *will* require you get me under oath. What *is* all this fuss about?" He patted his knees.

Grout showed him Mandy's photo. "Have you ever seen this girl?" he said.

Pratt took the photo and looked at it, handed it back. "No."

"It wasn't her you *visited* at the resort that day, or any other day?"

"She's twenty-five years younger than I. At least. She could be my child." He pulled a tuft of grass from the ground and tossed it in the air, watching it. He was nervous. He was hiding something. Lying.

"Money makes up for a lot," Grout said.

"You're saying this girl was a prostitute?"

Maybe Mandy had been *working* at the resort. Is that how she got pregnant? A john? It would explain no apparent boyfriend but the use of birth control.

"You'd testify to never seeing her?" Grout said.

"If made to."

"But you were there to see . . . a woman."

Pratt wedged a blade of grass between his thumb and index finger and blew a high, sharp note, as if a child. "It's a private matter. My wife and I—well, marriage isn't easy."

No, Grout thought, *it isn't*.

"Though I do all I can to make her happy," Pratt added.

"I'm sure. You're hosting an upcoming fund-raiser for Senator Renstrom. Yes?"

Pratt leaned back and spread his arms over the back of the bench, trying to strike a confident, casual air but trying too hard. Covering.

"So?" Pratt said.

"He's quite the lightning rod."

"A person who has unwavering beliefs contrary to the masses often is."

"You support him, personally?"

"I believe in much of what he represents. Solid American principles. Tradition. Family."

"Do you know Betty Malroy personally?" Grout asked, dropping her name without warning to watch Pratt's reaction.

Pratt's eyes glided toward the lake. "I've never met the woman."

"Do you know her?"

"No."

"Are you involved with The Better Society in any way beyond this fund-raiser?"

"Hardly." Grout was cold, freezing, out there in the fucking wind but dared not show it. His nose was leaking. His toes ice. Pratt seemed unfazed, sitting out there in his dandy duds. "I'm no good at being involved," Pratt said. "I'm good at giving money away. That's about all I'm good for."

Ah, poor lad, Grout thought. *Douche.*

A gust blew a fine spray from the lake, ice crystals now, that stung his face.

"What does this have to do with the girl?" Pratt raised his voice over the wind so it squealed.

Grout shrugged. His feet ached. He blew in his cupped hands. "There are some loose ends. It's my job to tie them all up."

"Have you?" Pratt said.

"Time will tell." Grout held out his cold hand in departure, but Pratt ignored it.

"We'll be in touch," Grout said.

CHAPTER 48

The meeting was held, of all places, in a defunct church rectory, a stone building next door to St. Catherine's Catholic Church that had been shuttered in 2008 after a pedophile-priest scandal.

It felt weird to have the meeting in a place associated with a church. As if the eyes of God were upon her. Except the eyes of God were supposedly everywhere, Rachel mused as she strolled up the walk.

To her relief, there were no protestors tonight. She entered the rectory's long, empty hall, hit with a glary fluorescent light from the suspended ceiling. She was early, not wanting to be The Late Girl, and found herself alone.

The hall was bare except for a ring of folding chairs at the far end, near a counter that bordered the back kitchen. The stained indoor/outdoor carpet gave off the odor of damp laundry. Rachel smelled something else, too. Coffee. She walked to the back, peeked into the kitchen to see only a Mr. Coffee chugging away. A water stain darkened the ceiling. The coffeemaker belched.

"Not the tidiest locale," a voice said behind her.

Rachel spun to see a woman blocking the doorway.

"Sorry, thought you'd heard me," the woman said.

"My mind was someplace else," Rachel said.

"Of course."

The woman was perhaps thirty, with a sense of fashion, for Vermont: Smart, purple eyeglasses, black hair cut in a severe bob not unlike Rachel's cut. It made Rachel feel self-conscious. She'd had a crazy notion she had sole claim to her new do, and that illusion was shattered now. The young woman wore a trim-fitting Patagonia fleece jacket and slenderizing, charcoal wool pants with cuffs that fit snugly over black Sorels with faux-fur collars. "I'm Jolene," the woman said, as if this explained her presence.

Rachel wanted to squeeze past Jolene, escape into the open space of the hall. But Jolene did not budge. She leaned against the jamb, blocking the exit. "Don't forget to sign in," she said, nodding at a clipboard on the counter as she straightened and slipped past Rachel to the coffeemaker.

Rachel stepped out to the dining hall, frazzled. What was wrong with her?

The meeting started with three other girls joining, none older than sixteen, all of them twitchy and tense, chewing fingernails or teasing the ends of their long hair with their fingers, eyes wandering, all bundled in winter coats they left zipped as if they could not wait to flee. None of them had been at the other meeting. Why would they have been? It was an hour away.

And none was Mandy.

With all who were coming apparently in attendance, Jolene started. "You're not alone . . ."

Halfway through the meeting, in the midst of a girl

speaking of her pending abortion as if discussing having to return a dress that didn't fit, the door blew open.

"Sorry!" a girl's voice rang from the darkened entrance. Purple Hair. She strode in, shaking off snow and stomping her feet, the tip of her leaky nose red as a cherry. When her eyes caught Rachel's, she froze, startled, then joined with an apologetic smile.

Rachel looked away as her mistake smacked her in the face: If it was odd that Purple Hair was here, how odd was it that *Rachel* was here? What reason could Rachel give to be forty miles from the other meeting just two nights before? She tried to form a plausible excuse, but her mind was a Fourth of July sparkler, spewing spastic sparks of thought that died as quickly as they were born. She had no *story*. She swallowed sticky spit. Purple Hair winked at her, and Rachel felt her heart flip the way it did whenever she was caught lying.

The rest of the meeting, Rachel's mind was stuck on the wink, the other girls' stories a muddle of background noise. She declined to tell her own story. Did other girls attend other meetings to get a rounded perspective, or preserve anonymity? Maybe attending multiple meetings was common.

Jolene was wrapping up, saying something about staying strong. Rachel eyed the exit, willing herself to breathe normally but nearly panting with anxiety to escape.

She was about to make quick flight when Purple Hair mouthed: *Let's talk.*

Well, so what if Purple Hair sensed something was off? Rachel was here to investigate. Rachel was the hunter, not the prey, as her father would say.

The group was disassembling.

"Sign in if you haven't," Jolene said.

Rachel tugged on her peacoat as she approached Purple Hair. "Hey there," Rachel said. Her tone was wrong. Too casual. Be serious, she reminded herself: *You're pregnant.*

"Hello back," Purple Hair said. Jolene strode over with the clipboard. "If you would," she said, and tapped a pen on the clipboard for Purple to use. Purple Hair paused, then took the pen and jotted her name. "There's coffee left. If anyone wants some before I throw it out—" Jolene said, and strolled into the kitchen.

"What brings you here?" Rachel asked Purple Hair, to get the upper hand.

Purple Hair shrugged. "I make it a point to come to as many as I can. Reach out."

"They let you do that? I mean—"

"*Anyone* is welcome. As long as you are respectful and preggers." She laughed.

"What's that called, infiltrating?"

Purple Hair's eyes went cold. "Where'd you get that language?"

Rachel felt panic leap into her chest. "I read somewhere online that—" She'd done her due diligence. She and Felix had researched how radicals did this sort of thing.

"That's *not* me. What about *you*? Why are you *here*?"

"It, the other place," Rachel began. "It was too close to home. I thought, what if someone sees me? It was our conversation that made me think of it."

"Really?"

Rachel nodded, getting hold of the thread of truth in the web of lies. "We were talking about my going to Middlebury, and one of the reasons I didn't go to a meeting there was I didn't want to be seen by friends or professors."

"Mmm." Purple Hair cocked her head like: *Go on, I'm listening. I don't believe a word, but I'm listening.*

"And when we came out of the last meeting, I saw someone I knew. Luckily before they saw me. And I thought, this town is *way* too small."

"Mmmm."

"You act like you don't believe me."

"Why should I not believe you?"

Rachel glowed with panic.

"I wouldn't want to be seen if I were *you* either," Purple Hair said, her voice metallic.

"What do you mean?"

Purple Hair cast a look to the last two girls heading for the door. "I have to talk to those two," she said, and charged after the girls. *What did she mean?* Rachel realized she was alone with the list, took her iPhone, out and clicked a quick pic.

Outside, the winter wind bit Rachel's face. She spied Purple Hair across the street under the pulsing light of a streetlamp, speaking to one of the girls.

As Rachel advanced on her, the other girl shuffled down the walk, her head down.

Rachel came up, ready to assail. But Purple Hair smiled, and said, "Oh good, you haven't trucked off just yet."

"I'm parked over there," Rachel said, angered. She'd come alone tonight. Felix had been swamped with a lab and two papers due the next day. He'd not wanted her to come alone, but she'd insisted. What could possibly happen? "Look, I—"

"I was rude. I apologize," Purple Hair said, her voice soft as kitten fur now. "If I were you, I'd have changed meeting places, too."

"Why do you keep saying, if you were *me*—" Rachel said.

"Who you *are*."

"Who I *am?*" A bright star of fear stabbed at the front of her skull.

"Yeah, who you are."

Purple Hair looked at her, quizzically.

"I don't know what you're talking about," Rachel said.

"If what had happened *when you were a baby* had happened to me, I'd be even more ashamed about killing my baby, keep it a secret at all costs."

Before she knew what was happening, Rachel had Purple's wrist squeezed in a pit-bull grip and was twisting.

"It's all right to be angry," Purple said, her voice steady, tranquil. "I'd want to hurt someone, too."

"What are you *talking* about?"

"What happened to your parents when you were a baby. How lucky you were to survive it."

Rachel's grip eased, her fingers sore from clutching so hard.

"I didn't *survive* anything," Rachel said. "I wasn't even in the car."

"Car?"

Rachel felt something inside her shift; her guts wormy. Recently, the idea to find out more about her parents had slipped into her brain. She'd gone through old photos and watched old videos, heard her mother's voice, her laughter. She'd studied her mother's face, set to memory her expressions. She'd watched the video of her mother in the hospital minutes after Rachel's birth, cuddling Rachel, who was all kicking legs and pumping fists. And, just before Rachel had left for school, she'd wanted to ask her father about the details of the wreck. Felt that the gnawing emptiness inside her would go away if she knew more. She'd typed her parents' names into Google but had never hit SEARCH. In the end, as much as she *needed* to know, she did not *want to* know. She'd turned her parents into romanticized idols. Victims. But what if the crash had been their fault? What if they'd been drunk? Or killed someone else in the crash? In the end, she hadn't wanted to taint her ideal with fact.

Rachel's eyes teared in the stinging cold. "Right," she said. "It's not like I was in the car."

"The house, you mean."

Rachel felt the ground turn to quicksand.

"Your parents didn't die in a car crash," Purple Hair said.

The wind was howling in Rachel's emptied skull.

"They were murdered," Purple Hair said, "stabbed to death by a monster."

RACHEL STALKED DOWN the sidewalk blindly, tripping and falling, picking herself up, buttoning her coat up tight for once against the sudden cold she felt. She sensed a sob working in her chest, wanting out, but her mind had not quite grasped what she'd been told. Not quite believed it. Every time she thought of what Purple Hair had said, she grabbed the sides of her head and squeezed, as if trying to rid herself of a migraine. She called Felix and got his voice mail, left a brief but babbling message. She tried to calm herself, breathe deeply.

From behind her she heard Purple Hair calling after her.

Rachel hurried along.

What Purple Hair had said rooted in her mind like a malignant tumor. She wanted to take a knife and cut it out.

CHAPTER 49

Rath sat slumped in a recliner in one of the Spine Center's inner sanctums, recovering from the procedure, his stomach oily, his skin hot and sticky. What an embarrassing display he'd made, vomiting at the tail end of the procedure. The nurse had told him all would be fine in a few days, he'd never even know his back had hurt. But that *needle*. Fuck. It had jammed in there so deep inside him, he had felt it piercing what could only be marrow. Or raw nerve. It *killed*. Rankin had been right. Pain could always get worse.

CHAPTER 50

Grout tossed a dart at the board in his office. He'd just gotten off the horn with Jen and was fried from her asking where the force budget was at and when the new positions were going to open up, both of which he had no control over or information to share. She'd said she'd seen a position online, for security, at the Littleton, NH, mall. *A mall.* In *New Hampshire.* Was she trying to give him reasons to strangle her? Had she not heard him all these years about how New Hampshire was the state they were forced to drive through to get to the Maine coast and back for vacation.

A fucking mall.

Fucking New Hampshire.

He thought about Boyd Pratt. Something was off about that one. Grout tossed a dart and almost struck Larkin's eye with it as he poked his head into the office.

Larkin looked at Grout, who held a pair of darts, his feet propped on the desk next to a growler of his home-brew stout and a half-tanked pint glass of the beer beside it, and said, "Am I interrupting something important?"

"What's it look like, given the evidence?" Grout said, and finished his pint.

"I guess not, sir."

"Skip the 'sir,' will you?"

"Yes, sir."

Grout sighed. "What is it?"

Larkin produced a folder from behind his back and slapped it against his thigh. "I got her."

"Got who?"

"Betty Malroy. I know where she lives."

Grout sat up, nearly knocked over his growler, just saved it with a lucky, buzzed grasp. "I thought I put you on the satanic bullshit deep dive."

"I finished with that, last night."

Grout eyed him skeptically.

"This morning, I should say, at 4 A.M., I've been on it like a beagle on a bunny straight out, like you asked," Larkin said.

Grout had no doubt it was true. It was clear the young officer had stayed up all night not just to impress his superior, or for any delusion of advancement at this stage in his career, but because he loved the work. And was thorough. He'd pulled an all-nighter, and he looked as scrubbed the day after at two in the afternoon as an altar boy at Sunday Mass. And he'd beaten Detective Test to the punch.

"How'd you find her?" Grout said.

"Tax filings. I tried mortgages, car registration, and the like. Nothing doing."

"Where is she?"

"Connecticut. Newbury. She also is the backer of another entity, sir, called Better Days. A very exclusive, very private adoption agency."

Grout gnawed his lower lip and processed what he'd just heard. He clapped his hands together. "Shall we pay her a visit?"

"Us, sir?" Larkin blushed.

"Unless you have plans."

"No, sir, not at all, sir."

Sir, again.

"But. It's another state," Larkin said, "we don't have juris—"

"Let me worry about that."

"What about Detective Test?"

"She fell sick yesterday afternoon. Her loss." Grout stood. "How long a drive you figure to Newbury?"

"It's two hundred and twelve miles, sir. About four hours and thirty-six minutes. Give or take."

Grout smiled at Larkin's preparedness as he looped a finger through the growler handle and hefted it up off the desk. "Ready," he said.

Larkin eyed the growler as he allowed Grout to pass into the hall.

The young officer fell in beside and a step behind Grout down the hall.

"Question," Grout said. "What about the sadist deep dive?"

"Plenty of sickos, sir. But nothing linked to Julia Pearl." He paused, slowed his pace.

"What?" Grout said, slowing his pace.

"There was this old case. It seemed a lot like Pearl, but. But it was too long ago and in another state. Halloween of '85, in Wayland, Massachusetts. It involved a Marianne King, thirty-two years old, and *not* pregnant.

An apparent isolated incident. But. *Look*." Officer Larkin handed his iPhone to Grout.

Grout stared at the image on the screen. "Christ," he said.

"All sincerity, sir. I don't think Christ had anything to do with that. But, other than somewhat similar wounds, there are no commonalities. Whoever did this to Marianne King and carved Miss Pearl, maybe had one thing in common though, if I may posit my own theory. The carvings weren't done by Satanists carving *their* mark of Satan on the girls, but rather by religious fanatics marking their girl, or woman in Marianne King's case, as the evil entity."

Grout studied the pic. The *carving* into the woman's belly looked disturbingly similar to the mess found in Julia's decomposed flesh. "It looks a lot like our girl's wounds," he said.

"But," Larkin said. His voice was low, as if he were a boy telling a horror story around a campfire. "It was twenty-six years ago."

"This woman on Halloween. Did she say *anything* before she died?"

"That's just it, sir. She *didn't* die. She's alive."

Grout gaped at Larkin.

"She's fifty-eight years old and lives in Beacon Hill in Boston," Larkin said. "A domestic-abuse advocate. Her husband is a star prosecutor."

Grout gawked at the .jpeg. That this woman had survived such a butchering could only be considered a miracle.

"I haven't spoken to her, sir, but I have set up a time to do so," Larkin said. "I hope that's OK. I don't want to step on toes, but—"

Grout nodded. This kid had something Grout lacked. Something the best detectives possessed: conviction. Instead of feeling jealous of it, however, Grout felt what, exactly? Proud.

"Mrs. King," Larkin said. "From the reports. She swears a child did this to her. Experts say she remembers it wrong; they attribute it to shock and blood loss scrambling her memory."

Grout looked at the .jpeg again. A child? No. Nothing could drive a child to such violence. "Well, even if there's no real tie to Julia Pearl, good work," Grout said, and started down the hall again, Officer Larkin a half step behind him now.

As Grout pushed open the door and strode out into the cold and darkening afternoon, he said, "Another question, Officer."

"Yes, sir?"

If he said *sir one* more time.

"And I want you to think hard about it."

"Of course, sir."

"What do you think of New Hampshire?"

"I'm from New Hampshire, sir."

"I see."

"That's why I moved to Vermont."

CHAPTER 51

Under a foreboding sky, Rath sauntered out to the barn, carrying a pry bar and a hatchet. He would get the deer unstuck from the frozen ground. He'd be lucky to salvage any meat now. But his back felt good. His back felt grand. His back felt *nothing*. He realized in the last day that something was missing from his routine, and it had taken him a while to realize what. The pain. When he turned or bent or reached, he found himself flinching against a pain that never came. The pain was simply, miraculously, gone.

He felt liberated, ready to do now with ease what he'd been unable to do at all just two weeks before. It would take a while to get the deer unstuck, but he wanted to get a start on it before the snow came. The area was due for a storm, and snow was already swirling down from the ominous sky.

He stood over the deer. His cell buzzed.

He didn't recognize the number.

"Yes," Rath said, his voice ringing, matching his high spirits.

"Mr. Rath?" The person on the other end was winded, gasping.

"Yes," Rath said.

"I've been trying to reach Rachel and keep getting her voice mail. And I left messages on your home machine, and—"

"Who *is* this?"

"Felix."

"Who?"

"You met me on campus—Rachel's boyfriend."

"Right. I hardly ever use my landline and check messages even less. Why were you leaving messages for me?"

"I wasn't; I was leaving them for Rachel."

"Rachel's not at the house."

"Well then, where *is she*?"

Rath dropped the hatchet at his feet. "She's not with you?"

"No." Felix nearly shrieked. "She went home."

"What are you talking about?" Rath stared out blankly at Ice Pond.

"She left a voice mail saying she wanted a few days alone. She hasn't been to her dorm so . . . I thought, when I didn't hear, I thought maybe I'd said or done something to make her mad. I've been calling and texting her cell and—"

"For how long?"

"Nearly three days."

"You haven't heard from her in three days?"

"I thought she was at home and wanted space."

"Christ. Did you have a fight?"

"Not really."

"What does that mean: not really?" Rath was shouting now, stalking back and forth across the barnyard, tapping the pry bar against his kneecap.

"She didn't want to tell you until we got concrete proof. Something that could help."

"Proof of what?"

"She went, well, undercover."

"What are you talking about?"

"She went to those Family Matters meetings."

"No," Rath said. He went stiff as pain shrieked in his chest, as if he were stabbed. "No. She didn't."

"It was probably stupid. You don't think her attending those meetings has anything to do with it, do you? Rachel's disappearance?"

Rachel's disappearance.

CHAPTER 52

Grout pulled the cruiser up in front of Betty Malroy's residence in Newbury, Connecticut. He'd expected a trophy home, perhaps an estate, from what he knew of her relentless fund-raising and her prominence among the Beltway crowd, not to mention the generosity her rabid cult followers would undoubtedly bestow on her if called upon.

She must be hiding the money somewhere, Grout thought as he looked at the modest raised ranch that sat on perhaps a half acre of land among similar houses at the end of a respectable but unremarkable cul-de-sac.

"This is it?" Larkin asked, glancing at a map on his iPhone.

A light glowed in the home's living-room window. No car sat in the driveway. Grout was tired; they'd hit snow in Vermont, then freezing rain down here. The going had been torturous, and Jen had called his cell and texted him every ten miles, asking where he was. Getting more strident with each message. Her voice all but screeching on the voice mail, her texts in all caps: WHERE ARE YOU? WHAT ARE YOU DOING?

He hadn't answered the phone or returned her messages. He was on a case, is what. He was doing his job.

"OK, let's go," Grout said, and opened his door, the McDonald's bag from the drive-thru they'd stopped at in White River Junction blowing out of the car on a gust and tumbleweeding down the street.

As they approached the porch, Grout heard a TV from inside, the volume cranked. He knocked hard on the door. They waited, Larkin with his hands jammed in his coat pockets and rocking on his toes. He was amped. Grout was, too. This woman, one way or another, she was behind these missing girls, behind the dead girl. Though he was still unsure how Mandy fit. She doesn't fit, he thought as he knocked again, louder.

The sound on the TV fell away to a murmur, and Grout knocked again.

He heard a chain lock slip from its slot, then the door was opened, and Betty Malroy stood before him on the other side of the storm door.

The fourteen years since the video he'd watched of her had been taken *had* aged her; but even standing there now with a terry-cloth robe clutched at her neck, she possessed an air of refinement, and it was easy to tell she had been stunning in her youth. Her luxurious silver hair was swept up in a carelessly attractive heap that on most women would look dumpy. Her face was pale, the skin a bit slack and her cheeks and forehead marred with age spots. But her eyes possessed the bright alertness of youth, and her posture was erect, delicate shoulders squared. She looked perhaps fifty-eight though Grout knew she was in her early seventies.

"May I help you?" she said through the door, glancing from Grout to Larkin, to somewhere behind them on the street, the car, perhaps, then back to Grout.

Grout displayed his ID, and said, "We need to speak with you. It's urgent."

She stared at them, her eyes going dim, the brightness gone in a blink, and Grout thought she was going to shut the door on them. Instead, she said. "Let me see the other gentleman's identification, if I may."

Larkin showed her his ID.

"Fine," she said. She allowed them into the foyer, reluctantly. Then she climbed the stairs without a word. Larkin and Grout followed, took a left at the top of the stairs as she did, Grout looking to his right, down the hallway for a long moment, to ascertain as best he could, if anyone else was in the house. Then he went into the living room.

The house was warm. The floors were a blond, handsome wood. The place was finely appointed with modern furniture that featured a glass coffee table and glass end tables. A sofa along the wall was sleek and angular; its pewter-colored fabric had those tufted buttons Jen thought were fancy in a way that escaped Grout.

It was all glaringly impersonal.

A white brick fireplace with a slate hearth and a simple white-painted mantel stood empty. No fire screen. No fire. Where the fire would have been was barren and cold, black from the soot of fires long extinguished.

Above the mantel hung the largest crucifix Grout had ever seen. It looked like it was made of solid gold and gleamed in the light thrown by a floor lamp at either side of the fireplace.

Betty Malroy sat in the matching chair to the sofa,

beside the fireplace. She wore a crucifix around her neck.

She turned the TV off with the remote, settled herself against the back of her chair, and nodded at the sofa.

Grout and Larkin sat. The room was too warm. Hot. Larkin took out a notepad and clicked a pen.

"What's happened?" Ms. Malroy said.

"Ms. Malroy," Grout said.

"Yes?" She looked Grout directly in the eye, unflinching, confident. Superior.

"You founded The Better Society, is that so?"

"Yes," she said, bored with him already. Dismissing him with a word.

"And you also are the primary source of financial backing for Better Days Adoption Agency?"

"True." She had not yet blinked since sitting.

"The Better Society, it's—" Grout began.

"I won't speak about it," she said.

"About what ma'am?" Larkin said.

"That organization."

"Your organization," Grout corrected.

She lifted her chin at Grout. "You've not done your homework, Officer."

"Detective."

"You've not done your homework, *Detective*." She sniffed.

Grout realized then that the house gave off no odor that he could detect. No aroma of food, or a pet, or perfume, or life. He glanced around. Besides the crucifix, the white walls were bare. Pristine. Sterile.

"How do you mean?" Grout asked.

"It's not my organization," Malroy said.

Grout leaned forward, elbows on his knees. "You

founded it. Your photo and biography are prominent on the home page."

"They can post what they like."

Grout was getting a slippery, uneasy feeling. This woman was sharp. This woman had threaded the eye of the needle in DC's political game. She'd swum with sharks and looked pretty good for having done so. Unscarred.

"There's a video of you that—" Grout began again.

Betty Malroy leaned back, drumming her fingers on the arms of the chair, imperious. "What does that video have to do with anything? What can a video from fourteen years ago possibly have to do with anything today, or with why you are here? Why *are* you in my home? Speak up. Don't dawdle. What do you want with me? I've done nothing."

Grout felt his skin tighten at the arrogance of her act. "Wrong," he said, projecting his voice as he lowered it. "You have done a great deal. You make it your life's work to foment hatred and violence, to create and grow an extremist organization that takes pride in terrorizing young women. Victimizing girls and young women who are already scared enough." His blood was up now. "You pushed forward a radical, spiteful agenda, created an army of young girls who infiltrate meetings of a very private nature. I saw that video. You know how to work up a crowd. A crowd made up of people who brag openly about calling men who murder doctors in their home—*saviors.*"

"Did," she whispered.

"Excuse me?"

"Did. I did know how to work up a crowd."

"I'm sure you are still capable."

"Capable. Yes. Willing. That's another matter. I perhaps *did* push forward a mad, as you put it, agenda."

"And how would you put it?"

"Ugly."

Grout was taken aback.

"Despicable," Malroy said. "Regrettable. Sinful even."

What was she saying? Was this a ploy?

"Detective . . ." she said, implying she had not caught his name.

"Grout."

"Detective Grout. As I said, you have not done your homework."

Grout glanced at Larkin, who seemed at a loss. Mystified.

"I have had nothing to do with that organization for years. Nothing to do with it except in trying to distance myself from it."

"I saw that video."

"I *made* that video. I know what you saw and felt. The same thing I feel now. Disgust. Repulsion. Hatred toward the hate. I know."

Grout could feel Larkin's eyes on him, but Grout kept his own eyes locked on Malroy. He wasn't buying her speech. Not yet.

"You can look into it easily enough," Malroy said. "Lawsuits are public. I tried to sue them for keeping my likeness and that video on there. I tried to put an injunction on them using the name of the society. Do your homework, Detective."

"You don't believe in what the Better Society stands for?" Larkin said.

"Let me put it this way. Do I believe in abortion? No. Do I believe in the right to protest? Yes. Do I believe

our Lord and Savior Jesus Christ is the Son of God? Yes.
With all my heart. What I don't believe in, Detective,
is murder. I do not believe in what The Better Society
promotes now. I haven't since '98. If you knew anything,
you'd know I 'disappeared' then. Of course, I've lived
right here all along. What I did was distance myself
from the society."

"Why?" Larkin said.

"Because of Kopp. Because of what he did to that
doctor. And because I was appalled so many of my followers would take a stance of support for such an act,
a sin. When that doctor, that father and husband, was
killed. In his own home. There was no justification for it.
None. And I said that, and they turned on me. My own
people. Like snobby, spoiled little brats. They turned on
their mother! I hadn't raised them like that!" She gave
her head a brisk shake, as if to snap herself back into a
state of propriety, but it was too late. The lunacy, the
zealotry, had flashed.

Grout ignored it. "Why not start a new society?"

Malroy swept her hand at him. "I'd already spent two
decades building the society from the ground up with
all the love I had in my heart. I wasn't starting over."

"Tell us about The Better Society, as you saw it,"
Grout said.

"So you can mock it?" Malroy sniped.

"So we can understand it."

Her eyes darkened.

"Our protests were legal. We abided by the law. We
were peaceful. Respectful."

"I see," Grout said.

"You're blind," she spat, further shedding her mask
of decorum.

"To what?" Grout said, easily, enjoying it.

"The true workings of evil."

Grout had her now, had the snake slithering out from under its rock.

"Please. Open my eyes," he said.

"See, you mock."

"He's not mocking," Larkin said, patiently. "The mission statement on the Web site says it's to 'confront abortionists and abortion promoters wherever they go: clinics, abortionists' offices, and even homes.' Was that your creation, or is that new since you left?"

"That was mine, but they warped it," she hissed. "They bastardized it."

"Do you know a Mandy Wilks?" Grout said.

"Who? No. I don't know Mandy anyone." She puckered her lips, homely, fishlike.

"She was possibly pregnant and seeking an abortion," Grout said.

"Possibly?" Malroy said.

"And she was seen with an elderly woman on a bench outside a clinic soon before she disappeared."

"There are lots of old ladies in the world, detective. I don't know any Mandy. I haven't laid foot in Vermont in a decade."

"Who said anything about Vermont?" Grout said as his blood pressure spiked at her slipup.

"What?" she said. "No one. I just. Your IDs."

"Right." Sure, Grout thought. The old woman was burying herself deeper with each word, each lie, she spoke.

"Don't you *right* me," she said. "Don't you dare. What is this *about* anyway?"

Grout took out the photo of Mandy, strode across the

room, and snapped it in front of Malroy's face. "Her, do you know her?"

"No," she said, without looking at the photo.

"Look at it," Grout snapped.

She looked at it. "No."

"I don't believe you," Grout said.

"I don't care. And I won't be interrogated in my own home, I won't—"

Grout slapped his thigh and laughed, openly mocking now. Malroy shrank back like she'd been cut. "This," Grout said, "is hardly an interrogation. An interrogation would be much different than this. You wouldn't want that. You wouldn't like that."

Her face was carved of stone now. Fixed. Immutable.

"Perhaps you know her?" Grout showed her the most grisly of photos of Julia.

Malroy's stone face was suddenly flesh again, quavering from a blast of unexpected shock. She looked away and set her mouth tight.

"Someone is killing girls up where we're from. All of them were in meetings where you have infiltrators."

"I have nothing to do with the society! I told you that!"

Malroy was trembling, her bottom lip quivering, but her eyes remained locked on Grout's. They shone with conviction.

"These are your followers," Grout said. "Your *apostles*. You taught them to be this way."

"I did not, I—"

"Shut up." Grout stuck a finger in her face. "Unless you're going to say something useful, shut up, you old windbag."

Malroy shook as if she might break apart, her face

going purple with silent rage. Her mouth working as if her dentures were loose.

"Now listen to me," Grout said. "These girls are being killed, their babies cut from them, and, well, you have an adoption agency, yes?"

"No. I mean, yes I do, but no. You couldn't possibly think. No. Never."

"Liar. You better start telling me something I can believe. Tell us who of your minions you think is capable of such a thing."

She clutched her face in her hands now, her fingers claws, as if she wanted to tear the flesh from her skull. And for a moment, Grout was afraid she was trying to do just that. She pulled her hands away, and her face was livid where she'd clawed it. "He."

"Who?"

"Oh God. No." She clutched her crucifix in her fingers. Kissed it. Wept.

"Tell me, Ms. Malroy." Grout touched her shoulder lightly. "Who?"

"He." She sobbed. "He's not doing it for—" She hung her head, shaking it as if she were able to rid her mind of whatever wretched thought was in it, she could rid the world of the reality. "He's not doing it for reasons you think."

"Who?" Grout squeezed her shoulder. She was frailer than she looked. He could break her shoulder easily. She was old. An old, wicked woman.

"It's not what you think. He would never do—" She sagged in the chair, and Grout thought she might expire. Feared it. But he squeezed her shoulder tighter anyway.

"Who? Who would never do what?"

"My. Monster."

CHAPTER 53

Rachel's disappearance.

The words slammed in Rath's brain as he drove Moose Alley at a reckless speed.

Rachel's disappearance.

RATH MET FELIX at his apartment, a tight one-bedroom tucked under the steep eaves of a Victorian attic, a living area just spacious enough to wedge a futon couch and stretch your legs without quite touching the opposite wall.

Rath did not sit and stretch his legs. He paced as Felix told him what he knew about the meetings and the strange girl Rachel had met at both meetings. The girl didn't match Mandy's description, but she'd been at two different locations. She'd been forceful and insistent, trying to convert Rachel.

A sound in the apartment came from the bathroom. A sharp squeak.

It festered in Rath's ear.

"Why was this girl at two different meetings?" Rath asked as he trod back and forth.

"I don't know," Felix said.

Rath paced. The odd chirping sound came again from the bathroom, needling. "What's that damned noise?" he said.

Felix looked at him, confused.

"Can't you hear that?" Rath said. "That noise in the bathroom."

"*Oh,* Ernie and Bert. Canaries. We have two canaries."

"I can't think in here." Rath clunked down the steep staircase.

Outside, he paced on the icy sidewalk. The snow was falling harder, in ghostly motes.

"Tell me more," Rath said, "about this girl."

"She doesn't fit the girl you thought. She was older, mid-twenties. Lived somewhere closer your way than the second meeting place."

"Where was that?"

"Danvers. Some old church rectory. I was supposed to go, but Rachel insisted I study. I couldn't stop her, she's—"

"I know."

"She left a message on my cell after the meeting sort of in hysterics, about how this girl was evil. And how she, Rachel, needed to be alone. Needed a break."

"Did you check to see if her car was parked near the rectory?"

"I don't have a car, and I just found out she wasn't at home when I called you."

Rath wasn't thinking clearly, his mind a walled maze that led to the center of one chronic thought: *Rachel's missing.*

"Fuck." Rath ran to his Scout and jumped in, fired her up. "Get in," he barked. As he pulled onto the street, he snapped his fingers at Felix. "Tell me more."

"I don't know more," Felix said. "I should have never talked her into doing it."

"You talked her into it?"

"She wanted to. She just needed a nudge. Because of what happened last month. I told her that was exactly why she should do it."

"What happened last month?" Rath wanted to throttle Felix.

"The pregnancy."

"Pregnancy?"

"That's why Rachel was so *busy* not returning your calls." Felix's voice was shaky.

"You got my daughter—"

"Not Rachel. Penny. Her roomie."

"You got another girl—"

"*No*. Penny got pregnant on a one-night stand. And she went bat shit, screaming how her life was over. Rachel thought Penny was going to hurt herself, so she finally dragged Penny to Family Matters. Just to get, you know, perspective. While we were at the place, these protestors kept calling Penny and Rachel sluts and murderers who were going to burn in hell. It was a shit show. We went a few times, but Penny miscarried, so—"

"You went, too?"

"Rachel needed me."

Rath shook his head, just when he wanted to kill the kid. "This girl Rachel thought might be our girl. Did she have any tattoos? Piercings? Scars or birthmarks? Anything that sets her apart?" Rath said.

"Purple hair."

"OK, good. Anything else? The way she talked?"

"Nothing."

"Did she dress weird? Slutty or like a Quaker? I don't know. Anything."

Felix rubbed his face. "There was one thing."

"Tell me." Rath squeezed the steering wheel.

"She wore the same shirt, just two days later. I mean, I've done that. Who hasn't?"

"What kind of shirt?"

"A New England Patriots jersey."

Rath stared ahead in astonishment. It hit him like a sledgehammer in the chest. The baby seat. Gale, Mandy's roommate, had said she worked for a day care. She had claimed she was a virgin. She'd ripped him for thinking she was easy, for judging her. When she'd talked about Mandy's books, she'd said it wasn't like they were copies of the Bible. The plaque on the wall, for Race for Life and the trophy for Hero for Life. Not for cancer. But for saving lives of the unborn. Pro Life races and rallies. Gale had told Rath it was Mandy's note on the refrigerator. Mandy's handwriting. And he'd taken her word for it. Mandy hadn't written the notes. Gale had. It all fit.

A truck horn blared behind, and a logging truck whooshed past him. Rath slowed to dial Grout. The call didn't connect. No bars.

He hit the gas, the Scout chugging up to 67 mph when it started to shake. He kept it pegged at 67 mph and dropped the cell in Felix's lap. "Check for bars and hit redial as soon as you see even one; when it rings, give me the phone."

They didn't get service until an hour later, five miles outside of Canaan.

Felix hit redial, and Rath held his palm out for the phone.

Voice mail. Damn it. "Grout. Call me. Now. Rachel's missing."

CHAPTER 54

Rath yanked the car into the driveway behind Gale's VW. *Got you.* He jumped out, commanded Felix, "Stay put!"

He stalked across the yard, eyeing the baby seat in the car, and something else, too. The black beads he'd noticed the first visit, hanging from the rearview. Rosary beads.

Rath pounded so hard on the screen door, he dented it.

The front door opened, and Gale stood there, sleepy-eyed and mussy-haired, her lips dry and split as she cracked her back, her vertebrae making tiny popping sounds like bubble wrap twisted in a fist. "What's with the pounding?" Her eyes were bloody egg yolks, her hair streaked Patriots' red and blue. Purple, where it had run together.

Rath pushed past her, inside.

She spun on him, an athletic move that belied her heft. "You can't just—"

Rath crowded her. "Why do you have the baby seat in your car?"

She blinked her eyes clear.

"Why do you have that baby seat in your car?" Rath repeated, squeezing her shoulders.

She shook his grip free. She was *strong*, easily strong enough to overpower other girls. "I *told* you. I work at a day care."

"What day care?" Rath turned toward a movement to see the cat batting a paw at his boot. He kicked at it and sent it skittering under the couch.

"Hey!" Gale screamed.

"Answer the question."

"Better Days Play School," she snapped.

"Sit," Rath ordered.

Gale's eyes searched his face for a sign of weakness then flopped into the chair. "Happy?"

"No," Rath said. "You're a liar, and my daughter is missing because of you."

"Your daughter?"

Rath held up his phone screen to show Gale a photo of Rachel. Gale swallowed.

"Know her?" Rath said.

Gale shook her head.

"Liar," Rath said, pacing, wiping spittle from his mouth. "Goddamned liar."

"Don't take the Lord's name in vain in my home."

"The Lord?" Rath wagged a finger, nicking the end of her fat nose. Gale's face was rigid with offense and insolence. Rath drew a deep breath, the pissy odor of the cats' litter box burning his nose. "I'm going to check with that day care," he said.

"*Go* for it."

"You said you were a virgin," Rath said, jabbing a finger at her.

She looked like she might bite it off.

"I am."

Rath's hand buzzed to smack her. "Did you have an immaculate conception? Did your Lord's hand anoint your womb? Because that Post-it was yours, with the word Erythromycin on it."

"Fuck you."

"There's our saintly virgin showing her true face," Rath said. "The liar."

"I am *not* lying. I *am* a virgin. In the eyes of the Lord, which is all that matters." She pressed her face in her hands, sobbing. Rath was too intimate with grief to be fooled. It was genuine. It shook him. She looked up, face flush. "I am a born-again virgin. OK? I had sex. *Once.* Four years ago. Before I found God. I fell for a guy's sappy lines, convinced myself he cared. He didn't. Not about anything besides my flesh." She wiped her nose on her sleeve. "All I could think was I was carrying a problem. And." Her face grew ashen. "All I wanted was to be rid of my problem. Getting pregnant was a mistake. What I did after was a sin. Jesus forgave me. But I can't forgive myself. I walk around like my heart's just been cut out."

Sob story, Rath thought. "We have a list of missing girls, all of whom you met at those meetings. *You* are the link."

"After what I did to my own baby, I'd never harm another soul after that."

Rath didn't believe her. She wasn't beyond hurting others, not in the name of a higher purpose, her zealotry a prism through which evil could be construed as godly. If she could convince herself she was a virgin, she could convince herself of anything.

"You're part of The Better Society."

"Yes." She lifted her chin in pride.

Rath could feel the violence trembling in him. "You met my daughter at meetings."

She nodded.

"Did you harm her?"

"*No.*"

"When'd you see her last?"

"I was trying to talk to her after the meeting, and she freaked and ran off."

"Why have you been going to these meetings if you aren't pregnant?"

"To save souls."

"And how do you *save souls*?"

"I let girls know that the thoughts in their heads are the Devil's thoughts. Not their own."

"Why'd Rachel freak out?"

"I mentioned what happened to her mother, your sister, and—"

Rath watched her mouth move but heard no more sound come from it. He shook his head clear. "How do you know about my sister?"

"Rachel used her mother's married name on the sheet. I googled it and found the story—"

Rath stared in horror.

"*You* told her it was a *car wreck*?" Gale said. "And you call *me* a liar?"

Rath slapped Gale across mouth. She stared at him blankly as her lip swelled with blood.

"Where's my daughter?" Rath said.

"I don't *know.*"

"You lied about being a virgin. About the Post-it note and handwriting. How do I know you're not lying now?"

"I am a virgin, in our savior's eyes. I admit I omitted the earthly truth because I'm ashamed. I do pretend I'm pregnant now, at the meetings, God forgive me. But I kept the Post-it stuck to my bathroom mirror to remind me of my sin every time I look in the mirror. When you asked if you could keep it, I couldn't say no. I had to act nonchalant. I'm ashamed. And when you asked for a handwriting sample, I wrote the grocery note to continue to cover."

Rath pressed his thumbs to his temples and looked out the window. The wind was up, rocking the trees. Snow blew like white ash of nuclear fallout. From his cortisone injection site a wave of heat radiated down the back of his legs now.

"Where did you get the idea to go to these meeting to save souls?" Rath said.

"Leslie, my boss at the day care."

"Tell me about her." If it wasn't Gale snagging these girls, it was someone using her for information. Manipulating her.

Gale exhaled. "The day care is for young, single moms who want to finish high school or need to work. Moms like I could have been. And for pregnant girls who decide to have their child and place them into adoption. We give refuge." She touched her swollen lip and winced.

"Tell me about your boss."

"She's taught me so much. She was a missionary in the most *primitive* places, where savages still believe in multiple gods or no god at all. She brought Jesus into my life when I confided in her about my own abortion—"

"How did you come to do that?"

"I was saying one day how I could relate to these

girls. And she read it in my face. She's seen it all. She's like a Mother Teresa. She even *met* Mother Teresa. She touched my hand. It was the kindest touch I ever felt, and said, 'You're a lost soul in Satan's grip.' That got me pissed. We snakes, we don't want to hear the truth. *Satan, the serpent of old, who is the real enemy of God, will not share in his peace.* She told me I was a godless serpent because I had killed my own baby." Gale took a breath. "I got up to leave, but she convinced me to stay, and she read me Bible passages. She gave me her very own personal pocket Bible and told me to read some myself and think on it, and I did, and it spoke to me."

Gale plucked a dog-eared pocket Bible from between the couch cushions. "This is it," she said, setting the Bible in Rath's lap as if he needed it more than she. He fanned the page edges with his thumb, the inside marked with red ink. He slipped it in his pocket.

"She was right," Gale said. "I was a serpent. And had to ask forgiveness. You see?"

Rath saw. He saw Gale really didn't know where Mandy or Rachel was. She was a pawn. "How long before she suggested you save souls?" Rath said.

"A month? There's only so much I could do picketing. I didn't want to be a screamer. I wanted to reach out with love and truth. So, I went to meetings. And reported on them. Which girls could most likely be brought to the side of God. Which ones are lost to Satan."

"And you give your boss names?"

"From the lists. They aren't always accurate. But I befriend the girls, and they confide, tell me their real names and stories. That's why I googled Rachel, to find out more about her so I could befriend—"

"*Manipulate.* What else do you share with this boss?"

"Everything. Backgrounds, families, boyfriends, grades, trouble with drugs or alcohol. It helps us understand how hard it will be to deliver them to God."

Good genes, Rath thought. That's what each missing girl had in common. Each had a trait that set them apart in some respect. The Star Athlete. The Gifted Musician. The Honor Student. The Beauty.

"Did you tell her about Rachel?" Rath said.

"Not yet."

"What does your boss do with the information?"

"What else is there? She determines which ones might be most likely saved, along with their unborn child of course."

Rath took out the photos of the missing girls and fanned them out for her to see. "Have you seen any of these girls since the meetings?"

"Why would I? We couldn't save them. They had their abortions."

"How do you know?"

"They stopped coming. I assumed—"

"These girls have never been seen again. Except…" Rath tapped a finger on the photo of Julia alive. "… Her."

"Well, good, see—"

Rath handed her the photo of Julia's corpse. Gale's face collapsed in a ruin of shock.

"A goat's head was carved into her belly," Rath said, "her feet cut up as if she'd fled for miles over every mountain—" A thought skittered across his brain. *Every mountain.* But the thought escaped.

Gale bowed her head, murmuring, in prayer, tears dripping into her lap.

"Mandy," Rath said. "Do you know if she was pregnant?"

"She had no boyfriends and . . . No."

Rath's cell buzzed. He grabbed it. A text. Grout.

Busy busy. With Betty Malroy in CT.
Recognize this mug?

Rath opened the .jpeg. Saw the photo. An old one.
From the eighties perhaps. A boy. His face disfigured.
He looked vaguely familiar. But the photo was bad.
Grout must have taken a photo of the original with his
camera, and the original looked like a Polaroid. Washed
out. Still there was something about the kid. His.

"Fuck," Rath said, and burst out the door.

CHAPTER 55

Rath was startled to find Felix in the Scout; he'd forgotten all about him. He fired up the engine as another text came in from Grout.

FYI This is from a crime Halloween '85

Rath studied the pic. If he hadn't known otherwise, he'd think he was looking at the carving in Julia's body. Rath knew who the boy was in the first pic. The pieces fell in place: shards of the frail and ghostly bones of facts, from which he pieced together the skeleton of the monster. He could envision the monster: how it lived, what it preyed on and why, the conditions needed for its survival, its lair. He knew where Mandy was. And Rachel.

He could only hope they were alive.

If Rachel had been taken just after the meeting, the monster would know by now she was not what he needed. She was useless. Dispensable.

The Scout skated on the steep, icy hill. Rath countersteered, but the Scout drifted sideways, picking up speed as it spun around on itself, sliding backward, shuddering and threatening to flip. Rath, powerless, let the Scout skim along until it jammed hard against the guardrail and stopped with a crunch of metal.

Felix gaped at him, terrified.

Rath righted the Scout, turned it around, and headed back down the hill, as fast as ever.

In town, he stopped and shouted at Felix, "Get out!" and Felix got out bewildered.

Rath didn't need or want the boy along for this.

CHAPTER 56

The snow lay deep, virgin, unmarred on the dark road as the white madness heaved against the windshield. The wipers groaned. If they quit, Rath would be stuck.

Rath drove over a covered bridge spanning Canaan River, the road turning from asphalt to dirt as the Scout's back end slid, then trundled up the steep dirt road. Hemlocks bowed under the weight of wet snow, choking the road down to a dark throat. Ahead, a stately, wood-carved sign proclaimed: RAVENS WAY. PRIVATE. TURN BACK.

Rath turned onto Ravens Way.

The road grew steeper.

Every quarter mile or so, Rath passed a driveway that went back into an estate, each residence announced with an ornate sign. He saw no lights in the trees. Was the power out? Rath drove, his hands gripped on the wheel like an old-time sea captain at the helm on monstrous seas. The wind rocked the Scout on its sad springs and swept the snow to obliterate visibility.

Slowly, out of the snow, a wrought-iron gate with colossal marble columns materialized. Rath tapped the brakes, and the Scout slid greasily to rest before twisted black bars that rose twenty feet into the night air, tapering to fearsome points. Atop the inner spire of each gate sat a raven sculpture, their savage beaks open wide, calling to the sky. At the center of the gate, the number 4915 was shaped of more wrought iron. Rath wondered why the numbers jumped so much from the last residence, whose sign read 795. The new address numbers for the fire and emergency folks was a fiasco.

He killed the headlights and engine.

The wind bayed in the trees, laces of fine silver snow spilling down.

The Scout's radiator pinged.

Rath took his .22 revolver from the glove box, snapped open its cylinder, and walked it around with his fingers. The brass rounds winked under the cab light. He sneaked out of the Scout and shut the door softly. The night air had a brutally cold edge to it that penetrated his jacket and stung through his jeans.

At the gate, he feared floodlights would flash on, or a surveillance camera would capture him, triggered by motion sensors. He looked for a way around the gate, but the iron fortress disappeared into the woods.

Rath threw a snowball at the gate. No lights came on. He threw several more snowballs along the entrance gate. The world remained dark. The power must have been out.

Scurrying to the marble pillar, he felt above his head, fingers aching with the cold, until he found a crevice. He fixed his fingers into claws and pulled himself up, pushing off with the toe of his boots and groaning. He inched his way up.

He was nearing the top, feeling around with deadened fingers, when his boot slipped, and he slid downward. His chin cracked hard on the stone, and his vision exploded with a lightning flash. He held on and caught his breath, waiting for his vision to return. Then began upward again.

When he at last gained the flat-manteled top of the pillar, he perched on it like a gargoyle, looking back to see his stark tracks in the snow.

There was nothing he could do about them. If Langevine was not home and drove up after him, he'd see Rath's Scout and tracks. But by then, Rath would be waiting for him.

Rath draped over the other side of the wall, dangling. It was his fingers that gave way this time as he plummeted to the ground in a heap. His revolver came loose and spun away in the snow. He felt around for it, his pulse beating fast. He found it and blew snow from it and tucked it back in his waistband. He stood gamely and loped along the edge of the drive.

The drive ribboned lazily, as if to build drama for what was around each next bend. When the house came into view, it was, indeed, dramatic. It rose out of the dark and snow, into view. Except it wasn't a house. It was a Gothic stone manor that would have been more at home among the moors circa 1867. The drive swung in front in a continuous sweep that brought it back on itself, in the center of which a Gothic marble fountain with a winged angel bubbled and steamed.

Rath felt insignificant. The wind blew motes of snow around him. The manor's dark windows shimmered like mercury. So many rooms. So many chambers and hallways and doors. He had to find a covert way inside. He could not simply knock. Surprise was key. How would he find them, Mandy and Rachel? He thought about calling Sonja, but he was out of cell range. He should have called. He should have told Felix where he was headed. But he hadn't. No one knew where he was.

His jaw was stiff where he'd cracked it on the marble stone.

Snowflakes melted in his eyelashes to blur his vision. Gauging by its vaulted leaded windows, the manor was three stories tall, each story at least fifteen feet in height. A watch tower with a marble balustrade sat at each end of the manor, perhaps three hundred feet apart. Rath walked to Tudor doors, set back in an imposing, shad-owed, marble alcove, each door's tiny rectangular win-dows adorned with Roman-cross iron hinges and an iron-ring door knocker.

He studied the immense Tudor doors, whose wood was as dark as dried blood. Where was the crack in the manor's armor? How could he get inside? A structure of solid stone and hardwood doors as thick as cinder block, first-floor windows far out of arm's reach.

He was just stepping off the walk to peer along the shrubbery skirting the front wall when the yard lit up like daylight. He froze and pushed back in the shrubs, leaving behind clear boot tracks in the snow.

The wind cried, his heart dropping into his gut. And over the crying wind, another sound: the sigh of hinges as the front door swung open.

Rath slid his hand down to the revolver's cold handle and waited. A shadow stretched on the walk nearby like a long, accusing finger.

Another sound, dampened by the rising wind. A snuffling.

A dog appeared. Feet away. Black and packed with

powerful muscle, its tail shorn to a blunt thumb of fur. A Rottweiler.

Rath slipped the revolver from his waistband. The dog lifted its wet, leathery nose to the swirling wind. Snot drooled from the nose as it worked eagerly in the air, the dog's blunt, triangular ears cocked forward, its massive chest seemingly carved from black granite. The dog rolled its upper lip back to reveal a jaw like a bear trap. It growled and swung its head toward Rath.

Rath held his breath, set his thumb on the revolver's hammer, inching it backward.

The dog stepped, tensed, growling. Gearing to lunge.

"Come inside," a voice said, freezing Rath in place. The voice had a shrill sting to it. The dog whined, muscles rippling below its coat. "*Inside*," the voice cried. The dog locked eyes with Rath. Its ears flattened.

"*Inside!*"

The wind sagged, and the night fell silent and still.

"He'll tear you apart," the voice said, emotionless now, tempered and cool. "If *you* don't come inside. Show yourself. Otherwise, I'm afraid I'll have to command him to *contain* you."

The voice was talking to *Rath*. Not the dog.

"He'll be on you in a blink, and I'm afraid while we have him trained well to attack, he's frightfully difficult to beg off once he's set his teeth into an intruder. I've phoned the state police. They won't be here for a good half hour. In that time, Brutus will either have made a meal of your innards or you'll have frozen to death. So. Please do. Come. Inside. We'll wait for the police in here, where it's warm and civilized, shall we?"

The police? Why would he call the police if he had Rachel and Mandy inside? Unless he thought Rath was

just some trespasser. A nuisance. He could not know it
was Rath in the hedges. Still, would he want the cops
here under any circumstances if he were holding girls
here? Unlikely. Still. Rath tucked the pistol in the back
of his waistband. Let the cops come. But he needed a
story. Fast.

"I'll give you to the count of three," Langevine said.

"Call the dog off," Rath said.

"Step forward where I may see you."

"Call him off."

"Not till I see you and know I am under no bodily
threat."

"It's me. Frank Rath."

Rath blinked, his eyelashes heavy with ice crystals.
He heard a faint snap.

The dog sat, and its jaw went slack and sloppy, all
dopey jowls, its muscles slackening.

"Dear me!" Dr. Langevine said. "Mr. Rath! Get out
here where I can see you. It's scandalous to be out in this
maelstrom! Whatever are you doing?"

Rath crept out from the bushes, his flesh crawling.
Play it dumb, he thought. He gave Langevine a meek
look, cupping his hand over his eyes against the blowing snow.

"My word!" Langevine said, and snapped his fingers
twice. The dog heaved itself to its feet and clomped inside with a lazy moan, its balls swagging back and forth.

Langevine glided out in slippers that looked like bear
paws and holding the collar of a plush bathrobe to his
turkey's throat. His big, round eyeglasses fogged up.

Rath did not move, the revolver pressing into his
spine as Langevine whooshed toward him. "Come in,
come in! Heavens!" Langevine exclaimed, his voice

bubbling with apology and decorum. Before Rath knew what to do, Langevine had slipped his arm through Rath's own and was ushering him in like a father giving away the bride.

Inside, Langevine shut the door, the echo of it sounding all too much like a door slamming behind a death-row prisoner. Stepping inside the great hall with its flying ceilings was like stepping into a cathedral, a hush falling over him and granting a sense of privacy and reverence. The checkerboard floor of veined white and dark green marble gleamed beneath crystal chandeliers suspended high above, lit weakly, as if by a backup generator. Antique pieces of dark wood and royal blue upholstery, benches and settees, lined each wall. A grandfather clock stood at the far end, its *tick tock* floating up from the hush like the manor's heartbeat.

Langevine's face was as undefined as a charcoal sketch in the ill lighting. A shadow of a Roman cross spread across the floor, caused by the outside lights shining through the Vermeer pattern of the leaded window high above.

Langevine faced Rath with his hands on his hips. "What the *devil* are you *doing*?" he inquired, seeming genuinely mystified. "You scared me half to death, Mr. Rath."

"I came to ask a few more questions, and—"

"You indeed pick the most inclement of conditions to visit." His tone was convivial, percolating with easiness, not the least bit tense or tight with guilt or suspicion, just simple curiosity and bafflement.

"I apologize," Rath said. What was going on here? Had he pegged it all wrong? No. No way. Langevine had to be the boy in the photo, and—

"It's nothing to me," Langevine said, his shoulders

quivering in a sudden, spastic manner, like a bird shaking water from its wings. "I was just nesting next to my toasty fire, indulging in a trashy novel and enjoying a nip. It's not I who braved the elements."

"When questions pop into my mind, I have to ask them. Otherwise, I'm haunted."

"You should have phoned and saved yourself the adventure. I'd have been happy to answer." Langevine delved his fingers into his deep beard, pulling at it as if a sage philosopher.

"I felt it best to ask in person," Rath said.

"I quite understand. After all, *I* can't diagnose my patients by speaking to them over the phone. I need to see them to ask the right questions. Hypochondriacs aside, of course." He smiled and scratched Brutus's head. "But why ever didn't you call to say you were on your way, I'd have fixed you a nip, too. And why ever were you hiding in my bushes? It is peculiar, I have to confess."

Rath's mind spun. He was off course now, knocked unsteady by this unforeseen turn, the congenial welcome and breezy manner of Langevine. He'd have known better what to do if Langevine had sicced the dog on him, or if Langevine himself had brandished a weapon or acted defensive or suspicious in any way. The questions Langevine asked were prying, but he had every right to pry; it was, after all, Rath hiding in the bushes and coming unannounced. Still, Rath didn't like it. It felt like a performance. If it was, Langevine had a career waiting for him on Broadway.

"I tried to call, but my cell had zero bars," Rath said.

"This state could stand to dip its toe a bit more in the twenty-first century, yes?"

"That it could. And I *had* knocked. Before stepping in the bushes."

"Oh?"

Rath nodded. "Likely not loud enough. For the racket the wind was making."

"I doubt I'd hear a knock back where I was. Did you actually scale the gate?" He let out what could only be called a giggle.

Rath shrugged, *guilty as charged*. "Yankee ingenuity," he said. "I'd not expected a gate like that. But I'd come all this way in such shit conditions, and it's still quite early in the evening, so, I climbed it." He shrugged. *I'm a dope.*

"But," Langevine said, "why were you in my shrubs?" There was nothing, not a speck of indication on Langevine's face or in his body language or eyes that betrayed the notion that he thought Rath was a threat, there for his daughter, or that, in fact, Langevine had anything to hide at all, whether he suspected Rath knew about it or not. He simply looked like a man whose sleepy weekday evening had been abruptly interrupted by an unexpected visitor on a night of godforsaken weather that no one in their right mind would brave; and he was acting his best to be understanding and cordial. In other words, he was behaving normally. It was Rath who was not, and who was on defense.

"After I knocked," Rath said, "I attempted to look into a window, see perhaps—I thought maybe there were some windows behind the shrubs or another entrance I could knock on. Then the yard lit up, and"— Rath glanced at Brutus—"he sauntered out, and I froze. I don't care for mean dogs."

"He's not mean. Are you Brutus?" Langevine said, scratching the dog's ear.

"I thought you said—"

"That was when I thought *you* were an intruder. I've been known to fib, if circumstances warrant. But. He's harmless. He acts the part. But. We're a long ways up here; isolated, nothing to the west or east or south for miles. Behind the house, you could tramp for miles before you hit a road. But given the slim odds that someone would actually do something *bad,* I can't balance that against the cost of a lawsuit if I were to have a killer dog on the property and the errant UPS man got gobbled up!" He giggled again, slapped Rath on the back, and said, "Come relax by the fire while we wait for our friends, the state police."

"We shouldn't waste their time," Rath said, wanting to call his bluff, if it was a bluff. "We should call and tell them what happened. Not to come. On a night like this, they've probably got plenty to do with—"

"I called 911. You can't undo 911, as I'm sure you know. We can wait for them in comfort, then explain it all. Have a guffaw. It is rather humorous. Don't you think?"

Rath did know. Once 911 was dialed, the police showed. No matter what. Rath was torn. He'd come storming up here with a loaded gun, certain his daughter was housed here, a prisoner along with another girl. Locked away in a manor where he suspected at least four other girls had been kept to . . .

"Everything okay?" Langevine asked, blinking up at him. "You look . . . stunned."

"I am," Rath said. "From staring out the windshield at a blizzard."

"Let's have that nip." Langevine clapped Rath on the back again, then led him to a tight hallway cast in a muddy light from frosted-amber sconces. The hall was so small, Rath could drag his fingertips along each wall and touch the ceiling.

Langevine opened the door and swept his hand to permit Rath to enter first into a library lit in the same dull, amber glow as the hallway, the source of which was now a fire in a massive stone fireplace at the far wall. Shadows and light danced together on the teak paneling and woodwork.

"Warm up. Be comfortable," Langevine said, permitting Rath to enter. The fire alone lit the room, shadows and light playing about the room as the flames leapt.

"Sit," Langevine said, "goodness."

Rath sat hesitantly in the wingback chair that faced the door. The fire roared and cracked and threw off its intense heat, which blasted Rath's icy face and hands, making his skin itch to life. The revolver dug into his back. He felt disarmed, but he could not just sit and have a drink. If Rachel wasn't here, Rath was wasting time he couldn't afford to waste. Yet. Everything had pointed to it. All the facts. Or, the facts as he'd arranged them in his mind. Now he had enough doubt that he couldn't just brandish the revolver in Langevine's face and demand he take him to the dungeon, just in time for the state cops to witness it. It seemed outrageous now, that this meek man of medicine was responsible for missing girls, that as a child he'd sliced open a woman, and—

An idea struck him. He stood.

"Sit, please," Langevine said as he swept his tiny, manicured hand toward the chair. He tonged ice cubes from an ornate silver bucket and dropped several tidy cubes into a snifter, lifted a bottle of scotch from among a collection of bottles. He poured two fingers of the honeyed liquid slowly, the cold ice cracking with a snap as the scotch slipped among it.

Langevine pushed the drink toward Rath, scotch sloshing at the rim. Rath took the glass.

"Shit," Rath said.

Langevine raised an eyebrow. "You don't care for ice? A *neat* man. I should have sussed."

"No. It's fine. I prefer it. I just think I left my dome light on." Rath needed an excuse to get outside to meet the cops alone and explain his suspicions in private. Have them *radio* Sonja. Since they'd been called to the house, anything deemed suspicious while on the premises gave them authority to search. It was the legal equivalent of a vampire needing to be invited into your home to have access to its powers.

"Excuse me?" Langevine said, confused. He poured himself a neat scotch from the same bottle.

"Before I got out of my Scout," Rath said. "I was rummaging for my notepad, and I turned on my dome light. If I left it on like a dimwit, the battery in that old jalopy—"

"The police will surely jump-start you," Langevine said.

A thought snapped to attention in Rath's head then was gone.

"I'd rather not look the fool," he said, and sipped his scotch. It was the smoothest scotch he'd ever tasted, the booze going straight to his brain, seemingly not obliged to take the trip through the circulatory system to which the Islays Rath drank were subjected. He glanced at the bottle: Glenmorangie 25-Year.

"Sublime, yes?" Langevine said, smiling.

"Mmm," Rath said, and indulged in a second longer sip before setting down his glass on the marble table-top. He worked his jaw back and forth to stretch his face muscles, the wonders of the scotch making fast work of him, the gums of his back molars feeling puffy, his face lax and numb.

Langevine glanced at the wingback chair. "Sit," he said. "Please."

"Look," Rath said. "I'll be straight. I didn't leave the dome light on. I'm embarrassed. I came up here and barged in planning to ask what I now see were weak questions at best."

"Ask them anyway."

"No."

"No?" Langevine's face squirmed beneath his beard, his eyes pinched down behind his large eyeglasses. His flop of bangs stuck to his forehead with sweat.

"I've bothered you enough," Rath said. "The fact is, I've already made a big enough fool of myself. I'm sorry I bothered you at all."

Langevine stared at him for a long, steady, uneasy moment. "Well," he said, and sighed. "We all make mistakes. Yours is quite inconsequential in the scheme of things."

Rath blinked. For a moment the room listed, then righted itself. It wasn't just the scotch. It was absolute exhaustion, and not having had anything proper to eat in days. Rath took one last long pull of his scotch, reluctant to relinquish it, and said, "I really must go. I've imposed enough."

Langevine made to put a hand to Rath's back, where the revolver was snugged in his waistband. Rath dodged him, squirted past, out into the hall, which seemed to have grown to the size of Penn Station after the tight quarters of the fireplace room.

High above, chandeliers swayed on a draft.

Rath walked down the hall, his footfalls echoing in his ears though he could not actually feel the marble floor beneath him. Langevine followed at his side, drinking his scotch. Rath's throat felt scratchy and choked, as if he'd swallowed steel wool. He cleared his throat, the sound a *whoosh* in his brain.

At the door, he gave his best smile, the smile feeling loose and manic, and said, "Again, I aplog-apologize."

"Do not fret," Langevine said. "Drive safely. I'll work the gate for you so you don't have to climb back out." He giggled and opened the door, and a gush of wind was sucked into the house as if the manor were a beast sucking in a terrific breath.

The wind nearly knocked Rath over as snow swirled in. "Sorry," he said, and stepped out into the rejuvenated storm.

The door closed behind him with a solid, deadening *thunk*.

CHAPTER 57

Rath pushed headlong down the walk, disoriented and depressed. He jammed his hands into his jacket pocket and waited for the gate to open. It didn't. He stared back at the manor, his footprints already blasted to oblivion by the blowing snow. He pulled on the gate to see if maybe it was frozen in place. No. Locked.

The front light in the alcove blinked out, and the walk fell dark. What was going on? Did Langevine suspect Rath was going to wait for the cops? The snow was falling so hard and being blown so fiercely now, Rath could not see his boots. He put a foot up on an outcrop of the marble pillar and was reaching up for a finger hold to attempt to climb again when he heard a sharp metallic clank and an electric whir as the gates spread open.

Rath fought against the gale to the Scout. He started up the rig and cranked the heat, waiting to thaw, his head sodden. He ran the wipers and watched the gate yawn shut as he waited for the cops.

And waited.

Until it hit him like an anvil from the sky. *You don't close a gate when cops are expected any minute. You leave the gate open.*

No cops were coming.

They'd never been called.

Langevine had deceived him, lulled him with his smiling mug and his cloying nonchalance. Langevine had known, or suspected at least, why Rath had showed up at his door. The doctor had played up the casual, befuddled reception, welcoming Rath with an air of natural curiosity, clapping him on the back and feeding him top-shelf scotch.

Rath's gut seized with nausea. He shut his eyes and leaned forward, breathing hard through his mouth to calm his guts, which felt as if he'd drunk down bacon grease now congealing into a lump of hard fat in his intestines. His head clanged. His vision was watery. He spit up bile. Was that blood in it?

The scotch. If Langevine himself had not drunk from the same bottle, Rath would have suspected perhaps. But he had drunk from the same bottle.

The ice. The melting ice. Langevine had his scotch neat. No ice.

Fuck.

Rachel was in there. And Mandy. Rath felt it. Knew it.

His guts heaved, and he stumbled from the Scout and shoved his fingers down his throat, past his tonsils, and vomited until there was nothing left to vomit, until he was emptied and feverish. Then he did it again, gagging dryly.

He stood, leaning on the Scout's fender, and rubbed snow on his face and neck.

He stared at the gate, thinking, recalling what Langevine had said with a chill in his spine: *Behind the house you could literally tramp for miles before you come to the nearest road.* It struck him, what had skittered in his brain earlier when speaking with Gale. *Every mountain.*

Rath plucked his Gazetteer from under the Scout's seat. Yes, there it was. If you followed a line back up from where they'd found Julia's body, followed it up and back for miles, it took you to Canaan summit, a wilderness barren of homes or roads. But. Down the other side of that summit. This side. You came to Ravens Way. The back of Langevine's estate.

If Julia had escaped from here, she'd escaped out the back and immediately run straight away from her prison. There had to be a way out from behind. An in.

Rath stalked through the trees, mindless of the branches whipping his face. A warm trickle of blood slithered down his cheek as he staggered toward the iron fencing.

The terrain grew rocky with granite stone left behind by the glaciers. Ankle breakers. Head crushers. He picked his way, reaching into darkness as black as a covered well, and found the cold iron bars of the fence. He grabbed them, not wanting to fall off a ledge. His screams, his body, would be swallowed up forever.

He trudged along the perimeter, pulling himself forward by the iron bars, the snow deepening as he gained elevation, and the trees thinned. He stopped to gain his breath and peered through the iron bars. The cuffs of his wool pants were stiff as metal sheets with caked ice, his feet numb. The back of the manor had to be near.

He plowed through snow up to his thigh, the wind wailing, his frozen face and ears singing with pain.

The fence ended.

It was there, then gone.

Rath held on to the last bar and groped around for more fencing in the dark. But when he made to take another step, there was only empty air. How far down it fell, there was no way of knowing.

He held fast to the fence and inched around the end of it to solid ground. He was convulsing. Eyes burning. He tried to flex his fingers, but they would only bend at the first joints. The tips were dead.

He stared into the wind, toward where the house had to be. The snow stung his face. There. A dim light. He felt around in the snow. The ground was level. A lawn.

He pushed toward the pale light in the blizzard until he knocked up against a hulking metal contraption, a behemoth outdoor smoker, caked in ice. He slipped past it and came to the back of the manor, the wind flagging at the lee side, the snow falling gracefully. He stood in what looked like an outdoor patio, shaped in an arcing half-moon from a portico and edged by marble Greek balustrades capped with snow.

The light came from a window situated at least a foot above his line of sight.

He looked around for something to stand on.

There was nothing.

A shadow crossed a lit window upstairs, ghostlike.

Rath tucked close to the wall and found a door in the portico. He tried the knob. It was locked. He pondered breaking a windowpane, but he could not risk alerting Brutus.

As he walked the edge of the patio, he heard a flapping sound, like someone airing out a carpet. At the bottom of the door: a dog's entrance. The plastic flap slapped in the wind. Rath knelt and pushed the flap but was met with resistance. A piece of Plexiglas was screwed tight to the frame. He leaned against the Plexiglas with his shoulder, and it gave with a *pop*. Rath froze, waiting. When no light went on or noise came from inside, he squeezed through the dog door and lay on the floor, listening, hearing nothing but the whining wind. He was in. Thank you, Brutus.

Gingerly, he stood, his back protesting. The room was empty and cold, a three-season affair the size of a wedding banquet hall, the floor a jigsaw of multicolored slate. He stepped briskly across the room, feeling for his revolver with numbed fingers that stung ferociously as they warmed.

He worked the doorknob of a grand door. It turned with a click, and he pushed open the door and stepped deftly into a room with vaulted ceilings, gun drawn.

The room was dark, but he could make out a billiard table with the balls tidily racked at one end and a pair of cues crossed like swords at the other end. Beside it stood an ornate bar of dark wood, teak maybe. A flat-screen TV on the wall facing him was so immense, Rath at first did not recognize it as anything but a wall itself. It was the size of a drive-in movie screen. On the wall to his left was a stone fireplace with an elaborately carved marble mantel. This fireplace ran on propane gas, its pilot light pulsing in the dark room like a glowing blue eye of a madman. Above the mantel was hoisted a crucifix on which a life-size Jesus hung by the nails driven in his palms.

He slipped through a door into a hallway, revolver out, fingertips smarting with a prickling sensation, as if he were grabbing hold of cactus. Frostbite. He'd likely lose a finger, or two.

He prowled down the hallway toward a sickly light bleeding out from under a doorway at the end of the hall, stopped with his back to the wall to calm his breathing.

Light leaked from the antique doorknob's skeleton keyhole. He squeezed his revolver and put his eye to the keyhole as the woman's voice rose to a fervent pitch, words enunciated with a hard, precise bite of the teeth, as if each syllable were being punched out from a sheet of tin.

"Renstrom has led the way!" she bellowed. "He has soldiered in the trenches of the heartland for ten years. With steadfast heroism, he has enacted laws in his home state of Missouri to save our innocent unborn! He has been vilified and libeled and attacked for speaking the Holy Truth! For calling abortion what it is!" The woman's voice reached an incantatory crescendo, mesmerizing, orgasmic.

Rath pressed his eye tight to the keyhole but could make out only the jog of shadows on the wall. Rath lunged into the room, revolver up and swinging.

There stood Betty Malroy, wailing: "He has made it through his trials of fire *because* he speaks the Holy Truth. God's Truth! And he has made it nearly to the Promised Land, and if you get behind him, it is a win not just for the United States, no! But for God!" She sliced a finger through the air, as if to cut a throat. Her face was scarlet with fury. Insanity. A daub of spittle frothed at the corner of her mouth like a spiderweb.

She looked like she might faint from rapturous overload.

"We will win this war!"

Rath stared as Malroy continued her rant, oblivious to him because she was an image on a flat-screen TV that overlooked what could only be viewed as an altar, the room itself strung with pews, a small chapel with walls adorned with paintings of the Crucifixion.

Rath raced down the hall toward a spiral staircase where light from above pooled on the wrought-iron landing. He climbed the stairs quietly until he found himself in another vast corridor of marble.

At the far end, a single bright light shone like the lone headlight of a locomotive in a tunnel, casting a silver glow on the marble floor. A figure stepped across the light and was gone.

Rath hurried, the marble floors making it impossible to tread quietly, his footfalls seeming to boom around him. At the end of the hall, he panted and looked down the hall toward where the person had gone. Empty. He crept down the hall, looked left then right down the next hall. The place was a labyrinth.

He was about to venture left when he heard it: a weak, muffled sound, like a child sobbing into a pillow.

He waited.

There. A mewl.

It seemed to come from within his skull. A dream sob. A nightmare.

The sob floated along the floor, drifted from under the door like a sonic fog.

No. Not from under the door, from the vent beside the door. He crawled to the vent and put his ear to it. A girl's voice, pleading: "Help."

Rachel?

A voice, a woman's voice, not Malroy's, cried up through the vent: "For the body is not meant for sexual immorality, but for the Lord, and the Lord for the body!"

Rath was pushing off the floor to stand when the hall-way imploded in brilliant light, and the back of his skull cracked open.

He rolled onto his back, head screaming, and looked up to see Langevine standing over him, smiling.

In one hand, Langevine held a pool ball, slick with what Rath imagined was his own blood. Dangling from his other hand, a knife of gleaming steel, sterile, its blade long and slim. Wicked.

Langevine's face cracked open wider with a mad jack-o'-lantern grin. "It'd have been much"—he scratched his thick beard—"easier for you if you'd simply stayed and finished your scotch. You'd simply have slipped away and never awoken. Very peaceful. I had your feelings in mind. You'd never have had to suffer this indignity, as swiftly as I will try to make it for you now. I've grown quite adept at it. Surgical. Of course, if you care to drink the scotch, I'll permit that. I am not a cruel man."

Rath felt sure his skull was cracked open along its seams, his brain oozing out.

He kept his eyes locked on Langevine's eyes and crawled his hand in the shadows beside him, trying to locate the revolver.

Langevine stabbed Rath's hand and it burst with a supernova pain as he swallowed his scream, not want-ing to alert the woman, was it Leslie, Gale's boss, down there with Rachel?

Langevine picked up the revolver and fiddled with it, opened the cylinder and tipped out the bullets so they clacked onto the floor. "I hate guns. So . . . dispassionate. Cowardly even. Wouldn't you agree?"

He leaned down, his face inches from Rath's face, and smiled. Beneath the masking scent of mint mouthwash, his hot breath so rancid Rath recoiled. Langevine squeezed Rath's jaw and met Rath's eyes with his own. His eyes were . . . wrong. Somehow. The irises as black as the pupils. Lightless. Magnified by his thick eyeglasses, the blackness swam in the whites, an island of black in a puddle of white. Rath had taken Langevine's eyes as odd due to his eyeglasses magnifying them. He saw now the eyes themselves were abnormally large.

"Yes. My eyes," Langevine said, his breath caustic enough to shrivel a flower. "And. My breath. Side effects of Sjogren's syndrome, I'm afraid. An autoimmune-system disorder." He waved his hand around as if batting at phantom mosquitoes. "It affects the mucous membranes and moisture-secreting glands. Thus. No saliva. Dry mouth. Bad breath. No tears either." He shrugged. "Waa. An annoyance compared to the joint pain I suffer in my knees and hips, and the ongoing attack on my liver and thyroids. Rheumatism and arthritis since I was five years old. Dreadful." He giggled as if amused by an old joke.

Rath eased himself to sit against the wall. The pain from the stab wound volcanic. Blood spread out on the floor from where his palm rested.

A whimpering came from the vent, and Rath tensed.

"A shame," Langevine said. "It's a monstrous business, as I believe I mentioned in our initial interview."

"What?" Rath said. He wanted to keep him talking.

A whimper rose out of the vent. Rachel? Rath thought his heart might burst.

Langevine looked Rath in the eye. "I'd rather be alive and the way I am than have been murdered by my own mother."

Rath fought the urge to spring on Langevine. He'd

only be stabbed to death. He needed the precise moment if it came.

Langevine put his face close to Rath's again, smiling.

Rath squinted. There was something wrong with
Langevine's face, too. Up close, it was asymmetrical. As
if it were a mask that had been broken to pieces and the
pieces had been stitched back together again with meticulous precision, but with a few parts missing, so the
face did not quite add up.

"Your mother," Rath croaked, wanting to occupy
Langevine and take a shot at putting the doctor's narrative together. "Tried to murder you?"

Langevine grabbed Rath by the hair and knocked
his head against the wall, Rath's skull imploded in a
white-hot atomic blast in the desert of his barren mind.
Fluid trickled from the back of his head, down his neck.
Rath closed his eyes, the backs of their lids overexposed
X-rays of his capillaries. He opened his eyes again, the
lids leaden. Langevine's pale palm rose in front of his
eyes, as big as the moon, the knife in it looking sharp
enough to cut clear to the spine with one easy swipe.

Langevine smiled, languorously. He was enjoying
this. Enjoying sobs from the vent. Enjoying Rath's torment like a sick child torturing a frog.

"She," Langevine snarled, "that thing that carried me,
was not my real mother. My real mother"—he rolled
his eyes toward the ceiling, and Rath almost lunged—
"rescued me from the slattern that conceived me." Langevine cocked his head dreamily, as a woman's voice
drifted from the vent: "But the cowardly, the unbeliev-
ing, the vile, the murderers, the sexually immoral, their
place will be in the fiery lake of burning sulfur!"

"My *real* mother," Langevine said, "saved me from

that bloodless thing that *incubated* me and plotted to murder me when I was six months in her belly. Six months. A helpless, wee thing, I was."

Rath crept his hand toward the revolver while Langevine drank in his one-man audience. The revolver was empty, but it could break a nose if swung hard enough.

"My *real* mother saved me from that venomous bitch's womb," Langevine said, his voice dramatic, a PBS narrator's voice, as if he'd practiced all his life to tell his tale aloud. "I was an *innocent*. In the third trimester, when she'd learned I had . . . *issues*. Was *defective*. I fed on her blood. I shared her oxygen. I *lived inside* her. I was *of* her. And she wanted to pull me out by the root because I was a weed instead of a flower. Discard me on a compost heap with the other weeds. Kill me so she could try again. That's what they all say, when it's *inconvenient*. *I'm young, I'm healthy, I can try again. When the time is right.* Well, what about *my time*?" He slammed the blunt end of the knife handle down on Rath's stabbed hand and Rath thought he might pass out from the pain. Langevine leaned in close, his nose touching Rath's nose. The stench of his breath seemed to suck the oxygen from the hallway. "What about *my life*?" he said quietly, pleading his case. "I deserved to live. Didn't I?"

Langevine tore at his face as if to peel the skin from it, and his beard pulled free. It was a masterful fake.

Rath inched his fingers closer to the revolver. Felt its cold barrel touch a fingertip.

Langevine held the fake beard in his hand like the pelt of a skinned rodent. His jaw was squeezed at the sides, cheeks deformed and sunken, as if his head had been extruded through a straw. He grabbed at his hair and yanked free a wig and tossed it aside to reveal a frail, luminous skull hideously caved at either side just behind the temples, the pale skin a ruin of raised scar tissue as red and ragged as stitches on a baseball.

"My real mother saved me. *Loved* me. For a while. But. Even she proved not worthy of my love. Weak."

Rath sat spellbound by this creature before him. There was no other word for him other than *monster*.

"My face may be the face of a ghoul, but my heart is pure." He laughed. His eyes shone with elated glee, with love, as he licked his lips. "I am a doctor. I help people. I save lives!" he screeched, jutting a frail finger at the vent. Rath did not want to hear anymore. He wrapped his fingers around the revolver.

Langevine looked at Rath, lazily. "It will all be over soon."

"That's my daughter," Rath said.

Langevine stared at him blankly. "I don't know your daughter. It's unfortunate, if she is."

"She's not pregnant."

"Don't embarrass yourself by lying for her," Langevine snorted.

"She's *not* pregnant."

"She just goes to Family Matters support meetings for the conversation, does she?" Langevine giggled, lost in an insane hilarity. "Don't fret. God forgives. But *I* don't."

"Let them go," Rath said.

"Them?"

"My daughter and Mandy."

"Mandy? Mandy is my *patient*. I would never. Could never. No matter what sin she committed. What do you take me for?" His eyes were dazzling with wild madness. He closed them then, for just a second, as if in reverie, and Rath swung the revolver. Hard.

It struck Langevine's hand, the one that held the knife, with the cracking of bone.

Langevine peeled off a cry, pinwheeling with a look of surprise as Rath swung the revolver again, across Langevine's face, gashing his cheek.

Langevine squealed, and Rath pounced, pinned this sick, deformed child beneath him and struck his face and skull again and again with the revolver, smashing Langevine's face until he lay still on the floor, blood leaking.

Rath fumbled for the .22 shells on the floor in the dark hallway, but he was shaking too badly to get hold of them. He snatched up the knife and ran down the hallway and took the stairs three at a time, slipping across the marble floor of the landing before charging down a hallway, toward a door behind which a girl pleaded: "Someone. Help."

Rath burst into the room. On a flat-screen TV on the near wall, a very young Betty Malroy incanted, "Behold, I was shaped in iniquity; and in sin did my mother conceive me."

"Who's there," a girl moaned from behind a curtain.

Rath threw back the curtain to see neither Rachel nor Mandy Wilks, but a girl he vaguely recognized as Rebecca Thompson, her ankles and wrists bound with leather straps to a metal table. He went to her. Her face was gaunt and pallid, but her eyes lit upon seeing him. Then teared up.

Rath undid the girl's straps, and the girl draped her arms around him and squeezed him as Rachel had when she was a little girl, crying as Rachel had when she was a baby.

Where was Rachel?

Rath laid the girl back down and searched the room. Rachel was not there.

"Where is Rachel?" Rath demanded from the girl. "Where is she?"

"Who?"

"My daughter. Where is she?"

CHAPTER 58

The red and blue lights of the ambulance and the state-trooper cruisers kaleidoscoped across the snowy lawn and danced on the stone façade of the manor as the girl was wheeled out on a gurney, a nest of hoses and tubes hooked to pumps and IV bags as she was thrust into the back of the ambulance and driven away.

Rath saw a state trooper standing by his cruiser, speaking to a man cloaked head to toe in a white forensics jumpsuit, booties, and cap.

Rath strode over and interrupted. "Did you find my daughter?" Rath said.

"Excuse me?" the trooper said.

"Did you find my daughter? Did you find Rachel?"

"We found no one else, sir."

"You searched the place?"

"We had a team in there, sir. There was no one else but Dr. Langevine and his dog."

"You're sure?"

"Yes sir. Very."

"What about Mandy Wilks?"

"We found no other girls, sir."

CHAPTER 59

Grout shook his head, noting that Larkin was doing the same. Both were in disbelief at what Betty Malroy was saying.

"I thought my son was dead," she kept saying. "I thought Martin was dead."

"Tell me again, more slowly," Grout said. "So Officer Larkin here can get it all."

Betty Malroy nodded, her body wilting, a defeated woman. A woman at the end of her days, with nothing left to do but confess it all.

"I was a nurse living in squalor for all my good labor and godly deeds, and that rich, filthy Marianne King, she came to me and waved fistfuls of dirty dollars in my face, believing me, a good woman, a godly woman, would succumb to it, give up her God for money, and cut a child from her, a child *six months* in the womb.

"I couldn't *have* a child. But, I had prayed to God to provide. And God blessed me. You understand that, don't you? So. Instead of performing the evil she asked of me, I put her under and induced her, and I delivered my child. It was not easy. Mind you. It took great will. And. That baby. My son. He was not . . . ready. Things back then. Well. They were. Crude. I was forced to use forceps. And suction. I'm afraid it did not do him well. Physically. And believe me, it took a great deal to keep him alive. It took a lot of praying. A lot of God's graces. And I believed then that if God wanted him to live, he would live. And he did. God granted me a miracle. Or so I thought."

Grout rubbed his eyes and pinched his nose, disbelieving.

"Shortly after," Betty Malroy said, "I moved and got a nursing job in another hospital, and I faked a pregnancy.

"I kept him alive. As my own. Nursed and nurtured him, as any loving mother would. And he blossomed. Oh he did.

"I made one mistake. I was young. I was bitter and strident and so self-righteous. I told him."

"You told him what?" Grout said, prodding her, even though he'd heard her spew it earlier, in a state of foaming lunacy. He needed to hear it again, when she was calm, if in a stupor.

"I told him about her. His so-called biological mother. It was a mistake. He was too young to process it. Just thirteen, but so slight. So frail. Ill. He's always been ill. Weak. He was thirteen, but anyone who saw him would say he was an eight-year-old, a sickly eight-year-old at that. And. Well. He couldn't take it. And when I read in the papers about her on Halloween. I knew."

"So you sent him away soon after?" Larkin said, writing in his notepad.

"January of '87, yes, as soon as I was able. He had

some surgeries over there. Hormonal therapy, to help him grow. Plastic surgery to try to . . . correct his face. I—"

"You blackmailed Renstrom," Grout said, his anger steeping. His disgust.

"That was business. Renstrom sinned. Had an affair. The way you put it, it lacks decorum."

"Decorum?" Grout said, his voice echoing in the bared room. "You talk to me about decorum—"

"I'm a mother. Renstrom helped me and my son. But then. Well. Martin became . . . He was unmanageable. And we lost touch after he turned eighteen."

"Until?" Grout said.

"Until he wrote me from London, saying he'd become *someone else*, someone better than me, and if I did not give him—" She adjusted the chopsticks in her hair, patted the bun gently with the pads of her fingers. "An allowance. A significant allowance to be deposited regularly into an account. He would make it known. What I'd done."

"And you could not have that?" Grout said, stepping toward her.

The old woman shrunk into herself.

"No. I could not have that."

"You're coming with us," Grout said. He grabbed the woman's pale, fragile wrist and squeezed.

"Sir," Larkin said. "We have no jurisdiction, you can't just—"

"Get up," Grout ordered. He yanked on her arm, and her face fell slack, her eyes grew wide and vacant, and she began to shake.

"Sir," Larkin said.

The old woman slumped in the chair, eyes rolling up in her head.

"Sir," Larkin said, "something's wrong with her."

Spittle frothed out of the old woman's mouth, and a single thread of blood trickled from her nostril.

CHAPTER 60

As Rath drove through town, his eyes searched for Rachel's car, for Rachel walking along the dark street. He tried her number again and again and got nothing.

Pulling down his drive, his cell phone lit up, buzzing. He snatched it. Rachel's number shone in the dark of the Scout.

"Rachel," Rath gasped into the phone.

Static broke up a voice.

"Rachel?"

"Dad?"

Rath pulled the Scout to a stop. "Rachel, where are you? What—"

"I'm at the Monadnock Motel."

"I'll send the police, I—"

"I'm all right, Dad. I saw you on TV. And. I'm so sorry, you must have thought—"

Rath sagged against the steering wheel, bewildered and elated, feeling scraped out and raw as he fought to gain his composure and keep his voice from breaking.

"Come home," he said.

CHAPTER 61

Rath sat slouched on the floor, back against the couch in the darkened living room, blindly watching the TV on mute. Rachel was asleep in her old bedroom, but Rath did not want to chance waking her. She needed her rest.

The psychological and emotional toll she'd endured from learning the truth about her parents had scarred her. Changed her. Diminished her buoyancy and zest. Deadened her eyes. It had driven her to hole up in the motel, isolate herself from this man who loved her and had betrayed her. Rath could only hope her estrangement from him was temporary and his daughter would return. She'd not had the energy these past days to show the anger he knew she must have for him. There would be many hard days ahead. He was prepared for them. He'd wanted to talk to her about it when she'd come home, but she'd been too exhausted. All he could do was be there for her when she was ready. She had Felix, too. A good kid. A good young man. He cared for Rachel and had been there for her. He was out now getting her favorite take-out pizza from town for when she woke up. He was strong and nurturing and caring. Tender. Everything Rath had not been at his age.

The news came on, and Rath got up and crouched right in front of the TV, so close he could feel the heat of the screen. He turned the volume up the slightest so only he could hear it from a couple feet away.

A bleached-blond female reporter looked all of fifteen years old as she stood in front of the St. Johnsbury courthouse, her overly sprayed golden locks vibrating in the wind.

She messed with her earpiece for a moment then addressed the camera with her best serious, big-girl face.

"A Dr. Martin Langevine was arraigned today on shocking charges that rocked the small town of Canaan, Vermont, and stunned the entire country. The charges include kidnapping, torture, and one count of first-degree murder of a girl whose name has not been released. More charges may be pending."

The reporter paused. She looked bewildered.

"It was briefly thought that Langevine's mother was involved. Betty Malroy, seventy-two, a former nurse and the founder of The Better Society nonprofit for family values, and Better Days Play School, which caters to at-risk single moms and their kids.

"Dr. Langevine has allegedly made dramatic claims that Malroy is not his actual birth mother, and as a nurse induced his birth from a woman who had asked her for an illegal abortion. He claims Malroy kept him as her own, and that he knows this because she told him of it when he turned thirteen. He has also confessed to the 1985 Halloween attack on a Mrs. Marianne King, whom he claims was the woman carrying him at the time. Marianne King had no comment.

"It is known that Betty Malroy owns Better Days Adoption Agency, and it was thought there might be a connection between it and Langevine's motive. However—"

Rath drew closer to the TV, glanced back over his shoulder toward Rachel's doorway.

"—one Mr. Boyd Pratt III," the reporter continued, "a prominent Vermont citizen from a distinguished family who recently put in place plans to adopt a child from Better Days, has refused to speak with us. His lawyer insists Mr. Pratt met with Ms. Malroy at a resort in Stowe to finalize the legal adoption. But in light of the news, he will not be moving forward with the agency. It is alleged other girls might have met with Betty Malroy at the resort about possible illegal adoption, though what connection this has to her son's alleged crimes is yet unclear.

"It is also alleged that Dr. Langevine stalked his victims outside meetings for group counseling for pregnant women and lured the young girls with his slight physical stature by assuming the guise of an elderly woman in need of help. Dr. Langevine has allegedly said that he did what he did to save other innocents from dying. That girls 'like this' have many abortions and he was preventing many murders by doing God's work. He was quoted as saying: 'Now, we must rescue those who are unjustly sentenced to death; don't stand back and let them die.'"

The reporter tucked a length of hair behind her ear. She was outside in the cold, and her makeup was beginning to crack. Rath thought he heard a noise behind him and looked back toward Rachel's room, to find nothing but a dark hallway.

"It has been reported that the remains of two other

girls were found in an incinerator at the back edge of the estate on Ravens Way."

Rath knew from Sonja that the other girls were Sally and Fiona. Where was Mandy? Why had they not found her?

The reporter continued, "It is believed that each girl had been pregnant at the time of abduction, and that Dr. Langevine tried to keep the girls alive long enough for them to give birth, but—"

The reporter turned abruptly away from the camera toward the court steps, the camera trying to get back in front of her. "It appears Dr. Langevine is coming out now."

The camera swung and its angle went wide to capture both her and Langevine as he descended the steps slowly. His movement was stiff. His face was scabbed and bruised. A vicious zipper of stiches ran the length of his left cheek, from his eyebrow to the corner of his mouth. He looked washed out, until he stepped up straight to the camera, and flashed a look of supreme confidence and defiance.

"Today, I pleaded not guilty to these absurd charges, based on the defense of Vermont's Third-Person Defense Statute."

Rath blinked. This was insane. What was he possibly arguing? Was he setting himself up for an insanity plea, or something else much more cunning?

"This defense statute states—" Langevine squared himself: "'A person may defend the life of another third person when that third person is unable to defend itself against personal bodily harm. And if that third person is being threatened with mortal violence, they may be defended in kind.' That is *exactly* what the law states. And that is exactly what I did. I am a doctor. I heal people. *Save* them. I obeyed Vermont's law. God's law." His tongue flicked like a viper's.

Rath turned up the volume slightly, breathless at the words coming from this man's mouth and the certainty with which he spoke them.

Langevine smiled as if he'd just been elected president, and made the sign of the cross. "Psalm 82:4 reads: 'Rescue the weak and needy and innocent; deliver them from the hand of the wicked.' I tried to do just that, even if I may have failed at it."

Astonishingly, a smatter of cheers arose from the crowd.

The reporter looked as flummoxed as a cheerleader at a spelling bee, her heavily made up eyes batting, the mascara starting to seize in the cold, giving her a slightly frozen, frightful look. But, she jabbed a mike in front of a woman cheering and asked, if not in the most professional manner, perhaps the most sincere: "Why in the world are you cheering?"

The woman shouted, "He dares to do what is in his *heart*. We are——"

"Turn it off," a frail voice said, and Rath turned from where he was crouched, the TV's sick light playing on him, to see Rachel staring at him, hollow-eyed and brokenhearted, clutching her bathrobe to her throat. "*Please*, turn it off."

Rath picked up the remote and clicked off the TV, then turned back to Rachel. But she was gone, and all he saw was the light of her bedroom extinguished as her door shut with hard *click*.

RATH JOLTED AWAKE on the floor, blinking in the darkness.

"Dad," a voice whispered in the chilly room.

Rath rubbed his eyes and blinked in the darkness.

Rachel knelt beside him. She had a blanket, and she unfolded it now and lay it over him, making certain to cover his feet, pulling the blanket up to his chin.

He reached from under the blanket and touched her hand. It was cold. "How long have you been out here?" he said.

She shrugged. "Awhile."

He propped himself against the arm of the couch. He looked at his daughter, breathless before her. The humiliation he bore for jeopardizing her might have crushed him if it were not buoyed by the rush of euphoria he felt at her very presence beside him.

"I—" he began.

She took his hand and put it back under the blanket. "Rest," she said, and pulled the blanket to his chin again as she helped him lay back down. This was not how it was supposed to be. He was supposed to be comforting her.

"I should never have—" he began again.

But she would not let him continue.

"Rest," she said.

She laid her head on his chest, and he felt his heart pounding the way it had pounded all those nights the first months she'd been a baby in her new home with him.

"I should have protected you." His voice drifted from him. Soft. A whisper.

"You can't," she said.

No, he couldn't. It was the pain every parent must live with, always.

His chest rose, and she laid a hand on it to calm it though it would not calm. "I—"

"Rest," she said again. "Shhh."

"Thank you," he said.

She tried to speak, but her voice hitched, and he knew she was crying, could feel her starting to shake and sob. He reached a hand out from under the blanket and cupped the back of her head and held her close.

CHAPTER 62

Rachel moved back to campus the next day. Felix helped her pack up her few things, loaded them in her Civic, and helped her ease into the passenger's seat. He pulled her seat belt across her and locked it in and tugged it, checking to make sure it was secure. He loved her, that was certain. Whether it was a love that would last or be burned up by youth, Rath could not know. But Felix and Rachel shared something he'd never known, something good, and he was glad for that, at least. Maybe it meant he'd done something right. Maybe it was despite him.

He watched from the kitchen window as they drove away and noticed the hump of snow near the barn door. The deer. He'd forgotten all about it. It was surely rancid by now, having frozen and thawed several times. It was a shame.

But it was the least of his worries.

CHAPTER 63

Rath turned from the window and looked at the far wall, the display of missing girls' photos and the collection of random facts, of their lives, still pinned to it. It saddened him. There was so much more to each life than *this*. Scraps.

He began taking down the biographies and interview transcripts. The photos. He took them down with care, slid each piece gently into its respective folder, gave each photo one good, last look.

He saved Mandy's photo for last. The so-called "bad" photo. He preferred it. In it, she was less *perfect*, more human somehow. A girl. A pretty, innocent girl who'd known a hard, mean life and tried her best in the face of it. Fled, he hoped now. Left this town and her cruel family to start anew while she still could. New York, maybe. Boston. How he hoped. For her.

"Where are you?" he said, staring at the photo, of her at the beach cookout with others her age.

Something in the photo caught his eye. In the background, blurry. A couple. He peered more closely. Sat at his desk and dragged his lamp over to the photo to see it in a brighter light. Yes. In the background, just barely in focus enough to make out their faces. A young couple. Roughly Mandy's age. The boy a bit older than Mandy, a young man. The girl a bit younger than Mandy. The young man had his arm around the girl, in a sort of playful gesture, as if they were cousins. He was laughing. But his left eye. It was cut toward Mandy, looking straight at her, and the camera. The girl was looking up at the young man with one eye, and one eye was on Mandy too, just as she caught the young man eyeing Mandy. And her face. The hatred in it. The hatred for both of them. The young man. And Mandy. Not jealousy. But raw hate. Savage hate.

He knew both of the subjects in the photo. And thought about the question he'd asked himself when he'd first seen Mandy's Monte Carlo: *Why's it parked like that?* And he knew, in an instant, with a cold certain dread creeping in his marrow why the car had been parked like that, and that Mandy Wilks was dead. And who had killed her. And why.

He slumped in his chair and called Grout. Couldn't reach him. So tried Sonja Test.

"Hey," he said. "I got it."

"What are you talking about?"

"Mandy. I know who killed her. Can you meet me?"

"Of course."

He told her where.

CHAPTER 64

Rath waited outside, pacing on the street, smoking a cigarette. When he saw Sonja's Peugeot pull up, he flicked the cigarette into the road and joined her as she stepped out of the car.

"I still don't—" Sonja began, but Rath was already climbing the fire-escape stairs. Dad's F150 wasn't in the drive, but the Neon was. To be sure she was inside and alone, Rath had phoned moments before from outside. She'd picked up—and he'd asked for Dad. He wasn't in. He was at Jay Peak, helping gear up for the ski season.

Rath knocked on the door.

"Langevine," Sonja muttered absently. "Dressed as an old woman. I was running a while back and saw a man I thought was woman. Because of his long hair and, it bothered me, and—"

"I'll ask the questions," Rath interrupted. "She's sixteen, a minor. If you ask questions as a cop without an adult present, they may not hold up. But I'm not a cop."

"I—" Sonja began.

The door opened, and Porkchop, Abby Land, answered in a pair of sweats with CANAAN HIGH on the front. She looked like she hadn't eaten or slept in days. Her eyes were bloodshot and pale cheeks hollowed.

"Jesus," she said, "you—" She saw Sonja standing behind him then.

Sonja stepped forward and showed her badge. "Can we come in please?" she said.

Abby stared at them. "Sure. Why not?" She shrugged and went to the couch and sat on the edge of it, lit a cigarette she took from a pack lying on the old army trunk that served as a coffee table. She lit it clumsily. She didn't look familiar with lighting it, or with smoking a cigarette, coughing slightly and blowing out the smoke in a puff. "I already told you he was here with me that night," she said. She smacked her lips and doused the cigarette in a cereal bowl of milk.

"Right," Rath said. "We believe you."

"Good, *finally*. I'm telling the truth."

"The thing is," Rath said. He sat on the couch a foot from Abby and placed a hand on Abby's knee. Abby flinched and stared at the hand but said and did nothing. She seemed very far away now. Rath knew the look. Reality hitting home. Taking hold of the mind.

"The thing is," Rath said again, "you weren't here with him."

"What," Abby said. "What." Dazed. Disoriented. As if awakening in an unfamiliar bed with no memory of how she'd gotten there.

"You know you weren't here with him," Rath said.

"I was. He didn't *do* it. That's the truth."

"I know he didn't do it, dear," Rath said. "I know that much is the truth."

"Don't you *dear* me." She pulled her knees away from Rath's hand, squeezed them together. She began to tremble. "Who are you to—"

"I thought maybe when you gave him an alibi you were protecting him, or scared of him, because he was dealing coke or somewhere else he shouldn't be that night. But you weren't protecting him by lying about being here with him that night," Rath said. "You were protecting yourself."

"That's not true."

"Yes, it is," Rath said. Abby was sixteen, but looked no older than fourteen. What was he doing when he was sixteen? Still riding his Huffy 10-speed as fast as he could onto a ramp to see how many cardboard boxes he could jump.

He took out the photo of Mandy and handed it to Sonja.

Abby was staring at her hands in her lap now. She wasn't going to be able to keep the truth in her. In all probability, she wanted to vomit it up and out of her.

Sonja showed Abby the photo. Abby crumpled a bit when she looked at it. Then stiffened. "So," she said, a jolt of defiance steeling her. "So what."

"That's you in the background," Rath said.

"*So.*" She glared at him. "Big deal."

"And who's that with you?" Rath said.

She looked off toward the kitchen. "I don't know."

"You don't know?"

"Some guy. *So?*"

"No one important?"

"No."

"A good-looking guy like that. His arm around you."

"We were friends."

"Were?"

"Are. Were. Whatever."

"No. Not whatever. You cared about him."

"You don't know shit."

"I know this. He's a volunteer fireman. And he's stationed in the firehouse just up and across the street a door or two from the Dress Shoppe."

"Wow. Good for you."

"And I know that Mandy had bought raffle tickets from him."

"Big deal."

"And that Mandy saw him the last afternoon anyone ever saw her. Saw him walk past. And she wanted to tell him something, but by the time she got out there, he was gone, or she had lost her nerve. Maybe she even spoke with him. I'll know when I talk to him."

"Go ahead, talk to the asshole. What's it got to do with me?"

"You had a crush on him. But you were like his little cousin or something."

"Shut up."

"But Mandy. She was nothing like a cousin to him," Rath said.

"Shut up." She gritted her teeth at him and looked at him with eyes lost and barren. "You don't know *shit*."

"I know that when we check the battery on your Neon, we're going to see that the posts have marks on them from a recent jump start. Your car's got a bad battery. I tripped over the jumper cables coming out of here before. And those marks will match marks on Mandy's battery. And they'll both line up with the battery cables in your trunk."

Abby was tapping her bare feet on the floor now. *Tap tap tap*. Drumming her palms on her knees.

"I know it wasn't planned," Rath said. "I know it was a spur-of-the-moment thing. An anger rising in you, a jealousy. Your car is dead on the roadside after a party or something and along comes Mandy, and she knows you. Probably feels bad for you. She knows the shit you have to deal with being in the same house with her asshole father. So, of course, she stops and helps you out, and you can't stand it. You can't stand the sight of her. Little Miss Perfect. Everyone always drooling over her. Luke especially. Your Luke."

Tap tap tap. Abby's whole body shook now. Sonja put a hand on her shoulder.

"When we check the trunk of your car," Rath said, "we're going to find hair. Or blood. All kinds of it. What'd you do, after she jump-started you, did you have her help you get your tire and cables back in the trunk, and when she bent over, you hit her with something. The tire iron? And shoved her in and—"

"God," Abby moaned. "Please."

"We know you didn't *mean* it," Rath said.

Abby snapped her head up at him, locked her eyes on his, black with death, her face wrenched and wicked.

"The fuck I didn't," she spat.

"Where is she?" Rath said.

"Still in my trunk. The bitch."

EPILOGUE

"No," Rath said, as Barrons swiveled in his chair. "It's not for me."

"You're breaking my heart," Barrons said, and laid his big mitt over his chest as if to prove it. It proved nothing.

"I'm not a cop," Rath said.

"Bullshit."

"I was a cop."

"A good one."

"A cop has to believe."

"In what?"

"The law. The system. I don't. I can't. Not in a system that treats a sixteen-year-old girl as an adult. Or lets the Preachers of the world free to prey and victimize. Shit, even that crazy bat Malroy may have a shot at a cocka-mamie defense by perverting the system."

"If—"

"No. There is no if. This is life. You can't live life on ifs. Only *is*."

"Listen to you, professor."

"Yeah."

"Yeah. Well." Barrons leaned back in his chair and spread his arms wide. Behind him, on the sill outside, the pigeon strutted back and forth.

"Grout's not as green now," Rath said.

"Grout took a leave of absence after he fucked things up with that old bag in Connecticut. She nearly died. I don't think he's coming back. I think he's taking a security job. In New Hampshire."

Rath nodded. Nothing surprised him.

"Sonja isn't green anymore, either."

"What can I say or do to convince you?" Barrons said.

"*Nada*. You can invite me down to the Bahamas. We can fish. You can show me how to fly fish."

"You're ready for that? It's pretty refined."

"I'm ready." He was. He needed to get away to someplace he had never been before. Someplace hot and sunny and bright. A place to clear his mind and recalibrate. So when he returned he could focus afresh on what was most important. Ned Preacher.

"I thought you were seeing someone, had some lady on the line," Barrons said.

"That. Yeah. That I'm really not ready for."

"Have you told her that?"

"Not yet. She's called."

"You haven't called back?"

"Not yet."

"You should."

"She's seen the news. She must have an inkling that I've been a bit distracted."

"Call her."

"Right. OK. Can we plan this trip? I need it."

"We'll make a plan. Springtime is best for bones.

March. Do you good to get out of here then. Does me good. Can you wait that long?"

"Sure, yeah," Rath said. "I'm in. Were you able to get that address?"

Barrons grimaced. "I can, but I won't. You need to stay clear of him."

"I just want to make sure. Keep an eye on him."

"You can't keep an eye on him. Not forever."

"All I need is an address."

"Get it off the site," Barrons said.

"All the Vermont site for registered sex offenders gives you is the name of the town. No address. That needs to change. People don't need an approximation of where these cretins live. They need to know *exactly* where they live."

"You're a detective. You'll figure it out. But I'm a friend. I'm not helping you go down that rabbit hole."

Rath shrugged.

"March then?" he said.

"Plan on it."

RATH WAS DRIVING home from the station feeling uplifted. The sky was blue, a fresh snow sparkling under the sun in the fields. It was, simply, a beautiful December day. His phone buzzed.

"Hello," he said.

"How's my girl?" a man on the other end said.

"Excuse me?"

"I said, 'How's my girl?'"

"Who is this?"

"Don't tell me you don't recognize me."

Rath was about to hang up when he heard the laugh

on the other end. Guttural and soulless. Rath's blood drained out of him, and he knew if he looked down, he'd see a pool of it spreading out on the Scout's floor.

The laugh came again.

Preacher.

Rath killed the call and stopped the Scout, staggered out into a field, tracking up the pure snow. He braced himself against a lone oak tree out in the middle of the cold field.

His phone rang again.

He let it go to voice mail.

It rang again.

He let it go.

He was not prepared for this. Of all the scenarios he had run through his head, none had involved *Preacher* contacting *him*. They had all involved Rath's hunting Preacher, surprising him. Making his life hell. Now. This. Blindsided, he was not ready. He wanted it on his terms.

The phone rang. He turned it off and tromped back through the snow and got in the Scout and headed toward home.

At home, he plodded up the back stairs and set the phone on the kitchen table and sat with a bottle of scotch, poured a glass.

The landline phone rang on the kitchen wall.

Rath jumped in his chair and stared at the phone.

It rang and rang and rang. He'd discontinued the voice mail, so the phone would not stop ringing until the person on the other end hung up.

The phone rang and rang.

It couldn't be him. The line was private. Unlisted. There was no way. How could he have his number?

The phone kept ringing.

Rath jumped up and grabbed it, and shouted, "Listen you piece of shit, I'll find you, and—"

"Don't ever hang up on me again," the voice said, cold, reptilian.

"Who the fuck do you—"

"I asked you a question. 'How's my girl?'"

"When I find you—"

More laughter. "You? Find me? I've found you. Answer me. How. Is. My. Girl?"

"*What* girl?"

"*My. Girl.*"

"Who?"

"Rachel."

Rath's heart swelled in his chest, the blood trapped and pooling in it, the pressure terrific.

"Don't you dare speak my daughter's name."

"Your daughter?" Preacher laughed. "You ever ask yourself why I came back, to your sister's house?"

Rath wanted to hang up, but he heard a sound in the background that seemed vaguely familiar. If he kept Preacher on the line long enough, perhaps he'd be able to narrow down the type of place he was calling from if not an exact location.

"Well?" Preacher said.

"We know why you came back." Rath took a drink. What was that sound in the background? Focus, he told himself. Focus and keep him on the line, ignore his games.

"No, that's not *why*. That's the what. *What* I came back to do; but why did I come back to do it? Hmmm. *Why?*"

"You're evil."

"Tell me something I don't know, Frank."

Rath felt filthy hearing Preacher call him by name.

"You can do math, right, Frank? Simple math."

Rath said nothing, listening. The noise in the background sounded like a . . . he could not quite place it.

"Here's some simple math for you. How long was I gone from Vermont?"

The sound in the background where Preacher was became clearer as Preacher moved. A high scraping?

"OK. I'll tell you. Sixteen months."

Not quite a scraping, more like a—

"And," Preacher said, "how old was Rachel?"

Rath snapped to attention, his spine going cold and as rigid as a bar of iron.

An icy laugh came from Preacher. "And how long is the average human pregna—"

"You shut your mouth," Rath roared. "You shut your fucking mouth."

"I see I struck a nerve. Apparently, you can do math."

"You lying fucking—"

"You weren't the only whoremonger in your family, Frank. With women, of course, they don't call them whoremongers. No. They call them whores. Funny. No matter how you turn it, the woman is the whore. Why do you suppose that is?"

Rath couldn't breathe. The more he tried, the more he hyperventilated until he felt the bile burn his throat, and he spit it in the sink. What Preacher was saying was only to get a rise. Rath willed himself to ignore it. He had to get a grip, get leverage, the upper hand. This was not how it was supposed to *go*.

"Your silence is telling," Preacher said. "You're trying to tell yourself I'm lying, I'm fucking with you. But your body knows. It knows. Your sister *lied* to you. All those years. Your sister, the little angel. She didn't put her cheap ways behind her when she met Daniel, she was just more . . . hmm . . . discreet—"

Rath could hear laughter on the line. His heart was thundering. "Listen, you soulless—"

But Preacher ignored him, his voice cutting straight through Rath: "She told me all about you: Her sad little brother nailing pussy to make himself feel like a man, like your old man. How you thought she was such a saint." Preacher cackled. "But she. She couldn't stay away from the bad boys any more than you could from the bad girls. Well, she picked the wrong bad boy in the end, wouldn't you say? I came back through to give her some more of it. She turned me down. Gave me some holier-than-thou, prim-and-proper, Holly-fucking-Hobby *bullshit*. But I knew that was a mask. I fucking knew."

Rath was shaking so hard, his legs would not hold him, and he had to sit down on the floor. He was soaked with sweat. He tried to block out Preacher's voice and focus on the sound in the background. Focus focus focus. But he couldn't.

"What I didn't know," Preacher said, sounding as if he were speaking with a clenched jaw, "was about the baby. Until later, when I read it in the papers. My girl. If Laura was such a good mother, she should have just let me take her one last time on my way through, stopped pretending she was some born-again saint. If she'd just given in to her nature, let me have her like the old days, when she wanted to slum it with the bad-boy handy-man, I'd have gone off none the wiser. Instead, she had to resist. Play Good Girl. Cock tease. Force my hand. *Agitate*." His voice was distorted. Demonic. "I can do math, Frank. Even if you can't. I can do simple fucking math. Rachel's mine. Ask yourself how the mess I made of Laura and her husband differed from my MO."

Rath was gasping for breath. Every atom in him wanted to reject what Preacher said. But he couldn't. How could Preacher know these things from anyone else but Laura? And what Preacher had said, about the MO. It differed drastically from the coldness of the rapes. And age of the victims. They'd missed it before because Preacher had been so easily caught, he'd left DNA everywhere. They'd missed it for what it was: a crime of passion. A sense of dread hardened in Rath. His worry over Rachel's obsession with the twisted books and movies about sadists and depravity. He'd worried it had been because she'd heard about the murder of her parents. What if it was because she had Preacher's blood running in her veins? Focus, his mind screamed. Focus focus. *Focus!*

That sound. He knew it. It was coming to him.

"You won't tell me how My Girl is doing," Preacher said. "OK. I'll tell you. She seems fine. From what I see."

"How'd you get this number?" Rath said.

Preacher snorted.

"How did you get my fucking home number?"

PRIVATE. That's what the original call on Rath's cell had shown. PRIVATE.

"Tell me! Goddamn you, tell me!"

More laughter came, ringing and echoing in Rath's head.

When it died, Rath heard the sound again.

And suddenly, he knew what it was.

A bird. Birds. Two of them.

Canaries.

ACKNOWLEDGMENTS

My thanks to the many, many friends and family members who have encouraged and supported my writing over the years. There are so many of you, it would take its own book to list them all. But a special thanks to my wife. And a specific thanks to my agent Philip Spitzer and my editor Marguerite Weisman for taking on this book and believing in it.

Keep reading for an excerpt from
Eric Rickstad's

LIE IN WAIT

The baby was finally asleep and Jessica Cumber, forever restless and in need of busying herself, decided to wash a load of laundry before the Merryfields returned home. They wouldn't be long. Mr. Merryfield had been sick with the bug going around, and tonight was his first night out in a week.

Jessica worshipped Mr. Merryfield. Secretly, of course. He was so mature. Jessica found maturity very attractive. Plus, Mr. Merryfield was a *star.* He was on TV practically all the time because of The Case.

Kids at school, *teachers even*, pressed Jessica every day for info on the Merryfields and The Case. Jessica didn't know thing one about it and, would never ever betray Mr. Merryfield even if she did. Though sometimes, she had to admit, she enjoyed the attention and would give the impression she had some insight into The Case.

As she climbed the creamery's elegant staircase, her stomach bubbled. She hoped she wasn't getting the bug. In a town as small as Canaan, sickness spread swiftly.

Jessica stood atop the stairs, clutched the mahogany post to steady herself and peer over the banister. She was positively mad about the wooden staircase, its graceful curvature stretching toward the palatial foyer below. Light from the full moon outside lit the entrance door's windows and pooled on the marble floor, the marble quarried by young local men now a hundred years dead. Iron radiators clanked and hissed. Jessica shivered. She imagined the plumbing as the creamery's circulatory system, the coursing water its hot foaming blood.

Jessica slipped off her sneakers and padded shoeless down the hallway, trailing her arms out to the side, fingernails rattling on the wainscoting.

At the master bedroom's doorway, she drummed her fingernails on the doorjamb, then, with a dramatic flourish, flipped the light switch. Ta-da! Each time she did this, she couldn't help but marvel at the *enormity* of the room. Her mother's entire trailer would fit inside this one bedroom. The ceiling, which rose so high you'd need a ladder just to change a lightbulb, still had its original pressed ornamental tin and was trimmed with a white crown molding so glossy you'd think the paint was still wet. Decades' worth of paint had been stripped from the wainscoting to reveal mahogany beneath. Jessica knew these details because Mrs. Merryfield had made Jessica privy to them the first time she'd given Jessica the tour and interviewed her for the job; the whole time Jessica had been praying and praying she'd get the chance to babysit in *this* house. For this man and his family.

Now, here she was.

A dream come true.

When Jessica had told her mother about the grand

old home, her mother had said, "I wouldn't know how to live in such a place."

"I'd *learn*," Jessica had proclaimed.

Jessica tiptoed over to the sleigh bed, the carpet's lush pile squashing beneath her bare toes, cool and cushiony as a fresh bed of moss. The edge of the mattress rose to her rib cage. The frame was carved from the same wood as the wainscoting—manly, though the bedding, the duvet, was fluffy and flowery: *trés feminine*. Recently, Jessica had become taken with all things provincial. One day she would go to Provence. She was saving her babysitting money for it, and for college, of course. And veterinary school after that.

Jessica had lain on the sumptuous duvet just once. Briefly, and against her better judgment, with her beau. *Beau.*

Oh. She liked the sound of that! So refined. So mature. Even if her beau, in reality, wasn't either of those things.

When she'd lain in the bed that one time she'd felt like Goldilocks who'd found the bed that was *just right*. She hadn't wanted to ever get up.

Jessica started across the room to retrieve the Merryfields' laundry in the master bath. As she paused to view herself in the dressing mirror, she heard what sounded like the entrance door opening and clicking shut in the foyer.

Hot water gurgled in the radiators.

Jessica cocked her head.

Silence throbbed in her ears.

She stepped into the hallway and looked over the rail.

The radiators clanked.

The front door was unlocked, as was every front door in Canaan. This was Vermont after all.

The radiators quieted. The old creamery fell as still as a monastery.

"Hello," Jessica said, her voice echoing in the marble foyer.

The house did not answer.

The *baby*, Jessica suddenly thought, panicked. Something's wrong. Jessica felt it, queasiness rising from her belly to burst acidic in her throat.

She raced down the hall to the baby's room and stood at the doorway, breathless. Her heart fluttered behind her tiny ribs.

Not a peep came from the room.

Jessica tiptoed to the crib, frightened, not bothering with the light switch.

At the crib, she drew a deep breath and looked down.

The crib lay empty. The baby was gone. She knew it. As her eyes adjusted to the blackness, she saw, there in the low light, in the crib, beneath a mobile of prancing antelope, baby Jon, perfectly still, and breathing. Sleeping.

"Oh," Jessica said and sagged with relief against the crib. "Oh. Thank you. God." Jessica kissed her fingertips and touched them to baby Jon's hot forehead. She returned to the top of the stairs and stared at the unlocked front door.

"No one's here," she whispered to the empty house. She remembered her mother saying, "You can't make an old place like that new again. No matter how you pretty it up. It's always going to be drafty. Moaning all night. Haunted."

Jessica returned to the master bedroom.

A cold draft edged along the floor. Jessica shivered, wishing now for her shoes. With the new coldness, the duvet seemed all the more inviting. She could take a nice doze and neaten it afterward, she reasoned. Who would know? She sank her hand into the duvet and hoisted herself onto the bed. As she lay down, something dug into her side. She felt around the comforter and pulled out a hard plastic object. A woman's aid. She dropped it as if stung by a wasp, and sat up.

A month ago, her beau had shown her a Web site on Mr. Merryfield's laptop. The site sold all shapes and sizes of women's aids. When Jessica had used this term and told her beau to get out of the site, he'd called her a prude. "You're naïve," he'd said. "But I'll corrupt you yet. I bet the Merryfields have sex toys stashed all over the place."

"I hate that term 'toy,' " she'd said. "And the Merryfields aren't like that."

"We're all like that," he'd said.

She'd wanted to protest, but he was more versed in these things. That was part of his draw, wasn't it? His age? His experience? And the secrecy because of it.

For a moment, Jessica wondered if the noise she'd heard earlier had been him, slipping in the house. Had he waited for her to check the baby, then planted the aid in the bed and sneaked out, just to prove a point? He was always pulling pranks like that. He *always* had to be *right*. It was like a sickness with him. And he liked to scare people. Jessica, especially. He had a weird side to him that way. He got a real kick from it. Scaring her. Who did stuff like that? No one liked to be scared. But, the more scared she was, the harder he laughed. Sometimes, she realized, age did not equate to maturity; especially when it came to the male gender. Still, she loved him.

How she loved him.

Jessica had pushed him away that night, though,

made him shut down Mr. Merryfield's laptop. She wasn't supposed to use it. And soon he'd been kissing her. Whenever there was any silence between them, any downtime, he swooped in and kissed her, as if her silence were permission.

He'd ended up on top of her, then taken her downstairs to the couch. Again. His weight pressing. Her scent rising. She'd opened to him. Afterward, she'd felt guilty, as usual, like she'd let herself down, risked her whole future, veterinary school, a career working in equine breeding, her vacation home in Provence, all for a stupid selfish moment.

When the Merryfields' Land Rover had pulled up outside that night, the headlights swooping through the parlor, her beau had escaped out the side door just in time, the sensation of him still pulsing inside her when Mr. Merryfield strolled in the front door and asked, "Any trouble tonight?"

Jessica sighed now and extracted herself from the bed.

In the bathroom, she scrubbed her hands. She grabbed a load of laundry from the hamper and dumped it into a basket and lugged it out of the room.

As a precaution, hamper in tow, she called out over the stairway: "I'm coming down to do laundry! If you're down there and jump out at me, I swear to God, I *will* kill you."

Downstairs, she ducked low to avoid knocking her head on the beam above her as she managed the cellar steps, each stair creaking as if the nails would pull free and the treads collapse below her.

The old door behind her started to close, as it always did.

At the bottom, she had to stoop beneath beams and

hurry to the corner before she lost light from above. She pulled a string that lit a lone ceiling bulb. The bulb oozed a sick yellow light that was quickly swallowed by the dark, windowless cellar. The stone foundation sweated and seemed to pulse in the dimness. The air was close and greasy and smelled of mold. The stone and dirt floor was slimy and cold on her bare feet. She saw a mouse, dead in a trap, bloated, its neck broken, eyes popped out of its skull. Jessica's mother was right: There was no way to make a place like this new again. Jessica ducked beneath support beams. Cobwebs caught in her hair. The Merryfields had had plans to turn the kitchen pantry into the laundry room, until plumbing problems had arisen.

It was no wonder the Merryfields preferred Jessica not bother with laundry down here, where you could see the crumbling stone foundation, cramped and damp as a grave, on which the glamorous house stood.

The washing machine and dryer sat at the center of the lightbulb's pathetic yellow stain. On the crooked wooden shelf above them sat an old radio. Jessica turned it on, cranking the knob to find an upbeat pop tune from a Montreal station.

A heap of dirty men's clothing sat on the dryer. She picked up a pair of Mr. Merryfield's dress pants from the pile, checked the pockets for change and pens. With care, she sprayed stain remover on chocolate smeared on the front of the pants until it was saturated properly, according to the directions on the can. She liked doing Mr. Merryfield's laundry. She liked to defeat stubborn stains. The more stubborn the stain, the sweeter the victory. She picked up one of Mr. Merryfield's shirts and brought it to her nose, closing her eyes as she inhaled.

The shirt smelled of his aftershave and of his cigar smoke, yes.

But of him, too.

His body.

"Jon," she whispered.

She loved the sound of his name on her tongue.

Jon.

Her spine tingled to say it.

Jon.

She stuffed his pants and shirt into the machine, dumped in a precisely measured cup of detergent, shut the lid and started the machine on COLD.

She checked the dryer. The load in it was damp. She turned the dryer on to finish the load.

As she folded a shirt on the machine, she thought she heard a stair creak. Thought she saw a slice of light from above, as if the door to the upstairs had been opened. But it was hard to tell. She could see so little beyond her weak cone of light. The washing machine thumped. She returned to folding the shirt.

The noise came again. Jessica squinted into the darkness. Her blood felt hot. "Hello?" No reply came. "If that's you, say something. Don't scare me like this!"

Another noise came. The clearing of a throat?

Then. Nothing.

Her heart seized.

She needed to get out. Now.

Some animal instinct told her this: Get out of the house. Now. Run.

But to where? There was no escape up the stairs.

The bulkhead, her mind screamed.

As she moved swiftly toward the darkness where the bulkhead was, she smashed her forehead against a timber joist. A shattering of stars bloomed in her head. A hand grabbed her. She shrieked. She was spun around. A bright light shone in her eyes. She could not see beyond it. She looked down and tried to catch her breath as she saw the hammer held in the hand.